Dark Delicacies III
HAUNTED

EDITED BY

DEL HOWISON & JEFF GELB

Running Press
PHILADELPHIA · LONDON

To those horror writers who have worked hard and are yet to be published. The merry-go-round is tough, but keep reaching for that bloody ring. Perseverance and talent will win out in the end ... usually after you're dead.

—Del Howison

To Richard Matheson, Rod Serling, and Forry Ackerman who lit my lifelong fiery passion for all things horror.

—Jeff Gelb

Anthology © 2009 by Del Howison and Jeff Gelb
Each story remains in the copyright of its author.

All rights reserved under the Pan-American
and International Copyright Conventions

Printed in the United States

9 8 7 6 5 4 3 2
Digit on the right indicates the number of this printing
Library of Congress Control Number: 2009925848

Hardcover edition
ISBN 978-0-7624-3648-4

Paperback edition
ISBN 978-0-7624-3352-0

Cover design by Matthew Goodman
Cover illustration by Adam Fisher
Interior design by Matthew Goodman
Typography: Requiem and Historical

Running Press Book Publishers
2300 Chestnut Street
Philadelphia, PA 19103-4371

Visit us on the web!
www.runningpress.com

Copyrights

Contents

One does not become enlightened by imagining figures of light, but by making the darkness conscious.

—C. G. Jung

Introduction

Jeff Gelb

We are all haunted.

That's not to say we've all got ghosts chasing us around. That would be easy.

But we all are haunted by one thing or another. A deed we have done, or not done. An event in the past that changed us forever. A missed opportunity. A loved one's death. Our unhealthy desires and habits.

Or by our phobias. We all have them. Heights, spiders, snakes, food: you name it, we've got it.

And what we do about what haunts us makes us human. For better or for worse. Do we address these dark spots in our lives head-on? Or do we avoid them, or ignore them?

In any case, we're all haunted. Which is why this time around, *Dark Delicacies* is appropriately subtitled "Haunted."

Welcome to our third collection. And thanks for picking us up. This time around, our stellar group of contributors has cooked up a stewpot full of stories of people who are haunted. And yes, even by ghosts. But that's just for starters, as you will soon see.

Foreword

Steven Weber

When I was asked to write the foreword for this collection of stories, it felt like the time a stranger had approached me, his eyes hollow, desperate, and darting, muttering about unseen threats to his health made by unnamed enemies and otherwise causing me much alarm (as I am a classic coward), whereupon he thrust an object in a plain brown wrapper into my hands for safe keeping and, as quickly as he had appeared, fled into the murky night.

That never really happened to me, but I was stuck for a grabby opening. It's only a foreword, for chrissakes. All the good writing comes later.

Being a devotee of this genre is a lot like being a trafficker in porn (I imagine) in the days before its current ubiquity made it so commonplace that any eroticism has been mediocritized right out of it. And in spite of the recent glut of popular "torture-porn" films and their increasingly relentless sequels (I include any one of George Bush's State of the Union addresses in that particular genre), the real foundation of the horror/sci-fi/fantasy oeuvre (I just used "genre" a moment ago and couldn't risk the repetition) is more subtly invasive, its adherents less inclined to advertise their predilections so brazenly. Upon meeting a fellow connoisseur, there is a probing look into the eyes, an instant reading of the facial twitches, an understanding that we are . . . different. There's even a hint of sadness in the knowledge that we are lovers of images and ideas that the majority of the world views as repugnant, which ironically makes us embrace our choices even tighter. To me, it's this inherent push-me-pull-me nature of horror, science fiction, and fantasy literature and films that makes it so alluring, so forbidden. It's less the slashing knife or the rent flesh or the many other cruel, otherworldly acts themselves. It's the fact that they are the products of the same essential human recipe and therefore entirely possible. Because if it can be thought, no matter how insane or imaginitively deviant, it can be realized. *That's* terrifying.

Horror walks hand in hand with beauty, terror with contentment; neither could exist without the other. We who indulge ourselves in this world know this and know also that our counterparts would never admit as much. So why not scare the living shit out of them? Serves 'em right. And did I mention this volume would make a great gift?

Children of the Vortex

Simon Clark

"If you convince one normal, healthy individual that he is Abraham Lincoln, Picasso, or Elvis Presley, exhibit him on TV for the world's ridicule. Convince a million men that they are invincible warriors and you will strike terror into the heart of Man...."

—Dr. Hilda Lippisch, East Berlin, 1969

Isle of Rugen, Germany. Present.

"What is it, Leo? What's wrong?"

The old soldier regarded the limestone cliff that rose from perfect white sands. His respiration quickened. Either memory or the brilliant sunlight made him screw his eyes almost shut. His tongue ran from side to side over his lips as if it were a small creature searching for a means of escape.

"Leo. Is this the first time you've been back?"

"You know it is." Shuddering, he zipped his brown leather jacket up to a jaw that exhibited the prickly scarlet rash of razor burn.

"How far now, Leo?"

"I want to go home."

"You promised to help."

"After all these years I didn't think it would hit me as hard as this."

The Baltic surged over the beach with a roar that sounded distinctly ominous.

"Leo. Are we close?"

"Yes, Dominic. We're close. Far too close!"

Anger rumbled in the old man's normally soft German accent. *Old man?* This veteran soldier of the former German Democratic Republic, one of the Soviet puppet states, was only in his early fifties. Yet his white hair had molted to reveal a speckled scalp. Long-term usage of antidepressants left a glassy sheen in his blue eyes, which were apt to stare, unblinking, for so long it made Dominic uncomfortable.

Leo Fiedler awarded the tangled forest that topped the cliff a particularly long glare, then turned away, shivering. "I'm cold! There'll be nothing to see. It was dynamited after the Wall came down."

"Leo—"

"You see? It's a national park now. Just a nature reserve." His accent thickened. "Why be so damned stupid as to go back to the old places? Why dig them back up? Forget them!" The wind blew hard enough to tug away strands of the man's silver hair. They fled along the beach. "Get me back to the mainland, Dominic. This cold will be my death."

Dominic spoke firmly. "I know the place disturbs you, but we are under a legal obligation to investigate areas of public interest."

"Who do you work for? Army? Interpol? CIA?"

"Leo. Once we find the entrance to the complex, we can leave."

"And I told you that the sub base has been demolished."

"I'm not interested in submarine pens. It's the adjacent complex."

Leo's face turned gray. For a moment it looked as if he'd collapse. Dominic pressed on. "We are interested in the Vortex."

"No . . ." The man grimaced as if pains lanced his heart.

"We know you were present when the order came to terminate Vortex. You took part."

"I wasn't a proper soldier. Ha! They armed me with pencils; I audited military land holdings. I had nothing to do with Vortex! Now

. . . please, take me home." Anger turned to pleading. "I can't abide this place. Just the smell of it makes me ill. Please, Dominic."

Just then, a silver BMW 4x4 roared along the beach. When the vehicle stopped alongside them, three people sprang eagerly from it. Two men and a woman, dressed casually in jeans and sweatshirts. The woman's red hair was carved brutally short. The trio grinned at each other, then at Dominic, as if they'd brought him surprise birthday presents. In a way, they had.

"Good news, Scarlet?" Dominic ventured.

"We've got it." She brandished a memory stick. "The ministry biked it across twenty minutes ago." Then she glanced at the old soldier. "Feeling off-color, Leo?"

"Get me off this devil island!" He glared up at the looming cliffs as if he expected to see enemies there. "You should leave too."

Dominic shrugged. "I told him that we know he's linked to Vortex."

"Ouch." One of the men smiled. "That must have touched a nerve."

Dominic nodded at the memory stick. "Show us what you've got, then."

Scarlet waited, an impish smile on her face, as one of her companions brought out a laptop, flipped it open, then set it down on the car's hood. "It's classified. But you've clearance to watch it, Leo." Her green eyes were hard. "I hope you like horror movies."

As she loaded the data, one of the men advanced on Leo. Big boned, muscular, his manner suggested that of a policeman who'd peered too much into the world's nastier corners to be fazed by anything, no matter how bloody. "Leo. My name is Powell. This is my colleague, Larchette . . ." A thin, bearded man with anxious eyes nodded. "You've already met Scarlet. Now you're going to see footage from the communist regime archives. You will be asked questions during the showing of the film. Do you understand?"

Frightened, Leo nodded. The wind blew, tugging away more strands of silver from his mottled scalp. Meanwhile, the surf's roar grew louder. Waves smacked angrily against boulders. Gulls screamed.

"Best make it snappy." Scarlet glanced at the ocean. "Tide's coming in fast."

"This'll only take a couple of minutes." To the prematurely aged man shivering there in his leather jacket, Powell announced in aggressive tones, "Larchette will video your responses. Understand?"

"How can I stop you? I'm a sick man."

Larchette produced a digital camera. He aimed it at Leo's face, then nodded.

With the intense smell of brine in his nostrils, Dominic gathered with the others to watch the laptop perched on the car's hood. On screen, silver numerals counted down: *3, 2, 1*. B/W footage of a featureless room. No windows. A man sits to a piano. He plays— tuneless, discordant, an absence of melody. The camera operator is no expert either. The frame lurches left to reveal an attractive woman of around forty. She wears a clinician's white coat, carries a clipboard; long hair is pulled tight back from her face. Pianist remains in shot. Hunches shoulders, plays faster. An expression of ecstasy transforms his face.

Coolly professional, the woman addresses the viewer. "I am Doctor Lippisch. Senior MD, Project Vortex. Here you see subject seventy-two-stroke-nineteen-a, aged twenty-four. Upper mind successfully erased. Reindoctrination as musician. Subject had no musical training. Now, however, he is convinced that he is both a brilliant pianist and a renowned composer. Note: playing is discordant, totally unmusical, yet he believes he has written a beautiful sonata. Subject underwent C2 procedure: ECT, drug therapy, audio-corrective stimulation . . ."

As Dr. Lippisch continued her lecture, Powell fired questions at Leo: "Do you recognize that woman?"

"Never seen her before."

"Lippisch? Know the name?"

"You're going to get wet. Here the tide is fast. People have been swept away."

"How do you feel watching such a grotesque experiment? That man's brain was wiped, then reprogrammed."

"You think I'm intimidated by the tide, so you make me stand here. I don't fear the ocean. I wish I had the guts to drown myself in it."

"So you know something of Vortex?"

On screen, Dr. Lippisch seizes papers covered in delusional scribble and rips them apart. In grief, the pianist howls. "Don't! My music!" Heartbroken, he sobs as she tosses the scraps into the air.

Leo's glazed eyes were melancholy. "I know nothing of the scientific process. I was only there at the end."

On screen: Images of floating paper crash to black. Next: Dr. Lippisch in the same room. Instead of the piano there is a line of potted ferns on the floor: an attempt to create an outdoor scene. Three men in infantry fatigues crouch down. They hold AK-47s, which they point at the blank wall.

First soldier: "Enemy sighted."

Second soldier: "Permission to fire, Sergeant?"

Sergeant: "Short bursts. Keep them pinned down."

They rise above the tops of the ferns. Aim, fire. They mime recoil, but the guns do not discharge.

Dr. Lippisch steps screen center. "Three subjects medically unfit for military service. Twenty-two days of C2 has produced what you see here. Three men who believe they are soldiers, who genuinely believe they are on the battlefield. They hear gunfire, see shells detonate. Now watch." Off screen someone hands her a pistol.

Powell demanded, "Do you know the three men?"

Leo regarded the incoming waves. "We should get away. It's not safe."

"Vortex was based adjacent to the submarine pens. Why?"

"You can't interrogate me like this. You've no right."

Dominic felt stirrings of pity. Leo was agitated to the point where tears glittered in his eyes. Nevertheless, Dominic found his gaze drawn away from this brusque interrogation to the screen where Dr. Lippisch cocked a revolver. He'd heard legends about films that documented grisly communist-era experiments. However, he couldn't believe that the old regime hadn't incinerated the reels before reunification of East and West Germany. *They're evidence of crimes against humanity, for God sakes.* Even on this sunlit beach the first gunshot was startling.

Dr. Lippisch coolly shoots Soldier 1 in the back of the head. Though he slumps into the ferns, the others continue to fire—pretend to fire, that is. The docter aims at Soldier 2. He pauses, sensing something amiss. Lippisch fires. The bullet penetrates the top of his skull, then exits through his mouth, smashing his teeth. The round embeds in a wall, leaving a black mark.

Lippisch taps the surviving infantryman on the shoulder: "Sergeant? Where are your two comrades?"

Even though he looks around, he doesn't see the two men lying dead close by. Crisply, he states, "They've been redeployed to another part of the line."

"Don't you see them?"

"No, miss."

"If I told you that I saw them lying dead at my feet, how would you respond?"

"My response is that you are lying, miss. I see only two enemy dead."

"Look closer. Aren't those your comrades, Gruber and Istryn?"

"I know my comrades, miss. These are strangers. Gruber and Istryn moved off to support an assault on the enemy position. They are—"

Lippisch doesn't wait for him to finish. Turning to the camera, she states, "Picture an army of men such as these. Loyal, determined, fearless. They are incapable of self-doubt; nor can they comprehend the death of their fellow soldiers. If comrades die, the survivor truly believes they have merely been redeployed elsewhere." She smiles. "I take ordinary farm boys, prisoners, mental patients; I transform them into artists, scientists, warriors. Ladies and gentlemen, give me mortal clay; I will give you supermen."

"That's what I call an advertising pitch." Scarlet smiled. "Lippisch could sell condoms to cardinals."

On screen: The sergeant is suddenly puzzled. "But I'm not outside. This is a room." He stares at the assault rifle. "Why am I holding—"

Lippisch fires into the man's eye.

"Oh, my God . . ." Larchette, camera in hand, freezes.

"I told you it was bad." Powell nodded at the screen. "You should see the other experiments."

"What's wrong with his head?"

Powell shot a questioning look at his colleague. "What the hell's wrong with you?"

But then Dominic realized that Larchette was staring past the screen into the surf.

"Heaven help us," breathed Leo as he saw too.

By now the foaming tide rolled over the sand not ten paces from them. Dominic's scalp prickled as he saw what was being jostled by the surf. His gaze fixed on the head of the male corpse. The top of its skull had been sliced away. *What's wrong with his head?* Larchette had been right to ask the question. Looking into the open top of the skull was like looking into a cavern. The brain, eyes, roof of the mouth, tongue had all been scooped out to leave a void. When the sun struck the face of the corpse as it floated on its back, twin beams of light shone through lidless eye sockets to illuminate the interior of the head. The top of the spinal column formed a pearly white bud at the base of the skull. Wavelets made the empty head nod rapidly as if it agreed with their feelings of horror.

Leo cried, "See! I told you not to come here!"

The twentieth century is dominated by those who own oilfields. The twenty-first century will belong to those who control the human mind.
                                        —Dr. Lippisch, Moscow, 1972

Scarlet drove the car from the beach. In the front passenger seat sat Dominic. In the back, flanked by Larchette and Powell, Leo Fiedler slumped with an air of utter resignation. The 4x4 was scraped by branches along an overgrown highway. Rusty signs, in both German and Russian, warned unauthorized visitors: FORBIDDEN ZONE. ELECTRIC FENCES. EXPLOSIVE MINES. Dominic hoped that the military had been allocated sufficient resources to remove all the landmines. As a one-legged veteran had once dryly remarked to him,

"They only have to miss the one. . . ."

Then Dominic didn't avoid danger so much as render himself invisible to it. He'd attended the kind of school where you grew accustomed to the sticky sensation of spilt blood beneath your shoes. To survive, he merged with the background. Dominic was neither stocky nor skinny, neither short nor tall: the kind of guy that nobody ever picked out of an ID parade. As an adult he prided himself on slipping unobtrusively into situations where he could solve his employer's problems, then move on without anyone being exactly sure who he was. Similarly, his encounters with women were as fleeting as they were anonymous. He liked it that way.

Leo grunted. "Here it is. The road to the left leads to the complex that housed Vortex. Nothing will remain above ground. They used dynamite by the truckload." He sniffed. "The body of the fisherman. Why leave it on the beach?"

"The man died in an accident. We'll notify the police once we're done here."

"Strange kind of accident," murmured Leo. "If you consider the state of his head. All hollowed out like that."

Powell shrugged. "Obviously, the man fell overboard—a boat's propeller chewed up his skull."

"With surgical precision?" Dominic raised an eyebrow. Powell's arrogance had begun to grate. More than ever, he found himself on Leo's side rather than with these three. Officially, they were his colleagues, but in name only. As for trusting them? Well . . .

Wanting to get this case concluded, he said, "Scarlet, can't you go any faster?"

"Why the rush?"

Dominic kept his patience—just. "Haven't you noticed? It's almost dusk."

"If we're here after dark, promise you will shoot me." Leo wasn't joking.

It was obvious that the Stalin-era research complex had been obliterated. Apart from warning signs, sections of crumpled fence, and a few yards of exposed blacktop that had escaped the encroaching moss, there was little to see. Other than forest, that is. Beech trees engulfed the place. This area wasn't open to the public, but he knew that elsewhere the Isle of Rugen was a popular tourist destination. Most visitors were happy to stroll its white beaches or enjoy a refreshing dip in the ocean that was so often a dazzling turquoise. However, some visited grim regions of the island. Such as the Strength through Joy Resort: uncannily pristine buildings erected by the Nazis for party members when they needed a break from planning dark deeds. When Hitler exited, Stalin entered. He demanded his puppet regime build submarine pens (together with other sinister installations) on Rugen. Now this was what remained of Soviet domination. A thick forest that no doubt hid many a grisly secret. Project Vortex, for instance.

The team took the opportunity during the jolting drive to roll more footage on the laptop.

"Leo. Do you recognize the man in the right of the picture?" Powell asked. "The one helping carry the dead soldier on the stretcher?"

"It's obvious, isn't it? It's me. Only my hair is darker." He touched his own scalp, which shed its strands. "Dear God, I'm falling apart."

"Can you identify the corpse?"

"Otto Neumann. My best friend. By God, listen to what Dominic told you. Soon it'll be dark. Do you really want to be here in this damned forest when it is?"

"Why? What's so—"

"Enough of these games." Leo glanced through the rear window. It was as if he expected someone to be there. A *someone* he definitely did not want to see. "I'll tell you what I know. Larchette, keep that little camera of yours turning because I shan't repeat myself. After that, kill me if you wish. I shan't mind." He stared at the lens. "All I know of Vortex is that it took men and women, scrubbed away their minds, erased who they were, then replaced them with new identities. Vortex sucked ordinary people in, then it spat out soldiers, artists, musicians! You saw the film. Truthfully, even though I was military personnel, I only ever sat at a desk and compared title deeds with maps of military installations. When the Wall came down, we knew the communist government would fall and we were to be reunited with the West. There was total panic amongst party leaders and the generals. They were desperate to dispose of incriminating evidence. Senior Stasi appeared here on the island to terminate Vortex. You know of the Stasi? The East German secret police? Far, far more brutally efficient than the Gestapo, they had a staff of over one hundred thousand. They were rather good at repression, torture, and espionage. They even forced children to spy on their parents, and coerced wives and husbands to tell tales about each other." He sighed.

"Here on the island, regular troops were smart enough not to get involved with concealing human experimentation: they swapped uniforms for civilian clothes and simply returned home. I, and my fellow pen-pushers, were foolish enough to accept triple pay to tidy up some loose ends. What those loose ends were, we hadn't a clue." Leo glanced uneasily about the forest. Shadows there were altogether darker as dusk crept down onto this remote corner of the island: a place that no longer appeared part of the human world.

"Go on." Scarlet tensed with anticipation. "You saw Vortex?"

Leo shrugged. "New Year's Day, ninteen-ninety—we assembled in the Vortex block. Already, filing cabinets had been emptied into the yard, papers set on fire. The place was a mess. Its permanent staff had fled. It was left to us poor bloody clerks to bring an end to Vortex. Clearly, there weren't enough Stasi officers to do the job themselves. Already, most of them had deserted too. They knew we wouldn't have the guts to see it through, so they gave us bottles of strong Danish beer along with little pills that, they said, would give us stamina. Little and black they were, like berries that grow on juniper bushes. They ordered us to swallow them. Ack, bitter as aspirin! Within ten minutes my heart was racing—everything twinkled with silver stars. Amphetamine, I guess. Probably with a bit of acid, just enough to make everything unreal so we wouldn't be troubled by our consciences. Then they issued guns, and we went to work."

"What then?" Powell demanded.

"I should be asking *you* a question. You're so smart, but you've missed something blindingly obvious . . . something under your idiot nose."

"Leo. I ask the questions."

"Then be it on your head."

"What did you do once you were issued weapons?"

"We formed into squads of ten. The first squad was sent into the subterranean levels of the building to terminate the experiment."

"And?"

"Do I have to spell it out? They never came back."

Dominic shivered. The sun shone blood-red through the trees. Shadows fused, pooled, spread. *Time to go . . . it really is time to go . . .*

Leo suddenly took pleasure in this, as if he was close to springing a surprise on them all. "So the Stasi commander sent in the next squad of pen-pushers, toting their submachine guns. The drug made them laugh, a screaming laugh, to those men it became the most hilarious thing in the world. Those were strong drugs, huh?" He nodded, seeing it all again in his mind's eye.

Gently, Dominic urged, "Tell them everything, then we can leave."

"Only after he's shown us the Vortex site," Scarlet countered. "Once we get a fix, the excavation team can do the rest."

Leo groaned. "Why must I keep stating the obvious? The squads entered the complex. They never returned. Three officers went down there to find out what was making our soldiers vanish. One officer came back. His face was missing—only the eyes stared out from this red, dripping mask. We were high. We laughed like maniacs as we emptied our guns into his belly. Ha, the Stasi had a bellyful too." He chuckled. "They raced out to their big black cars, fled back to the mainland. I realized then that someone had a video camera—no doubt for the benefit of the top brass. They could see Vortex destroyed without having to actually step on tainted ground—at least, that's what they hoped. Eventually, a couple of us ventured into the first of the underground levels. Believe me, they went on for kilometer after kilometer. With big silver pipes that made whooshing noises. As we stood there . . . wondering what the hell we should do, we heard a humming sound. That sent us crazy . . . we fired into the tunnels . . . then I realized it was the elevator rising up through the levels to our floor. The doors opened. I found my friend Neumann. We carried his body out on the stretcher. You've video of us doing just that." He paused, smiling. "But I wonder why you haven't seen what I've seen."

"And what's that, Leo?"

"Look at the footage again of the corpse on the stretcher. See the state of his head. Now cast your mind back to the corpse washed up by the tide. Then compare the two."

To end Vortex is madness. See the films I have made. Visit my test subjects. Whatever it takes, find a way to continue this research—for I can give you absolute power over the human mind.

—Dr. Lippisch, 1989

Within five minutes of leaving the car, Leo pointed to the setting of the long-gone building that had housed Vortex. Now there were only beech saplings and stinging nettles. Hemlock gifted the evening air with a bitter scent. Scarlet wielded an aerosol to mark pink streaks on the turf where the walls and entrances had once stood. Soon, yet more weed-covered mounds of rubble were marked with splashes of fluorescent pink. Powell, still wearing his grim seen-it-all-before expression, employed a handheld electronic device to record the exact GPS coordinates.

Larchette, however, obsessed about the dead fisherman and footage of the corpse Leo had helped carry on the stretcher. "They had the same wounds," he insisted. "Both had undergone the identical surgical procedure. Their brains had been removed. It must have happened to the fisherman only hours ago. How can that be when this place was dynamited back in nineteen-ninety? Is there—"

"Larchette," Scarlet interrupted. "We can speculate later over a beer—you *clearly* need one."

Larchette fired anxious glances into the forest. "We don't know what happened to those test subjects. Leo told us the execution squads simply vanished. Except for the guy recovered from the elevator. He—"

Scarlet snapped, "That's enough." Even as she spoke, they heard a soft thump, one loud enough, nevertheless, to make birds in the trees screech in alarm. Dominic's three colleagues exchanged puzzled glances.

"Sounds like a big door being slammed shut—*underground.*" Leo chuckled. He'd taken satisfaction from Larchette's unease. "Someone just left the house. In a temper. A steaming rage."

Dominic shook his head. "That's no door." He raced back through the trees. By now, the sun had sunk behind the uppermost branches to stain the ground with shadows that stretched out like so many limbs, eager to seize unwitting victims. "Damn." He stopped dead. The big 4x4 had been waiting on the track to take them home. Now that would no longer happen.

Larchette howled, "I knew it was going wrong. I knew it!"

In the growing gloom, the car stood on its roof. Four tires, slashed to shreds, pointed forlornly at the evening sky.

Powell frowned. "Somebody's playing tricks."

"Tricks?" Leo smiled strangely. "This is no prank."

Scarlet seized his arm. "What do you mean?"

"You're in danger. Dreadful danger. Don't you understand?"

The sunset's bloody light gushed through the leaves.

Larchette trembled. "We've got to get out of here. Now."

"How, you idiot?" Powell bellowed. "Someone flipped the damn car!"

Leo chuckled. "See? This place unmans the strongest. Even Herr Powell is frightened now."

"Frightened." Powell sneered. "I'll do the frightening." He drew an object from under his fleece. Dominic saw the gunmetal black of a revolver.

"Useless." Leo's chuckle turned manic. "A child's toy."

"Quiet."

Leo pressed on, eyes bulging as memories flooded him. "My comrades went rolling into Vortex armed with AK-47s, those big, fat curving ammo clips full of armor-piercing rounds. Consummate widow makers. Yet only one man returned. With his brains scooped out. Hah, how will your little pistol save you? How—"

Powell slapped Leo hard.

He wiped blood from his mouth with grim satisfaction. "I am right, Herr Powell. You are frightened."

Powell raised his fist. "Stupid old—"

"Enough," Dominic barked. "Leo's no fool. You should be listening to him. Because right now you're the stupid ones. You're blundering round like you're playing spies in your own backyard. You've absolutely no comprehension about what happened in this place. The experiments! The atrocities! Even worse, you haven't realized something is *continuing*. There's an aftermath. Some agency is still at work in this forest. Can't you get the fact into your thick heads? People flipped that car. They shredded the tires. Therefore, someone wants to trap us here: *they have plans.*"

"He's right." Scarlet drew a handgun from a concealed holster. "Start watching each other's backs."

"This is connected to the fisherman, the one with the . . ." Larchette pressed the top of his head as if to check that it was still intact. "My God. We might be next."

"We could turn the car?" Powell suggested.

"Even if we can, how would it run on flat tires?"

"Walk," Larchette stammered. "Start walking now—we'll reach a road, at least." He pulled out his cell phone. "The police can have cars waiting for us."

As he pressed the keys, his bearded face quivered. "No signal. Damn, damn! Try yours, Scarlet."

It took moments to confirm that cells were useless in this remote quarter.

"Either shoot me or follow me," Leo told them. "But this is the way."

Renewed hope made Larchette eager to be friendly. "How long, Leo?"

"Twenty minutes, maybe."

"Then we should just make it before it gets properly dark," Scarlet observed.

"So?" Leo smiled. "You're trusting me with your lives?" The smile broadened. "Deliciously ironic."

The light turned deeper crimson: a congealed quality that became streaked with black as shadows lengthened. Rich, earthy scents of fungi thickened the air. Dominic noticed that the woodland crowded in as they moved away from the demolished complex. Here, a thick loam allowed trees to sink their roots deep underground. He pictured pale tendrils snaking down through dark, moist soil to penetrate Cold War bunkers. For all the world, it felt as if they'd crossed a threshold. They'd entered an alien landscape of dense, primeval forest. Here, the dead might sing melancholy ballads. A phantom wolf could swallow up the moon to bring an end to humankind. Or so it seemed to Dominic.

As they walked, a jittery Larchette sputtered, "It can't be far now, surely? See? This is the old route to the highway."

But the abandoned road had skinned over with moss. Brambles engulfed it, forcing detours. Boughs overhung it to form a tunnel that was so devoid of light that sometimes they stumbled. A cold wind, born in the Arctic, ghosted through the foliage. Timbers creaked. Twigs plucked at the strands of an old wire fence until it sounded as if a lunatic guitarist was seranading them with jangling metallic discord as they found themselves once more swallowed by an army of trees

Dominic noted that his three "colleagues" were well equipped. Soon they produced slender flashlights to illuminate the path. They trudged on as a rising gale cried through the wilderness. Flanking the way were steel signs that were slowly dying of rust; nevertheless, he could make out Russian words that must have spelled out ominous warnings. Beneath that rune-like text, etchings of death's heads underlined the threats of danger. Dominic glimpsed domed skull shapes gazing out from the bushes. These morbid, decaying objects were concrete machine gun posts intended to protect the military complex in the time of yore. Twin slits in the front, from which the guns would have been fired, resembled eye sockets that imbued the domes with a cold, hating stare. Trespassers weren't welcome.

Larchette was worried. "Surely, it can't be far now—hey!" He whirled round as if tracking an object that moved swiftly through the trees. *"Did you see that?"*

"For pity's sake, man, get a grip."

"I did see something," Larchette protested. "A flash of white . . . like bare skin."

"If you go chasing elves, we'll never get out of here." Powell marched away along the overgrown track. "You're a coward, Larchette. And that's the word I'll use in my report. You're fin—"

This time Powell stopped short. His anger vanished completely when he uttered, "I hope you've got strong stomachs."

"We're dead," Leo predicted with grim satisfaction. "As good as nailed into our coffins. As good as eaten by worms."

What blocked this weed-choked roadway to the outside world was a chain-link fence, ten feet high and topped with razor wire, clearly erected when the Cold War base was abandoned. This, however, hadn't triggered Leo's macabre statement.

Everyone stared at what adorned the steel mesh. At what had so grimly fruited there in the bone-chilling northerly. Their eyes absorbed every detail of the dozens of corpses that had been strung from the wire. From the tiny corpses of sparrows, to crows, to rabbits, to the bloated cadavers of reindeer that swung heavily—blood-filled pendulums that sprinkled maggots into the grass when the wind blew.

"Look at their heads," Scarlet breathed. "Every single one of them."

"Just like the fisherman back on the beach, eh?" Leo enjoyed himself now that he detected fear in his interrogators. "So? What does this evidence tell you? Are you sure you will be going home to your families, after all?"

Perhaps forty creatures hung there: tiny birds to man-sized deer. Each and every one mutilated. Probing beams from flashlights revealed that the tops of craniums were missing; the brains removed; eyeless sockets formed windows to redly vacant skulls.

The cold seemed to blow right through the five as if eager to tug souls free of all too mortal bodies. Tree trunks groaned deeply while beneath the endless clawing of the branches, the domed concrete bunkers stared coldly, sullenly, as if knowing what awaited the foolhardy as nightfall sent forth its invasion of prowling shadows.

A gunshot split the air. "There it is!" Smoke poured from Larchette's handgun. "You must have seen it!" Screaming, he ran into the bushes in pursuit of the flitting form.

Powell had seen it. Anyone could tell just by the expression on his face. Aghast, he backed off, then fled.

Dominic called to Scarlet and Leo, "Get back to the beach. We can follow the shore to . . ." He didn't finish the sentence. A spider scuttled out from the bushes.

"Oh, dear heaven." Like a frightened child, Scarlet's hand found his.

Because it wasn't just any kind of spider. There in the light of Scarlet's flashlight Dominic saw a crude spider shape. Only it was far too big, perhaps ten feet in diameter. Pale, almost hairless—flesh pulpy. Quite simply, the creature had been assembled from naked human beings, eight men arranged in such a way that they lay face down with the tops of their heads touching. Skulls had been top-sliced to reveal the brains. Then the craniums had been fused, while some abhorrent surgical technique extended the spinal columns so they were bonded together. Sutured scalps formed a yard-wide knot of unruly hair in the center of that raft of flesh. With their heads conjoined, the men were forced to cooperate as they moved on all fours. They ran on the palms of their hands and soles of their feet, like monkeys trained to perform some weird dance with the crowns of their heads touching. Frequently, they moved sideways—giant, soft-backed crabs, their backbones pressing against skin, each rib visible in their straining bodies, bare buttocks clenching-unclenching as they moved.

"They're dying," Dominic whispered. "They must only be able to survive like this a few days at most."

Already, the face of one man had turned a bruised purple. One eye had closed, the other bulged out, sightlessly, as red as a ripe cherry. A crash from their right heralded the arrival of another of these composite creatures. The eight pairs of limbs moved in a mad scramble, yet every so often the conjoined brains of the individual men must have bonded in perfect synch. Then legs moved with undulating precision, just as the millipede ambulates with a smooth, wave-like motion that carries it across the ground, while the arms that now protruded from what amounted to the underbelly of the beast supported its center where the eight heads were fused. When the gales stopped mauling the trees, a sudden quietude allowed the sound of the fused men to reach Dominic's ears. Each surgically joined man grunted, panted, or whimpered with pain.

He shot a glance back at the creatures adorning the fence. Bizarre trophies, or raw material for new experiments?

Five more of the creatures emerged from the forest onto the weed-choked road. The largest moved clumsily, one of its component parts long dead. Its limbs hung limp, while the other bonded men tried to compensate. The bloated corpse painted a black trail of slime across the grass. Another conjoined creature had also mastered locomotion, so each man moved with graceful precision: it seemed as if the multilimbed creature danced lightly through the dark toward them. Grunts of exertion turned into excited snorting as sweating torsos heaved upward to allow the faces, which were normally turned down toward the ground, to glimpse the intruders. With a cry, Larchette burst from the trees. In one hand he held the flashlight, in the other the pistol. Screaming, he raced toward one of these whirling stars of human flesh, their legs radiating outward. He fired into the press of bodies. With a roar of agony erupting simultaneously from eight mouths, it rose up onto two pairs of legs. Limbs writhed in the air, resembling the tentacles of some nightmare octopus. In the beast's center, eight faces of those conjoined men were clearly visible. The skin along the hairlines had been stitched. Now, stresses of the facial skin tugged features out of shape. Sixteen misshapen eyes glared in both fury and agony at Larchette. He fired his last two rounds into the center, where eight skulls met to form a single structure of bone. While the creature howled, its freakish companions cried out in dismay. Then the wounded beast slammed down onto the turf, feet kicking wildly at the ground until toenails were ripped clean away. A moment later it lay still.

The creature nearest Larchette pounced. As he lay beneath it, it began to resemble a huge pale fist that rested palm down on the earth. What its sixteen hands did to violate Larchette, Dominic had, mercifully, no way of knowing, but the man screamed in terror for a long, long time before his voice trailed into despairing, gulping sobs . . . then, at last, silence.

Dominic didn't know when he began running. Or where. Only that he ran alone through the nighttime forest. Pale tree trunks, phantom sentinels, darted by him. Cold gales provoked the branches to claw at his head as he ran. Twigs plucked the fence wire. Metallic notes punched his eardrums. Torrents of air raked the grass as if invisible claws were tearing at the earth in fury. He blundered by the skull-shaped domes of concrete bunkers, their gun slits watching his desperate scramble with mute amusement. Behind him, the stitched-together conglomerations of men followed. Once, he called out to Scarlet. In answer, the storm raised sounds that aped scornful catcalls.

On returning to what had once been the site of the Vortex buildings, he saw that running was a waste of time. A dozen of those fleshy man-crab creatures waited for him. Some had raised themselves onto two sets of legs so that limbs radiated like the petals of a sunflower. From its crowded center, a cluster of faces peered out, all those glinting eyes fixed eagerly on Dominic.

When they rushed Dominic, he didn't fight. In the face of those odds, what was the point? Powerful hands seized his limbs, then deposited him onto broadly muscular backs where they held him with strong fingers. Coarse body hair pricked his face. Man-sweat, spiked with hormonal excitement, filled his nostrils. As his consciousness retreated from the horror of it all, they carried him away. Like riding a dog sled, he thought dreamily. Low to the ground. Fast, smoothly fast . . . gliding . . .

Any regrets, Dominic? Despite the surreal journey through the dark forest, he found himself musing on his life. He'd no regrets about his clandestine profession. But he felt a sudden, profound sadness. All those casual encounters he'd enjoyed at hotels ... Why couldn't he have invested time in nurturing a meaningful relationship? Yes, he had one regret as his life neared its end: he wished he'd mated emotionally with a woman.

As he rode on the backs of the conjoined men who scrambled crabwise, he pictured himself opening the door of his increasingly lonely apartment to find, instead of emptiness, a smiling face. "How was your day, my love? Did you do anything special?" Briefly, he struggled to free himself. One of the beast's hands gripped his throat. Above him, the stars appeared to spill out of the sky: falling, falling ... they flowed through his skull until his brain was filled with fire.

Grainy VCR color footage. A superimposed date: 03/03/1991. One of the fleshy man-crab beasts lies dead on a tiled floor. Fluids leak from the corpses. Dr. Lippisch addresses the camera. "I don't have anti rejection drugs. So within days, these beautiful children of mine wither and die. But see what I have done. I can fuse separate individuals into a single, coherent being. I reprogram their minds, so they believe this is how they are meant to be." She laughs. "See the torso, then legs ... how they radiate outward like the limbs of a starfish. I name this creation Man-Star. A word play on monster, *of course. Man-Star, my Man-Star ... But one day this Man-Star race will be perfect."*
—VCR anonymously mailed to Leipzig University

To Dominic, it seemed a long, long night. One of absolute darkness. Then there were the dreams ... of blood, of restraint, screaming ... nightmares ... They stained his soul ...

At last: LIGHT. A light that drove incandescent torrents through his eye sockets. As he tried to force himself fully awake, he realized that a woman in a white coat stood near him. Silver streaked her long hair. As she held a clipboard, she addressed a camcorder set on its tripod in the room's center. "I am Dr. Lippisch, Senior MD, Project Vortex. Here you see my latest subject, aged thirty-three, a healthy male. Drugs, which I have at last acquired, will prevent the subject's immune system from rejecting my surgical grafts. Composite brain is healthy, tissue pink, arterial blood-flow satisfactory. Students, watch carefully. The abdomen wall is already clamped back in order to receive a very special passenger."

Dominic turned his head to one side. There on a line of tables lay Scarlet, Leo, Powell, and Larchette. The tops of their heads had been neatly sliced; empty skull cavities revealed that the brains had been removed.

Dr. Lippisch walked quickly to the camera, tilted it so its lens would capture images of Dominic strapped to the operating table. Then she switched on a TV bolted to a tiled wall. In vibrant detail, it revealed Dominic as he lay there supine. Naked. Blood-stained. Belly slit from ribcage to pubic hair. The mouth of the wound gaped huge and red as steel S-shaped clips tugged back the flesh. His stomach now formed a great crimson cave of a thing. A gory void. A roomy vault from which arteries, expertly clamped, protruded.

At that moment Dominic understood many things. An epidural killed any sensation below his collarbone. (Lippisch: *"See the regular rhythm of the diaphragm. All is well."*) What's more, he knew that the woman—utterly insane—had remained in the bunker after the fall of communism. There, she'd secretly continued Operation Vortex. She had built her Man-Stars. (*"Watch how I insert the grafted matter into the space once occupied by the right kidney. Now I connect blood vessels, which once fed that kidney, with the carotid and jugular stubs of the conjoined brains."*) Worse, he would know what it was like to carry the brains of Leo, Scarlet, Powell, and Larchette in his belly. And for those four, moistly pink brains to be fed by his own lifeblood. (*"Viewers, please check the website for updates. I fully expect this subject's nervous system to gradually connect with those of the brains implanted in his abdomen. Soon, he will establish communication. The integrated brain in his stomach will talk to him via his own neural highway. . . . Just imagine the nature of such a conversation!)*

Lippisch was mad, of course. Completely delusional. An opinion proved when she accidentally caught the epidural embedded in his upper spine; the long loop of tubing had been left to hang carelessly down to the floor, and her foot had done the rest. Once the needle had popped out, his healthy liver stopped efficiently filtering the drug from his bloodstream. Pain was quick to show its unwelcome face. Within moments, the agony of the vast surgical wound in his stomach became a Pentecostal fire. Unconsciousness stayed cruelly at arm's length, so he felt the nettle-like sting of the scalpel part yet more muscle. Then came the cold mass of his companions' brain tissue being forced through the gory hole into his abdomen. Dr. Lippisch happily sang a Bavarian folk song as she operated. Dominic's scream carried upward through the clay to the surface. Momentarily loud enough, it made Lippisch's monstrous creations pause in surprise before they slid back into the all-engulfing shadows of the forest.

Success is sweet indeed. And with that success, even I am transfigured.

——Dr. Lippisch

"What is it, Dominic? Are we close?"

"Yes . . . too close."

"Are you frightened?"

"Terrified. If you believed me, then you'd be terrified too."

"Show us the site of the Vortex compound, then you're free to leave."

How similar the replacements to Powell, Scarlet, and Larchette sounded. They looked the same too. HQ must use the same recruitment template. The woman was a career-driven ice maiden. One man appeared queasy at the sight of everything here on the beach.

The third wore a permanently bitter expression.

"You haven't asked to see my scar," Dominic began. "I can prove—"

"We've been through that," said the woman. "An old surgical wound proves nothing."

"Show us the Vortex site." The queasy man switched on his digital camera. "You will be questioned and your responses filmed. Do you understand?"

Dominic grimaced. "Follow me."

He led them up the beach, over piles of seashells that were as white as fresh snowdrifts, to a break in the dazzling cliffs, for which Rugen is justly famous, then he guided them into the forest. There, its silent, shadowed interior embraced them.

The bitter-faced man spat questions: "You came this way with Scarlet, Powell, and Larchette?"

"Yes." The twelve-pound brain mass inside Dominic's stomach grew hot, itchy; it began to pulsate. His inner companions were full of anticipation.

"You found the site of the Vortex lab?"

"As you will see for yourselves."

Overarching tree branches formed a tunnel of near darkness.

"Do you know the nature of the Lippisch experiments?"

"Oh, yes, indeed."

Dominic led the way. Contentedly, he rubbed a big, tightly full stomach. Behind him, a white-coated figure fell in behind his little, unsuspecting party. Hair tied severely back, she walked silently with a clipboard hugged toward her chest. When she lifted a hand, her Man-Stars sidled out of the undergrowth. The trio hadn't yet noticed they were being stalked by naked men conjoined at the head, their long pale legs stepping in unison through the gloom. But they would see them soon enough, when it was far too late to do anything about it.

"When the Man-Stars make their move, I'll let you watch."

"What was that you just said?" asked the nauseated-looking one.

"Oh." Dominic didn't turn round. "Just talking to the inner man, so to speak."

When Lippisch's Man-Stars launched themselves on his three new "colleagues," that's when he turned to watch the one-sided struggle. As he did so, he found himself recalling the increasingly lonely hours at home; the pointless encounters with strangers in airport hotels; the click of the hotel room door, closing on a woman whose name he'd already forgotten. "Be sure you don't injure the female," he told the Man-Stars. "Dr. Lippisch has promised me a bride." He smiled fondly. "A bride with brains."

Dominic began to laugh. A huge, hearty laugh that scared the birds from the trees. This, he knew, was the start of beautiful new world.

Mist on the Bayou

Heather Graham

Moss draped the trees like crystalline spiderweb's, caught in the eerie glow of a full moon made misty by low-hanging clouds. The water appeared to be black, with an unearthly sheen just hovering above it; the air temperature had cooled, creating the fog.

As the pontoon boat moved down the Pearl River, even I, who have known this area like the back of my hand since childhood, thought it was the perfect venue for a "Haunted Happening"—as the ghoulish, year-round attraction to which we were headed, Labelle Plantation, was being touted. It had opened last year, but closed right after Halloween. We'd had some trouble then in the city—folks coming down and disappearing—and though they might have moved on elsewhere, everyone was glad that Halloween was over. But that was last year, and this is now, and people have to make a living. Those who had come had spread the word about the fantastic haunted house created out of the old plantation on the bayou, and everyone had been on board to entice more tourism.

In retrospect, no one had known just how good it would be, or that it would attract such a huge crowd.

Now, the publicity the place had garnered was bringing people in by the hundreds, and thus the determination that it would stay open all year. And that was why I was aboard this first "midnight bayou" tour of the place. It could be reached by the road. It could also be reached by the river. Ben Perry, who owns the boats at the boat slips on the bayou, is one of my best friends. He's been doing simple bayou tours for years. Ecology just isn't as big as scaring the pants off people. Since I've been known for my "Myths and Legends" walks in the city, my old friend thought he needed me on his inaugural voyage for the event.

I had just finished conducting a tour of the French Quarter, and there I was on a pontoon boat on a chilly night, dressed in my Victorian waistcoat and top hat. Not such a bad outfit for the walks—but strange when I was going to be hopping to the sandy beach area that fronted the plantation. Ah, well. I did have my Victorian boots on too.

So up ahead was Labelle Plantation.

A screech owl let out a mighty call, as if it had been paid to add to the eerie environment.

A pretty brunette jumped and let out a little, "Eek."

Ben laughed, pleased. "Hey, we haven't even gotten there yet," he told her.

Most folks around New Orleans and environs had thought for sure that the old plantation would be condemned, and that the Boudreaux brothers' attempts to buy the place and set up shop would be denied. But apparently, despite years of neglect, a reputation for the truly horrid even among the legends in the realm, and a history that might be conceived as the epitome of evil, the structure had been deemed sound. The place had been repaired, reconstructed, and set up as a haunted house. A haunted history house, so they said—with every creepy possibility and nightmare thrown into the mix. Hell, if someone had so much as a *thought* a hundred years ago, it had to be history now, right? Anyway, the brothers decided that making a big creepy tourist attraction out of the place would be good for everyone. The economy just kept taking a beating because of the storms, even the country needed a good fix, and whatever works is what we need. That was the logic behind it all. I couldn't argue that much; I was thirty, and I owned my own tour company. I only had two full-time employees now; once, I'd had ten.

I had known Ted, Fred, and Jed—no kidding—Boudreaux since I was a kid. They were hellraisers—the kind who had spent years shooting up beer cans in the bayou, talking tough, and looking like cast members out of *Deliverance*. Ted was my age. I knew him best—he was the one with the business expertise. Fred was the oldest—dangerously psychotic, in my opinion—while Jed had actually made it through eight years of college and a residency to come home as a doctor and was now a beloved GP.

With the motor purring, the boat moved slowly along, and those twenty folks aboard the pontoon kept a wary eye out. Gators slithered about in the night. There were "oohs" and "aahs" as they did so. They were mostly little guys, three and four feet, but their eyes glowed gold when caught in the lights, and there was something primeval about the way they moved. Ben was making a big deal out of them; I caught his gaze as he pointed out one of the creatures. He gave me a silent shrug: *We all have to make a buck. So what if the little gators are ten times more scared of the people?*

The screech owl was on our side; he let out another eerie shriek. In the brush that bordered the bayou, a wild pig rustled through the foliage. It couldn't get much better.

I grinned at Ben in return. I wasn't a native of this area just east of Slidell, not like Ben and the Boudreaux brothers. Ben had a degree in business; he'd actually spent a few years on Wall Street, but he loved the bayou too much, so he was back. I had been born just outside the French Quarter, and I'd lived there all my life, except for a stint up north for college—I had been a history major at Columbia, no less. But this was my home too. I knew all the stories; I had grown up with them. I knew all the crazy folk in town too—the harmless loonies, the true psychopaths; most of them were imported these days, and worse. I love all of this area, The French Quarter, the bayou, the Garden District, all of Orleans Parish and the parishes beyond. It's my home; it's where I belong.

"We're coming up on the Labelle estate," Ben announced to the tourists. "My friend Dan, from the Myths and Legends Walk, is going to give you the story on the old plantation. The truth, my friends, is far scarier and creepier than anything you'll see tonight."

I winced and smiled at the girl who had been seated near him on the pontoon. She was a pretty thing, blond, with enormous blue eyes and a strange air of fragility. We'd talked for a few minutes earlier. I knew she was staying at one of the old B and Bs near Rampart Street.

I found her fascinating. Most people on the tours came in a pack—or at least in twos and threes. They liked to hang on to one another as they walked through a creepy haunted house; guys loved for their girlfriends to be scared and grab them.

The girl smiled back at me tentatively. It was strange. She was so pretty, so fragile, and yet she had a look of resolve about her—as if she could do this; she *would* do this. Something about her touched me. I wanted to assure her. Hell, I wanted to put an arm around her and protect her from all the evil in the world.

But it was just a haunted house, and it sure didn't seem as if there was anyone with her to whom she might have something to prove. She had come alone. Being alone on this tour was not good for the fainthearted. The Boudreaux brothers had done an entirely gruesome and ghastly workup on the place. The brothers created a maze that contained all kinds of wicked and evil tableaus from history and also from their imagination, which allowed the costumed actors to run around and scare the daylights out of everyone.

"The truth, and nothing but the truth!" came a cry from the back of the pontoon. Great. The guy in the back was drunk. That happened when you picked up your tours on Bourbon Street. Lots of people had some kind of fortification. Most didn't come plastered.

"The truth," I announced. I have a good voice for a tour director, something for which I am grateful, since I do love my company and telling all the wild stories about my homeland. I have a deep baritone that projects well—a damned good voice for ghost stories. But the story I was about to convey wasn't paranormal. It was certainly about evil, but it wasn't paranormal.

"The plantation was completed in eighteen fifty-nine by a wealthy French merchant," I began. "He and his wife moved in, along with many of their servants. The wife was the descendant of one of the French Quarter's famous octoroons, said to be a voodoo queen who didn't recognize all the goodness that might be found in the spiritual sense of the religion. She had charmed a rich Frenchman, and thus gone on to be rich herself and produce rich descendants, such as Madame Labelle. All manner of visitors left the city of New Orleans to visit Labelle plantation; many were never seen again, but as communications were not what they are now—no cell phones or e-mail, you know— their disappearances weren't suspected to have been at the hands of the Labelle family. Strangely, many of their contemporaries had thought the Labelles were active in the Underground Railroad, so many slaves seemed to disappear from their homes. Although she entertained lavishly, was known for her incredible beauty, and seemed to be a powerhouse in society, folks were a little frightened of Madame. Then the Civil War rolled around. Soldiers were sent out to the plantation to find quarters and food; they didn't return. When more soldiers were sent out, they didn't return either. Finally, several companies of soldiers went out. Apparently, the Labelles knew they were coming. They fled. When the Yankee captain in charge searched the barn, he found dozens of men hanging from meat hooks; their throats had been slit and their blood had been collected in troughs. But there were worse discoveries to be made. There were bodies and body parts found buried throughout the house. Upstairs, in Madame's boudoir, there was a massive wooden tub stained with blood. Bones had been utilized to make lamps, an altar, and other decorations. Shades and even a macabre quilt had been made from the skin of those she and her husband had murdered. She was practicing black magic more than voodoo; her blood sacrifices were necessary, according to the ancient Haitian text she had left behind."

I paused. Even the drunk had grown quiet.

"Not even the Yankee commander would stay at the house, or take anything from the house. It was left empty. The war raged on. People said the place was haunted, and no one wanted to go near it. They heard screams of terror—which turned out to be real. Twenty people or so had been left to die, chained to walls in a root cellar at the rear of the property, beneath the slave quarters. Those people are long since gone, and the outbuildings have fallen to the ground. The root cellar has been filled. Only the house remains today."

A gator slid into the water from the embankment, making a slithery sound. The drunk jumped.

Some girls laughed.

"Hey! That's a crock. No one bought it until now?" the drunk called, trying to regain a semblance of he-man fearlessness.

"Oh, yeah," I said. "A fellow named Sullivan bought it during the eighteen-eighties. He died from a fall off the roof. It was vacant again until nineteen-twenty. A family lived there. They moved out a year after they purchased the place, saying that the ghosts were shaking their children in the middle of the night. The little girl, according to police documents, was bruised and beaten."

"Yeah, I can tell you what happened there," one of the drunk's more sober friends said. "I think they call it child molestation these days."

"Maybe," I agreed. "But the family moved on to Mobile, and there were no more incidents. I'm only telling you what really happened, or what was documented. The home was purchased by an American oil tycoon, but he never lived in it, and he lost it to taxes during the Depression. Another speculator bought it in the nineteen-forties, but he was killed in World War II; the house went to taxes once again. A cultist bought it in the early seventies, but he and his harem drowned in the Mississippi—he was convinced that the aliens were due down to earth to pick him and his women up in their spacecraft. Since then, it's been vacant." I smiled. The blond was staring at me. I remembered then, when Ben had taken her ticket, she'd said her name was Callie. She didn't seem horrified by the truth—she had seemed more frightened earlier, but I still didn't see her taking a casual, fun-but-super-scary trek through the old plantation.

"Oh, that's just bull!" cried the drunk.

I could see Ben at the tiller, shaking his head. He was probably thinking about losing the drunk in the water. And maybe one of the young gators hanging around had a big hidden mama who might take a bite out of him.

That would be one mean lawsuit.

I shrugged at him. People often came to New Orleans just to get blitzed. Those of us who lived here didn't have to be saints, but we usually knew how much to drink, or at least when it was appropriate to get wasted. I said, "You can check parish records, folks—I'm just telling the truth."

I smiled again at the blond. *Callie.*

She rolled her eyes. "Ass!" she said softly to me, indicating the drunk at the other end with a nod of her head. She shivered.

"Listen, they keep a snack bar opened in the second formal parlor. It's to the left of the house after we enter," I told her.

She looked at me gravely, then offered up a slow grimace. "Ghosts certainly didn't perform any of the evil you just talked about," she said. "Madame Labelle was a human monster. And the cultist was a psycho, and sadly, the girls with him were idiots."

"So who actually owns the place now?" a thirty-something fellow called out. He looked as if he had been a linebacker in college. He was there with his wife, a pretty redhead who had certainly been a cheerleader, and another young couple.

I laughed and couldn't help looking at Callie again. I really liked her, everything about her. "Believe it or not, folks, and this is the absolute truth, it's owned by Ted, Fred, and Jed—known as the Boudreaux brothers in these parts. Born and bred right here along the bayou. They saw a chance at a good income, and they took it."

The ex-linebacker's red-haired wife shivered. "You are making all this up! What bad taste to open a haunted house in such a terrible place."

"Ma'am," I assured her, "I am not making it up. Please, think about it, there are lots of other places like this one. If you reserved a room, you know, you could spend the night in Fall River, Mass, where Lizzie Borden allegedly gave her stepmother forty whacks."

"Ooh, creepy," said another pretty brunette. She had a drawl—not Louisiana. Texas, I thought, and I'm pretty good at accents. She was with two friends, and they all seemed to be flirting with a few Wall

Street types on vacation, who in turn looked to be happy to have the three flirting with them. "But, yes, you can stay there! I've heard that it's true."

Murmuring went up as the rest of the boat agreed; they all knew that what I had just said was true—they had watched the Travel Channel.

"Yeah," the linebacker said "And I saw on one of those shows that the Labelle plantation was one of the spookiest haunted houses in the country!"

"There it is!" Ben announced. "And careful getting off, folks. This isn't Disney World. We're on a real pontoon boat, and that's real Pearl River sand. The brush has been cleared off leading up to the plantation house, and there's plenty of light, but still, be careful stepping on and off."

The pontoon slid hard onto the sand, hitting an uneven area; the drunk had started to rise, and he toppled onto the linebacker. They might not have to worry about the fake blood in the house; the two men might come to blows before they got off the boat.

Stepping to the stern, I reached for the drunk's arm and steered him from the linebacker.

"I got it, I got it," the drunk grumbled.

The linebacker stared daggers at the fellow, looked at me, and held his peace.

I leapt off the pontoon, landing on the soft sand and hurrying around, swearing quietly as my boots hit the water. No real biggie; I'd clean 'em up later. I didn't want Ben's first evening on the river as a tour guide to the dynamo haunted house going sour.

"The footing is uneven here—everyone has to be careful," I said, reaching for the first tourist.

Ben and I helped the rest of the bayou tourists off the boat. "We get to hear the skunk ape story on the way back, right?" one of the women asked.

"Oh, yes, ma'am, yes, ma'am," Ben assured her. "You can head right on up the walk," he added. "There will be a zombie or witch to greet you at the door, and Dan will be waiting at the snack and gift shop for you all when you get through. Bayou guests get to break the line!" he added.

I watched the group start up the walk for the house. People could come by car, but this really was the best way to see the place; plantations had been built near the water. Long ago, the river had been the way most folks traveled, so the grand entrance actually faced it.

The eerie mist still hovered above the water and seemed to encroach on the land. Not far up, though, the "ghost" lights were switched on; plenty of illumination, but in a strange shade of blue.

For a moment, the house was caught in that eerie glow of blue light and fog. It was majestic; a Colonial with wraparound porches and a grand entryway. The door stood open; it appeared for a moment as if the fog issued from the house. The mist seemed to swirl around the front door and weave in circles around it.

There were plenty of people in the house. The Boudreaux brothers were invested in it; Ted was a good businessman. He'd brought in professional designers to lay it out. Then he'd kept the costs low by hiring the slashers, victims, zombies, voodoo queens, movie monsters, and what have you from the ranks of our local college kids.

I realized that I was staring at the house, thinking that the mist made it appear to be really evil. Ben was doing the same. Our group had already gone up the foggy walk—and had disappeared into the house as if they, like the fog, had been swept in by a spectral force.

"So," Ben said, a little anxiously, "it's going to be good, right? These folks don't mind paying the money for the boat trip over. It comes with good stories, real history, and bless those alligators!"

I didn't answer him at first. The house was disturbing me. And I still felt a little "haunted" myself by the lovely Callie. I didn't understand why she was doing this when she looked so scared. I found myself thinking back about the comment the other woman had made, about it being in bad taste to make a haunted house out of a place where so much terror had occurred. Ben was worried. Why not? Times had been hard.

"Sure, it all went great, will go great," I told him. "Hey, I'm going to go on. I've heard about it, but I haven't been through it. I'm worried about the blonde."

"What blonde?" Ben asked.

"The one at the front of the boat."

Ben shrugged. "Frankly, the only girls I really noticed were the three brunettes with the football players. They were from Texas." He grinned broadly. "And one of them had a pair of jugs on her the size of Texas too."

"She looked scared—Callie, the blonde. I'm going to try to catch up. It won't be good if she has a panic attack, or something."

Ben shrugged. "Go for it, dude. So, I like the jugs, you like the blondes. I'll be here. Oh, hey."

"Yeah?"

"Thanks for coming tonight. I know you're juggling your own stuff. But tonight, seemed important to have the best."

"Sure. No problem," I told him.

"No. I mean *thank you*. Really. Tonight, it had to be *you* out here."

"Like I said, no problem at all, Ben."

I strode up the path, hurrying to catch up. The haunted house was hotter than hell as a tourist attraction right now. Ben had made a deal to get his people in right away for the twenty bucks extra they paid to come by the bayou.

They had already been greeted by the zombie at the door. It was actually Darla Boudreaux, a cousin of Ted, Fred, and Jed. I told her hello, and she gave me a gooey kiss—she was wearing a lot of makeup. "Hey, you. Trying to catch up? Your group are is already in the Egyptian gallery, screaming away. Our mummy jumps out of his sarcophagus."

"Thanks, I'll meet up with them," I told her.

The lighting was done extremely well, the outside in the blue light that enhanced the fog, the inside hallways bathed in a crimson glow. The house was never so dark that you couldn't see where you were going, but it was plenty dark enough to make you wonder just what was lurking around the next corner—indeed, just who or what was walking next to you.

There was a crowd ahead of me, not my crowd, trying to slow down so that the costumed monsters would jump out and scare them. I excused myself and made my way around them. It wasn't difficult; I was in my tour clothing, so I looked like an employee.

The Egyptian room was first. The mummy started to scare a tourist but saw me and stopped. "Hey, Dan!"

"Hey. Roger?" Roger Thompson worked for me part-time. I hadn't had enough business lately to keep him on as full-time staffer. He was twenty-four, still a kid enough to really love dressing up as a mummy.

"Yeah, yeah, it's me. Cool place, huh?"

"Yeah, get back in. The next crowd is coming through."

Roger lay back down, bringing the top of his sarcophagus along with him.

It was well done. The walls here, false walls as they were, had hieroglyphics covering them; it appeared to be a section of a tomb. A lifelike Cleopatra had eyes that followed me as I moved—I expected her to be real, she was so lifelike, but she wasn't. A partially mummified cat screeched from its wrappings as if it were being buried alive, and the soundtrack was an eerie Egyptian theme.

The Egyptian area was followed by an old Celtic-slash-druid-slash-pagan arena, based on the bodies found in the bogs of England; a poor farmer was garroted, sacrificed to a harvest god. There were peat bog monsters running around there, scaring folks, along with a few druid priests.

I moved on. The Inquisition happened again here in Louisiana, complete with some really scary inquisitors. In a tableau where the French Revolution was reenacted, an actor lost his head over and over and over again. Fake blood spurted, and the floor was filled with it in the area surrounding the guillotine's basket. A few girls were screaming their heads off as they passed through, jumping, knocking into each other. The Boudreaux brothers had done exceptionally well with the sound system; each new era of death, dismay, and torture brought in a new and very creepy soundtrack.

I don't know why, but as I moved through the maze seeking my people, I felt a growing sense of restlessness. Something about the place just wasn't quite . . . right. I told myself I was a fool. The sins of the past were not going to come back and make the walls of the old house come to life, seeking blood, or anything of the like. People just loved haunted houses. They loved to be scared. It was cool, and that was it.

Famous murderers followed the French Revolution; I was in a street where Jack the Ripper was roaming; the Countess Bathory—a gorgeous young girl in a mammoth wig—walked the maze, studying all the young women, as if seeking their blood. New Orleans' own Madame LaLaurie wove through the thrill seekers as her husband performed mutilating surgery on an actress laid on a slab. The actress screamed and writhed, and it was a horrible sight.

I finally caught up with my own group; I saw the drunk and his pals. Seemed they were sobering up a little. Then, the Wall Street types, and the girls who had been flirting with them. We had come to another tableau; here, the one-time owners of the plantation were depicted. Madame Labelle was in an old-fashioned wooden bathtub; blood spilled everywhere around her. She lifted her bloody fingers and pointed out the women in the crowd. "Oh, do come over for dinner!" she said, licking her lips lasciviously.

"Move, move, let's get on!" The linebacker's red-haired wife urged. She was snuggled up against her husband's back.

"Actress, honey, she's an actress!" he murmured.

But even the linebacker seemed to be unnerved.

I skirted around them; I brushed against the wife, and she cried out, then smiled ruefully as she saw me. I grinned and excused myself, moving on.

In the next scene, Monsieur Labelle was torturing a victim, a beautiful young woman. He was in a nineteenth-century waistcoat, much like my own. His white cotton shirt was stained with blood. His victim was on a marble table, and he was leaning over her, deciding whether to draw blood from her wrists or her throat.

There was only one person in the area before the tableau: Callie. She was staring on with absolute horror.

I was about to reassure her; I saw that the actor playing Monsieur Labelle was none other than Fred Boudreaux. I didn't recognize the girl on the table.

"It's just a scene," I told her, setting my hands on her shoulders.

The others were starting to fill in behind us.

Callie didn't seem to know I was there. "No!" she cried. "No, stop him, stop him, it's real!"

The young woman on the table let out a horrible shriek as the knife touched down on her shoulder. The linebacker, who was behind me, let out a nervous laugh.

The girl cried out again hysterically; she was naked beneath a sheet, and she was tied down with rope. She couldn't move, but she thrashed about screaming. "Help me, help me! For the love of God, help me!"

I smelled the blood; I can definitely smell blood. I know the scent of it inside and out.

"It's real, damn it, somebody help her, please, yes, for the love of God!" Callie shouted.

I leapt over the velvet ropes that separated the "guests" from the actors. Fred Boudreaux looked at me, stunned. Then he smiled.

I'd always known that the sucker was psychotic.

"You want some of the action, Dan, is that it?" he asked me softly. Then he wielded the knife in my direction. It was a period piece; an antique knife with a sharp blade. It gleamed in the red light. And it came down at me before I could move, slicing across my collarbone.

Blood spurted, but not as it might have. He'd been aiming for my jugular.

I flew at him, bringing us both down on the floor. I didn't have a weapon; I used my fists and my teeth. Everyone around the two of us was screaming and shouting, crying for help. A lot of the folks thought it was all part of the haunted experience.

Some knew it wasn't.

I was already on top of Fred; he hadn't been able to kill me with his first stab, and he hadn't been prepared for the force of the attack I made. Fred should have known better when he saw me; he should have known what he was up against. I'd managed to rip out half his throat with my teeth, and not even his feeble attempt to skewer me in the gut caused much damage. I was still stunned that he'd really gone so mad, that he'd actually made use of the house to vent his sickness and attempt a murder before an audience.

And yet, where else could you murder in plain sight and get away with it? Listen to a victim's frantic and desperate screams, watch the blood flow, and have an audience screech and scream as well and then walk on by?

The linebacker knocked down the velvet rope. Great. Big help. I was already lying on top of Fred, and he didn't have much throat left, and the blood was spurting insanely from him. I didn't know if I had meant to kill him; I only knew that he had meant to kill me.

Chaos reigned. The linebacker held Fred down to help me, and he, too, became covered in blood. Someone went to help the girl who was tied to the table. People ran from the house, screaming, trampling one another. Ben had called the police. Cops were suddenly flooding through, bright lights were on, and eventually, the plantation emptied of tourists. The hysterical girl was not an actress; she had been one of the first to come through *alone* when Fred grabbed her. She gave a choppy version of events to one of the cops and was taken away in an ambulance. Finally, it was me, the linebacker, the cops, and Ted and Jed Boudreaux. They were horrified, claiming they'd known Fred was a little crazy, but in their wildest dreams, they had never imagined this. I'd gone to school with Ted, as I said. I believed him. He told the cops his brother believed the house was evil; he'd even believed evil could slip into people, but . . . well, everyone knew that the economy was in the dumps and . . . they'd needed to make a living.

It was three a.m. by the time I was able to leave. Ben had been waiting for me, trying to find out what the hell was happening at first, then just pacing the beach in a state of horrified anxiety. I couldn't calm him down. We didn't have any more "guests" for the boat. They'd all been taken back to their various hotels and B and Bs by the cops.

"Jesus," he kept saying, sitting at the back of the boat. "Jesus."

Neither of us noticed the alligators slipping now and then from the bank to the water.

The screech owl was still crying out, but the shrill and haunting sound just bounced off our ears.

"Jesus," Ben said again as we finally got the boat back to the landing.

He looked at me then, shaking his head. "You saved that girl—he stabbed you. There's blood all over you."

"I'm all right. Ben, go to bed. No, drink yourself to sleep. There's nothing else you can do now."

"The cops . . ."

"I have to make an appearance and another statement in the morning," I told him. "They've got the linebacker. They think he did most of the subduing—and that he killed Fred because he had to," I assured him.

"Jesus," Ben said. He blinked. He seemed to be past some of the shock. He shook his head. "I guess it's true. Old Fred never knew that you were a vampire, huh? Hey—there's no chance that he can come back, right?"

"I'll see to it," I assured him.

There were several of my kind living in New Orleans. I mean, where else did you go where you could act out all the time? I wasn't a killer; I had never taken a life that didn't need taking. These days, there were blood banks everywhere. We all knew each other, avoided each other, and kept a watch out for any of our kind who might show up in the city and ruin the good thing we had going.

I could live off the blood banks—as could the others. And when there was a shortage, well, we had prisons with some of the meanest rapists, killers, and child molesters in the country. If one of them committed suicide, most folks felt that it was good riddance.

"You always told me not to say anything to anyone," Ben said. "Hell, when we were in school—wait, just how many times have you been through school?"

I shrugged. "Several."

"I thought it was the coolest thing in the world, to have my best friend be a vampire. But you wouldn't let me tell anyone, no matter how cool I thought it was. A good thing, huh? I mean, he might have killed your average guy, you know?"

"Yeah, thanks, Ben. Look, it's thanks to you that no one else was killed tonight, right?"

He grinned sheepishly. "Not really, but I'll take it."

"Ben, go get some stiff drinks, and go to sleep," I told him.

I had work to do.

Problem was, there were usually a lot of folks around a morgue. It wasn't really an easy task to get into one.

I was noted by one of the cops when I arrived; I told him that one of the other fellows had been questioning me, I couldn't remember his name, but he'd asked me to hang around. It wasn't until the coroner and the cops started talking about the events in the reception chamber that I was able to slip back and get into the coolers.

Fred was on the table, missing half his throat. But when I looked down at him, his eyes popped open. I was just in time.

"You freak! I always knew you were a flipping freak!" he told me. Then he started to laugh. "So now . . . now, I'm immortal, right? Oh, Danny Boy, you've given me exactly what I always wanted. I can kill and kill and kill . . . and eat and eat and eat—until I *don't* die!" he gloated.

He started to rise.

"No way, asshole," I told him. The good thing about a morgue is that you can usually find a good scalpel. And, as you can imagine, I'm pretty damned strong.

For most people, it's really a task to cut off a human head. A burly murderer actually has to work really hard at a decapitation.

But I'm good. Before he could begin to rise, I'd reached down, pinned him, and worked the scalpel.

I left him with his head cleanly severed. I went back to the reception area, where no one seemed to notice that I had been gone. In fact, Jeff Major, a homicide detective, looked at me and set a hand on my shoulder. "Come on, Dan, I'll get you home."

In the morning, there was only one thing left to do. I had to find Callie.

I went to the B and B where she had told me she was staying. I knew old Mrs. Llewellyn who ran the place; she greeted me with hugs and a kiss on the cheek. The events of the previous night were the talk of the day. The story was on all the news stations, AOL, Yahoo, and so on.

I was glad that the linebacker was happy to take the credit for bringing down the psycho. But Mrs. Llewellyn knew that I had been the first over the velvet rope.

When she finished gushing over me, I told her I was looking for Callie.

She groaned. "Not you, too!" she said with dismay. "What, is this going to start it all up again about that runaway?"

"What are you talking about?" I asked her.

"Last year, the cops were all over this place. Don't you remember? There were a few girls who were reported missing. I had rented a room to a young girl named Callie Davenport. But she checked out of here, packed up her car, and left."

"What?"

"Dan, she wasn't anywhere near here this year."

"But I saw her last night. She was on the boat. She was the one who started screaming, letting everyone know that it wasn't just a scene, that Fred Boudreaux was attempting to murder a girl right in front of our eyes."

Mrs. Llewellyn shook her head and smoothed her silver hair behind her ears. "Dan, if Callie Davenport is your Callie, then she's back in town, she isn't missing, and she's staying somewhere else. Dan! I wouldn't lie to you, you know that!"

No, she wouldn't.

I went back out to see Ben. He'd taken my advice and started drinking. It was morning, but he was still drinking. He'd be all right; he'd just need a day to pull himself together.

What I wanted was his list of reservations.

He gave it to me. And I found her name. Callie Davenport. She had her local address listed as Mrs. Llewellyn's B and B.

"Did she say anything to you?" I asked Ben, puzzled.

"Bro, I never even saw the chick you're talking about," he said. "I told you, I was into the girls with the huge hooters."

My fault; I had told him to drink. I wasn't going to get anything out of him.

I called Jeff Major at the police department. I didn't tell him that I'd seen Callie; I just asked him about folks who'd supposedly disappeared from the area a year ago. I rather vaguely suggested that they might want to find out if anything had gone down the year before.

I waited.

They found Callie—and another three missing girls—in the ruins of the root cellar in the back of the plantation, slashed to pieces and mostly decayed.

When I heard the news, I decided to drink also. Vampires can; we only need blood so often, and I sure as hell do enjoy a double malt scotch.

So I took Ben's boat out to the "beach," Pearl River's sandy beach where we had been the night before. The same place where the night is eerie as all hell and gators slip and slither in the water. The place where the screech owls cry out, and the brush rustles while the mist rises into a fog when the water temperature is higher than that of the air.

By day, I could hear the traffic going by on the highway just beyond the bank and the strip of trees and foliage.

I sat there, with my scotch.

She found me.

She sat down beside me, and she didn't speak. She set a hand gently on my thigh. She leaned over and kissed my cheek. "Thank you," she told me.

I looked at her. "Can't you stay?" I asked her huskily. My heart was sinking as I did so. I had to joke. "I do believe in mixed marriage, you know."

And she laughed. "It would have been nice," she told me.

She stood. I didn't. She smiled as she walked away. Toward the light. Oh, yeah, toward the light of the sun.

Then she was gone, just a wisp of fog that didn't belong by day.

In the Mix

Eric Red

East St. Louis in August was like drowning in snot, Underdogg thought. The choking summer humidity was a smothering wet blanket on his head and shoulders. It weighed the scrawny black teenager down onto a squalid gravel of empty plastic crack vials that crunched under his stolen unlaced sneakers as he walked the sidewalk. Underdogg's jeans were hanging off his ass, and his turned-around baseball cap was bathed in sweat. Voices pounded inside his skull, forming words, lyrics to his rap song. With every step he took on the street, he looked at the words written in black Magic Marker on his wrist, palm and back of his hand.

"Dust the motherfuckers with my nine."

"Gonna get paid, it's gonna be fine."

No, that wasn't right.

He glowered as he trudged on through the punishing heat. A car lumbered past with low sonic boom beat blasting out of the speakers. It fueled Underdogg.

"Dust the motherfuckers with my nine . . ."

"Gonna get paid, gonna get mine."

The sixteen-year-old looked up.

There he was, above it all.

Scratchmaster ruled over all he surveyed.

The peeling billboard was a giant picture of the local music producer impresario that loomed over Missouri Avenue by the congested overpass of the 55-64 freeway interchange. Yellow smog and wet waves of heat rising off the simmering asphalt distorted his looming, melting figure. Scratchmaster was tall, thin, dapper, a full grill of gold teeth glinting. He struck an iconic figure. Bald. Black shades. Black leather suit. Two bimbos, one black and one Latino, stuck their exaggerated big butts out, thongs jammed up their cracks, one on each elbow of the producer. One of the bitches' faces was by the Man's crotch, looking like she was about to start sucking him off. *Shee-it,* Underdogg thought. *The Man had bank. The Man had bitches. The Man was not down here in the motherfucking shit, that's for damn sure.* The kid sighed.

The billboard boasted that the top rap record on the charts was produced by legendary producer Scratchmaster, recorded and released on his independent 666 label. The local music mogul's rap songs owned a dark and disturbing power. There was an indefinable something behind the sledgehammer bass, pounding funk drumbeats, and brutally assaultive exclamations in the vocals. It was a subliminal suggestion in Scratchmaster's popular records that got listeners' blood boiling to where they sometimes were driven to acts of violence. It was the primal jungle beat in the bass-heavy sledgehammer pounding rhythm. But there was something else. Something in the mix, under the music. Like the sound of breaking bones and squishing guts. It gave the listener the satisfaction of a pipe collapsing some motherfucker's jaw and teeth. Or their skull caving in with a brick in your hands, brains flying out. Shit, sometimes it was like you could hear the screams way back in the music underneath it all.

That was Scratchmaster's genius, Underdogg knew in his gut, and what made him a great rap producer. The 666 label's patented brand of Rap Music was the real deal. To be a Gangsta Rapper, you had to be hard core. Any dumb niggah can spell and some who can't could write and perform a rap song. But Scratchmaster, nobody could do what he could do in the studio. His mix. It was all in the mix.

Scratchmaster's music was everywhere.

Pumping out ghetto-blaster boomboxes on gangbangers' shoulders.

Pouring out of the sweltering open windows of the tenements.

Thundering out of cars with huge backseat speakers.

It provided the depressed streets violently vital sonic lifeblood, the deranged musical pulse of a psychopath strung out on crystal meth.

It was what Underdogg was listening to on his iPod when he got the gun and robbed the liquor store. He was so high he was halfway inside before the boy realized he was busting into the Dry Spin Laundromat instead. Bunch of stupid-ass old lady faces and homeless mofos giving him blank looks when he was going for his gun. Sheee-it. He was this close to putting a cap in the ass of the old bitch cussing him out like she was his mama or something, but he didn't have no mama, so he just grabbed her purse and knocked her on her bony ass. Then he walked out to find that liquor store. Underdogg had smoked so much weed in his sixteen years he could barely remember his birth name of Rufus. He didn't do crack though. Well, maybe just a taste now and again. He had to keep his head straight, not like the other niggahs on the block.

After all, he wasn't going to be pulling holdups and robbing old ladies his whole life.

This was just something he was doing until he became a rap star.

And his dream was, Scratchmaster would be his producer.

Just needed to use the holdup money to buy a huge ghetto-blaster radio.

Underdogg looked up at the billboard across the street and made eye contact with the Satan in satin and shades.

Payday, motherfucker.

He wrote down some rap lyrics on his hand with a Magic Marker.

"Got that welfare check from the old bitches' bag."

"Stuck up the liquor store grab the swag."

"Don't mind no life of crime."

"Gonna get paid, gonna get mine."

"Indeed."

"Indeed."

The recording studio was the basement of a boarded-up bombed-out crackhouse on Ohio near the train tracks. Recording studio was what Underdogg called it anyway. He lived there too. His equipment basically consisted of an old beat box and a CD recorder. The kid would prance around and punch the air and yell out his rap lyrics as the beat box backed him up with an electronic drumbeat. He would grab a hammer and pound on the bricks and pipes. This shit was on.

Wiping sweat from his face with a filthy towel, Underdogg took a seat and pressed Play on the CD recorder.

His teenage crew, Infamous DKX and Hi 5 Jam Boy, hunkered in the darkness, lounging on the junkyard sofa, their shades and jewelry glinting. A black steel Beretta 9mm sat on the table. The powdered remains of a few lines of cocaine on a mirror were beside it. Empty McDonald's and Popeye's food containers were everywhere, along with half-eaten food. The teens passed a jay and listened to the primitive rap song their friend recorded on the boom box. Thick, noxious smoke filled the air. Somewhere outside, backfire or gunshots sounded, and then a dog barking, then a siren wail. Underdogg took a hit. *This weed is rank,* and he struggled not to cough as he held the smoke in his mouth and breathed out. One day he was going to afford the good shit. That day was going to be a great day.

Infamous DKX shook his head. "Niggah, them lyrics of yours is some nasty shit."

"Tru dat," nodded Hi 5 Jam Boy.

"What the fuck you talkin'?" Underdogg shot them a defensive glance.

"I'm talkin' you be all rapping about beatin' your 'ho's brains in, and then fuckin' her after you killed her shit because the bitch held out on you the money she made turning tricks for you. Damn, boy. That's harsh."

"To be a Gangsta Rapper you gotta be *hard core*," Underdogg told his crew.

"Tru dat," nodded Hi 5 Jam Boy.

They listened to the tape, and Underdogg heard how cheap it was compared to the violent subliminal force of a Scratchmaster CD. He got up and paced around his filthy basement crib, making a long expression. "Man, listen to that Scratchmaster *mix*, y'all, it's all in his *mix*. If my record had the *sound* that Scratchmaster gets, I'd be there. I'm gonna get him to produce my record."

"How you gonna do that, dawg?" jibed Infamous DKX. "Scratchmaster is big time and he ain't gonna bother with your scrawny ass."

"Scratchmaster listens to my stuff, he'll know I'm his *boy*," Underdogg bragged, squeezing his package with one hand and pointing two fingers with the other. "He'll beg me to produce *my* record."

"You'll be Scratchmaster's *bee-yach* you go messin' with him," said his friend. "He been in jail for murder, and they say he had three East Coast rappers capped in drive-bys last year."

Underdogg grinned approvingly. "Like I said, to be a gangsta rapper you gotta be *hard core*."

"Tru dat," Hi 5 Jam Boy nodded.

Underdogg and his peeps hung out on a street corner across from the 666 studio, scoping it out. The record company was in a local warehouse down on State Street and Gray Boulevard. There was a fence topped with razor wire around the alley. Doberman pinschers skulked behind the chain links, choke chains on their necks. The area used to be a meat-packing district, and heavy rusted hooks hung in the heat of the abandoned loading bays. The boys knew this hood. After-hours clubs kept popping up around here until cops busted them, and crack and pussy was always available for a price. The rappers had the ghetto blaster with them, with Underdogg's CD. They had been waiting for hours, and no sign of nobody.

Soon, a huge, garish limo rolled up and parked.

Scratchmaster got out. He looked smaller and older in real life than Underdogg figured he would. The music producer was a tall, rather sunken man with a black leather coat and rings and jewelry on his neck and fingers. He had a voluptuous 'ho on each arm, each wearing a mink coat. As he helped one of the girls from the backseat, her fur opened along with her legs as she stepped out, a flash of bush on her naked thighs underneath. Across the street, the three boys silently eyeballed their appreciation to one another. The girl licked her gloss lipstick, tossed her frizzed hair, and walked toward the building wearing only the coat and high heels.

"I'm gonna go get up in his grill," says Underdogg, and crossed the street. "Hey, Scratchmaster, lemme talk to you a minute."

The music producer turned, radiating intimidating boss-man charisma. "What do you want?"

"I want to play my tape for you. I'm Underdogg, a rapper from the 'hood, and after you hear my sound you'll wanna make my record."

"Send me a CD."

"No, I want to play it for you now. I got it right here on my box."

Amused at the kid's juice, Scratchmaster exchanged a wink with his ladies. "Okay, my man, let's see what you got."

"Check this out." Underdogg pressed Play and held up his boom box. His crude song blasted out of the speakers.

Not for long.

Scratchmaster winced in pain. "Turn that off. That is the worst thing I ever heard. Boy, get yourself a real job." The foxy women on the producer's arm laughed derisively in the gangsta rapper's face.

Underdogg cringed in humiliation as Scratchmaster and his women turned their backs and walked into 666 Records. When the disgraced kid turned around, he saw his crew, Infamous DKX and Hi 5 Jam Boy, buckled over in laughter. "So Scratchmaster give you a record deal?" they chortled, and headed off down the street.

"Screw you man, *you'll see*," the embittered Underdogg called after them. His eyes turned to flint. "To be a gangsta rapper you gotta be *hard core*."

Night.

Underdogg stood across the street from the quiet warehouse. He kept his mouth closed so his gold tooth wouldn't catch the light.

He had the nine stuck in his pants.

He knew Scratchmaster was in the building and that he was alone because the bitches had gone in the limo hours ago. Once, the record producer had come out the back, behind the barbed wire, and fed the Dobermans some kind of meat. The dogs were insane the way they chewed it down, getting blood everywhere, but they licked that up too.

He was glad he was packing the nine.

Presently, the front door opened, and Scratchmaster left the studio alone.

The gangsta rapper walked up to him on the sidewalk, fearless belligerence on his face.

"What do you want now, sucka?" whispered the producer.

Underdogg pulled the gun and aimed it at him sideways. "You gonna produce my record, Scratchmaster. Right now or I'm gonna go hard core on you."

"Take it easy," Scratchmaster said, looking like a very old man.

Prodding him in the chest with the barrel, the kid forced the heavyset producer back in the building. "What's your plan, my man?" Scratchmaster said. "This a robbery? We ain't got no money here."

"This ain't no robbery, like I told you. Don't you listen? We gonna go into your studio, and you gonna set me up on the mike, and I'm gonna do my rap, and you gonna record and mix it with that Scratchmaster sound that you do. Then you gonna gimme the masters, and I gonna split."

"That's your plan?"

"And I'm gonna take the tapes with me and go get it released and the record we done gonna go platinum."

"That's it?"

"Indeed."

"Boy, I thought I seen some far-out things people do to be breaking into the business, but this takes the cake."

Underdogg followed Scratchmaster down the hall, gun in hand, but spoke with reverence. "I jus' wanna say I respect you."

"Say what?"

"I respect you."

"You gonna put a cap in my ass and you say you *respect* me?" The old man shook his head.

"I didn't want to do it this way. You watch. You listen to what I record. You gonna make a million dollars. I let you manage me."

"I 'preciate you *manage* not shooting me in my damn head is all. Watch that gun. Studio back here."

All along the wood inlay walls were 60s- and 70s-era music posters of R&B and soul stars. There were mounted LP records from that time on all the walls. Several framed photographs showed a much younger Scratchmaster with a huge Afro and sideburns and mustache, standing and grinning with Smoky Robinson in one and Sly Stone in the other. But Underdogg's blank stare showed he didn't know who they were. The music producer shook his head sadly. "Boy, bet you don't even know who those people are. Hell, bet you don't even know what an LP is."

"Shee-it, what I don't know is how motherfuckers *dressed* like that."

Scratchmaster seemed eerily cool as he did as he was bid and took them into the secluded, soundproofed recording studio of 666 Records.

"Yo, Scratchmaster, what's the secret of your sound?"

"It's all in the mix."

"I knew that!" Underdogg chortled. "I tell all the motherfuckers that! Scratchmaster's music, *it's all in the mix!* Don't I tell everybody that! Damn. You 'n me, Scratchmaster, we gonna be *boys.*"

"In my day, we said brothers."

They went into the darkened, low-tech room filled with tape reels and mixing banks. Underdogg ordered Scratchmaster at gunpoint to get the tapes and put them up on the reel-to-reel. "Don't you use digital? This shit looks like what they used in the seventies."

"No." Scratchmaster smiled. "I'm what you call old school." The music producer showed Underdogg into the recording booth.

The teen gangsta rapper noticed that the floor was covered with sheets of black plastic. "Y'all got plastic on the floor."

"We doing some renovations," said Scratchmaster.

He checked the levels on the mixing board. And pressed Record . . .

"Sit down by the mike. You ready."

Underdogg sat down in the chair behind the microphone, his eyes filled with excitement. "Hot *damn,*" he chortled.

Sticking the pistol in the belt, the kid eyeballed the producer through the booth window. "Don't try nothing funny, dog, I got my nine right where I can get it."

Then Scratchmaster pressed another button.

Four steel clamps shut over Underdogg's wrists and ankles. He was firmly pinned. "Wha—?" he gasped.

Scratchmaster turned up the lights.

The walls were covered with all forms of knives, scalpels, cleavers, drills, truncheons, tongs, and death apparatus. Some still had dried blood.

The recording studio was a torture chamber. Underdogg whimpered, completely pinned. And suddenly realized why there was plastic covering the floor.

Scratchmaster tugged on rubber surgical gloves.

"Helllllllllppppp!!!" screamed Underdogg.

"The studio is soundproofed, fool," said Scratchmaster as he moved some microphones into position and turned on the recording machines.

"I'm sorry I'm sorry!!!"

"Please scream a little louder," said Scratchmaster as he tweaked a knob. "I need to get a level."

Underdogg looked on in shuddering, helpless terror. Scratchmaster perused the torture implements and selected a power drill.

He approached with it.

The tape rolled, recording.

"Maybe I was wrong about you," said Scratchmaster. "Could be you do have what it takes to make a hit record."

Underdogg screamed hysterically as the producer revved on the power drill with a hideous *whirrrrrrrrrrr.*

"Nnnnnnnnooooooooooooooooooooooooooooooo—!!!"

"This is a take."

The reel-to-reels turned.

The drill cut.

The microphone was splashed with blood.

". . . Because it's all in the mix, baby, all in the mix."

"Ohmigoooooood!" The drill bit stopped, caked with blood-ribboned flesh as it was ripped out of the reamed cartilage of Underdogg's kneecap. "Please stop please stop why you doing this to me, man, why why?"

Scratchmaster laid the power drill on the splattered, black plastic duct-taped to the floor. A jet of pumping blood ejaculated out of the kid's knee. The record producer went out of the booth and got behind the mixing board, checking some levels. "You want to know why I'm doing this?"

"Please don't hurt me no more, man. Why?"

Straightening up, Scratchmaster removed his shades. He eyeballed Underdogg through the glass. "Because *I hate rap music!*"

The kid's eyes blinked incredulously through his agony. "But . . . you Scratchmaster, man. That's what you do, bra, that's what you do!"

"I'm gonna *school* you, boy. Rap ruined the *music.* Back when I started out, we knew how to play. R and B. Soul. Even funk. Motown. Smokey. Aretha. Even Teddy Pendergrass. Even Sly. You know those names? I sessioned with them. I was by their side in the recording studio making their records. And it didn't start with them. Shit no. You know who Robert Johnson is, boy? Sonny Boy Williamson. Howlin' Wolf? They was giants. That's who we listened to when we was comin' up. Then you dumb fuck *can't-play-a-note-crackhead-rap-motherfuckers* come along with your bullshit rhymes and your 'hos and you ruined the music. Put me out of business." The venomous old man spewed bitterness and bile from a ruined, disappointed life, twisted into insane viciousness. "Nobody puts me out of business."

"I don't know what you're talking about, you crazy old niggah, *I don't know what you're talking*—!" Underdogg twisted in the chair in the mechanical restraints.

Scratchmaster continued on his bipolar rant, his mood veering schizophrenically from righteousness to murderous fury. "All you rap motherfuckers want to do is wear your chains and smoke your crack and act like gangstas with your bitches. We was musicians in my day, boy. We learned *guitar*. And we *learned* piano. We could play. And we hung with *cats could play*. And we toured *our shit*. We worked hard. Hard work. And now it's all gone. The *music* is gone. *Because. Of. Rap.* You punks all think it come easy. You think you put on chains and strut like an ape to a beat box with a cheap rhyme and you *get yours*. I'm getting mine. The people want this rap shit, I give the people what they want. *Always give the fucking fuckers want they want . . .*"

The record producer returned to the booth. Opening a closet, he pulled out a stand with a saline drip on an intravenous tube.

"W-what's that?" Underdogg mewled.

Taking the hypodermic syringe at the end of the tube, Scratchmaster injected it in the kid's forearm. "Why, this here is saline drip. Make sure you don't go all into shock and pass out on me. You got a lot of screaming to do, and for that, your ass gotta be awake." The record producer looked disgusted when Underdogg began to snivel. "Don't you want to be a star, boy? Don't you want people to listen to you on the radio?"

"I-I just want to go home. Please let me go." The kid was bawling like a bitch.

"Well now, that's no way for a . . . what do ya call it . . . *gangsta rapper* to act. What would 50 Cent say? He'd say 'see ya wouldn't want to be ya.' I want to hear what you got!" Scratchmaster's bony fingers closed on the long handle of a fire hatchet.

Underdogg's vision blurred as he saw the tall and skeletal old man grab the heavy axe from the table, heft it high above his head, and swing it down hard. *Wfffffft.* The kid heard a wet snapping crunch and watched the front of his sneaker shoot like a rat across the floor with his severed toes and half his foot still in it.

The last thought that passed through his mind was, where was he going to steal a new pair of Nikes.

Then he wasn't thinking anymore. Just screaming. Someone was screaming louder than him. "And my name *ain't* Scratchmaster, *boy!* You *hear* me?" roared the old man as he swung the bloody axe home again and again in red volcanic eruptions of gore. "*My fucking name is Leon!*"

He hacked and hacked until the tape ran out.

The following morning, warm summer rain pelted the decrepit warehouse of 666 Records. The rundown area was bleak and deserted. From somewhere in the building, the cool R&B strains of Smokey Robinson floated out into the humid air. Behind the rusty razor-wire fence, the feral Doberman pinschers skulked, drenched. The heavy industrial rear door creaked open and Scratchmaster stepped out in his robe. The air blossomed with Smoky's lyrical falsetto in an old Motown classic song pumping from the stereo inside. The guard dogs snapped and growled hungrily, straining on their chains. Adjusting his shades, a cigarette dangling from his lips, the Afro'd record producer carried a bucket of chopped meat he dumped in the dog-feeding trough. He got away from his animals quick as they attacked the meal. Scratchmaster hummed "Just take a good look at my face" along with the music as he went back inside. The feral canines dug into the bloody chum slopping out of the trough, digging their jaws into the red, dripping shags of flesh. They devoured all traces of it in a few bites.

One of the Dobermans suddenly yelped, whimpering as it spit out something hard lodged in its molars.

A gold tooth.

Snow fell on the peeling billboard for 666 Records lording over the frozen December Missouri Avenue. Cars hissed by on the slushy sleet-encrusted street.

A local record store was open.

Posters were everywhere for the new "Underdogg" CD.

Blasting out of the store speakers, a song with the vaguely recognizable hideous screams, power drilling, and hatchet chops of Underdogg's dying moments.

A line of local teenage boys and girls were waiting outside to purchase the first copies, shivering in the cold.

Scratchmaster watched from his heated limo, puffing a cigar. He wore his black suit and fingered his ivory cane.

"Excuse me."

Scratchmaster turned to see the eager face in the opposite window.

"You Scratchmaster, ain't you?" It was another belligerent young gangsta rapper holding a homemade CD. "Would you listen to my stuff?"

The record producer watched the kid, and he sort of smiled.

Then opened the door to his limo. . . .

How to Edit

Richard Christian Matheson

The Problem

So. Let's get started.

My name is Bill Wiley and I'm a professional writer. Perhaps you are too. Or perhaps you want to be. It is a noble calling. Right up there with opera and giving blood. However, there is a dark side, which you indulge at your peril.

The lure of elaboration.

I speak from experience. Despite efforts to condense, I just couldn't seem to wrap it up. If a period is the STOP sign in a sentence, I have run too many. Engulfed in heightening and widening, I have creamed readers like innocent pedestrians.

Writers can't resist. We explain. Then we say it again. Then we say it once more . . . just in case we missed anything salient or pithy. And by the way, *salient* and *pithy* are similar enough that I could have used one rather than both in that sentence. More on this often irresistible, self-destructive tendency later.

The problem: we are hemorrhaging words. The solution?

Read on.

How Serious Is the Problem?

It is suffocating our world.

Without being melodramatic, for writers, the issue is toxic and ubiquitous. We even use words that annoy our readers like toxic and ubiquitous. Yes, I'm aware writers claim that explaining at length improves clarity. Or enhances style. I've heard it all. I've said it all. I've gushed and exceeded word count with oblivious verve.

But let's take off the long-winded gloves (a labored metaphor I will cut and, if you'd written it, I'd hope you would too) and be frank:

Here's what is really going on: 1) narcissistic indulgence, 2) self-adoring excess.

Which, by the way, are basically the same description expressed two different ways, an aggravating variation on the "pithy/salient" syndrome alluded to above.

On your path to good writing, always remember: pencils have erasers to eliminate mistakes. They also have them to erase ego, crud, and prolongation.

A Handy Tool for You

For illustrative purpose, I am weaving writing misdemeanors into this piece so you can see them up close. Like swollen, unsavory lab specimens. Scrutinize their lack of discipline, poor execution, and general sloth. If you play close attention, you can learn from my bad examples.

Remember: good writing is taut. Embrace exactitude. Purge the superfluous. And get serious about it. No more false promises. No more lip service.

Another sentence I will cut, as the point it makes is redundant.

How Widespread Is the Problem?

Are you kidding?

It's everywhere. Brochures. Menus. Deodorant instructions. Horoscopes. Writers are drunk on self-expression. Awander in word thickets. High on adjectives. Mainlining verbs.

See, I'm doing it again. It's as bad as heroin.

What Is Good Writing?

Your eyes waltz across it. It has music, balance, and depth. It provokes thought and feeling. Not resentment and stupor.

It paints pictures, dodging images strung together like a charm bracelet from Honolulu. It doesn't overuse commas, underlining, italics, similes, gassy embellishment, big words, or bludgeons of obscure reference: all the tricks of a neophyte, transparent and uninvolving.

I do think that sentence will ultimately be cut or made into three sentences, but let's move on.

Good writing also avoids the overt in concept and execution. It remains subtle while intense. Miscellaneously, it should swerve around exclamation marks, which are like loud drunks screaming in your face, and minimize use of the word "because"; it's an indolent crutch.

But none will resuscitate the truly mediocre. Good writing, thus, is hard to achieve. Why? Partially because writing, per the insight of our betters, is rewriting. Consolidation. Sculpture . . . if you are inclined toward the metaphoric.

And there I go again. Caught in my own florid avalanche. This is to be scrupulously avoided.

Here's why:

Author's Disclaimer

No one publishes my work anymore.

They used to. I sold lots of books. Eleven novels, thirty-six short stories, eight articles about writing technique. Critics of my fiction said I had edge. Immediacy. I got fan mail. I was stalked by a busty chiropractor from Portland who thought I was the new Cheever. John. Not Susan. A big New York editor wrote a letter to me about a suspense novel I'd written. Said my voice was a "hypnotic scalpel." Did that make my day? I thought I was headed for the top. A sure clue, life has taught me, that everything is about to crumble.

Two tanked novels later, even my stalker went home.

Now they tell me my work is chubby. A yawn. "A wanton spill of exposition," some critic at *Publishers Weekly* wrote. How did it happen? My ex-agent says I fell in love with my voice; tumbled into the reflection of my own bloated verbiage, drowning in self-regard. My word bulge numbed minds. That sentence needs some work, by the way.

The point is: it half ruined me.

Don't make the same mistake.

How Do We Correct the Problem?

First we acknowledge it. Do not run the other way. It can run faster.

Then we roll up our sleeves. And we stop whining. Don't you hate that? I hate that.

Our vow? To excise linguistic sludge. Be precise. Not sloppy, nor diffuse. Either of which, by the way, would have sufficed in making my point. Again, witness the problem and try to deny its strangling enormity.

That sentence, by the way, though self-conscious, has some style.

What Holds Us Back?

Ourselves.

If you blame others, you are naive. Not to say there aren't plenty of unhelpful types who get in our way. I had mine. You've got yours. You know who they are. Make a list. And commit to doing something about it.

No one said writing or the writing life was easy.

Personal Discipline for Writers

In the spirit of the aerodynamic, let me mention some of my bad habits and how I have endeavored to correct them.

For starters, in my quest for the succinct:

1) I sleep less these days. Three hours a night. When I can ignore the constant pain. But that isn't your concern. Then, I'm up, and I'm editing.

2) I stopped seeing people I don't really enjoy. Not a long list to begin with. Now blank.

3) I quit drinking and smoking. Both distracted me with their expense and ritual. They also required time that was better spent

writing and rewriting. Also, they probably led to my cancer diagnosis. You remember cancer? Cells that just keep multiplying, spreading uncontrollably all over the goddamned place like an Ohio flood.

Where was the editor when cancer got invented?

Simplicity Is Your Friend

In mastering the art of editing, compress. Eliminate. Streamline. And don't use three words like I just did.

Ditch all but the vital.

Did you know Michael Crichton ate the same thing every day when he was writing, in order to edit out needless decisions—allow his mind to think only about what he was writing? He did not regard food as sensual treat nor friend. Simply as fuel.

Tactical isolation. It is your ally.

Trust me, no one else in your life is.

Insider Tips

I now eat once a day. I also stopped calling my mother. Easy considering the things she did to me when I was little. I know it's hard to draw the line. Old habits die hard. But then I suppose everything that doesn't want to die dies hard.

Taking Action

Which brings me to Linda.

She was never a creative person, even when I married her. To make matters worse, she has zero sensitivity to the new novel I've been working on. How it is going to launch my comeback?

Her lack of vision vexed me. I took action.

Make sure you do the same.

A Few More Words about Using Fewer Words

Never underestimate the profound effect of eliminating the needless. Particularly from your work environment. I heartily recommend removing distractions. TV. Music. Barking dogs.

Even people. Ask yourself: who is really there for you when the chips are down?

A friend? Or yourself?

A perfect example is those annoying creeps at the coffee shop last Thursday. I was in my booth, just back from radiation therapy. Feeling sick. But in the middle of an important chapter. I was on fire; my inner Cheever was back.

I savored the thought of my ex-agent seeing this new novel, falling back in love with my writing, and being informed to eat shit. I savored my stalker resuming her obsession. I savored the prospect of the critics drooling at my incandescent reentry. Watching their snide eyes narrow with envy, their ulcers bleed.

But none of that was going to happen because as I sat at the booth, trying to write, the little girls wouldn't pipe down. Giggling. Jumping. Fake sneezing on each other. Mom busy on her cell phone in the smoking section patio, talking with some douche bag.

I ask you, what's more important? Novels or annoying, obnoxious little girls?

Yeah, no kidding.

Can You Overedit?

No. That's a rumor perpetuated by hacks.

You can always edit more. A word that gums up flow. Waxy dialogue. A pudgy phrase that slows sleek thought. Be ruthless. Do not become so fond of things you thought you cared about that you aren't willing to nix them.

Opportunities are everywhere.

Another example taken from real life? This morning, as I was about to write, I looked into the mirror and realized something. Two eyes? Maybe I only need one. Why use the excess energy blinking? Just because we're born that way?

We need to think outside the box. Before that box is our casket.

Your Writing Future

As you cultivate your future career as a writer, learn to never use two words where one will do the trick. Or several ideas to camouflage the absence of a true one.

Remember, the amateur overwrites. The professional edits. My new novel is a perfect example. The first draft was over nine hundred pages. After a thorough, unsentimental edit, it has greatly improved. I even sent it to my ex-agent to torment him.

Every life has twists.

Wrapping Up

Editing is a philosophy of life.

For example, last night I realized that, in theory, I don't need legs. Writers sit, not walk. Even two arms, for a scribe like me who writes by hand, is overkill.

But these are my musings. Arrive at your own. We are the architects of our own fate. As you deepen your commitment to the brief, forge a unique path. Don't copy mine or someone else's.

The key is to discover your own methods. Look for whatever slows down your writing or gets in your way. And eliminate it. Accept no intrusion on momentum. Which I basically already said in the prior sentences, so that one is a goner.

As a famous wag once said about editing our writing, ". . . we must be willing to kill our children."

Well, that's a start.

When all is said and done, there's only one golden rule: no loss, no gain. If it doesn't contribute anything, cut it.

Until it hurts.

Happy writing.

The Los Angeles Times

WRITER'S BODY FOUND
Novelist Was Plagued by Problems

Former best-selling, critically lauded suspense novelist Bill Wiley was found dead in his North Hollywood home Tuesday morning. His badly mutilated body, which police investigators said was missing an eye, arm, and legs, was discovered by shocked neighbors. Investigators reported Wiley had used pliers and a jigsaw on himself and bled to death. A final article he wrote about editing was found in his blood-spattered office.

Wiley's last two years were riddled with tragedy. Bad sales, poor reviews, and a terminal cancer diagnosis beleaguered him, and in June, his wife of thirty years, Linda, hanged herself in their home. Wiley was not a suspect in her death but remained a person of interest in the ongoing investigation of two young girls who vanished from a coffee shop in which he often wrote.

His longtime agent said Wiley's new novel, *Small Print,* an avant-garde work in which each chapter is one sentence, was purchased, after his death, by his former publisher.

The novel is seven pages long.

Resurrection Man

Axelle Carolyn

"The dead don't feel. The dead don't talk. The dead don't walk, and no matter what your confessor may tell you, they won't rise from their graves on Judgment Day. Dead bodies are nothing but toxic waste, bones, and decaying flesh. When Our Lord Jesus Christ returns to earth for our final hours, He will judge our immortal souls. And leave the bodies in my care."

The students laughed. Nervously, for the most part, but some with genuine enthusiasm. Alistair S. Cooper, Great Britain's leading surgeon and anatomy teacher, knew how to tell his audience a good joke. He knew his pupils needed the release when confronted with their first dead body, cut up and open, naked and on display on the dissecting table.

He also knew he needed to make his point loud and clear. Too long had primitive beliefs hampered the progress of medicine. The mere idea of physical resurrection was absurd, so he couldn't fathom why Londoners still insisted on burying their dead at the eve of the nineteenth century. It was to him little more than a hazardous and archaic practice. Why not let him study the bodies and then cremate them? His students had to understand that science should not be strangled by tradition or religion. Cooper was a modern man, liberal and devoted to rationality. Having to struggle for each corpse because the good people of London wanted their mortal shells to stay whole for their presumed apocalyptic return was illogical and frustrating.

"Society tells us we should be buried untouched," he said, "yet the law does not protect the dead. Steal a shroud, they will judge and condemn you. Steal a cadaver, you'll walk away free. A corpse is worth nothing—it belongs to no one. Even grave robbing, this most despised activity, isn't illegal. If justice does not give bodies any value, why should science?" As if to illustrate his point, he plunged a pair of forceps into the gaping thorax of his subject, a murderer known to the public as the Dockside Butcher. The students, sitting in rows around the slab, winced when the dead man's vertebrae creaked under the tool.

"It is far more important to save the living than to preserve the deceased," the surgeon added. He pulled out the heart from the ribcage and after a somewhat lengthy analysis, concluded the lesson.

A brilliant anatomist, Cooper had devoted his life to the advancement of knowledge, and had never let superstitions get in the way of his research. He had thus autopsied his share of criminals—the only corpses automatically delivered to him, straight from the gallows— and a fair number of innocents, stolen from their graves by a gang of professional robbers. Dealing with body snatchers was unpleasant, though, so the surgeon had limited his interest to those unfortunate few whose deaths had resulted from some incurable disease or rare malformation. Only they presented an acute challenge to modern science.

But it was another type of challenge that Cooper contemplated that evening, sitting in front of a pint at the local inn, his head bowed, his usually exceptionally steady hand trembling with anticipation. The passing of Ben Vaughan, an eight-foot-tall, deformed giant, had been a local tragedy. The carnival man was adored by his peers and had made quite a name for himself among the public. His formidable stature and oddly shaped bone structure, however, made him the perfect object of study for Cooper. The surgeon had at once contacted his grave-robbing partners to acquire the precious skeleton. But ever since Vaughan's death six weeks prior, the answer had been the same from every gang: all deemed the tomb too dangerous. The giant, terrified that his eternal sleep might be disturbed by the sting of the scalpel, had taken special measures to ensure the safety of his resting place. The exact nature of these measures was unknown, but various traps and a lead coffin were near certainties. Yet the scientific discoveries his autopsy could lead to were too important for Cooper to be so easily deterred.

"Cowards, all of them," he said, and he lifted his glass to his lips.

It was already dark when Cooper left the establishment. The flickering streetlights shed long shadows across the path, illuminating the drizzle that hit the surgeon as he looked around the sinuous cobbled street, making sure no one had recognized him. It was a moonless night, perfect for tonight's enterprise. Cooper lifted the collar of his gray frock coat and started his way to the churchyard.

The church grounds were plunged in obscurity. It was one of London's poorest areas, where lamplighters did not venture. Obviously, the giant had chosen to spend his meager earnings on safety mechanisms rather than a pricy location. A mistake perhaps: the place was deserted at night and police officers were seldom spotted in the neighborhood. The squalid houses nearby, separated from the graveyard by a wide and badly paved avenue, were all decrepit. They gave shelter to an army of beggars and delinquents who lived in fear of wall collapses yet gave extravagant sums for their overcrowded accommodation. Paying little mind to his surroundings, Cooper picked up the sack, pickaxe, and shovel he had hidden in a bush against the iron fence of the cemetery. The gate creaked as he pushed it open, and he cast a furtive look over his shoulder to make sure he hadn't been followed. Then he took a few steps inside the churchyard. The gate closed behind him with a metallic clang.

The little graveyard was so dark that the surgeon could hardly make out the outline of the gothic church in front of him. He stepped away from the fence, put down his tools, and rummaged blindly in his sack until he found a small copper lantern. He lit it as fast as his trembling fingers allowed, and in the vacillating light examined the burial grounds. All was still, yet no peace emanated from the place. The poor's refuges in death were as overpopulated as their habitats in life. London was overflowing with corpses, their coffins piled up on top of each other in each grave, their bodies often prematurely decomposed by quicklime. Cooper lifted the lantern above his head. He glanced at the sea of tombstones around him. On each side of the narrow path that led to the massive edifice, not a stone had been left unturned, and every square inch of muddy earth hid a tomb, even if none was visible. There was something undeniably eerie about the little cemetery, and for a moment the surgeon thought of turning back. Then he remembered the purpose of his mission and the higher interest he was serving. He gathered his spirits, and without wasting another minute, scurried toward a carved headstone a dozen yards to the right. The giant's headstone.

Cooper started using the shovel right away. No need for the pickaxe; the ground was soft and soggy. Given the size of the cadaver and the possibility that the coffin might not be made of wood, the doctor had decided against the resurrection men's common method. They would have dug up the head of the casket, broken it with a crowbar, and hauled the body out of its box. The surgeon, on the other hand, would dig a hole the length of the whole grave. Sweating in the cold and stopping often to look out for strange noises, he was waist deep in the grave when, with a screeching sound, the shovel scraped a surface. Kneeling in the mud, his heart beating fast and loud in his eardrums, he removed some of the earth with his leather-gloved hands, revealing a wooden lid. He knocked twice with his clenched index, and the coffin gave a hollow sound: the layer would not be thick or heavy to lift. Could it be the body snatchers' fears were unjustified? Comforted by this discovery, he went back to work, clearing away the rest of the coffin. The rain redoubled, lashing his back as he hunched over the tomb.

Cooper scooped away the last spadeful of soil and stood at the edge of the casket, catching his breath. Thoughts raced through his mind. What if the coffin was booby-trapped? Would he have time to jump out of the hole? He would have to take the risk. Shifting around in the tomb to face the part opposite the hinges, the surgeon stuck the crowbar in the slit below the lid and pushed down with all his weight. The wood creaked and split, a couple of inches at first, and then the cheap locks gave. The smell of decay emanating from inside instantly gripped Cooper's throat and he coughed, his eyes welling up. He threw the crowbar to the surface and wiped his forehead with his right sleeve. He sighed deeply, refilling his lungs with fresh air before going back to his gruesome task. But as he looked down at the coffin, something moved in the bushes to his right, in the periphery of his vision. The surgeon turned. Nothing. His gaze roamed around the place. All seemed quiet.

"Probably just a fox," he said to himself. His voice seemed unusually loud to him, but he forced himself to repeat. "Just a fox," and with a last look around the cemetery, he knelt down in the grave.

Cooper gripped the lid of the coffin and carefully pulled it open. The stench was hard to stomach. The surgeon, used to the sight and smell of the recently deceased but unaccustomed to corpses in such an advanced state of decomposition, gagged as he removed Ben Vaughan's shroud. The face of the giant had already rotted away, his features unrecognizable, his lidless eyes sunk back in their sockets and gnawed at by myriad insects. Maggots crawled in his hair, in his half-eaten ears and exposed ribcage. The flesh of his fingers had all but disappeared; the cheap suit he had been buried in was now little more than shreds. Yet his skeleton was intact, protruding through the moldering skin, shiny white in the timid light of the lantern. His upper torso was twisted, his shoulders hunched, his frame narrow: despite the pestilence and the horror of the place, Cooper couldn't help but admire the uniqueness of the specimen. Struggling to subdue his jangling nerves, he was preparing to lift the body's head and place a rope underneath its armpits when he heard a crack somewhere above him. Leaning on the side of the box, he stuck out his head, looked up, and saw nothing. He listened intently. At first, all he heard was the sound of his own breathing. But after a few seconds, as his breaths became longer and more subdued, he made out a crackle in the bushes to his left. He squinted. Another sound to his right. He spun around quick as lightning to catch the source of the noise, and as he shifted, his left hand slipped from the coffin to the head of the corpse.

The cold, moist feel of putrid flesh startled him, and his hand brushed the cadaver's blackened lips . . . which suddenly snapped shut, entrapping three of the surgeon's fingers. Cooper howled in pain and surprise. He tried to pull his fingers out, but the teeth dug hard into his skin, and the dead jaws held on too tight. Doing his best not to succumb to panic, he knelt in the mud and brought his face near Vaughan's. Tugging repeatedly and wincing with each failed attempt, he noticed a little piece of metal at the edge of the giant's mouth. A trap! How could he not have noticed it sooner? How could he have been so naïve, assuming the casket would be the only potential danger? Absorbed in his fight against the corpse, he was only vaguely aware of the shuffling above him. He jerked his hand one last time, leaning on the cadaver's upper arm, and triggered another hidden mechanism. The dead man's putrefied fingers caught the intruder's right arm, gripping him in an inextricable clench. Transfixed with terror, Cooper yelped and pulled, but the grasp only tightened. Tears of frustration welled up in his eyes. He inhaled deeply and took a moment to calm down. In his own relative silence, he finally registered footsteps around the tomb. He froze, his heart skipping a beat. Then he slowly looked up and saw the wavering lights of approaching torches. He had been found.

"Who goes there?" Cooper cried, hoping against hope that the newcomers would deliver him from his gruesome predicament.

No reply. The footsteps had stopped; the lights were right above him.

"Who are you?" he insisted, craning his neck, trying to see at the surface.

Without a word, the intruders stepped into view. The nightmarish vision made Cooper scream, and he pulled at the corpse's hand and mouth again, desperate. They were a dozen around the tomb, of all shapes and heights. A couple of dwarfs, one of them bearded and haggard, the other slim with long hair, flanked twins whose heads came out of the same body. A woman the size of a child, her face covered in thick brown hair, stood by a man whose scarred features, disfigured by smallpox, were crowned by a pair of black horns. An obscenely obese woman held the hand of a small, bald creature with hog like teeth coming out of its lower jaw. The only one who didn't carry a torch was a torso with a head and one arm, crawling on the grass.

Medical marvels. Vaughan's sideshow companions.

Cooper's cries and supplications stopped when the horned man swung a wooden board down into the grave, hitting the surgeon's right temple and knocking him unconscious.

The world was gray. Cooper looked around, but in the first seconds after he'd awoken, he couldn't see past the dense mist that clouded over his vision. He blinked and shook his head. Once he'd fully regained consciousness, he tried to move his arm. He was stuck. Twisting his neck, he saw that his wrists and ankles were tied to the table he lay on. A thick rope was wrapped around his naked waist.

The room was dark, but he recognized it at once. He was bound to the slab in the auditorium, where he had taught countless students and given numerous public lessons. He smelled the chemicals used in dissection and heard the clanging of instruments—scissors, blades, forceps, scalpels, picks, and probes—against the pans, and the chatter of the audience in the rows around him. Sideshow freaks occupied every seat around, from the front steps to the ceiling. Three figures in medical apparel stood a few feet away, caught in a debate. Cooper moaned. The monsters fell silent and turned to him.

They approached.

"Sssso Missster Cooper, you are awake," said the tallest, thinnest of the three, revealing a forked tongue. He held out his scaled hands. His companions, a dwarf and a creature with a mustache, broad shoulders, and large breasts, passed him a scalpel and a pair of forceps.

"You don't believe in the afterlife, Mister Cooper, sir," the dwarf said.

Cooper shook his head and groaned. He was desperate to argue his case, but terror blocked all coherent thought.

"Ben Vaughan did," the hermaphrodite added in a low voice. "He believed."

"In fact, he believed sssso much he made ussss promisssss we'd keep hisss remainsss sssafe from your . . . kind," the Lizard Man explained, spitting the last word with disdain.

"We knew you'd come," the little man said.

"And we have instructions," the she-male added.

The Lizard pressed the tip of his scalpel on the surgeon's sternum. A single pearl of blood formed between the blade and the skin.

"In God's name, leave me alone!" the doctor pleaded, as loud as his exhausted lungs allowed. He could feel long drops of sweat running down his forehead onto the slab.

"In God'sss name?" the Lizard repeated. "That's exactly what we will do. Act in God's name." In one quick, brutal gesture, he slid the scalpel down his patient's thorax, opening him up from the middle of his ribcage to the lower part of his stomach. The prisoner yelped, the last sounds he could emit. The audience applauded and nodded in approval.

"You sssee, Missster Cooper, we're going to give you a tassste of resurrection," he hissed as he put down the scalpel and prepared to plunge the forceps into the wound.

Alistair S. Cooper fought the ropes around his wrists, but the bonds were too tight and there was nothing he could do. He was above all a practical man, and he could tell his body had reached its limits. As the cold metal of the extractor touched his chest, he knew his mortal shell would soon be clay, an empty carcass left to decay. Worn out, resolute, he closed his eyes and prayed for a quick death, and the salvation of his soul.

A Haunting

John Connolly

The world had grown passing strange.

Even the hotel felt different, as though all of the furniture had been shifted slightly in his absence, the reception desk moved a foot away from its previous position, the lights adjusted so they were either too low or too bright. It was wrong. It was not as it had once been. All had changed.

Yet how could it be otherwise when she was no longer with him? He had never stayed here alone before. She had always been by his side, standing at his left hand as he checked them both in, watching in silent approval as he signed the register, her fingers instinctively tightening on his arm as he wrote the words "Mr & Mrs," just as he had done on that first night when they had come here on their honeymoon. She had repeated that small, impossibly intimate gesture on every similar occasion thereafter, telling him in her silent way that she would not take for granted this coupling, the yoking together of their two diverse personalities under a single name. She was his as he was hers, and she had never regretted that fact, and would never grown weary of it.

But now there was no "Mrs.," only "Mr." He looked up at the young woman behind the desk. He had not seen her before, and he assumed that she was new. There were always new people here, but in the past enough of the old had remained to give them a sense of comforting familiarity when they had stayed here. Now, as his electronic key was prepared and his credit card swiped, he took time to take in the faces of the staff and saw none that he recognized. Even the concierge was no longer the same. Everything had been altered, it seemed, by her departure from this life. Her death had tilted the globe on its axis, displacing furniture, light fixtures, even people. They had left with her, and all of them had been quietly replaced without a single objection.

But he had not replaced her with another, and he never would.

He bent down to pick up his bag, and the pain shot through him again, the sensation so sharp and brutal that he lost his breath and had to lean back against the reception desk. The young woman asked him if he was all right, and, after a time, he lied and told her that he was. A bellhop came and offered to bring his bag to his room for him, leaving him with a vague sense of shame that he could not accomplish even this simple task alone: to carry a small leather bag from reception to elevator, from elevator to room. He knew that nobody was looking, that nobody cared, that this was the bellhop's purpose, but it was the fact that the element of choice had been taken from him that troubled him so. He could not have carried the bag, not at that moment, even had he wanted to do so. His body ached, and every movement spoke of weakness and decay. He envisaged it sometimes as a honeycomb, riddled with spaces where cells had collapsed and decayed, a fragile construction that would disintegrate under pressure. He was coming to the end of his life, and his body was in terminal decline.

He caressed the key card in the ascending elevator, noting the room number on the little paper wallet. He had been in that same room many times before, but, again, always with her, and once more he was reminded of how alone he was without her. Yet he had not wanted to spend this, the first wedding anniversary since her death, in the house they had once shared. He wanted to do as they had always done, to commemorate her in this way, and so he had made the call and booked a room. And in a kind of fitting symmetry, he had been given a junior suite that was familiar to him.

After a brief struggle with the electronic lock—what was so wrong with metal keys, he wondered, that they had to be replaced by unappealing pieces of plastic?—he entered the room and closed the door behind him. All was clean and neat, anonymous without being alienating. He had always liked hotel rooms, appreciating the fact that he could impose elements of his own personality upon them through the simple act of placing a book on a nightstand or leaving his shoes at the foot of the bed.

There was an easy chair in a corner beside the window, and he sank into it and closed his eyes. The bed had tempted him, but he was afraid that if he lay down he might not be able to rise again. The journey had exhausted him. It was the first time he had traveled by plane since her death, and he had forgotten what a chore it had become. He was old enough to remember a time when it had not always been so, when there was still an element of glamor and excitement to air travel. On the flight down he had dined off paper, and everything he ate and drank had tasted faintly of cardboard and plastic. He lived in a world composed of disposable things: cups, plates, marriages, people.

He thought he must have slept for a time, for when he opened his eyes, the texture of the light had changed and there was a sour taste in his mouth. He looked at his watch and was surprised to see that an hour had passed. There was also, he noticed, a bag in his room, perhaps brought by the bellhop while he slept. It was not his.

Silently, he cursed the young man. How difficult could it be to bring up the correct piece of luggage? The lobby hadn't even been very busy when he checked in. He got to his feet and approached the offending item. It was an unopened red suitcase, and it lay on a baggage stand beside the closet. It struck him that perhaps he might have missed it when he entered the room, wearied by his trip, and it had been there all along. He examined it. It was locked, and there was a green scarf tied around the handle, presumably to help to distinguish it from similar baggage at airports. There was no name upon it, although the handle was slightly tacky to the touch where the airline label had been removed. He glanced into the trash can beside it, but it was empty, so he could not even find a name to identify its owner.

The telephone in the bathroom was closer than the phone beside the bed, so he decided to use it to call reception. He was about to do so when he paused and looked again at the bag. He experienced a brief surge of fear: this was a big hotel in a large American city, and was it not possible that someone might deliberately have left this item of baggage in one of its rooms? He wondered if he might suddenly find himself at the epicenter of a massive terrorist explosion, and saw himself not disintegrate or vaporize, but instead shatter into pieces, like a china statue dropped onto a stone floor, fragments of his being littering the remains of the room: a section of cheek here, an eye, still blinking, there. He had been rendered fundamentally flawed by grief; there were cracks in his being.

Did bombs still tick? He could not say. He supposed that some—the old-fashioned kind—probably did. Just as he had relied upon his windup alarm clock to wake him for his flight that morning (he lived in fear of power cuts on such occasions), then perhaps there were times when only a straightforward, tick-tock timepiece with a little keyhole in the back would do the trick when failure was not an option.

Carefully, he walked over to the bag, then leaned in close to it and listened, holding his breath so that any telltale sounds would not be masked by his labored wheezing. He heard nothing and instantly felt silly for even trying. It was a forgotten case, nothing more. He would call reception and have it taken away.

He stepped into the bathroom, hit the light switch, and stopped, his hand poised over the telephone. An array of toiletries and cosmetics had been carefully lined up beside the sink, along with a hairbrush, a comb, and a small vanity case. There were moisturizers and lipsticks, and in the shower stall, a bottle of green apple shampoo alongside a container of jojoba conditioner. There were blond hairs caught in the hairbrush. He could see them clearly from where he stood.

They had given him an occupied room, a room that was temporarily home to a woman. He felt anger, on both her behalf and his own. How would she have reacted had she returned to find an elderly man snoozing in the armchair by her bed? Would she have screamed? He thought the shock of a woman screaming at him in her bedroom might have been enough to hasten his mortality, and he was momentarily grateful that it had not come to that.

He was already composing a tirade in his head when he heard the hotel door open and a woman stepped into the room. She was wearing a red hat and a tan mac, both of which she discarded on the bed along with two shopping bags from a pair of chichi clothing stores whose names were known to him. Her back was to him, and her blond hair was tied up loosely at the back of her head, held in place by a leather clip. Now that the coat was gone, he saw her lemon sweater and white skirt, her bare legs and the tan sandals on her feet.

Then she turned and stared straight at him. He did not move. He felt his lips form a word, and he spoke her name, but she did not hear him.

No, he thought, this is not possible. *This cannot be.*

It was her, yet not her.

He was looking not at the face of a woman who had died barely a year before, her features heavily lined by old age and the depredations of the disease that had taken her, her hair thinning and gray—her body small, almost childlike, where she had shrunken into herself during those final months—but at the face of another who had lived by that name in the past. This was his wife as she once was, as she had been before their children were born. This was his wife as a young woman— thirty, perhaps, but no more than that. As he watched her, he was taken aback by her beauty. He had always loved her and had always thought her beautiful, even at the end, but the photographs and memories could not do justice to the girl who had first entranced him, and about whom he had felt as he had never felt before about a woman.

She walked toward him. He spoke her name again, but there was no response. As she reached the bathroom he stepped out of her way, performing a neat little dance that left him outside the room and her inside. Then the door closed in his face, and he could hear the sounds of clothing being removed and, despite his astonishment, he found himself walking away to give her a little privacy, humming a tune in his head to cover any stray sounds that might emerge but also to distract himself from his own confusion. In the short time he had been asleep, the world appeared to have changed once again, but this time he had no understanding of his place in it.

After a minute or two, he heard the toilet flush, and then she emerged again, also humming the same tune, an old sixties thing they had both loved. *She cannot see me,* he thought. *She cannot see me, but can she somehow hear me?* She had not responded when he called her name, and yet now here she was, sharing a song with him. It might have been coincidence and nothing more. After all, it was one of their favorite pieces, and perhaps it was hardly surprising that, when she was alone and content, she would hum it softly to herself. He had, by definition, never seen her alone. True, there were times when she had been unaware of his presence and he had been allowed to watch as she moved unself-consciously through the rhythms and routines of her day, but such occasions were always brief, the spell broken either by her recognition of his presence or his realization that there were important matters to which to attend. But how important had they truly been? After she died, he would have given up a dozen of them—no, a hundred, a thousand—for another minute with her. Such was hindsight, he supposed. It made every man wise, but wise too late.

He shook his head. None of this was relevant. What mattered was that he was looking at his wife as she had once been, a woman who could not now be but somehow was. He went through all of the possibilities: a waking dream, a sleeping dream, a hallucination brought on by tiredness and travel. But he had smelled her as she passed by him at the bathroom door, and he could hear her now as she sang, and the weight of her footsteps left impressions on the thick carpet that remained visible for a moment before the strands sprang back into place.

I want to touch you. I want to feel your skin against mine once again.

She had unlocked her suitcase and had begun to unpack her clothes, hanging blouses and dresses in the closet and using two of the dresser drawers on the left for her underwear, just as she did at home. He was so close to her now that he could hear her breathing. He spoke her name again, his breath upon her neck, and it seemed to him that, for an instant, she lost her place in the song, stumbling slightly on a verse. He whispered again, and she stopped entirely. She looked over her shoulder, her expression uncertain, and her gaze went straight through him.

He reached out a hand and brushed his fingers gently against the skin of her face. It felt warm to the touch. She was a living, breathing presence in the room. She shivered and brushed the spot with her fingertips, as though troubled by the presence of a strand of gossamer.

A number of thoughts struck him almost simultaneously.

The first was: *I will not speak again. Neither will I touch her. I do not want to see that look upon her face. I want to see her as I so rarely saw her in life. I want to be at once a part of, and apart from, her life. I do not understand what is happening, but I do not want it to end.*

The second thought was: *If she is so real, then what am I? I have become insubstantial. When I first saw her, I believed her to be a ghost, but now it seems that it is I who have become less than I once was—and yet I can feel my heart beating, I can hear the sound my spittle makes in my mouth, and I am aware of my own pain.*

The third thought was: *Why is she alone?*

They had always arrived together to stay in this hotel to celebrate their anniversary. It was their place, and they would always ask for this room because it was the room in which they had stayed that first night. It did not matter that the decor had changed over the years or that it was, in truth, identical to almost every other room in the hotel. No, what mattered was the number on the door, and the memories that number evoked. It was the thrill of returning to—how had she once put it?—the "scene of the crime," laughing in that low way of hers, the way that always made him want to take her to bed. When the room was not available, they would feel a sense of disappointment that cast the faintest of shadows over their pleasure.

He was seeing her in their room, but without him. Should he not also be here? Should he not be witnessing himself with her, watching as he and she moved around each other, one dressing while the other showered, one reading while the other dressed, one (and, in truth, it was always he) tapping a foot impatiently while the other made some last-minute adjustment to hair or clothing? He experienced a sensation of dizziness, and his own identity began to crumble like decaying brickwork beneath the mason's hammer. The possibility came to him that he had somehow dreamed an entire existence, that he had created a life that had no basis in reality. He would awake and find that he was back in his parents' house, sleeping in his narrow single bed, and there would be school to go to, with ball practice afterward, and homework to be done as the evening light faded.

No. She is real and I am real. I am an old man, and I am dying, but I will not let my memories of her be taken from me without a fight.

Alone. She had come here alone. Alone, for now. Was there another coming, a lover, a man known or unknown to him? Had she betrayed him in this room, in *their* room? The possibility was more devastating to him than if she had never existed. He retreated, and the pain inside him grew. He wanted to grasp her, to demand an explanation. Not now, he thought, not at the very end, when all I have been waiting for is to be reunited with her at last—or, if there is nothing beyond this place, to lose myself in a void where there is no pain, and where her absence can no longer be felt, merely absorbed into the greater absence beyond.

He sat down heavily in the chair. He raised his hand to his brow and tried to remember what was real. The telephone rang, but whether in his world or hers, he did not know. They were layered, one on top of the other, like twin pieces of film, just as in old movies an actor could play two parts in the same scene by being filmed against an earlier image of himself. His wife, her shoes now discarded, skipped across the floor to the bed and picked up the receiver.

"Hello? Hi, honey. Yes, everything's fine. I got here okay, and they gave us our room." She listened. "Oh no, that's too bad. When do they think they'll be able to fly you out? Well, at least you won't miss the *entire* weekend." Silence again. He could hear the tinny voice on the other end of the line, and it was his own. "Well, it makes sense to stay at an airport motel, then, just in case. It won't be as nice as here, though." Then she laughed, sensual and throaty, and he knew what had been said, knew because he had said it, could almost remember the exact words, could recall nearly every minute of that weekend because now it was coming back to him, and he felt a flurry of conflicting responses to the dawning knowledge. There was relief, but there was also shame. He had doubted her. Right at the end, after all of their years together, he had thought of her in a way that was unworthy of himself, and of her. He wanted to find a way to apologize to her, but he could not.

"I'm sorry," he whispered, and to acknowledge his fault aloud gave him some relief.

He went through his memories of that weekend. Snow had hit the airport, delaying all flights. He had been cutting it pretty tight that day, for there were meetings to attend and people to see. His was the last flight out, and he had watched the board as it read "delayed," then "delayed" again, and, finally, "canceled." He had spent a dull evening at an airport motel so he would be close enough to catch the first flight out the next morning, if the weather lifted. It had, and they had spent the next night together, but it was the only occasion upon which they had found themselves apart in such a way on their anniversary, she in their room and he in an anonymous other, eating pizza from a box and watching a hockey game on TV. Recalling it now, it had not been such a bad night, almost an indulgence of sorts, but he would rather have spent it with her. There were few nights over the entire forty-eight-year history of their marriage that he would not rather have spent with her.

There was something else about that night, something that he could not quite remember. It nagged at him, like an itch in his mind demanding to be scratched. What was it? He cursed his failing memory, even as another emotion overcame him.

He was conscious of a sense of jealousy, of envy toward his younger self. He was so brash then, so caught up in his own importance. He looked at other women sometimes (although he never went further than looking), and he sometimes thought of his ex-girlfriend, Karen, the one who might have been his wife, the one who went to a little college in the Midwest with the expectation that he would follow, when instead he had gone elsewhere, choosing to stay closer to home. They had tried to make it work, but it had not, and there were moments in the early years of his marriage when he had thought about what it might have been like to have married her, of how their children might have looked and how it might have been to sleep each night next to her, to wake her in the dark with a kiss and to feel her respond, her hands upon his back, their legs slowly intertwining. In time, those thoughts had faded, and he had dwelt in the present of his choosing, grateful for all that it—and she—had brought him. But that young man, carefree and careless, would arrive the next morning, and he would take his beautiful wife to bed, and he would not yet understand how fortunate he was to have her.

She hung up the phone and sat on the bed for a time, running her fingers across the stone of her engagement ring and then tracing circles around the gold band that sat above it. When she was done, she stood, finished unpacking, and then, as he remained in his chair, aware now of flurries of snow falling outside, she drew the curtains, turned on the bedside lamps so that the room was lapped by warm light, and began to undress.

And it was given to him to be with her that night, both distantly yet intimately. He sat on the bathroom floor as she bathed, his cheek against the side of the tub. Her head rested on a towel and her eyes closed as the radio in the room played an hour of Stan Getz. He was beside her as she sat on the bed in a hotel robe, a towel wrapped around her head, painting her toenails and laughing at some terrible comedy show that she would never have watched had he been with her, and he found himself laughing along with her as much as at it. He followed the words on the page as she read a book he had given her, one he had just finished and thought she might like. Now he read along with her; the contents of the book he had long forgotten, so they both discovered it anew together.

At last, she removed the towel and shook out her hair, then took off the robe and put on a nightdress. She got into bed, turned out the light, and rested her head upon the pillow. He was alone with her; her face was almost luminescent in the dark, pale and indistinct. He felt sleep approach, but he was afraid to close his eyes, for he knew in his heart that she would be gone when he awoke, and he wanted this night to last. He did not want to be separated from her again.

But the itch was still there, the sense that there was an important, salient matter that he could not quite recall, something linked to a long-forgotten conversation that had occurred when he had finally found his way to this room and they had made love. It was coming back to him: slowly, admittedly, but he was finding pieces of that weekend in the cluttered, dusty attic of his memory. There had been lovemaking, yes, and afterward she had been very quiet. When at last he had looked down at her, he saw that she was crying silently.

"What is it?" he had asked.

"Nothing."

"It can't be nothing. You're crying."

"You'll think I'm being silly."

"Tell me."

"I had a dream about you," she had replied.

Then it was gone again. He tried to remember what that dream had been. It was relevant, somehow. Everything about that night was now relevant. Beside him, his young wife's breathing altered as she descended into sleep. He bit his lip in frustration. What was it? What couldn't he remember?

His left arm felt numb. He supposed that it was the position in which he rested. He tried to move it, and numbness became pain. It extended quickly through his system, like acid injected into his bloodstream. He opened his mouth and a rush of air and spittle emerged. He groaned. There was a tightness in his chest, as though something were now sitting astride him, coiling around him, constricting his breathing, compressing his heart so that he saw it as a red mass grasped in a fist, the blood slowly being squeezed from it.

"I dreamt that you were beside me, but you were in distress, and I couldn't reach you. I tried and tried, but I couldn't get to you."

He heard her voice from afar, recalling now the words, remembering how he had held her and stroked her back, touched by the strength of her feelings yet knowing in his heart that he thought her foolish for responding to a dream in this way.

She moved in her sleep, and now he was crying, the pain forcing tears from the corners of his eyes.

"I dreamt that you were dying, and there was nothing I could do to save you."

I am dying, he thought to himself. *At last, it has come.*

"Hush," said his wife. He looked at her, and although her eyes were still closed, her lips moved, and she whispered to him: "Hush, hush. I am here, and you are here."

She shifted in the bed, and her arms reached out and enfolded him in their embrace, and his face was buried in her hair, and he smelled her and touched her as the agony grew, his heart exploding deep within him, all things coming to an end in a failure of blood and vein, of artery and muscle. She clasped him tightly to herself as the last words he would ever utter emerged in a senseless tangle, and then the darkness took him, and all was stillness and silence for a time.

"Hush," she said, as he died. "I am here. . . ."

And now you are here.

Hush. *Hush.*

And he opened his eyes.

Church Services

Kevin J. Anderson

As soon as his shouted prayer reached a crescendo in tandem with his silent internal plea, Jerome Tucker opened his eyes and watched the demon leave the young man.

Inside the canvas revival tent, the blasphemous thing emerged from the teenage boy's nostrils and throat like poisonous smoke mixed with a swarm of bees, crackling, buzzing, and writhing. Demonic whispers built to a scream. A trickle of blood followed the thing as it slid and tore its way out of the possessed young man.

The demon had no choice but to obey. Jerome had commanded it with the compulsion of God Himself.

He had lost count over the weeks, but he had summoned and trapped at least a hundred demons on the long and slow wagon trek across the farmlands of Illinois, across muddy and rutted roads to the wild lands and new homesteads of Wisconsin Territory. In this new and barely settled land, there were many secrets, many buried shadows of times past. So many demons had been cast out in Biblical times, and the evil had to have gone somewhere. What better place to seek refuge than among the heathen in the New World? It made perfect sense.

Inside the large tent crowded with farmers, their wives, their children, and a few shopkeepers from Bartonville (the closest thing that could have been called a town), he raised his hands. His full, rusty red beard stood out like flames on his chin.

"Leave this boy, I command you!"

Even after the demon had fully emerged, the teenager continued to spasm and moan, his jaws clenched, lips drawn back. The audience gasped; several women fainted, while others uttered their own prayers. Two lanky farmers swore with coarse language that would not have pleased an eavesdropping God.

"As Jesus Christ trapped the demon Legion in a group of pigs, so I contain you here, where you can do no further harm." With an imperative gesture, Jerome stuck out his hand, touched the ornate potbellied clay jar covered with runes and designs, symbols now rusty with dried blood.

The demon struggled and wailed, shifting and convulsing like a tornado of flies, and, inexorably, the crackling black mist was sucked into the containment jar—the holy relic from ancient Egypt, or Babylon, or Assyria (Jerome wasn't exactly sure which). Like smoke swirling up a chimney in a harsh draft, the indefinable thing vanished into the clay vessel with a last alien howl, and when it was trapped completely in its new prison, the maddening sound stopped with the abruptness of a slammed door.

"Glory to God on high!" called out Jerome's wife, Mollie. She dutifully stood beside him at the pulpit, holding open the tattered Bible, knowing exactly which verses Jerome would need for the next step of the process.

The teenager's weeping mother rushed forward, knocking over one of the thin wooden benches as she came up to throw her arms around her limp son. "Oh, he's saved, he's saved!"

Blood dribbled from the boy's mouth as he groaned, then opened his eyes. He stared around with a sparkling awareness, as though he'd been asleep for months. The audience applauded wildly, called out choruses of "Amen!"

Mollie read aloud from the Twenty-third Psalm, not because it was especially appropriate but because it was her favorite passage. Her high and musical voice gained strength as she read verse after verse.

Jerome was the more forceful personality with a passion for his calling, but he couldn't have done this without Mollie's help, without her faith. She had followed him from their home, leaving everything behind to journey across untamed country, staking her future on him.

Jerome Tucker had always wanted to be a preacher, but he'd needed a flock. And with so many homesteaders moving west to stake their claims in uncharted lands, *those* people needed to hear the Gospel. So Jerome had gathered up his savings, took the last of the money he needed from his parents, and bought a wagon and horses, a large tent, and Bibles—everything he needed.

He went to the land surveyor's office to study maps of Illinois and Wisconsin all the way to the Mississippi River. The owlish-faced clerk had shown him available plots and already claimed areas where farmland was being cleared by hardworking pioneers. Jerome did not want acreage for himself; he just needed to find a large enough group of people who required his services.

He knew he would find the right place. He'd been so eager to grab the plat books that he'd cut his finger on the countertop's ragged wooden edge. Sucking on the wound absentmindedly, he had turned pages, following the geography up into south-central Wisconsin. By smeary light that passed through flyspecked windows, he stopped to study farmland, roads, and neighboring towns.

A droplet of blood fell and splashed on one particular area, a bold crimson mark on the map. Jerome considered it a sign, a position chosen by his blood. *That* was where he would go.

As they made their way westward, he and Mollie had preached to crowds, and Jerome did God's work, casting out and capturing many demons to purify the population along the way. The cross-country journey had taken months, through falling snow and over slushy roads, through heavy rainstorms and a miasma of humidity and mosquitoes. He felt as if he and his wife were required to pass through the very plagues of Egypt to reach this particular Promised Land.

Finally, on a low hill that overlooked recently claimed farmlands, sprawling fields of corn, and uncleared trees that marked land boundaries, Jerome and Mollie had erected their big tent for the last time. There, he held nightly services. When the people began to understand that Jerome could truly cast out demons, that he could take away their sins and purify their thoughts, his flock began to grow. . . .

Now, seeing the teenage boy get shakily to his feet and collapse in his mother's arms, both of them crying, Jerome felt tears roll down his own cheeks. He had saved at least thirty people in this area already, and they all owed him a great deal. He would forge them into a community, a town, a new place.

Smiling, he lifted his hands and called out once more. The canvas tent had been old when he'd purchased it secondhand; now it was patched and stained—by no means was it an adequate palace for worship. Now that he knew with all his soul that this was the place, now that all the people in the revival tent listened raptly to whatever he had to say, he called them together and he made his request.

"I must ask something of you, my friends. This ground has been consecrated enough with all our prayers. Now, I require your help, your wood, your tools, your labor, and your love. We will build a church here, and then we will establish a town."

During their journey west and north through Wisconsin, at the edge of a river that drained into the Mississippi, Jerome had found the ancient symbol-bedecked urn that had changed his life.

He and Mollie had stopped for the night in a small town where flatboats delivered cargo downriver and brought new supplies back upstream. There, they had met a man with clumpy brown hair and three fingers missing on the left hand. His face was weathered and more deeply tanned than could be explained by any Midwestern summer, and his eyes had a distant stare, focused on memories rather than the landscape, as if he had already seen more than his share of wonders and nightmares.

The man struck up a conversation with Jerome but did not introduce himself. He explained how he had traveled the Ancient World looking for oddities and treasures.

"Pharaoh held the Israelites in Egypt," Jerome said. "In ancient times."

"Egypt is an ancient place full of dead things. I'd heard rumors that there were so many treasure-filled tombs scattered across the desert that a man could simply walk along and pick up gold and jewels. There are tombs, all right. The entire land is like a skeleton."

Jerome knew about wealthy Europeans, gentleman archaeologists who explored Egypt and returned with mummies and artifacts, telling ludicrous tales of curses and the revenge of ancient gods. Jerome knew all such stories to be false, of course, because he had read the Bible—carefully—several times.

The man held up his left hand, showing the three stumps of his fingers. "A jackal did this. Bit them clean off when I tried to retrieve a demon jar from a tomb."

"What's a demon jar?" Mollie asked. The man looked at her, surprised that she had spoken.

Jerome had no patience for those who didn't respect his wife. "What's a demon jar?" he repeated.

The man opened the large trunk that held his belongings and moved a rolled rug and some cloth aside to extract an ivory-pale urn made of ancient clay; it looked as if it had been cast from liquefied bone. Its surface was stippled with indecipherable writing, odd designs, one of which Jerome recognized as the Star of David; another, prominent in the center, was unmistakably the Cross.

"Moses wasn't God's only prophet in Egypt," the man said soberly. "This jar was created by one such holy man as a vessel to capture and hold the demons that filled the land." He lifted the lid of the urn and gazed into its dark interior. "It's empty now—either the demons have escaped over the years, or it was never used. But you can tell by the symbols that it must be a sacred relic."

Mollie was more skeptical. "If this was created in ancient Egypt or Sumeria, that was many years before Christ died for our sins. How could it carry the symbol of the Cross?"

The man regarded Mollie with no small amount of annoyance. "And what is it, ma'am, that a prophet *does*? Why, he *prophesies!* He knows the future. Wouldn't God's chosen know about the impending arrival of God's son?" He turned back to Jerome. "If you are a preacher, and if you are truly guided by the Holy Spirit, then you must know already how to cast out demons."

In fact, Jerome didn't, though he'd always thought about it.

"But any preacher can *cast out* demons," the man continued. "And then what? They are freed from one host and sent to wander the world, where they continue to wreak havoc. With this urn, however"—the man patted the rough clay surface—"you not only withdraw demons from the possessed, you also imprison them, seal them in this jar, where they will cause no further harm."

The man sounded tired and disappointed. "To be honest, I have no use for this relic. I am not a holy man." With a smile, he extended it toward Jerome. "Take this as my gift. It is better off in your hands, since you can do God's work with it."

Suddenly embarrassed or shy, he added, "However, if you could spare some coins, I need to buy passage back home. Thieves in Constantinople took my last money, and I have had to beg my way, working for passage across the sea, then on riverboats down the Ohio, then across country, finally to here. My mother has consumption, you see. I am trying to get home so I can be with her before she dies."

Jerome felt the earnestness in the man's voice, and he knew how much good work he could do with this demon jar.

"Whatever you think the jar is worth . . ." The man left the idea hanging. Mollie shot her husband a sharp glare as Jerome enthusiastically opened his money pouch and withdrew far more coins than they could spare. Jerome was sure, though, that once he began casting out demons, grateful parishioners would quickly contribute to the offering plate.

"How do I use it?" Jerome asked.

The man regarded him earnestly. "You'll know. God will show you."

Late at night, under a buttery-yellow moon, Mollie found Jerome within the framework structure of the nearly completed church. The glass windowpanes had not yet been installed, but the walls were finished and the roof partially covered. The smell of sawdust mingled with sweat hung in the air: aromas of sweet pine and devoted labor. People volunteered their time, several days a week, to finish the great work.

In the large window opening that would soon be filled with beautiful stained-glass panels shipped all the way from Chicago, Mollie could look down the hillside to the silver-lit fields and small cluster of new buildings, the embryo of the town that her husband had coaxed into existence.

The altar had been completed first, covered with an embroidered, lace-edged cloth: a gift from three farmers' wives who had worked their fingers sore to finish it. In the center of the altar lay the large old Bible next to the pale demon jar. Jerome had held regular services here as soon as the framework was erected, and he had packed away his tattered old revival tent for good. He expected his brother Clancy to bring their parents any time now.

Now he knelt before the altar in the dark. Unlit candles stood in freshly lathed wooden stands. As Mollie entered the skeletal church behind him, her step softly creaked the new-laid pine floorboards, but he did not stop his muttered prayer. Eyes half shut, he pulled out his knife, touched the razor-edged tip to his thumb, then sliced. The blood looked like black molasses as it welled up.

Mollie stood behind him, bowing her head, not interrupting the sacred ceremony. Jerome extended his thumb and pressed the warm wetness to the Cross that stood out in sharp relief among the other designs. The ancient jar seemed to draw the blood, drink and absorb it greedily.

"God will protect us from demons," Jerome muttered. "God will contain them inside here."

It wasn't exactly a recitation from the Scriptures, but the demons could hear him. Trapped in their jar, they would be afraid.

The Scripture had a long tradition of blood sacrifice: just as Abraham had been willing to make a blood sacrifice of his son Daniel, just as Moses marked the lintels of the Jews with lambs' blood so that the Angel of Death would pass over their homes, just as God had demanded the blood of his own son Jesus to save humanity, so Jerome was willing to give up a small amount of his blood to strengthen the demon jar, to keep the evil things inside.

He slowly regained his feet, turned to his wife. "Every demon I've removed and imprisoned is one less soldier Satan has for the Final Battle. Not only am I making my new town a pure and holy place, I am aiding the whole world."

Mollie, though, was concerned. "All the times in the Bible where a godly man casts out demons, he never tries to *collect* them. He never keeps them like old coins in a purse. And what happens when the vessel is full? Do you know how much evil it can contain? I'm worried about what that jar really does."

"Why, it imprisons demons, Mollie." Jerome leaned closer in the deep shadows of the unfinished church. "And when we bless this new house of worship, when all of the congregation comes from miles around, they will join together and make a similar sacrifice. We'll purge this area of all sins and evil thoughts. This land, this town of Tucker's Grove, will become a new Eden." His eyes were shining in the moonlight. "Yes, I'm sure, Mollie. I'm sure of our future, I'm sure of this place, and I'm sure of my mission. Not a shred of doubt."

"That's all I wanted to know," Mollie said with a smile, "because I have news for you as well, joyous news." She took his hand and a smear of blood went down the front of her palm. "I'm pregnant, Jerome. I'll have our first child in your new town."

When the church was finished—when all the siding had been painted white, the black shingles laid down, the bell installed in the steeple that perched like a triumphant hand raised toward Heaven—it was time for a great celebration. The three men who had delivered the stained-glass window from Chicago stayed for the festivities; Jerome hoped they would remain permanently, since the town needed glaziers.

Jerome felt that he had lived all his life for this day. His clothes were freshly laundered, his hair combed, his beard trimmed. Mollie had sewn herself a fine new dress from a bolt of pink fabric she'd purchased at the general store in Bartonville. She had left the waistline loose, because now the curve of her belly was becoming noticeable. Jerome thought she looked radiant.

The bell pealed out a shrill, melodic tone as two young farm boys took turns yanking the rope to set up a clangor that rang from horizon to horizon. The people streamed in: more men, women, and families than Jerome had thought lived in the area. They came to dedicate the church they'd helped to build. Though Jerome had not yet secured a piano to lead the music, they would sing familiar hymns in unison. That was all a church really needed.

Jerome spoke up when they had squeezed into the pews so that everyone could have a seat. "This place of worship stands on holy ground, for I have made it so. All of your crops will be blessed, and all of your children will be strong and protected from evil. I will make it so. *We* will make it so. We will be a community, a bastion against darkness."

He turned to the altar and touched the demon jar. "You have all seen me cast out demons. The most powerful and most dangerous of those evil fallen angels are here, trapped inside this urn." He brushed the surface of the vessel. "They are locked there by the grace of God, by the holy symbols . . . and by the gift of blood."

Jerome extended his thumb toward the congregation. "Today, we make one grand final summoning to draw out all the evils and ills that permeate this land, that permeate our hearts. We will draw away the pain and darkness so that Tucker's Grove can be a perfect place, a shining example for mankind."

The people in the church shouted their amens. Some stood in the pews.

"A drop of blood," Jerome said, "from me, from you—from all of you—and this town will lock away those evil spirits forever." With a flick of his knife, he sliced open his thumb once more, this time a little more extravagantly than he'd expected. The blood flowed, and he touched it to the Cross so that the ancient, mysterious urn drank the scarlet liquid. He held up the knife. "Who will be the first to join me?"

The people in the front pew nearly fell over themselves to come to the altar. Each took up the knife, drew blood, and touched red thumbprints or fingerprints to the pale ivory curves of the ancient vessel.

The second row of people came forward, jostling and pushing each other. Some wept with joy, while others closed their eyes and prayed as they made their offering. This was not like a somber Communion ceremony: they were an army laying siege to the evil things that had troubled them all their lives.

With Jerome's command, a great wind of shadows, dark thoughts, evil deeds, frightening memories—the very manifestation of sin—swept up the hills and blew like a quiet winter wind into the church. The congregation could sense how much more darkness the demon jar was drinking, but their blood maintained the seal, trapping the bad things forever.

Jerome felt his heart swell with love for these people, his people. Mollie stood looking preoccupied, maybe a bit worried. Beaming, he slipped his arm around his wife's waist. "Why are you so quiet, my dear? This is our finest, most perfect hour."

Mollie bit her lower lip and shook her head, afraid to answer at first. Finally, she said, "All that blood . . . Instead of trapping the demons, what if it's *feeding* them?"

With a great outcry, the last of the parishioners stumbled back from the urn. The incredibly old Egyptian—or Sumerian, or Assyrian—vessel had begun to glow a faint orange, like fire within an eggshell. The embellished clay walls began to pulse in a heartbeat, as if the demons inside were fighting and struggling to break free.

Jerome took a deep breath but could find no words. He had gathered numerous demons from all across the countryside on his travels up to Wisconsin, collected them from suffering people over the course of his journey. Victims had come to him from far and wide, and he had torn out the demons and imprisoned them in the vessel, carried them here to his new town.

And they were all furious.

Cracks appeared in the ivory ceramic; then fire belched out of the fissures. The demon jar exploded with a thunderstorm whirlwind of black, screaming voices, buzzing flies. Howling anger and dripping vengeance roared out with enough force to snuff a tornado.

Parishioners ducked, throwing themselves onto the pews, onto the floor. The unleashed demons filled the church and swirled around; some streaked through the open front door. A black, smoky jet smashed through the stained-glass window, sending jewel-toned shards flying in all directions.

The evil blackness whistled around Jerome and Mollie. He grabbed his wife, tried to protect her, but he didn't know how. A murky, miasmic face that seemed made of fangs rose up before them, screaming: a scream that sounded more like laughter.

Mollie cringed. The shadows pummeled her, wrapped about her as though she were being sprayed with mud. She collapsed to the floor, crying in terror.

Jerome balled his fists and shouted, "Begone, I command you all! *Begone!*"

And the demons fled the church, racing out and away to find new hosts in the vicinity of Tucker's Grove.

The evil storm subsided just as abruptly as it had begun. The interior of the new church had been shredded, leaving clouds of dust, splinters, and fear. The people were stunned, moaning, touching small cuts, and inspecting tattered clothes. As Jerome ran among his people to help, some of them looked away in deep shame, afraid to let him see the shadowed hollows in their eyes, the new darkness that glinted from their gaze.

Jerome felt his bones turn to ice and understood that his dreams had been dashed. He had meant to establish a perfect town, to create a new Eden completely free of sin or evil or hate. Instead, he had brought more darkness to the area and saturated this very place.

He clung to the sharp foundation of his faith. He would not surrender. He refused to leave his town. He had far too much work to do here.

Crumpled and sick, Mollie retched onto the floor, cradling her abdomen. Jerome knelt beside her, helped her to her feet. She swayed against him. "Are you hurt? Are you all right?"

Mollie drew a deep breath. "I'll be fine. I just felt the baby kick, that's all."

He didn't ask her why she was shuddering.

And she didn't tell him that the kick had felt distinctly like that of a cloven hoof.

Starlets & Spaceboys

Joseph V. Hartlaub

The sky looked as if it had been splattered with multicolored droplets, a light blue background for the hot-air balloons decorated with all manners and sorts of colors and patterns. It wasn't even noon on Saturday, yet the wide-open space over Festival Park seemed improbably jammed to capacity, with even more balloons rising majestically upward to the oohs and aahs of the crowd below. Sparkle, too self-consciously hip at age eighteen to make noises of approval like she had when she was five and six (and maybe even twelve or thirteen), nonetheless felt an internal thrill as she watched the spectacle of it all, both in the air and on the ground. She wasn't ordinarily given to thinking ironic thoughts, not even when asked to do so in her senior English class; Sparkle considered, however, if only for a second, that she was all alone in a crowd of thousands.

The day hadn't started that way. She had ridden the Sun Tran with her friend Marie to Festival Park early that morning, looking forward to a day of hanging out at the Balloon Fiesta and staying loose. They had done just that for a couple of hours, wandering through the park, taking in the hot-air balloons decorated like people and the crowds of people dressed like balloons, all of it framed against the backdrop of the Sandia Mountains rising so majestically out of the desert to the northeast of Albuquerque.

Their pair-up had abruptly ended, however, when Marie spotted Michael, her all-too-recent ex-boyfriend, strolling through the crowd and not even ten feet away from them. Marie had a hurried conference with Sparkle (who assured her friend that she would be fine, just fine, on her own) and had walked up to him. Michael had smiled, said something, and the last Sparkle had seen of either of them, they were walking hand in hand into the maw of the crowd, which quickly swallowed them up.

Sparkle took stock of things. She was beginning to feel a bit overwhelmed by the crowd and by some hunger pangs that were starting to hit. She had left the house in a hurry that morning, taking a whore's bath and then quickly applying all over herself the sparkle makeup that had earned her the nickname, and she hadn't had time to eat breakfast. She was looking for a food vendor who didn't have a mile-long line when she felt a hand grip her shoulder.

She turned around and there was Rod, all decked out in his gray slacks and Pep Boys shirt with his name emblazoned in an oval patch on the left side.

"Hey, there, Sparkle," he said, his grin revealing what her friends called summer teeth—summer here, summer there—stained with tobacco. "What are you doing here?"

"Wussup, Rod, no lube jobs stacking up?"

"Funny girl." He paused and took a drag on a cigarette, reached into his pocket and pulled out a wrinkled pack of Chesterfields, offering her one, his eyebrows going up. She shook her head no. He put the pack back in his pocket and asked, "Your mom around?"

"You know she isn't," she said. "She's at home waiting for you."

"Yeah, well, I got off early, thought I'd come down here for a little while before I went out to see her." He took a long drag off the cigarette and blew the smoke out while he smiled at her. "It's great running into you out here. I've been wanting to talk to you anyway. Get to know you a little better."

Sparkle just shook her head, thinking, so fucking obvious, this guy. "You're really smooth, Rodney," she said, using the name he hated. She had turned eighteen in July, three months ago, and she had caught him looking at her more than once since then, always when she was in profile to him and always when her mom wasn't looking. She would rather be dry-humped by a Walmart greeter than by this grease monkey.

"I gotta go," she said. She turned to leave and took a step away, her forward progress interrupted when he grabbed her upper arm and turned her back around, not hard but maybe a shade beyond friendly.

"Hold up a minute," he said. "I just want to talk." His mouth was smiling, but there was something in his eyes that looked angry. "There's no reason to get hostile here, pretty lady."

She looked around, saw everyone moving in different directions, heading here, heading there. She was all alone in a huge crowd of people. People in different parts of the crowd were shrieking happily, one girl squealing "Heelllp!" with some others laughing. Sparkle tried to pull away, but Rod's grip just got tighter, like one of those paper Chinese handcuffs. The grin was frozen on his face, but it was more of a weird-pissed look than a happy one. Sparkle had seen the bruises on her mother's upper arms, the evenly spaced dark marks that looked like fingerprints, and she was pretty sure that they weren't the result of erotic exuberance. At least, not always.

"Don't pull away, now, there's no reason for that, and no reason to tell your mom. This is just between you and—"

Rod stopped talking suddenly. His mouth was open, but no words were coming out of it. His head was turning to the left, looking at a set of fingers that had curled over his shoulder, a set of fingers attached to a hand, which in turn was attached to an arm, which itself was attached to one of the most beautiful guys Sparkle had ever seen. He was an inch or two shorter than Rod's six feet but somehow seemed to tower over him. All sharp angles, like he had been carved out of stone, he had deep-set blue eyes that peered out from under the shelf of a shaven head, eyes that looked directly into Rod. Rod let go of Sparkle's arm, his fingers not so much releasing her as falling off her, as if some strings in his arm had been cut.

"Leave," the guy said to Rod, his face about an inch away from his. "Now." Rod stumbled, as if he couldn't get his feet and legs moving properly, and the guy righted him and turned him, almost gently, in a direction opposite of Sparkle and gave him a soft shove. Rod took a couple of steps away and the crowd enveloped him, as if he were a beaten dog accepted as a nonthreatening presence by a larger pack.

The guy turned back around and looked directly at Sparkle for the first time. His eyes were like pools; they had lost the laser-beam intensity they had possessed when he was looking at Rod. Looking at her, they were just . . . warm. She wanted to dive in and lose herself in them forever. He smiled at her, a genuine smile that didn't overdo it, yet lit up the day and everything in it.

"Are you okay?" he asked.

"Yeah, I'm fine. He's just a creep."

"Do you know him?"

"He's a friend of my mom's."

"Ugh." The guy's smile went up another hundred watts. "I hope you have better taste."

They shared a laugh.

"I'm Nick," he said. "Nice to meet you."

"I'm Sparkle," she answered.

"And so you are, indeed," he said. They both laughed and shook hands. Nick's hand was warm and strong, but didn't grip hers so much as gently encompass it.

"My pleasure," he said. "This"—he gestured to the balloons, the costumes, the people all around them—"is amazing, it's overwhelming. This is my first year here. Have you been here before?"

"Oh yeah," she said. "I live in Albuquerque. I come every year."

"Well . . ." He hesitated a minute, then dialed up the wattage of his smile yet again.

"Look," he said, "I'm starving. I'd love to hear more about all of this, and about you."

He looked around at the food vendors, at the impossible lines in front of all of them. "Would you care to have lunch with me, and talk?" Nick had wanted to go someplace quiet, away from the noise. He was staying in Old Town and had seen a restaurant there he had wanted to try, so they caught a southbound bus and then walked over to the

Church Street Café. Taking her hand as if it were something they did every day. The two of them sat down at an outside table underneath a hanging basket of flowers, sharing chips and a hot bandito pie and drinking frosted glasses of San Felipo Lemon Tea while they talked.

Nick told her that he was an advance man for a rock band called Starlets & Spaceboys. Sparkle had never heard of them. He told her they were trying out a new marketing model: get on a bus, go to a big open space where there were a lot of people, and put the word out that they were going to have a rock concert. No tickets, just contributions. He had been in town for about a week, putting the word out, waiting for the band to catch up with him. They were going to play a midnight show out under the Sandia Mountains the following Saturday. Maybe, Nick said, looking into her eyes, you'd like to come. She said she'd love to, both of them knowing without saying it that they weren't just talking about a rock concert.

Nick never asked her how old she was, or if she was in school, or anything like that. He never asked her about the Balloon Fiesta or about her life or anything else. And Sparkle never asked him about his accent—British, maybe, or Australian—or about how he happened to enter her life at exactly the right time. They simply finished lunch, and she reached for his hand, but he put his arm around her. She melted into him and they walked out of the restaurant and down the sidewalk to his room at the Hotel Albuquerque.

Sparkle loved hotel rooms. She had only been in one a couple of times, both of them on so-called vacations with her mom, one of them at a Comfort Inn on the outskirts of North Phoenix, with a real pool bizarrely located in the parking lot, the other one in a Days Inn outside Oklahoma City. Sparkle liked the sheets and the wrapped soaps and the plastic cups wrapped in cellophane, and the way a maid would come in and clean up after you.

This was different, however; it was even better. Nick's room was on the top floor of the hotel, the bedsheets crisp and starched and smelling fresh and clean, the air conditioning just high enough to be comfortable, the room bright and airy. And Nick was different. She knew what roofies were, and Nick hadn't touched her drink, spending the whole meal just paying attention to her and answering her questions, looking into her eyes and not at her tits, though she could tell he wanted to.

Sparkle was not a virgin, but she was used to furtive groping and quick thrusting by guys her own age, thirty-second encounters that were over before she even got wet. Nick was different there, as well. He took his time with her, exploring her slowly but with a confidence that was an aphrodisiac all by itself. He kissed her gently on the mouth while he unbuttoned her blouse, ran his tongue over her rosebud nipples as he unbuckled her jeans, slowly tickled and tongued her pussy as his hands tweaked her breasts. When he entered her, his cock felt like a fire inside her that she never wanted to put out. There was a part of her that was terrified, that was screaming that this was too pitch-perfect, being in bed with a guy who looked exactly like the guy she had always wanted, someone who made her feel safe, and desirable, turning her inside out with pleasure. It was like that amusement park ride, the Demon Drop. Nick took her higher than she had even been in her life and then dropped her down into a hole that was so deep she passed out.

When she woke up, the room wasn't quite as bright. Nick was lying next to her, his arm around her, watching television. He looked down at her and smiled as she moved up against him. "What year is it?" she asked.

He smiled down at her. "This one," he answered. She laughed and smacked his arm.

"It's actually five-twenty p.m," he said.

"Ghod, what did you do to me? I'll never fuck again."

"Don't tell me I've ruined you," he said with mock dismay.

"I'm afraid so," she responded. She looked at the television. Nick was watching some sort of science channel. There was a commercial on for a video, one of those wonders-of-nature things with footage of bears catching fish in their mouths in midair. Sparkle and Nick watched as a large fish swam by a rock, which turned out to be a fish itself. A large mouth suddenly materialized, swallowed the fish whole, and settled down into rock shape again.

"That," Nick said, "is what I am going to do to you."

Sparkle laughed. "I think you already have," she smiled.

"No," he said, "not yet. Not quite yet."

They both laughed and he kissed her and then helped her out of bed. He led her into the shower—where, under an endless stream of needles of water, they began swallowing and soaping body parts and entering orifices until Sparkle thought her bones had turned to rubber. Nick carried her out of the shower and laid her on the bed, draping a towel over her. He called room service and ordered a light supper for the both of them, which got to the room just as they finished dressing. They ate quietly: steak and steamed potatoes and vegetables and bottled water. They sat on the bed and fed each other, watching the sun set.

Sparkle was halfway through dessert—a large piece of banana cream pie—when she turned to Nick and said, "I don't know how to say this, but I'm going to have to go home at some point."

"I know," he said, "and I have to earn my keep as well." He walked over to a suitcase and opened it, taking out a plastic bag. There were seven capsules inside.

"The band is working on something, a new type of music delivery system, if you will."

If you will, she thought. She loved his accent, his eyes, his body, the way he treated her, everything about him. She could almost feel tendrils, ley lines, snaking their way across the space between them, connecting them invisibly.

He held the bag up to her. "These are not drugs. I swear to you. But take one each day and you will hear a different Starlets and Spaceboys track in your head. It may take two or three days, but it will be like nothing you have ever experienced."

Nick took her hand and placed the bag, the capsules inside, on her palm. Then he gently closed her hand around the bag and kissed her.

"Endings," he said, "and beginnings."

The words were out of her mouth before she even knew it. "Will I see you again?"

Nick looked her directly in the eye. "Oh yes," he said. "And before the concert. We'll hook up before Saturday.

"But now"—he stood up, offering her his hand to raise her gently off the bed—"we both have to go."

They caught a bus back to Balloon Fiesta Park, and they held each other and kissed under a sky full of balloons and stars.

"I'll see you out there," Nick said, pointing to the Sandia Mountains. He squeezed her hand one more time, looked into her eyes, turned, and became one with the horde. Sparkle, for her part, felt like she could have died right there.

By Monday, Sparkle couldn't get the music out of her head.

It wasn't so intrusive at first. She took her first capsule late Sunday morning. When she had come in on Saturday night, her mother had been passed out in the living room of their shotgun double-wide, an empty liquor bottle on the floor next to her. There had been no evidence of the Rodster in sight; apparently, he hadn't had the nerve to show up after trying to pick up his girlfriend's daughter. Sparkle wasn't sure whether she would tell her mom or not, thinking, wait and see, keep it in reserve for an argument. There was no point in waking her mom up in any event. She was snoring to beat the band; she always did after a bout of heavy drinking, and Mom liked that Captain Morgan Spiced Rum. Tonight, Sparkle had thought, she'd been the one with the Captain in her, oh dear ghod yes. Sparkle had gone to bed and enjoyed the sleep of the well-fucked and satiated.

When she woke up on Sunday morning, the sun was high in the sky and the air was warm. There was a message on her cell phone; Sparkle hoped that it was from Nick, even though she hadn't given him her number. It was not from him at all, of course; it was from Marie, asking if Sparkle wanted to go to the Fiesta today. Fat fucking chance of that, Sparkle thought, though she couldn't really be mad at getting left high and dry. Well, high anyway, she laughed to herself.

Sparkle had wandered into the kitchen looking for something to eat. There was no cereal, no Pop-Tarts, only some toast that looked like it had been found during an Anasazi dig. She remembered the capsules in the plastic bag in her pocket and got a glass of water from the faucet, thought for a moment about taking all of them, then remembered what Nick had said. *Jesus*, she thought, hugging herself for a second at the memory. *What a great fuck he had been*. She unclenched herself and swallowed a capsule. *And a nice guy, too.*

Sparkle had believed Nick, but she was still surprised when the music started in her head. It began not so much as a melody but as a discordant series of notes heard from afar, like a car radio heard from the distance of a couple of blocks that never gets any closer or farther away. The sound didn't interfere with her thoughts; it was more like background music that almost wasn't there. She spent her Sunday afternoon hanging out at a Starbucks and then surfing the net in her bedroom, all of it with the music, some sort of ambient rhythm with deep thumping bass and drums, faintly playing in the background of her mind.

Nick hadn't told her about the video. Sparkle didn't see it until she closed her eyes, but then, all of a sudden, there it was, synced to the music that she could barely hear. A bunch of guys who looked like Vikings—long beards, horned helmets, swinging axes and swords—were in a pitched battle with these things that looked like women, except that they were . . . off, in a way that Sparkle couldn't quite put her finger on. The Vikings were getting their asses kicked royally, literally being eaten whole, the almost-women screaming and laughing with blood smeared around their mouths, biting the heads off the Viking guys in one chomp. It was vivid, yet repetitive after a fashion: a Viking would lose his head and his body would jump around for a few seconds, blood spurting out of his neck, and then fall over.

The music in the dream video got louder and Sparkle suddenly recognized the song. It was a cover of a song her mom had played for her once, had told her that she played in the birthing room when

Sparkle was born, something called "Thursday" by Morphine. Nick was in the video as well, standing off to the side, laughing at the carnage, urging the women-things on at the top of his lungs.

Sparkle sat straight up in bed, wide awake. The Vikings, the carnage, the women bitches . . . were all gone. The music still echoed in her ears, and for just a second she saw Nick standing in the corner, smiling at her. He disappeared, but the music played on, loud and proud, inside her head.

Sparkle lay in bed for a moment before she realized it was Monday, a school day. She looked at the clock and reluctantly rolled out of bed. She stripped, applied her sparkle glitter, then quickly rooted through a pile of clothes on the floor of her closet until she found something reasonably clean and got dressed. She stopped in the kitchen, but there was still nothing there for breakfast; she hesitated a second, then filled a glass from the faucet and took a second capsule.

By Monday afternoon chemistry class, the music was drowning everything else out. Marie had come up to her in the cafeteria at lunch, wanting to talk, but hearing Marie talk was like listening to some garbled radio station from a foreign country: it made no sense to her at all. What she wanted to hear was the music. It was like she had an iPod in her head set on Repeat, and it wasn't playing the quietly creepy Morphine song anymore. It was a track she'd never heard, faintly like "The Four of Us Are Dying" by Nine Inch Nails but more sinister. She loved every note; she found herself bopping along to it. Her lab partner, a Native kid named Cristos, kept looking at her, and he raised his eyebrows at her once in question, as if asking her if she was okay. She just nodded her head yes. She had never felt better in her life. She couldn't wait until Tuesday morning so she could take another capsule.

Sparkle was dream-free Monday night, but taking another capsule on Tuesday seemed to open a part of her brain that she hadn't known existed. It was like she was split into three parts. The song in her head could have been an unreleased Puscifer track, while off to the side— there was no other way to describe it—the battle scenes from *300* seemed to be playing in silhouette. And in front of her was this world.

Then, of course, there was Nick, always Nick, who seemed to be whispering to her. She didn't even think about how she looked to the other kids at school—Marie tried to talk with her a couple of times, but Sparkle blew her off without even knowing it—until Cristos blocked her way in the hall after chem class on Tuesday and got in her face. She could barely hear him over the music, sensing rather than understanding what he saying.

"Hey Sparkle, wassup?"

"Hey, Cristos." She tried to walk around him, but he wasn't having it. The Native kids always kept to themselves, unless they played sports or something. Sparkle hadn't said two words to any of them in her entire three years of high school, and she saw no reason to break the record in her senior year. She didn't like Cristos blocking her way; it was like she didn't have enough brains to handle it. But he wouldn't give way.

"Listen to me . . . you been swallowin' music, haven't you?"

"It's none of your fuckin' business!" She tried to pull away, but he quickly nudged her into a corner and began speaking low and quickly. The music abruptly faded away, though it was still there. She wanted it back, loud and now. Cristos was somehow interfering with the transmission.

"Listen, it's bad shit." He looked around, to see if anyone was listening. "I've got a cousin, Miguel, he worked at the Dancing Eagle out in Casa Blanca, at the restaurant?"

Sparkle didn't say anything to him, not even a nod, so he kept talking. "He kept talking to his boss about some woman he met who was playing the slots, some Anglo who looked like she stepped out of his dreams. She was with some rock band or something, looking for a place to have a concert, and she had these fucking pills she gave him so that he could hear the band's music. It's some band no one ever heard of, Stardust and Spacedreams, or something—"

"That's enough—"

"—and after just a day or two he's bouncing around, dancing, not paying any attention to anything but this music he's hearing in his head. So he starts wandering off into the desert, looking for this bitch, this Nikki—"

Sparkle grabbed him. "Wait a minute. Who?"

"Nikki. Miguel kept talking about this woman named Nikki. And then he just wandered off, looking for the band, and they haven't seen him for two weeks and now you're acting—"

"Shut up!" Sparkle pushed him away, crying, and ran up the hall and out the door. She had walked halfway home before she realized it.

The music had come back, full volume and then some, as soon as she had cleared the school doors, and now there was just the road, the music, and the video playing behind her eyes. She found that with some practice she could control the volume of the music just by thinking about it, almost like the sensor-touch volume on the Bose MP3 player she and Marie had seen at Target a couple of weeks before. She wondered how loud she could make it, and kept pumping it up, not stopping even when the blood started to drip out of her left ear. By the time she had walked to the gravel road that led to the double-wide, her T-shirt, the one that said "Your Mother Is a Bitch," was ruined. It made it look even better. She stuck some toilet tissue in her ear to dam up the blood and went to bed.

When Sparkle woke up hours later, it was dark outside, just a faint hint of daylight peeking out from the east. She went into the bathroom and got a glass of water and swallowed all of the remaining capsules at once. The music stopped suddenly, and for just a second she felt as if she could unzip her skin and crawl out of it. She didn't know what to do about it, not at first.

Then she walked over to the window and looked out across the city toward the horizon, where the Sandia Mountains rose from the desert and met the sky. She knew it was impossible, but she thought she could see Nick out there, standing at the base of the range, his arms crossed against his chest and smiling at her as if he was waiting for her. An electrical storm was starting up off to the west; she thought it might get to Albuquerque in an hour or two. Maybe, she thought, I can get to the desert before then.

She slipped back into her room and put on a dirty pair of jeans and a Coke Dares shirt. She felt small and helpless, but there was a comfort to it as well; she was so insignificant that the universe would never notice her, never stoop so low as to hurt her. And, she thought, who would hurt me, with Nick to protect me?

She opened her bedroom door quietly and slid out and down the hall, trying to be quiet, though her mom was snoring so loudly that Sparkle could probably have stomped out and she never would have known. Still, Sparkle padded quietly down the hallway, past her mother's room—peeking in, she saw no sign of the Rodster—and walked into and through the living room.

It never failed to surprise her how quiet everything was at this time of night, just before dawn. And it was even more so now that the music had stopped. Or maybe it hadn't. Sparkle seemed to hear some sort of low "thrum" interspersed between the rush of blood into her ears, and wondered if this was what snakes felt, the pulses that attracted them toward the highway where they would get run over.

At least, she thought, *my ear has stopped bleeding*. She felt a slick wetness between her legs, however, just as she reached the front door. *Shit*, she thought, *pretty soon there'll be no point to leaving*. She hurried to the bathroom for a quick cleanup and a tampon insertion, and after changing her underwear she slipped quietly out the front door.

The sky was jet black with a swirl of stars through them, kind of like the cake mix Marie's mother had used for birthdays, Funfetti or something, where you mixed colored sprinkles in with the chocolate cake mix. Sparkle thought for a moment about Marie, who seemed more like someone out of dream than a friend she had shared things with, and then the moon went behind the cloudbank that was the source of the electrical storm that was approaching. Sparkle could still see the desert gleaming across the road, a solid black with scraggily patches of sagebrush.

She was deep into the desert within a few minutes, far enough from the highway to feel enveloped in the dark and solitude. She maneuvered around the slightly elevated mounds that bespoke of ant or spider nests and began walking toward the mountains.

What would happen, she thought, if I just kept walking and never came back? She imagined that if she did that, she would eventually die out here. Not a bad way to go, she thought. A sophomore girl at school last year had gotten into her mother's tranks and deliberately overdosed; Sparkle also remembered a senior boy who had hung himself in the closet a couple of years ago. There were rumors, though, that the hanging had been an accident, that he had slipped while whacking off. A couple of the football players said his body had been found with gay porn, but in the end, it didn't make any difference. Dead was dead. There was an appeal, though, to dying under the sky, falling asleep and never waking up, the last thing you felt being the sun and the heat.

Sparkle kept walking toward the mountain range off to the north. In the distance she could see Indian School Road winding off toward it, vanishing behind it the mountains which interrupted the horizon. She thought she saw a twin smudge of headlights back on Interstate 40, someone leaving this place. *Land of Enchantment, my ass*, she thought. She didn't feel like going to school today.

Maybe, she thought, *I'll just stay out here until around ten o'clock, then start walking back home.* Her mom would be at work by then. It was kind of a sweet deal. Her mom got up around 8:00 and left for work a little after 8:30, and would figure that Sparkle had gotten up and left for school. School wouldn't call the house and report her missing until around 9:15 or so. She could erase the message from voice mail and then write a note or something. She'd figure it out later, like she always did. *If I figure it out at all*.

The music suddenly started up in her head again at the same time Sparkle saw Nick, smiling, standing on a pile of rocks practically next to her as if he had been waiting for her. It wouldn't be cool to run to him, but she did smile back at him.

"I missed you," she said—so uncool, but so true—and hugged him against herself.

He seemed to melt into her and asked her as if from a long way away, "You took all of the capsules, didn't you?"

He wasn't mad about it, not at all, his voice rumbling gently through his chest and into her ear. He was wearing cargo pants and a tan T-shirt that said "Starlets & Spaceboys—Millennium Tour" across it, the lettering curved over a tour bus whose front grille resembled a gaping, leering mouth.

Sparkle nodded yes into Nick's chest, and he laughed, saying, "It's okay, everybody does."

A part of her brain, the little corner that was still, somehow, working properly, wondered at that, even got briefly angry over it—*like this is something he does all the time,* she thought—but the emotion was quickly shouted down by a hundred different voices, and she just pulled him tighter to her.

"C'mon," Nick said, still sounding happy. "It's time to meet the band!" He gently disengaged from Sparkle and, turning her toward the Sandias, took her by the hand and began walking with her.

The bus seemed to materialize out of the rock at the base of the mountains. One minute there was thin air; the next a sleek black bus was moving toward them. There was a flash of lightning off to their left, and a few seconds later she heard a clap of thunder that coincided with the roar of the bus engine. The bus came right at them, the blinding shine of the headlights in her face looking like a set of glaring yellow eyes, the grille looking just like it did on Nick's shirt.

It was one of those large passenger vehicles like Greyhound used, except the front and side windows were not just tinted but blacked out. Music was blasting out of some hidden speakers, so loud it was almost distorted, yet the beat of it coincided with what she was hearing in her head. A random thought, so faint and distant that it seemed to come from a well inside her that was a mile deep, said that something was off about the whole thing, but she didn't have time to wonder about it. The bus headed straight for her, and she jumped back just as it pulled up in front of her and the side door folded open.

Sparkle immediately became enveloped in a burning cloud of scent not unlike dope—the good stuff, not the Mexican crap the beaners and the niggers at school were selling for a quarter a joint, but the quality Jamaican stuff she had been able to score once or twice from the guys who hung around the college when she able to hitch a ride down there: the type of shit that gave Bob Marley brain cancer. She took a deep breath of it, letting it settle into her lungs, feeling the ganglia open, the synapses sparking.

Nick got up on the first step of the bus, made a mock bow, and held his hand out to assist her up—courtly like a gentleman, grinning at her all the while. Sparkle noticed for the first time how pointed his teeth looked, how sharp, and wondered why they hadn't cut her while he had been sucking on her nipples, on her clit. For just a second, her feet almost seemed to jump off her, running away of their own volition, but she overrode the impulse and stood there, wondering what was causing her to freak on some level.

She suddenly remembered a dream she had had a couple of months before, about a magic bus coming out of the desert and taking her away from everything: her mom, her school, the boys who were always looking at her tits and never at her eyes. And here it was, right in front of her. There was dope—and it was good shit, heavy and sweet and totally, absolutely intoxicating—and now there was Nick, who looked like he had stepped right out of her wish book, standing at the top of the stairs leading up to the bus, one hand holding hers, the other on the old-folks rail, standing there, all of the answers to all of her problems.

Sparkle stepped past Nick into the bus. The door folded shut and Nick was suddenly gone, swallowed up by the dark interior. She could barely see the driver, who smiled at her over a white shirt and dark tie and jacket, giving a jaunty wave and a "Welcome aboard!" even as she felt the bus begin to move beneath her.

The odor of the ganja was overpowering and caused her to stumble as she made her way down the bus aisle. She turned around and Nick was gone, not just out of sight but gone, and she was standing alone in the aisle. She could make out dim shapes on either side of her, fuzzy and indistinct, and there was another smell now, one she was trying not to think about.

Somehow, Nick was in front of her again, and he had her gently but firmly by the arm—*almost as tight as Rod,* she thought—and was walking her down the aisle, slowly. The aisle seemed to go on for a mile or two, and Sparkle thought that it must be the effect of the secondhand smoke from the dope; she wondered what it must be like to actually smoke the stuff. Nick seemed to know what she was thinking and winked at her, holding his finger up to his lips and smiling, playfully raising his eyebrows and wiggling them. It reminded her of that comedian, the one with the bushy eyebrows and mustache and cigar who was in the old black-and-white movies.

The music was even louder now, dark and moody, like Bauhaus or Marilyn Manson, thumping so loud that it felt as if it was coming from within her instead of from the floor- and ceiling-mounted speakers she could barely make out in the corners of the bus. Sparkle wasn't focused on the music, however.

The other smell she had been trying to ignore was almost scrubbed out of the air by the odor of the marijuana, but it was something that bespoke of things dark and foul, and for just a second the odor got down into her stomach and flipped it over, almost making her want to throw up. It seemed to be coming from the seats on either side of the aisle, or rather, from the shapes in the seats. To Sparkle, the shapes looked like people sleeping, but there was something off about the whole thing. The seats looked as if they were stained with something dark in big splotches, and the people weren't sitting in them, not exactly. It was more like they had been . . . stuck on them.

Sparkle's eyes suddenly focused in on the seats that were not seats; they looked more like teeth, with bodies in various states of rot and decay on them. They suddenly jumped into focus, as if a veil had lifted, and the shapes began to look familiar: one looked like Rod, and those two, across the aisle, looked like Cristos and another Native. All of them didn't sit upright so much as . . . jiggled, as if they didn't have any bones holding them together. Sparkle's stomach lurched, and a scream rose up in her throat, but it died as Nick put his hand on her shoulder and turned her slowly to him.

The light in his eyes caught her, impaled her, and from far away she heard him say softly, but somehow over the roar of the music, "You're my starlet, and I'm your spaceboy."

Something soft broke inside of Sparkle, and then there was nothing, nothing but Nick and the music, the beautiful, loud, roaring music. Sparkle smiled at him and closed her eyes. She loved him so much. But she did not want to watch as Nick's jaws closed over her head.

A Nasty Way to Go

Ardath Mayhar

Being a constable in a bump in the road like Hackberry, Texas, is mostly boring. Drunks and wife beaters and kids who steal watermelons are about the worst criminals you ever set eyes on. Burglars wouldn't find anything worth stealing here in the middle of the East Texas woods in the middle of a Depression that busted even the single local millionaire. Old Buzz Gurley never spent a dime anyway, so nobody missed any business he might have sent their way, and nobody else had much more than a nickel for a can of Levi Garret Snuff.

The Pindars, though—nobody had a clue how they were making out. In a town of two hundred people, everybody knows everybody else's business, but the Pindars had been a mystery ever since the old man's grandpa moved here over a generation ago. Nobody knew how he got the money he used to buy their farm, but there must have been enough to allow his widow to control her sons and their wives for over fifty years. And she drove those people like a hitch of mules, as if they had no say in their own lives. Long as she lived she held the whip hand over her grandsons too.

The question of the Pindar money, whether it existed or not, about drove a generation of old geezers at the barbershop crazy. Their sons were still at it when I was a boy, jawing away with guesses and getting no answers, and it looked as if their grandsons might still be doing it when they got old—if we all didn't starve to death in the meantime. There were four Pindars still living, but two of those moved away up north as soon as their grandmaw died and never came back. We were left with Dennis Pindar and his wife, Gladys, and she was a pistol, you'd better believe.

She used to beat the bejeezus out of Dennis every Wednesday night after prayer meeting at the Baptist church, that being almost the only time they ever went off their own land. What there was about prayer meeting that always set her off, I couldn't tell you. Nobody else could, either, because that was the only time they showed up, though the way the preacher kept mentioning tithing and offerings and slanting his eyes at them, we were all pretty sure they never gave him anything.

There's nothing in the world, I'd guess, that frustrates folks like something they can't have—or can't find out. What little the Pindars bought in Hackberry they paid for in old, wrinkled, musty-smelling greenbacks. As not one of them had ever had a lick of work except on that farm, and as they never produced anything extra to sell, the townsfolk couldn't figure where those greenbacks came from. There was talk of a trunk full of money somewhere on that farm, but as nobody ever succeeded in getting past the front porch, or at the most the front parlor, they couldn't even guess where that trunk might be. If it existed at all, of course.

Being a kid in the early days, I didn't pay much attention to the gossip in the barbershop or on the porch in the evening. Not until I was twenty-six and they got me appointed constable was there any reason for me to pay any attention to such things. But when the county decided to put a constable in Hackberry to cover the twenty miles of surrounding farm and woodland, the three old guys who ran things in town didn't want that man to be an alien, which anybody from outside our exact area was considered to be.

I was the right age, the right size (big and strong), and not bright enough to realize what a bore the job would be. I was cutting firewood at the time to trade for garden produce or corn or whatever foodstuff folks could spare, because there were just no jobs to be had. I'd even thought about moving to one of the bigger towns, like Tyler or even Dallas, and I jumped at the chance to make that fifteen dollars a month.

I have to admit that my job began pretty excitingly, too, thanks to Gladys Pindar.

You have to remember that this was 1933. Nobody that far out in the country had telephones or electric lights or any modern conveniences to speak of. So when little Uneeda Ralston came pounding up to Ma's front door that Wednesday night, his eyes wide in his mahogany face, and yelled that Miz Pindar was likely going to kill her husband if somebody didn't come right quick, I was pretty happy to be needed. I took Papa's old Colt .45 and set out after the boy through a big patch of woods, across a creek and a field, and onto the Pindar property. Near as it was, I'd never been there before, because Ma didn't like Gladys one bit.

That meant that I saw for the first time the famous windmill that pumped water into a tank on a tall metal frame, giving the Pindars running water inside the house. I had heard the rumors that they shit inside the house! Which seemed unreasonable to a boy raised with the old reliable privy, though Pa had explained the principle of a septic tank. It still seemed unsanitary to me.

I didn't have time to gawk at the windmill, though, for it sounded as if a war was raging inside the big house with the dog-run down the middle. Screams, some of rage and some of pain, were mixed with bangs and clatters and the sounds of breaking glass. If they did this every week, I couldn't see how they might have anything breakable left. Still, I gulped once, got out the Colt and checked the load, and moved toward the scene of battle. The boy crept behind me, at a safe distance.

As I climbed the steps, a fruit jar came whizzing out of the open door and shattered against one of the porch posts. I figured it was time to stop this, so I yelled, "Mister and Miz Pindar, this is Cal Hampton, the new constable. Please quiet down so I can talk to you. This is no way to settle anything. Come on out here—or I'll come in, if that's all right with you."

There was no answer, but the noise stopped, so I took that as an invitation to come in. That room was a mess! Broken glass, furniture upside down, they'd spared nothing. It was a good thing the coal oil lamp that lit the place was way up on a shelf or they'd have burnt the house down. I squinted through the dimness to find some human shape, but one poked me in the chest. I looked down and there was a tiny little woman, still young, who weighed maybe eighty pounds; she was glaring up at me with black eyes that could have drilled through cast iron.

"What business is it of yours, boy?" she shrilled.

Behind her there was movement, and a lanky young man dragged himself onto a battered sofa and groaned. "How 'bout savin' my life?" he croaked. "That seems to be somethin' the law should take some notice of."

I never really heard anybody grind their teeth before, but she did, and it wasn't a nice sound at all. She drew back her arm, and I didn't like the look of her fist. I could see its marks all over her husband, and I didn't want to carry her brand on my hide, so I reached down and lifted her and set her down beside Dennis. It was like handling an angry cat, but I managed without getting scratched or bit, which was something of a marvel all by itself.

Well, that was my first encounter with that pair, and I managed to get them settled down without any more bloodshed. But I knew it wouldn't last, and it didn't. Dennis wouldn't leave his family farm, and she wouldn't quit wiping up the floor with him every Wednesday night, so I quit bothering with them at all. I figured if they killed each other it would be a good thing, all around.

Things rocked along normally after I quit trying to tame the Pindars. The public works programs began to hire men to build some roads and bridges and even put up nice little roadside parks, with stone tables and benches, and people stopped having to live on catfish and possums and garden sass. I got married and moved into my own home, had a few kids, and kept an eye out for moonshiners and watermelon thieves.

'Course there were always families like the Peddys and the Venders, who took advantage of every chance to make trouble, but I knew how to handle those. I'd just grab the first Peddy or Vender I could locate and whip the bejeezus out of him, and the rest would settle down for a month or two. It was a shame I couldn't do that to Gladys Pindar, I often thought, but the one thing that was knocked into me from my first birthday was that you couldn't go hitting a girl or a woman. Just couldn't seem to get over that, though I knew many a man who whipped his wife regular and never got any jaw about it.

By the time the Second World War came along, I was just beyond the draft age and had a family, so the draft board let me be. Nobody else wanted my job, as I now made only about thirty dollars a month, which was just about survivable if you raised your own vegetables and meat. All in all, I was better off than anybody I knew had been for a long time, and though there were now kids who drove their dads' cars too fast on our dirt roads and wound up in ditches, things were fairly calm.

Then the government decided to put a prisoner-of-war camp in the middle of the woods about six miles from Hackberry. In a way, that was good. They needed workers to build the road to it as well as a narrow-gauge railroad line to carry away the timber those prisoners were supposed to harvest. There were a lot of mixed feelings about that. The old geezers in the barbershop, all of them past doing any work to speak of, were mighty skeptical about lodging a bunch of young, strong Germans way out here where our young women had never known anybody but neighbors and kinfolk. Most of us married cousins of some kind, simply because there wasn't anybody else to marry, and gasoline was rationed so nobody traveled much. And with the draft taking all the young men into the army, even I could see that having so many strangers so near might be a problem the government never thought about.

I never dreamed what a problem it would be. I spent a lot of time rounding up girls who were out picking blackberries (even when they were out of season) and got themselves hung up in sawvines and thickets. I spent some time locating POWs who had no problem getting out of the stockade around the prison camp—one reason it was placed out here was that there was noplace to go. Once they were in the woods, they had no idea how to handle themselves in the sort of wild woods East Texas produces. Even the ones who had been country boys were used to tame forests, and they were mighty glad to be taken back home to their camp, believe me. They might have been hunting girls, but what they got was chiggers and water moccasins and bobcats.

All this meant that I didn't get around to the barbershop and the Baptist church nearly as much as I used to, and for a year I didn't think once about the Pindars. That was why it came as a shock when Mattie, my wife (and third cousin), said one evening at supper, "You know, Cal, the Pindars haven't been to prayer meeting for a month. Miz Carey even suggested we send somebody out to check on 'em, but we couldn't get anyone to volunteer. Gladys is such a mean little woman, we can't know what she might do."

That came as a bit of a shock. The weekly Pindar appearance at prayer meeting and the follow-up beating were as much a part of our world as the mosquitoes and the heat.

"You want me to go out there and see about 'em?" I asked her. "That would be a nice change. I'm just about worn out with chasing girls and Germans through the woods, I have to admit. It will surprise me if we don't have a crop of big blond babies in the next year, 'cause there's no way one man could keep up with what's goin' on."

She leaned over and squeezed my hand. "I'd appreciate it, Cal. Somehow when something that has seemed as regular a sunrise all of a sudden stops happening, it shakes you up. Maybe one of them is sick, or she has finally killed him . . . ." She went silent, as if her own words had scared her.

The next morning I set out for the Pindars. I now lived in Hackberry instead of on Papa's farm, so it took me a while to drive the 1930 Plymouth over the rutted roads and through the wagon track that led through the woods to their house. It was around 8:30 when I pulled up in front of the gate and honked the horn. That isn't polite, I know, but too many of the country folks keep a dog that'll eat your leg off while you're trying to introduce yourself. No dog showed itself or barked, and nobody came to the door, so I got out and went into the yard.

"Miz Pindar? This is Cal Hampton!" I yelled, not knowing just what sort of firearms she might have in the house. "Mister Pindar? You all right?"

There was a long silence. Then feet tap-tapped toward the door, which opened a crack.

"We're fine. Go away!" that unforgettable voice snapped.

"Folks kind of got worried about you when you quit comin' to prayer meeting," I said as soothingly as I could.

"Tell them we're just fine. We need nothing at all, now or ever. Now go away."

I did, because that woman had more authority in her little finger than General Rommel did in his entire body. And there things stood for several months, because my work got more complicated when they assigned me to help out with Precinct Three, whose constable had been drafted.

Uneeda Ralston got old enough for the draft, and they took him off for basic training. I'd been using him from time to time when I needed somebody to give me a hand, so I made sure to see him when he came back for his final leave before being sent overseas. Turned out I didn't have to go looking for him, because he came to see me on his last day at home.

He looked mighty trim and clean and military, which was good, but he also looked pretty upset.

"Come sit down, Uneeda," I said, leading him to the bench on the porch. "You bothered about somethin'?"

"Mistah Cal, I think I done seen a ghost. " His voice shook, and I could see he figured I wouldn't believe him, but I knew that boy well, and I knew he wouldn't lie to me.

I put my arm around his shoulder and felt him shaking. "Tell me about it," I said.

He straightened up and took off his cap. "You know my mama lives nearest of anybody to Mister Dennis Pindar's place. We kin see their backyard from our cow lot. I went out to milk old Daisy for one last time, just after daylight. I got settled and was milkin' away when I realized I was lookin' at somethin' tall and skinny that I could see clean through. Not only that, but after a little it begun to moan, like as if it was hurtin'. Sounded plumb pitiful."

Uneeda looked into my eyes and spoke carefully. "My mama says she ain't seen Mr. Pindar for months, though she used to wave at him sometimes when he was workin' in their garden or fixin' fence. Mama thinks . . ." He seemed to be gathering his nerve, but then he went on, "Mama thinks Miz Pindar has kilt him and put him down that there septic tank she's so proud of."

I must have jerked, because he nodded slowly. "She thinks so, Mistah Cal, and you know my mama ain't one to holler before she's hit. Kin you do somethin' to check up on it and see? Mama is pretty upset over this thing. She's goin' to do enough worryin' about me, once I get over to Yurrup and the war. She don't need no extra to worry her."

All the while we said our good-byes and I called the kids to shake his hand, I was thinking about the problem he'd brought to me. I'd been constable, by now, for eight years, and I'd never had a murder to handle. Killings, yes, over fences or stray cattle or wives caught with the wrong man. Many hunting accidents, of course. But no deliberate murder—I shivered at the thought.

As I waved to Uneeda, and his uncle Ned's car carried him away toward Templeton, I was still thinking about the Pindars. How in hell was I going to find out what, besides crap, was down in that tank?

Then, of course, things got busy for me. Old Man Ellison went deer hunting to get his family some winter meat and found a body in the woods. It wouldn't have been such a big deal, but that body turned out to belong to a federal agent who had been on some assignment for the government—they wouldn't give even a hint as to what that might be, and that got the sheriff and the Texas Rangers (one of them, anyway) and even some men from Washington down here getting in my hair and making a lot of unnecessary trouble. Except for the ranger, a little guy about shoulder high to me, none of them had any idea how to get around in the woods without getting snakebit or stuck in briar patches.

Even worse, the fellow had been dead for a couple of months, so the chance of finding who killed him was pretty slim. If he'd been local, it would've been different, but this man was from Wisconsin, of all places, and nobody here had ever seen or heard of him. I believed that too. What in tunket could be a reason for one of our folks to shoot somebody from Wisconsin, anyway? Most likely he got killed by whatever outfit he was investigating, and that was finally what everybody decided after wasting most of the winter with useless messing around in the woods.

By the time that was over, I'd just about forgot about Uneeda's ma and her ghost. That boy surprised the tar out of me, though. He wrote me a letter! To find a colored kid who could write wasn't all that common, because the school for Negroes was pretty sorry back then. He'd managed it, though, and once I figured out his spelling, I realized that the boy was really concerned about his ma, who'd evidently written him letters of her own since he left.

I decided that I ought to do some quiet investigating of my own, since nobody in this part of the county would want to run afoul of Gladys Pindar. I talked it over with Mattie and even asked my ma what she thought. Ma is a mighty clear-headed lady, and she said, straight out, "I've knowed Minty Ralston since she was little, and I never knowed her to tell a lie. If she says she's seein' somethin' over there, she sure enough thinks she's seein' it. But be careful, Cal. I figure you might hide out someplace close enough to see good but hid enough so Gladys won't know you're there. I s'pose the deputy out of Templeton wouldn't give any help?"

I shook my head. It would take a lot more than a letter from a black boy, soldier or not, and the word of his ma to get official help, particularly now that the law was so shorthanded and wore out from thrashing through the woods for weeks. I knew I'd have to do this by myself, with maybe some help from Minty Ralston.

It's funny how different it feels to sit in the early dawn chill waiting for a deer or a flight of ducks and doing the same thing waiting to see if there is a ghost dancing around on the top of a septic tank. By now

I was familiar with the things . . . since moving into Hackberry my family had used one, and even my folks had put one in and were surprised at how nice it was not to have to trudge out to the privy in the dark and cold on a winter night. I knew the old man who had dug the pit for the Pindars, and I looked him up and got a clear notion of where the thing was and what kind of lid it had on it. He promised not to mention my visit to anybody, and I trusted him.

So there I was, crouched behind a clump of yaupon bushes, trying to see through the dimness. After a little I heard Minty going out to her cow lot to milk Daisy, and I took a deep breath and came to attention. Now was the time, if it was going to happen today.

But it didn't. Nor the day after either. Not until the fourth morning did I hear, over the squirt of milk into Minty's bucket, the sad wail coming from the Pindar place. I stood up to look over the yaupons, and there was a drifty sort of shape out in the backyard of the Pindar house, directly over the spot where the old fellow had told me he'd dug that pit.

I slipped off toward the cow shed and hissed at Minty, "Is Ned able to come out and be a witness for me? It's there, and I need another person to testify to it."

"He's not feelin' too swift, but he'll go with you. I'll get him." She took her bucket of milk into the house, and soon old Ned came limping out, walking stick in hand, and waited for orders.

I took up the bag holding my shovel and pick, and together we went quietly toward the Pindars' back gate, slipped inside the yard, and stopped. The figure was still drifting above the septic tank, moaning very softly. It didn't seem to care that we were watching it, and I asked, "Dennis Pindar? You in there?" I nodded toward the dirt-covered lid of the tank.

He went out like a bubble popping, and I knew he had to be there. "You sit down, Ned, while I dig. I know your heart won't stand hard work, but you can swear to whatever I find in there . . . if I find anything, of course."

It was easy to get to the tank lid, though it should have had thirty years of washed-in dirt on top of it. The lid had been a sheet of corrugated iron, and it was rusted almost into brown lace. The smell was unbelievable when the shovel blade punched through it and let the accumulated stink out. That had strong hints of privy in it, but overriding even that was the overripe smell of dead flesh. That's something you never could mistake for anything else.

I sent Ned home to alert Minty, while I took down a washline pole and dredged the tank with it. With a bloop of released gases, the body came up to the surface, and it was nothing you'd ever want to see. Made that body old Ellison found in the woods look almost good, by contrast. And the smell was beyond anything I'd ever known before.

About that time, the back door of the house flapped open and Gladys came boiling out like a whole nest of wasps. "What do you think you're doing in my yard, digging up my—" Her voice stopped abruptly when she saw what I was doing.

"Miz Pindar, you're under arrest. One of Minta Ralston's children is on his way to town right now to telephone to Templeton for the sheriff. I just found your husband's body in your septic tank, and nobody could ever convince anyone that a man would open the thing up, jump in—and then close it after him."

She didn't say a word. Even when the sheriff showed up, sweating thumbtacks over bothering the Pindars, she kept her thin lips shut like a trap. But nobody could deny what was in that hole, and there was no one else on earth who had anything against Dennis Pindar. I was able to write Uneeda Ralston that his mama's problem was solved, because even the jury couldn't find any way to figure Gladys Pindar was anything but guilty as sin.

Now I've retired from being constable, the war is long over, and Uneeda has come home to take care of his mama and his uncle Ned. I can go to prayer meeting on Wednesday nights without worrying about poor old Dennis getting beaten like a rug by that skinny little wife of his. When they passed out mean, that woman went through the line twice. Maybe three times. I often wonder how she fares in prison, but not enough to inquire about her.

But I'll never forget the stink rising from that hole in the ground or the wispy shape of poor Dennis hovering over his dead body. We put him away real nice, once we got things sorted out, and he lies in the cemetery beside his daddy. If I have anything to do with it, Gladys can be buried in the Huntsville prison graveyard with the rest of the unclaimed murderers. I just wish I could stick her in her own septic tank!

The Flinch

Michael Boatman

Sonny Troubadour was waiting to cash what passed for his paycheck when Scrape Rifkin's Cadillac Escalade pounded up to the curb and disgorged three hundred pounds of human sewage.

Sonny's guts convulsed as he watched the rest of his day slide down the toilet.

Just what I goddamn need, he thought.

Sonny pocketed his check and cracked his knuckles.

The chronically discouraged patrons of the Windy City Cash-Rite Currency Exchange dropped to the floor as Norman Morris, aka *Nomo,* and L'Dondrell Witherspoon, aka *O-gazm,* burst into their midst.

"That's right," Nomo said. "I want every one of you ugly bastards to lick this dirty-ass linoleum. Keep your asses horizontal and I won't have to shoot nobody today."

Sonny remained vertical. Nomo noticed.

"You got a problem with yo' knees, motherfucker?"

Sonny shrugged. "Knees are fine," he said. "Just not goin' down today."

Nomo's brow crinkled. "You ain't *what?*" he said.

"What did he say?" O-gazm said.

"Big man say he ain't gon' *eat* no linoleum today," Nomo said.

O-gazm gaped.

"Watch the heifer," Nomo said, pointing to the manager, a big black blonde who peered out from behind her bulletproof plastic window. "She moves, kill somebody."

Nomo pointed his Sig Sauer 9mm at Sonny's forehead.

"Look like we got us a bad man here," he said.

Sonny stared down the barrel of Nomo's gun.

No kinda life for a man anyhow, he thought.

"He don't look so bad," O-gazm said over his shoulder.

Nomo's gold teeth bounced pellets of ghetto sunlight off Sonny's retinas. Notorious for spending other people's money on his smile, Nomo sported the kind of dental retrofit that makes racist South African gold exporters sing "God Bless America."

"Who you supposed to be?" he said. "Black Superman?"

"No," Sonny said. "But if you don't shoot me in the next ten seconds I'm gonna take that gun and whip your ass with it."

"Lord have mercy," the manager moaned.

Nomo shook his head as if he wasn't sure he'd heard right. His gaze flicked over Sonny's shoulder to where the Scrape's SUV sat rumbling at the curb.

"Five seconds," Sonny said.

"I'm gonna . . ." Nomo stuttered. The tip of his tongue poked out of the corner of his mouth, moistened his lips, and darted back into its golden cave. "I'm gonna—"

Then Sonny rushed him.

Nomo fired high and wide over Sonny's left shoulder, blasting a hole through the front window and setting off the burglar alarm. Then Sonny bitch-slapped the 9mm out of his hand.

"Hey! Hey, man—"

And that was *all* Nomo said, because his mouth was abruptly filled with Sonny's fist.

"Yo! Yo! Yo!" O-gazm said.

Sonny grabbed Nomo by the collar and swung him around in a wide, staggering circle. The barrel of O-gazm's Saturday-night special jerked back and forth.

"Stand still, goddammit!" he said.

Sonny launched Nomo across the room like an Olympic shot putter.

Nomo slammed into O-gazm, and they both went down in a flurry of flailing limbs.

Sonny bent and picked up Nomo's gun.

Sensing the ass-mangling trucking their way, the would-be bandits rose to the challenge, each according to his gifts: Nomo assumed a classic "Crane style" kung fu pose while O-gazm pissed his pants. Fifteen seconds later they resembled a half-assed reproduction of a lesser-known Picasso pencil sketch.

Sonny hauled the brigands outside and speed-plowed his right foot, size 16½, up their backsides. Nomo and O-gazm hit the Cadillac and crumpled, having been literally kicked to the curb. A second later, the street-side back door opened and the Scrape stepped out.

"Jesus," Sonny said. "You look like shit."

The Scrape looked . . . squeezed, like a half-eaten Florida grapefruit with its innards scooped out, leaving behind an empty bit of skin and a whiff of rotten produce.

I'm looking at the rind, Sonny thought. *Man's been sucked dry.*

Looking at the Scrape made Sonny's head hurt.

The Scrape squinted up at the sun like a groundhog that was shaky on the terms of its contract. Then he pulled a pair of designer shades out of the pocket of his imitation tiger-skin jacket.

"Fuck you," he said. "You look like you could use some scratch, brah. You want a job?"

Sonny scowled. But then he remembered the daily spine-grind that was his post office gig, surrounded by gibbering *sistahs* who treated him like an adopted teddy bear one minute and a complete chowderhead the next, all under the watchful eye of his supervisor, *Bobbi-with-an-i.*

Bobbi-with-an-i was a Jamaican ballet instructor moonlighting with the USPS until Baryshnikov died. The day before, he'd invited Sonny up to his place in Boy's Town for "cocktails and career counseling." Sonny was beginning to have serious questions about Bobbi-with-an-i.

Finally, Sonny remembered the disconnect notices piling up in his kitchen trash bin. His car, a brown Ford Fiesta with a death wish, was squatting in an impound lot on Randolph Street, banked for a D.U.I. he'd picked up a week earlier.

"Yeah," Sonny said. "What do you need?"

By the time he was fifteen, Tommy "the Scrape" Rifkin had amassed a small fortune selling black market ordnance. By his twenty-first birthday, he'd taken over the local crack/Ecstasy/crystal meth trade, all while managing to evade select representatives of Chicago's Finest.

This talent for skullduggery—plus an obsession with all things NASCAR that brought new meaning to the word *autoerotic*—had secured Rifkin's induction into the South Chicago White Trash Hall of Fame.

The Scrape's nasal whine complemented his lair: half trailer park chic, half ghetto-fabulous. A black leather La-Z-Boy sat between a framed poster of Malcolm X and a life-sized standup of Dale Earnhardt Jr.

"I need you to find my girl and bring her back," Rifkin said. "It's worth five large if you bring her back."

Rifkin swiped at his forehead with a paper towel while Sonny picked his jaw up off the table.

Five large, he thought, trying not to drool.

"Yo," Rifkin said. "You was almost the champ, right?"

Sonny tensed: people still recognized him three or four times a day, and it chapped his ass.

"Yeah," Rifkin said. "I saw your style back at the Cash-Right. You was a *contender*, bro. Don King called your right cross '. . . an extinction-level cosmic smackdown from the Devil Hisself.'"

"That was a long time ago," Sonny said.

"Bro, I remember the Champ chewin' on your ear like it was yesterday," Rifkin said. "Vegas o-six, right? Dude, that shit was disgusting."

"Five years ago," Sonny said. "Past is past."

It was during Sonny's last shot at the title that the reigning champ, a semihuman piledriver named Baron Flake, laid him low with a left-handed uppercut to the occipital that detached his right cornea. Sonny woke up to find Flake gnawing on his left earlobe, his demolished eye spitting blood, while faerie lights popped and fizzled along his optic nerve like a paparazzi assault from hell.

The hospital stay sucked and blew at the same time.

Afterward, Sonny attempted a comeback, but every time he heard the bell clang he would rush to the side and puke over the ropes. Finally, Sonny's trainer, the inimitable Sharkey Washington, took him aside.

"My three-legged Pekingese got a better shot at a title bout than you do, boy," Sharkey growled. "It's over."

Then Sharkey, who was the closest thing to a father Sonny would ever know, wiped his protégé's secondhand breakfast off his polyester warm-ups and dropped dead from congestive heart failure.

"Ahem," Rifkin said. "Yo, Troub, you with me?"

Sonny shoved his memories aside to consider the matter at hand: Rifkin looked wobbly as Commander-in-Thief of this shitty little outfit. His focus fluttered around the room like a fruit bat on steroids.

Why won't he look me in the eye? Sonny wondered.

Rifkin noticed Sonny noticing him and—*flinched*. Nomo and O-gazm grumbled. Post-pistol whipping, the brigands looked surlier than ever.

Better close the deal now, Son, Sharkey advised from the Great Beyond, *'fore somebody separates this fool from his pointy little head.*

But Sonny was curious.

"Why can't you go and get her yourself?" he said.

"Mooother-*fucker*," Nomo hissed.

O-gazm spat on the floor.

Rifkin *flinched*.

"Yo, Black Superman, you ask a lotta dumb questions," Nomo said.

"Sit your stupid ass down, Mo," Rifkin said.

Nomo backed down. The Scrape peeled another paper towel and went to town on himself. Sonny winced.

Sounds like sandpaper scratchin' at dead wood.

"You wouldn't understand," Rifkin said.

Sonny agreed and decided that he was officially ready to get away from these people.

"Where was the last place you saw her?" he said.

Rifkin shook his head. "She stole something from me," he insisted. "Two weeks ago. I need it back."

"She s'posed to be dancin' around the titty bars in the Loop," Nomo said.

"What's her name?" Sonny said.

"Her name is Harmony," Rifkin whispered.

"Harmony Tremontane."

Twenty-seven hours later, Sonny was standing in the main room of The Shakedown, an upscale gentleman's club off Rush Street, waiting for another hardbody to take her clothes off and trying not to puke.

Innards were never the same after that last bout, Sonny thought. His stomach rumbled in agreement. These days, a night spent partying with a pint of Jim Beam always preceded a morning spent clutching the ky-bowl with one hand and a bottle of Maalox with the other.

Seems you just about livin' on J.B. and Maalox, Son.

Sonny shook Sharkey's voice out of his head, but he was staring at the bar, and his mouth was watering.

Focus, he reminded himself.

The dancer on stage swept up her cash and ran off to a smattering of applause.

"This next young lady joins us after a whirlwind national tour of *Oh! Calcutta!*" the announcer said.

You gotta be kiddin', Sonny thought.

"Men, lets get it up for—Harmony Tremontane!"

Sonny's focus snapped toward the stage.

The music started. The red curtain parted. Sonny stopped breathing.

She was more than beautiful.

Earlier, Nomo had told him that the Scrape's woman was a slag: skinny, with faux-luscious breasts that looked ludicrous on her shriveled frame. But this Harmony Tremontane was tall, with lithe brown legs that swept her across the stage. Her thighs were full but taut. A red-gold Afro framed her face like a halo made of sunfire.

"I'll be . . . damned," Sonny whispered.

If anyone could steal something from a freak like the Scrape and survive, it would be a girl who looked like that.

"Yep, that's her," one of the bouncers volunteered. "Harmony Tree-mon-taaane."

The bouncer was wearing a black T-shirt with the words "Does Not Play Well with Others" emblazoned across his seventy-five-inch chest.

"I heard she did pornos out in La- La Land before she blew into Chi," the bouncer said. "Very talented. You feel me, Troub?"

The bouncer held up a hand in a high-five gesture, but Sonny was in no mood for camaraderie. Besides, he advocated rough disemboweling for anyone over thirty who didn't have time to say "Chicago."

"But ain't nobody gettin' within a mile of that tonight," the bouncer said. "She's with Block Tokomatsu."

High-Five pointed a sausage-thick finger toward a table near the stage. Seated at the table were five of the biggest human beings Sonny had ever seen.

Block Tokomatsu was a half-Japanese/half-Samoan Player down from Milwaukee. He'd done a stretch out at Marion State Correctional on a murder-2 convic, plus stints here and there for all manner of antisocial activities.

Block Tokomatsu regularly beat the melanin out of *scores* of brothers for light exercise. He doled out ass-whippings the way the Pope dispensed benedictions at Christmas: he was the Supreme Pontiff of the Righteous Beatdown.

"Hey, Black Superman."

Sonny turned to find Nomo lingering like a bad fart.

"That's the homely bitch right there."

Homely? Sonny thought. *Who's he looking at?*

"Hold on a minute," Sonny cautioned. But Nomo whipped out his wireless and pushed *Send*.

"Yo, she's here," he said. "At the Shakedown." He nodded, twice, and disconnected. He glared at Sonny with reefer-enriched rancor.

"Scrape say you better do yo' job," he said. "Else I'm gon' handle you like I *shoulda* handled your big ass back at the currency s'change."

Do it, the Troub urged in Sonny's mind. *Just reach over and pop that neck like a chicken bone.*

Sonny savored the fantasy for a moment and decided it wasn't worth the shit storm that would follow. He needed to be shut of this crew like nobody's bid, but there was still the matter of five-large-plus-expenses to settle before he could call it a night.

"I'll get her," he rumbled, certain that this was all going to end badly. "And the word is *ex*-change, idiot."

While Nomo tried to figure out if he'd just been insulted, Sonny advanced toward the black leather hillock that was Block Tokomatsu's back.

Let's do this.

James Brown was extolling the virtues of being both Black *and* Proud via the state-of-the-art sound system. The DJ worked two turntables with one hand and a hard drive with the other, a digital raindance that filled the Shakedown with hip-hop thunder. Relentless rhythm jiggled Sonny's organs as he sat at a table behind Tokomatsu and his cronies.

How the hell am I supposed to get her past all those big Samoans? he wondered.

A bevy of the prettiest dancers adorned the Block's table, laughing too loudly, casting fox-eyed glances in the Block's direction even while they flirted with his lieutenants.

Tokomatsu looked oblivious to the cold war of sexual innuendo being waged around him. He tracked Harmony's every move, his eyes flickering between her and the main entrance the way a nervous pimp guards a hooker with her original teeth.

What have you gotten yourself into? Sonny thought.

Harmony finished her number six feet up the "fireman's pole," her legs spread wide, toes peaked in an exquisite dancer's "point." She slid to the floor, gathered up her cash, and vanished behind the red curtain.

The lights changed and the mostly male audience erupted into a barnyard cacophony.

A flash of silver drew Sonny's focus down to the waistline of one of the Block's lieutenants. A quick glance around the Samoans' table confirmed the sinking sensation in his gut.

They're all strapped, he thought.

Brute force was not going to get him around the Block.

Gotta think, boy, Sharkey might have said. *Can't punch your way outta every fight.*

Sonny gritted his teeth and closed his eyes.

Sixty seconds later he borrowed a pen from a passing loser, scribbled a note on a cocktail napkin, and handed it to one of the uglier waitresses along with a twenty for her troubles.

Two songs died before the waitress returned and Sonny learned that his night was about to get a lot more complicated:

Dear Shithead,
Do the world a favor and blow your goddamn head off.

H.

Gotta do this the hard way then, Sonny thought.

You don't "gotta" do anything, Sharkey said in his head.

Sonny waved the ugly waitress over again.

"J.B. *straight,*" he said. "Make it a double."

The waitress nodded and waddled off.

A few minutes later, Sonny was staring at a tall glass of the straight medicine, and marveling at how the overhead disco lights made the ice cubes twinkle.

"Merry Christmas," he said, even though it was July.

He emptied the glass and gestured a cute little Korean import over.

"Buy me a drink?" the stripper said.

"Private dance," Sonny rumbled. He got to his feet and the stripper's eyes brightened.

"Ooohh, you're a *big* one," she said. Then she smiled, straightened Sonny's collar, and led him into the back room.

Red lights and naked women were everywhere.

In the corner off to Sonny's right, two strippers were dancing for a man and his date, a redhead with no lips.

"Like redheads," Sonny said. Meanwhile, the animal crouching behind his eyes stood up and tugged on the bars of its cage.

Wish Flake was here now, he thought, recalling the human piledriver and his unholy uppercut: the red thunderflash that blew out the last candle on Sonny Troubadour's cake.

Feed him his own damn ear he was here right now.

Sonny sat on a red velvet chair and the stripper started to gyrate. "My name's Douglas," she said. "Twenty dollars for one dance?"

"Okay," Sonny said.

He reached into his wallet and gave over.

Then Harmony glided past his cubicle.

Sonny shoved Douglas out of the way and stood up.

"Hey, Hercules, no rough stuff!" she chirped.

"Sorry, Doug," Sonny said over his shoulder.

He crossed the room in four strides and headed Harmony off at the bathroom door. She almost bumped into him before she looked up.

"Well?" she said.

Sonny grabbed her around the waist, swung her over his left shoulder, turned, and froze: about two dozen fake fornicators frolicked between him and the door.

"Move!" Sonny bellowed.

Strippers and suckers scattered like roaches.

One girl screamed, then they all chimed in. High-Five, the bouncer from the front, appeared and blocked Sonny's path.

"Freeze, asshole!"

Sonny uncorked a right cross that lifted High-Five out of his shoes and put his lights out before his ass hit the cheesy red carpet: the Troub was open for business.

Move, he commanded. *Move-move-move.*

Sonny kicked the exit door open and lunged into the alley. The woman hanging over his shoulder remained silent. She didn't struggle or scream.

Too scared, Sonny thought.

When Nomo saw Sonny chugging toward him, he dropped his cigarette and jumped into the driver's seat. Sonny threw open the back door, tossed Harmony inside, and dived in on top of her.

"Goddamn, Black Superman!" Nomo said. "You take yo' work serious!"

A hail of bullets peppered the right side of the Cadillac. Sonny whirled to see the Block and his lieutenants stampeding toward them, firing as they came.

"Drive!" he shouted.

Nomo jammed the accelerator and laid a smoking trail of burnt rubber across Rush Street. He blew through a red light and headed toward State Street.

"You're goin' the wrong way!" Sonny said. "Rifkin's place is on the West Side!"

"Rifkin don't want Tokomatsu heatin' up his territory," Nomo shouted. "I'm takin' her to another spot!"

Sonny squinted as the headlight glare from the Block's black Mercedes shrank his pupils. Adrenaline burned the alcohol haze from the surface of his brain. The fighter's focus that once helped the Troub inflict brain damage on dozens of opponents cleared Sonny's head in an atavistic attempt to save his ass.

"You better drive like your nuts are on fire!" he said.

"Don't worry about my drivin'!" Nomo hollered. "You just keep Ol' Yeller in check!"

But Harmony was staring at the tenements whipping by. Nomo wrestled the Cadillac down the entrance ramp to a fuck-you chorus of blaring horns. While panicked drivers swerved and collided as Nomo shoehorned the Cadillac onto the expressway, Harmony studied her nails.

Nomo thumbed a red switch on the steering wheel and ignited the illegal afterburners in the Cadillac's engine. The ninety-second "burn" that followed punched Sonny into the leather seat cushions. Nomo left the black Mercedes on the far side of a snarl of crushed metal and bleeding citizens dwindling in the distance.

"He's wrong, you know," Harmony said.

"What?" Sonny said.

Harmony smirked. "What's mine is mine."

Sonny winced. He shook his head at the bloom of pain that blossomed behind his right eye.

"You his woman?" Sonny said, trying to distract himself.

Harmony sucked her teeth. "I'm nobody's woman, fool."

"You ripped him off."

"I don't steal."

The girl's eyes flashed.

Sonny shrugged. One thing was certain: once the Scrape had Harmony back in his camp, he'd never let her leave with her skeleton on the inside of her skin.

Harmony shifted, moved closer—Sonny was uncomfortably aware of the heat from her body—and *something*, a squiggle of quicksilver, shimmered in the woman's eyes.

"What's—" Sonny said. "Your eyes . . ."

"You want some of this, fighter?" Harmony whispered. She reached up behind her neck and undid the straps of her bikini top.

"Hey," Sonny said. "Hey now . . ."

Harmony let the top fall. "You're the same as Rifkin," she said.

She'd been pretty a moment earlier, but the woman who faced Sonny now might have danced for kings instead of kingpins and dope slingers.

"Your eyes," Sonny said. "What are you doing?"

Sudden, murderous desire ambushed his common sense. Enflamed, stupid with need, he reached for the stripper.

"What the hell are y'all *doin'* back there?" Nomo said.

Sonny's hand halted a hair's breadth from the stripper's thigh. Then something inside him flipped over and he puked onto the floor of the

Scrape's Cadillac.

"Heeeyyy!" Nomo screeched. "Hey, motherfuckahhhh!"

"What . . ." Sonny gasped. "What happened?"

The air inside the Cadillac was suddenly too dry to breathe. Sonny's vision doubled, then trebled, Harmony splitting into triplets as he watched.

Nomo screeched. "Rifkin gon' have my ass behind this, you big dumb bastard!"

"Hush," Harmony snapped.

And something *happened*. Nomo shut his mouth and turned around. His head slumped forward onto the steering wheel.

"Hey," Sonny moaned, guts burning. "What's goin' on?"

Harmony was staring at him as if he'd just appeared out of thin air. Her clothing was completely intact.

"I—I—" Sonny stuttered.

He looked out the window.

They were sitting in an abandoned grocery store parking lot, but Sonny didn't remember leaving the highway.

"Lady, who the hell are you?" he said.

Harmony's smile slashed a bright afterimage across Sonny's vision, like lightning gouging the spectral flesh of midnight skies.

"That's easy, Andrew," she said, though he'd never told her his real name. "I'm your dream date."

It was then that Sonny noticed two small crystal vials dangling from a leather string tied around the woman's neck. She fingered the vials as she spoke.

"Why don't we go someplace quiet?" she said. "Where I can show you what you've been dreaming about."

Sonny swallowed, cleared his throat. "Skank," he said. "Parasite."

"Oh?"

"You're Rifkin's whore," Sonny snarled. "Or Tokomatsu's. Either way, from what I can see, you ain't worth the trouble."

Harmony laughed. The vials around her neck chimed. To Sonny, the chiming sounded like screams.

"We're not so different, you and me," she said.

Sonny shook his head, tried to clear his vision. Nomo slumped across the front seat like a marionette with its strings cut. The black walls of the Cadillac pressed closer, stifling Sonny in leather and chrome.

"You don't know . . . anything about me," he said.

"I know you smell more like a distillery than a man," Harmony said. "But it's the smell of blood that made you what you are."

"Shut up."

"I know you sometimes wish that boy from New York had killed you dead rather than made you into the thing I'm lookin' at now."

Harmony's fingers stroked crystalline peals of anguish from the vials, each note an accompaniment to the agony in Sonny's gut.

"You drink to kill the *despair,* but you can't," she said. "You was bigger than this. Once upon a time you held power in your hand, power that set you above other men. Then the world moved on, left you bleedin' in that ring, half-blind, too old and too stupid to get up."

"Stop," Sonny said.

Harmony leaned over and placed her left index finger on Sonny's knee. "I can change all that," she said. "I can take you to a place where the dead dance in fields of blood-red violets. Where the air is black with power and the earth is seeded with ashes."

Sonny shook his head. But he was standing at ringside and watching himself bleed.

"I—I don't want to *see,*" he whispered.

"Oh, but you *do,*" Harmony said. "I know *that* too."

Sonny hovered, a dark Icarus above the ghost world in her eyes. Then his wings took fire and he fell, burning, into its swirling atmosphere, captured by the gravity of her gaze.

"Let's go."

He had nothing left to lose.

"Don't touch me."

They were lying on Sonny's sofa in the living room of his one-bedroom apartment. The stripper stretched her leg over his chest and straddled him.

Some instinct warned him at the last instant, and he tried to sit up. The woman set her hand at his throat and Sonny sensed the power to gut him tensed in her fingers.

"I *know* what you want," she said. "The smell of your dreams makes me want to puke."

Harmony reached back and undid his belt. She yanked at his pants as she held him down. Sonny bucked, trying to throw her off. Her nails cut deeper into the flesh of his throat.

"We *are* alike," she breathed. "I'm a survivor too."

The pupil of her right eye bulged outward, eclipsed both iris and sclera. In their place, a black orb shone wetly. There was a sound like the ripping of muscle, and a shock of red hair burst from her scalp.

Harmony clamped her fingers over Sonny's mouth, tore his flesh, and mashed his scream against his teeth.

"Be still," she moaned.

The taste of blood filled Sonny with manic strength. He freed his right arm and struck her across the chin. Harmony brushed aside his attack, held him down as her face ran like heated wax.

"You want to be with me, fightin' man?" the thing whispered. "I've been alone for soooo long."

A white tongue the length of a man's arm slid out of Harmony's mouth and dived between Sonny's lips, filling his mouth with the taste of ashes. He gagged, grasped the thick stalk, and bit down, trying to sever it.

Then something exploded in the hallway.

A high, bubbling scream pierced the red clouds in Sonny's mind. Pain beat back the shadows in his head. Harmony withdrew the tongue and spun toward the sound as the front door exploded off its hinges.

Nomo staggered through the doorway, clutching at the red hole in the center of his chest. Then he fell behind the sofa and the Scrape stepped into the room.

"Dude," Rifkin growled. "I'm gonna fuck-you-*up*."

Indeed, the shotgun he carried—a twelve-gauge Mossberg Bullpup with a twenty-inch barrel and walnut pistol grip—testified to the whole congregation that Mama Rifkin's baby boy had come to set things straight.

But playing spine-tag with Teflon-jacketed armor-piercing minimissiles was not on Harmony's "to do" list that night. She fixed Rifkin with a glare that would have given Siberia terminal freezer burn.

"Put that down, Thomas," she said.

Rifkin blinked, stumbled backward, and said "Daahh."

Sonny noted the scraps of white powder clinging like fresh leprosy to Rifkin's sad mustache: the Scrape had apparently snorted enough coke to make Condoleezza Rice sing "The Dreidel Song" at a Nation of Islam celebrity fundraiser.

"Shut up!" Rifkin howled. He lifted the Bullpup. "Me and Coco Chanel are callin' the shots, y'hear?"

Whatever magical influence Harmony normally wielded was gone, cock-blocked by redneck rage and third-rate Peruvian go-go powder.

"Baby, I'm gonna kill you, then him, then myself if you don't get up off him right now," Rifkin said.

Harmony got up, leaving Sonny exposed with a German tank ventilator aimed at his sack.

Sonny got to his feet.

"Yeah, punk," Rifkin crowed. "Ain't no dodgin' *this* smackdown. You feel me?"

Sonny nodded. "I feel you."

Rifkin smirked. "Damn right, you washed-up mother—"

Sonny charged.

At the same time, Harmony grabbed the Bullpup by the barrel. Coco Chanel blasted a basketball-sized hole through the ceiling and scared the holy hell out of Mrs. Gupta-Sung-Jefferson, Sonny's landlady, who lived upstairs.

Then Harmony grew a third arm.

Sonny braked hard as the stripper clutched the shotgun with her right hand, Rifkin's throat in her left, and Rifkin's *balls* with a third hand that was attached to the arm that extended out of her lower back.

Sonny's headache reached down, pulled his lower lip over his head, and spiked it to the nape of his neck: his bad eye was transmitting a sight that a man fighting to stay sober should miss. Something like a cross between Beyoncé Knowles and Kali the Hindu Goddess of Destruction was giving Rifkin the nightmare "reach-around" of all time.

Sonny's left eye, however, still perceived Harmony as she'd been back at the Shakedown: somehow, luscious dancer and tongue-raping grief freak were one and the same.

"Please—give it back," Rifkin whispered.

Harmony dug her nails into Rifkin's throat. In seconds, stripper and slinger were covered in blood.

Harmony's tongue lashed out and doublewrapped itself around Rifkin's throat. Rifkin turned purple and Coco Chanel clattered to the floor. Harmony hoisted the Scrape over her head and body-slammed him hard enough to crack Sonny's synthetic wood floor. Then she shook him until his mullet sprinkled white flakes like a snowstorm over Minneapolis.

An evil sound issued from Rifkin's backbone—

Crack!

—and his foot shot out and kicked the shotgun across the room. Coco Chanel slid to a halt at Sonny's feet.

Harmony dropped Rifkin while Sonny retrieved the shotgun. And before even *he* understood that he'd made his choice, she pounced, her face melting as she came for him.

Coco Chanel coughed and punched Harmony in the throat. The stripper struck the far wall and stuck. Sonny had five seconds to realize that he had not been dismembered; then Harmony slithered up the wall and disappeared in a patch of shadow near the ceiling.

Then the lights went out.

"Shit!" Sonny hissed.

He spun, trying to separate the woman from the shadows over his head. Then, *sound*, a sensation like a million fire ants strip mining his bones, filled the air. Something in Sonny's head ripped open, and blood filled his bad eye. He screamed and dropped Coco Chanel.

The hag-thing dropped out of the shadows and landed on his back. Sonny windmilled around the room, smashed into the walls, knocked over furniture trying to dislodge her.

"One way or another, fightin' man," she hissed.

Pain detonated against Sonny's spine as her tongue pierced the skin at the base of his skull. The tongue burrowed, widening the tear in his flesh.

Gotta stop her, boy! Sharkey shouted. Sonny felt the tongue shudder, a sandpaper rasp against his backbone.

"Stop her, booyyy," Harmony said.

Sonny dropped to his knees.

The shotgun lay a few feet away. Sonny reached for it and fell on his face. The thing on his back plunged its proboscis deeper.

Sleep, the Troub thought. *Be nice to just lay down.*

Don't be stupid, Sharkey argued. *You lay down now and whatever's left to get up, it won't be Sonny Troubadour.*

And because he knew Sharkey was right, Sonny stretched out his right hand, his joints creaking, and reached for the gun. Something in his shoulder popped and gave way: Sonny stretched further, touched cool wood . . . and snagged it.

He rammed Coco Chanel up and over his left shoulder, felt the barrel penetrate soft flesh a second before he pulled the trigger. Then Coco Chanel spat thunder and hag-slapped Harmony across the room.

Sonny leapt to his feet, his breath a dry heave, his bad eye sifting the darkness. Harmony lay against the doorjamb, her face a ruin. Her stiletto heels gouged twin ruts into the floor as she pushed herself halfway up. Then she uttered a thick grunt, and the back of her head dragged a red arc down the wall.

The lights flickered back on a second later.

Sonny touched the wound on the back of his neck and winced. Then he went to check on Rifkin.

Sonny had seen *dead* before, but the Scrape made Latin look lively. He looked like a man who'd slipped in a puddle of discount tomato paste, suffered a heart attack, and shat himself before dying from terminal embarrassment.

Sonny watched the last of his five-thousand-plus-expenses soak into the floorboards of the apartment he could no longer afford.

Then the Scrape sat up.

"That hurt, you bitch!" he hollered.

Sonny joined in: the two of them screamed like Billy Graham and Charlton Heston at a prison gangbang.

"Dude, you're freakin' me out!" Rifkin said.

Sonny shut his trap.

"Vials," Rifkin said.

"Huh?" Sonny said back.

"Crystal vials. You didn't blow them up, did you?"

Harmony slumped against the wall like a blow-up doll whose glory days have come and gone. A single vial lay nestled in the petrified valley of counterfeit cleavage rapidly deflating beneath her bloody halter top.

Sonny heard that tiny scream again, clearer this time.

It was coming from *inside* the vial.

"Well?" the Scrape said.

"One of 'em is gone," Sonny said. "The other one is—"

"Shit! Shit! *Shit!*" Rifkin banged his fist on the floor, each expletive provoking a mushy *pop* from his backbone. Then his spine gave way with a soggy lurch and his torso compacted a full two inches: Rifkin folded like an all-black revival of *Oklahoma* and slammed face first into the floor.

Sonny's guts did the Hokey-Pokey, and he let fly for the second time that night.

Outside, car doors slammed. The police probably wouldn't bother to show up till sometime in the early A.G. (After Gentrification), however, so no one was worried about *them* getting in the way.

Rifkin pushed himself up onto his knuckles and glared at Sonny from a vast puddle of blood.

"Bring that shit over here, goddamit," he snapped.

Then one of his hands slipped, and he fell on his face.

Sonny heard the *crack*, but he didn't believe it.

"Owww!" Rifkin screamed. "By dose!"

Sonny wiped his chin and zipped up his pants.

"You're pathetic," he said.

"Hey!" the Scrape shouted at the floor. "I'b dot bayin' you da backdalk me, dickwad!"

"Keep your damn money, man," Sonny said. "Just pull yourself together and get out."

Rifkin snorted. "Hey, genius, I'd love do, but she broke by friggin' deck and I can'd ged ub!"

"Sounds like a personal problem," Sonny said.

Rifkin screamed. The lightbulb over Sonny's head flickered.

"All right, *look*," the Scrape snapped. "There's half a million dollars *cash* in by trunk. Gib me the vial and it's yours."

Sonny's brow furrowed. "What's in it?"

Rifkin rolled over and spoke to the ceiling.

"Harmony feeds off the real part of a man, the part that *means* you. She keeps it stashed in those vials."

Some kinda fucked-up testosterone vampire, Sharkey grunted. *Like my first wife.*

"She told me that without my essence I'm doomed to wander the earth forever," Rifkin said. "Like the living dead, or the Wandering Hebrew or some shit like that."

Man gave you a second chance, Son, Sharkey opined.

Sonny cursed the day he let Sharkey lift him out of the gutter. Then he tossed the vial to Rifkin, who thumbed it open and inhaled like Marion Berry on a new crack pipe.

"Mmmm," he murmured. "Guess one's as good as another. Right, Troub?"

A second later, however, Rifkin shot to his feet, clutched his head, and painted the air with a fusillade of the finest Japanese profanity since Emperor Hirohito woke up on that fateful morning in 1945 and read in the *Tokyo Sun* that his monthly golf trip to Hiroshima had been postponed.

The Scrape made a sound like a yellow cat being strategically peeled. Then Mrs. Rifkin's gift to the dope trade fell dead to the floor.

Something flitted at the edge of Sonny's vision. He whirled, Coco Chanel at the ready.

Harmony's body was gone: The rump-shaker from Planet X had returned to the Great Beyond.

When Sonny stepped onto the sidewalk, he was greeted by half of the Samoan National Sumo Wrestling Team. Tokomatsu's men were pointing enough firepower to repel the French Navy at Sonny's Afro.

Tokomatsu stepped forward, his left hand raised.

"She dead?" he said.

"Don't know," Sonny said.

"Mmmmph," Tokomatsu grunted. "Rifkin dead?"

"Yup," Sonny said.

The Samoans observed a moment of silence. Then Tokomatsu hawked and spat on the sidewalk.

"Well, that's *somethin'*," he said.

Sonny noted that Tokomatsu avoided making eye contact. Testing a theory, he took a small step forward. Tokomatsu winced and took a step back.

The Samoans rumbled, and Sonny recalled that Rifkin had imbibed Tokomatsu's essence before he kicked.

"You *saw*," Tokomatsu whispered. "You saw what she was."

Sonny shook his head. "I don't know."

Tokomatsu considered his shoes. Then he shrugged.

"Yeah, brah," he said. "I don't think nobody knows."

And Sonny recognized the new thing in Tokomatsu's voice. It was the same thing he'd heard in Rifkin's voice the day before: the *Flinch*.

Tokomatsu glanced over his shoulder. "I could kill you now," he said. "You know?"

Sonny nodded. "I know."

Tokomatsu nodded. "I could use an intrepid brother such as yourself on my team," he said. "You want a job?"

Sonny took a deep breath. "Thanks," he said. "But I got some schemes working."

Tokomatsu shrugged. "All right then."

The two men shook hands. Sonny even managed a smile.

"All right then," he said.

But his gaze never wavered from the back of Rifkin's Cadillac, still idling at the curb.

Tyler's Third Act

Mick Garris

It had been sneaking up on me since Entertainment went online, but I guess the beginning of my end came with the Writers Guild strike in 2007. Not that I was a total Luddite; I did all my script work on an iMac, browsed my e-mails over hot green tea every morning, watched a couple of the funny videos that some other writers had forwarded to me. But if they were more than a couple of minutes long, I just couldn't pay attention to the little window on the monitor. It's hard for me to enjoy movies in miniature.

Why had I shelled out over ten grand for a new Pioneer plasma screen, upgraded uncompressed sound, and the whole Blu-ray thing, anyway? So I could watch a YouTube home video of some pudgy, pimpled adolescent acting out his Jedi Knight fantasies, blown up to sixty inches of stuttering, cubist blocks?

No. I love movies, even if they're on television; movies have scale and scope and an emotional investment in stories and characters. Yeah, yeah, I know all about that whole "convergence" thing, but it hasn't happened yet. I'm not going to watch *Lawrence of Arabia* on my iPhone, thank you very much. Movies are made for the big screen, and if it can't be a sixty-foot screen, sixty inches can still make due. Three point five won't cut it for me.

All right, I tend to digress. I promise not to lecture a couple of generations who can't pay attention to a film if it's not in full, blazing color. If you can find joy in homegrown cell phone movies rather than the craftsmanship of the best of Hollywood's greatest technicians, well,

I feel sorry for you, but the planet keeps turning. If cavemen had developed camcorders before cave paintings, there never would have been a need to write or paint to communicate; they'd have sent video of their latest kills instead.

Bitter? Hell no, not me.

But after the strike ended in 2008, my world, if not the state of photographed drama, changed for good, and that was bad. The great unwashed, uneducated, undead masses discovered reality TV in greater numbers than ever before, and rushed like lemmings to leap from the cliff of scripted dramatic entertainment. They hibernated to their computers and PlayStations, evacuating the cinemas and home theaters, their eyes fluttering in unfixed attention-deficited fragmentation, Blackberried and text-messaged to the point of cranial vacuousness. If it required brainpower, it was abandoned for a quick barrage on a tiny, portable screen: a snack, a punchline in search of a joke.

But like I said, the world turns with or without me, spinning into oblivion, choking on its own dust. Ashes to ashes, and all that shit.

When we emerged at long last from the noble fight against the studios and the producers, our Nikes worn thin as we marched obediently across the studio entrances, the viewing public had lost interest in my line of work. Life before the strike was remunerative, if repetitive, going into the second season as a staff writer on *Letting Blood*, a medical procedural on NBC that reveled in the viscera of forensic investigation and the hot young personalities behind it. Okay, hard to make a case for art in the sea of commerce, but still . . . better than a YouTube video of a colonoscopy, right?

Regardless. Life as I had known it, when I was about to enter my first season as a producer on a series, was shattered by the strike. The series, like most others, was shut down and replaced by *Dating Daddy*, yet another reality show, this one featuring young women paired unknowingly with their oblivious fathers who had abandoned them in their youth, set up on blind dates, hidden cameras catching them when they unwittingly engaged in daddy-daughter sex. *Dating Daddy*, while dutifully scorned by the watchdog critical press, was embraced in record numbers by a drooling, knuckle-dragging populace hungry for all but the nudity and money shots, which were tastefully obscured with a digital blur. The uncensored DVDs and pirated downloads alike scored record numbers.

So *Letting Blood* was put to a painless death, and the Nielsen families had either adopted the babies of reality or abandoned network television, never to return. While the networks, panicking to find they'd been forsaken by the brood they had so abused, tried in vain to find the lowest possible denominator to reach out to them, they were as savvy to the ways of the modern world as the soon-to-be-retired idiot president from Texas, and they, too, found their world collapsing.

Scripted series were still produced, but they were broadcast to the vast darkness of outer space, perhaps to be viewed eons in the future by multi-eyed alien lifeforms with perplexed interest in life on the primitive third planet from the sun. Even the successful creators of series and their showrunners struck out repeatedly with their pitches; new series from the prophetic geniuses of seasons past crashed and burned with an industry that collapsed in an operatic prelude to the 2008 housing industry and financial markets.

Sure, basic cable had a measure of scripted successes, but their audiences, as well as their paychecks, were minuscule by comparison. Only the self-congratulatory Emmy Awards noticed them.

So when work was available at all, which was increasingly rare, it was at a greatly reduced rate. No one was making the big dollars of just a year or two before. Even the feature film business was teetering: illicit downloads and gaming took over from the box-office figures that only a year earlier had reached record levels. The only way to get your movie green-lit was to anchor it to a star . . . but even that was no guarantee. And the indie market that had so powerfully reawakened with *Little Miss Sunshine* and *Juno* and other low-cost, big—box office Cinderella stories had collapsed in narcoleptic slumber.

So here I sat, watching the number of incoming e-mails decline as the Viagra spam grew in direct proportion to my depression. The house

I had bought to celebrate my newly acquired status of *Letting Blood* producer was already worth less than I owed on it, so I sold it at a loss of some three hundred grand and moved into an apartment on a shady street overlooking the Los Angeles River in Sherman Oaks. I know that sounds cozy, but if you're not a local, you should know that the Los Angeles River is not what anyone from elsewhere could possibly define as a river: it's a concrete trench that runs through the San Fernando Valley and overflows on the six days a year when it rains in Southern California but is otherwise a dry, baking cement gulf between nice homes and shitty little apartments. I now occupied the latter.

I went hat in hand to series I wouldn't even consider watching to get a single script assignment. Working for scale looked mighty good to me at this point. I wrote spec pilots, a couple of feature scripts, and was even halfway through a novel as my savings account stayed on a binge-and-purge anorexic diet . . . without the bingeing. I pitched all the broadcast networks, the Turners, the pay cablers, even the chintzy little digital channels way up at the end of the channel guide on your satellite system. I got the thumbs-down all the way down to the Fine Living Channel.

A bunch of my wretched brethren had turned to the great god of the Internet for solace, creating shows they owned and producing them on a shoestring. Maybe one day they would find a way to make a living off it, but I just couldn't get it up for that; that day, as sung by Ruby and the Romantics, was yet to come. I just didn't see a home for drama until true convergence had taken place, where everything from broadcast networks to YouTube came through the same pipeline to your giant screen in high definition. And that wasn't now.

Way back when, I'd had big dreams about writing movies, working my way up to directing my own original screenplays, a reflection of my own unique sensibilities. Of course, I never imagined creating blockbusters; I would be happy churning out my own Saylesian-Cronenbergian-delToronian-Allenian-Aronofskian indies that would find a small but devoted following that allowed me the freedom to do Work That Mattered. It wasn't much to ask, but I was on my knees for years before the growing Pisan Tower of rejected spec scripts landed me an agent and a freelance episode of *Charmed*.

So, my career history in a nutshell: a no-name, personality-free career bouncing from one television series to another, scripting for shows that *someone* watched, but no one I knew. The chapters of my existence were brief and relatively drama-free: a Writers Room Romance or two that never went anywhere, an expanding waistline and contracting imagination, and growing cold-pizza-induced carotid blockages. My bank account grew and life was predictably comfortable. I had coworkers and no real friends, could type a blazing fifty words a minute, and sat before my home cinema alone to appreciate the Blu-ray beauty of my John Ford collection.

And now, the rug of my life tugged out from underneath my unsteady feet, I was wedged alone into a Sherman Oaks two-bedroom-two-bath, with nothing but my movie collection at rest in the second boudoir. I felt like a mime in a shrinking-room routine.

It was getting scary; the residuals were shriveling and arriving less frequently. Most of the shows I'd worked on seldom lasted more than a year, and therefore were neither repeated nor syndicated. If I was lucky, they were bought by third-world nations learning about shitty television as they shuffled their way haltingly toward civilization, providing me with coffee money. Movies and television were all I knew; as the debtors grew more hostile in their collection techniques, it became clear that I needed a job. My agent was useless; he had more important clients than me breathing down his neck. My skills were limited, and, at the moment, had little commercial value. Movies and television turned a shoulder to me that was so cold it burned my fingers.

I sat in front of the twenty-four-inch screen of my iMac, fingers poised as if ready to pound out a polonaise, but there was no music. Fear and creative impotence froze me in the glare of the monitor, bathed in its icy blue glow, keyboard silently awaiting keystrokes that never came, daring me to unleash an unbroken flow of genius that would take me past the world of series television, to the toppermost of the poppermost, A-listing for the rest of my life, leaving the Conelrad

Agency for CAA and the heady aroma of true success.

I was not up to the challenge. My psychic dick shriveled, pulled back, retreated, went to sleep. Failure curdled my guts and I broke out into a sweat. I could not pull my eyes from the monitor, magnetized as I was to its beckoning, held prisoner by its insistent presence in the otherwise darkened room. The plasma wall screen in the living room behind me was dark; the cell phone and Blackberry had been silent for days; the Arclight down the street offered nothing but popcorn and projected pabulum. No, it was this glowing, one-eyed monster that held my future. I was no longer a child of cinema, not even the son of television. That night, after two acts of pleasantly dull existence, the third and penultimate act of my life was about to begin.

I could never love this virtual world of virtual entertainment, but I would embrace it. If I fed this cyclopean monster the blood of my being, it would feed me. And I had just the idea for the first course.

It was time to create a website. There had never been a reason in the past: I was too busy to put together a MySpace or Facebook page, and even if I had, who would have been drawn to it? Well, beyond my mother, who is in a home and wouldn't even recognize me if I stood right in front of her—and she has never used a computer in her life. The exes would just want to pelt me with nasty responses to my postings . . . if they were even that motivated. And there certainly were not any Tyler Sparrow fans out there clamoring for news on my work.

So I clicked on a GoDaddy ad on my Yahoo! homepage and registered TylersThirdAct.com before someone else beat me to it. Then I downloaded instructions on building a website and cobbled something together that actually was pretty attractive, filled with personal photos from my life's initial chapters, with liberal use of shots from all the series I'd worked on as well as some candid shots of a couple of the C-list actresses I had badgered into going out with me, and created the plan.

I'd discovered long ago that the most voracious Internet audience seemed to be those attracted to the seamier side of life, the brutes looking for a taste of forbidden fruit, uncensored looks at anything a civilized society would normally be denied, whether it's penetration shots of a famous but talent-challenged TV actress and her rock star boyfriend, or the beheading of a Middle Eastern hostage. The world is bloodthirsty, voracious in its appetite for the unappetizing, its collective stomach rumbling whenever scandal and viscera are about to be served. In a world where life is cheap and sanctity and decorum no longer existed, I was a self-appointed curator of the world zoo . . . and it was feeding time.

After clicking through my local Yellow Pages, I emerged from the destitute darkness of my humble San Fernando Valley abode into the scorching, relentless sun that shrank my underdeveloped pupils into pinholes. Sol's glare was so white-hot that it took several minutes before my brain could process my surroundings. When the world around me had irised back into visibility, I climbed into the Beemer to do some shopping.

One benefit of being out of work: traffic was light as I made my way over Coldwater Canyon from the Valley to the Basin. Pico Boulevard was filling with the kosher lunch crowd at its numerous delis that punctuated the car repair lots, the used-book stores, the faded fabric shops, and the medical supply houses. I parked and pumped the meter with all the change I could round up, and found that it wasn't the medical supply houses that offered what I was looking for, but *surgical* supplies I sought. I suppose Home Depot would have served my needs as well as what I was looking for here, but as a movie guy (okay, fine, television guy), the visual mattered to me. Well, normally the surgical supply houses were limited to those only within the medical profession, but after a couple of hours and a half-dozen triple soy latte espressos trolling the boulevard, I stepped into the dark, dusty, cobwebbed little den that proffered all I had hoped for and more.

Though the surroundings within the tiny Silver Elite Surgical Supply store were grimy and ill-attended at best, the displays of gleaming, hungry scalpels, cutters, and other flesh-rending devices were immaculate. They stopped the heart; these challenged the gorgeous, horrific creations of the Mantle Twins in *Dead Ringers*. As I stood alone in the shadowy, seemingly abandoned little shop, I felt the theatrical stillness rent by a ripple in the air and the shuffling of leather on the grimy floor.

"May I help you?" wheezed through the tiny shop, barely more voice than breath.

I looked up, then down to find the proprietor, a grizzled, hunched little man of indeterminate ancientness. His eyes, under the melting brow, were a pale ice blue beneath the milk of cataract, and peered out over the luggage of drooping lower lids. His liver-spotted scalp was studded with a few coarse white bristles pretending to be hairs, shellacked and pomaded across the cranium. He was bent over, a frail Quasimodo in the form of a permanent four-and-a-half-foot question mark. His surprising solicitous smile was toothless.

"I need some surgical instruments," I told him.

"Hence your presence in a surgical supply shop." But his sarcastic reply was delivered with such an ingratiating grin that I did not feel insulted. "Are you a member of the profession?"

"Well, I hope to be."

"Ah. A student."

"Exactly. A student." I stood over the display case, taking in the instruments that gleamed in theatrical light. "These are beautiful."

"Thank you. I've made them all since we opened, back in 1948."

"Wait—you mean you actually craft these instruments yourself?"

He smiled again, and if there were blood coursing through his Paleolithic veins, he'd have blushed.

"The finest in the world, if you'll forgive me the sin of pride." He looked at me, though I doubted he could recognize me a second time. "What do you need?"

"I need a couple of scalpels and a nice pair of cutters."

"Ribcage or smaller?"

"Um . . . digital? You know, fingers, toes?"

"It seems you have a very specific speciality." Yes, he said the five-syllable version. I didn't answer, and he went to the glass case and removed two gorgeous, gleaming scalpels and a pair of cutters that fit perfectly into the hand. Really beautiful craftsmanship, and I told him so.

"You'll swell my head," he replied. "So these will do?"

"Perfectly. What do I owe you?"

"Let's see, that's, oh, two thousand eight hundred fifty dollars."

"Yikes! I had no idea they were so expensive!"

He looked at me with some curiosity. "These are not surgical steel, young man. They are bladed in solid silver. Cleanest cut in the industry. Quality has its price. I'm not making much of a profit on this, you know." I didn't know what to say, so I kept my mouth shut. He peered at me in a face-rumpling squint. "Well, you are a student. I suppose we could call it twenty-five hundred and everybody goes home happy."

Yeah, well, everybody but me.

"Of course, I could send you to some mail-order shop, where you can get the same instruments used by the *hoi polloi*. Naturally, your student identification and medical cards are up to date for the transactions, right?"

Well, money wasn't going to mean much to me soon, anyway, was it? So the dregs of my savings weren't doing any good just sitting in another collapsing bank, were they? Visa could cover it for now, and when the time comes, let the devil collect his due.

"Do you take plastic?"

He sighed. "It's a plastic world now, and it breaks my heart." He took my card, ran it through the manual reader, scrawled the amount, and handed it over for me to sign. I scribbled my signature as he gently swaddled his creations in soft, elegant black velvet. It was obvious I was getting my money's worth. Transaction completed, I took the luxuriously bundled instruments under my arm as he shook my hand in his surprisingly soft one and bid me good-bye.

Ensconced in my meek little Sherman Oaks dorm, I sat in front of the iMac, seeking the sites that would most likely yield the quickest access to the Web's sanguinary sippers. I put together a little ad with a

PhotoBooth shot of my feigned innocence under the title *You want a piece of me? I will begin to remove my body parts live on webcam at 10 p.m. PDT Thursday at TylersThirdAct.com. The first one's free!*

After setting up a PayPal account that would be funneled to the home that lodged my demented mother, in the guilt-easing hopes that she could live out her waning and oblivious life in comfort and splendor, I purchased little animated spots on Fangoria, Bloody-Disgusting, Shock Till You Drop, Horror.com, Dread Central, Arrow Through the Head—all the horror sites—as well as the notably tawdry TMZ. This proved to be an auspicious and prescient choice. As soon as they began to run, literally within hours of them being posted, both Google and Yahoo! picked up the story and linked to my site, and the news went viral. Once CNN picked it up, there was no stopping the inferno that raged. Everyone assumed it was fake, of course; why wouldn't they? But it didn't keep them from checking it out. I did my best to exercise my constitutional right to privacy, so no one was going to track me down on this, not until I was ready. I was getting hundreds, then thousands of hits on the site . . . and it was only Saturday!

In five days, I fully intended to begin my own disassembly, my personal contribution to the world's culture, blood of the lamb spattered all over the screens of the lions. Blood, sweat, and self-sacrifice are the backbone of success in Hollywood, according to all the screenplay books. But I'll bet Syd Field didn't have the guts, the true intestinal fortitude, to put his internal self on the screen the way I intended to.

I didn't bother looking into the legality of this. I assume there are laws against suicide . . . but they must be pretty toothless, since if you succeed, prosecution would prove to be a problem. But I was only taking the modern primitivism of self-mutilation and skin art to my own personal level. It was artistic expression, damn it!

If you went to the site before its premiere on that fateful Thursday, you would have subjected yourself to a little dance of snapshots from my life to date, which gave way to a full screen with my face and hands taking the shape of a clock, ticking down the hours, minutes, and seconds until the first excision was to take place. Beneath my beaming countenance, a calendar clicked away the days. Other than that, nothing else, aside from the same words seen in the ads. In the upper right corner was a button to click to join, a $100 payment payable only through PayPal, refundable only up to the moment of the first shearing. The first removal, as promised, was to be free, but if you wanted to see more, well, open your wallet, pal. Nothing worth anything is free, especially my own Silver Diet. Its webcast would be live only, no video podcasts, no replay recordings available. Though I was sure there were hackers capable of capturing and rebroadcasting the events and posting them elsewhere, I thought there were enough of the famished, ghoulish public out there with enough disposable income to make it pay. It was a one-way site, clean and elegant: no postings or blogging from me and no comments from the peanut gallery. I had no interest in what they had to say anyway. It's my life, and I'll do what I want.

Thursday seemed endless, a train never to emerge from its tunnel. My guts were roiling in anticipation, and I was unable to eat a thing. I tried to go to a movie, just to get out of my little abattoir of an apartment and make the day pass before the ultimate curtain would be drawn. But I couldn't concentrate on a thing. The Arclight was buzzing with midday customers—mostly the elderly and the Hollywood-unemployed—and as I passed through them, I could feel the occasional burn of recognition. Eyes surreptitiously tracked me out to the parking structure . . . unless it was opening-day nerves and paranoia I felt on the back of my neck. I guess I was useless out in the real world, as usual, so it was back into the Beemer and the too-brief ride back to Valleyheart Drive.

The apartment was choking on itself, closed up and fetid. The air conditioning had broken down—again—so I opened a window, and curdled, beige, airlike San Fernando Valley fumes reached inside to caress me.

I hung a purple velvet curtain behind the Aeron chair that faced the computer and artfully trained a light against it. I positioned another light directly over the chair, which threw me into a cone of illumination. For further creative effect, I added a sidelight. I didn't want the audience to miss any of the salient details. A crystal bowl, which, at showtime, would be filled with ice, was placed on the desk right next to the hypodermic needle and attendant bottles of alcohol, anesthetic, and antiseptic. At the end of the row of implements, a George Foreman Sandwich Grill was plugged in and heating up. To give me strength and solace, a tall, unopened bottle of Jack Daniel's was placed close by, with a nice, clean glass.

So now, the only thing to do was wait for 10:00, and my first leading role.

I vacuumed the apartment, did the dishes, took out the trash, washed the windows, threw the newly acquired DVDs of the last few weeks into their alphabetical homes, whipped up a smoothie that I couldn't drink, took a shower, shaved, made my bed, turned on CNN, wiped the plasma screen, checked my messages (zero), washed out the blender, took a sip of my smoothie, and watched the clock.

It was not even 5:00.

So I surfed. I lingered over YouTube, got sick of the amateur-hour spoofs, the mediocre music, the decidedly democratic and creativity-challenged cultural contributions of the unpaid and unwashed, and listened to my stomach howl in protest. I scoured the more obscure sites that offered up the terrorist videos of physical disengagement, but I couldn't bring myself to watch. My stomach is tender when it comes to the real thing. Give me foam latex body parts and Karo syrup blood, and it's giggles and grins; show me the real thing, and I've passed out on the floor. So this was going to be a real event.

I checked the counters: more than a half million visitors had gone to my site! So far, I had fifteen hundred paid subscribers—that was $150,000!—and it was sure to go up after tonight's display. I could have quit now and suckered them, but making a profit for my incognizant Mommy—or even myself—was not the point. My meaning in life came in its disassembly.

It was now only half an hour or so before the curtain was to be drawn. I changed into my performance attire: a nice suit and a hand-painted Argentinean tie I had acquired on a trip to Buenos Aires. My fingers were uncluttered by jewelry, which would be important tonight. Running my hand through my thinning hair one last time, straightening my tie, I sat before the screen, counting down the seconds before activating the camera.

Finally, Act Two in the life of Tyler Sparrow had faded to black, and I typed, for the last time, "fade in." My third act had begun.

By the time the webcam was switched on, there were over nine hundred thousand ravenous denizens waiting online. I hated them for their lust, their tawdry, base instincts, their witless, plotless, pointless lives, their vampiric need for my blood. But I didn't have to like them, or even respect them. I could despise them, pander to them, and still fulfill my own destiny.

I did not speak. I did not perform. My face, hopefully expressionless, dispassionate, uninterested, stared back at me from the iMac as I took the hypodermic needle in hand, filled it with Lidocaine, plunged it into the base of the little finger on my left hand, and depressed the plunger. Shooting holes all around the base of the spastic digit, I emptied the hypo and jammed my protesting finger into the bowl of ice. As I waited for the anesthetic to take full effect, I looked into the lens of the webcam, into the greedy eyes of my audience, without so much as a blink. I cleaned the cutter with alcohol and a soft cloth, and it gleamed a silver grin. My whole left hand was going numb, as dead as my heart, so it was clear the moment was near.

No words, no music. Silent drama in its purest form.

I held up my insensitive left hand, and it shook in nervous anticipation. My mouth went dry, and I couldn't keep from repeatedly clearing the cotton from my throat. I splayed my fingers wide in front of my face and picked up the eager cutters in my right hand, which also betrayed me with nervous tremors. I swallowed, then drew the shining silver implement close and opened its rapacious maw. Perspiration besotted my brow and trickled down into my eyes, making them sting. I ignored it and drew the cutters closer. Now or never; the heat from the Foreman Grill broasted my right side.

I took a deep breath and . . .

Snip!

In a single cut, the shears clipped through flesh and bone, and my unappreciated left little finger plopped onto the small white satin pillow I had placed on the desk. It sat motionless in a crimson corona of my blood as the red stuff flowed mightily from the new stump at the end of my left hand.

Shock wrapped me in its shawl; there was no pain, only the dull throb of an accelerated heartbeat. Regardless, after holding it up on display for the voracious audience to prove to them that it was real, I brought it down to George's jolly little Grill and stubbed out the bleeding with a cauterizing sizzle. I screamed reflexively and gagged on the smell of my own burning meat, gulped down a double dose of Jack Daniel's, jammed my hand into the bowl of ice, and shut down the webcam.

I turned off the lights and sat in darkness, unable to stop the palsied shake that overtook my body. My hands shook most of all, and my heart was a rocket to the moon. Mission accomplished . . . its first chapter, at least. I took deep, ragged breaths, trying to bring down my pulse. Sweat broke out in a sheath over my body, cold and slippery, and I had to lie down on the couch. Still, there was no pain, though I knew it would come. Even pharmaceutically and alcoholically deadened, the thudding beat of my pulse was strong in my stump, and it felt as if it were trying to expand. So I swabbed it in antiseptic and wrapped it carefully in gauze and adhesive tape.

I lay staring at the cottage cheese ceiling, breathing deeply, not missing my useless finger, just trying to slow down my body's panic. Calm down, fella; it's over, it's going to be okay, you did it, just breathe, breathe, slower, slower . . .

It started to work; my eyes began to regain their focus, my brain turned off the olfactory assault of my burning flesh, and my heart began to give up its sprint for a jog. One more long drink directly from Jack's neck and I was nearing functionality again. When I was able to get to my feet, I returned to the beckoning eye of the iMac and woke it from its slumber.

Over one million six hundred thousand viewers had joined me for my little anatomical demonstration . . . and over two thousand of them had actually paid for the privilege! Which led to this realization: I had just been paid more to cut off my finger than I'd ever gotten for writing a script. I cogitated on that for a while, trying to put it all into perspective. That, however, proved impossible.

I had to get out of the apartment, which closed in on me, threatening to crush the life out of me. I stumbled to the carport and climbed into the Beemer, bouncing clumsily out onto the street and ultimately up Coldwater Canyon. The night atypically cool and the traffic thin. At the intersection of Coldwater and Mulholland Drive, I pulled haphazardly into the Tree People lot and stepped out into the last expanse of nature in the center of Los Angeles. Though the park was closed, I made my way through the valley oaks and piles of dog shit until I reached an open clearing. The San Fernando Valley was laid out before me, a dying harridan choking on her final gasping breaths. The NBC/Universal tower lorded over all it could see, a black obelisk of fortitude; lights twinkled and cars obliviously choked the Cahuenga pass into Hollywood. The city lay open and exposed, an autopsy pinned wide open for me to inspect. I saw the corpse decomposing before me, and its rot was contagious. A piece of me had been removed, and the course of action to follow was laid out. I felt lightened, relieved, excused from gym class. The network piranhas had been taking bloodless bites out of me for years; my destiny was now in my own diminishing hands. The Southern California sky wrapped me in its arms and put me to sleep.

"Roger, no!"

I woke suddenly to a new dawn and a stream of hot wetness. My furry alarm was a Jack Russell terrier relieving himself all over my head, its horrified owner, two hundred fifty pounds of jogging jiggle stuffed into the finest lululemon athletic wear money could buy, screaming to wake the dead.

"No! Roger, bad dog! Get over here!"

I stood, hung over, my face dripping with Roger's pee, and remembered where I was and what got me there.

"Oh, God, I am so sorry!" She pounded across the dirt path and chased the prankster terrier in a circle as he easily evaded her, laughing a maniacal doggie laugh. I stood, weaving, glaring through confused, bloodshot eyes as she handed me a towel from around her neck. "*Roger!*" She shot away in pursuit of her little urinating monster, never to return, and I wiped away its possessive piss, fully humiliated, before vomiting all over the ground.

I climbed into the Beemer and joined the sardines that choked the only artery into the valley. Naturally there was rush hour construction on Coldwater, but again, there was no hurry to get home, was there? As it turned out, there was.

When I arrived, media trucks surrounded the Valley Vista Apartments. News crews were buzzing on Starbucks and scandal. I parked and was immediately engulfed by a ravenous cadre of cameras and slick, sexless, Barbie and Ken news monkeys, each shoving their phallic microphones into my face for a multinetwork blowjob. They shouted at me, rolling tape and demanding my cooperation. I was not up for this impromptu press conference and shoved my way through them and into my apartment, locking the hollow plywood door behind me. Who had known I'd be so easily found?

This was not what I had expected.

Though I had sought the spotlight as an artist, I had grown accustomed to the relative comforts of anonymity, and resigned to being a meaningless cog in the entertainment wheel. Suddenly, the spotlight glared on me, and I sought the shadows. This is what it took to get their attention? My blood? Jesus, you guys are *easy!*

The thin door and single-paned windows did little to muffle the roar of the needy tabloidmeisters outside, but I pulled the curtains and threw the chain bolt and retreated to the comforting glow of the iMac.

It awoke with a click and showed me a list of dozens of unexpected e-mails, mostly from unfamiliar addresses, and almost none of them Viagra spam. I guess I was not so difficult to track down: my e-mail address was *tylersparrow@ymail.com* after all. My answering machine blinked "full." This lonely little hovel had suddenly overflowed with unexpected popularity. I had been elected King of the Prom! And all it took was the excision of a relatively useless digit (well, useful if you want to type *A* or *Z* or *Q*, but otherwise overrated).

The phone kept ringing and the knuckles rapping on my chamber door, but I blocked it all out. I disconnected the telephone, shut down the cell phone, and ignored the invaders until they at least quit knocking and shouting for me.

Muzzy-headed, with the remnants of Jack seeping out through overactive pores, I hovered over the iMac and scrolled through the messages. Most of them were from the anticipated crazies, a bunch of fundamentalist Christians spewing hateful fire and brimstone, print and website reporters looking for a quote from the Crazy Cutter, a few friends and coworkers from around the various writing tables I'd occupied over the years looking to have coffee and talk. As I had no family beyond my mother in the home, there were no outpourings of love and concern. Just more people who wanted something from me. Which is why I was where I was in the first place.

I opened my website and found a spike in the visitors. Five thousand people had now Paypalled to see the continuing dismemberment! Tonight's installment was an important second step. It was time to grow the audience, to bring eyeballs and open wallets to the site, to feed the chattering, nattering diners a second course to their virtual feast.

Ding!

The computer alerted me to more e-mail, and I returned to find a message on top of the new pile, with an attachment. The address caught my eye: *piecemeal82@gmail.com.* Surely a kindred spirit.

I clicked it open. The attachment was a photo of a young woman, very attractive but not in the obvious Hollywood manner of TV bimbo: no blond hair, no boob job, and slightly snaggled, imperfect teeth. She had dark bobbed hair, glasses, seemingly flawless skin, and a face and body that offered hidden promises that could be missed on first appraisal. Of course, this was only a still photo, but it looked like it had been snapped privately, certainly never retouched, and had a sense of very personal outreach. Her gold eyes looked directly into the lens, as if defying me to find her irresistible.

The message was simple: I admire what you're doing. Want to videochat? Sally.

I stared at her picture, which stared back, expressionless. There was a trace of the Mona Lisa about her. Was that hint of a smile conspiratorial, a secret bond between us, or was she mocking me? I couldn't take ridicule right now; I was feeling very vulnerable. What was it exactly that she admired?

I looked back into her inscrutable face.

What the hell? How many attractive young women actually go to the trouble to seek me out? My life was now a deck of cards cast to the wind; there was no structure, no timeline, no appointments (at least nothing before 10:00 tonight), no *anything*. So I hit Reply and wrote her back:

Sure, let's chat. Where do you live? In LA? When would you like to webcam?

Her response was immediate.

You took my breath away last night. I'm in Ojai, but I feel much closer to you. Are you by your camera now?

My heart started pounding. I reeked; I was shrouded in Jack Russell pee and Jack Daniel's vomit.

Give me half an hour, I typed.

Ignoring the mounting streamliner of e-mails and the scarlet flash of phone messages that pulsed beseechingly, I lurched into the bathroom, and after an endless strone of relief, submerged myself under the stinging nettles of a hot shower. Revived if not refreshed, I blew myself dry and climbed into presentable attire before taking my place before the computer. Breathing deeply to slow my heartbeat, I typed in her iChat address and activated my own.

Her face filled the screen, looking directly into mine. And she was lovely.

"Tyler," she said. "I can't believe it's you!"

Her voice was husky, smoky, seductive. And Jesus . . . she couldn't believe it was me!

"Yeah, it's me," I answered. "I can't believe it's you."

She smiled, and I was delivered unto her. My heart was imprisoned in her cage from that first grin.

"You're beautiful," she said.

"You must be looking in a mirror," I told her. "Did you watch last night, Sally?"

"I did. You're very brave. It was quite a performance." She paused and bit her lower lip before she went on. "It . . . excited me." It was obvious; she was breathing more heavily, and her face betrayed a sudden flush of passion. Cutting off my finger excited her? What was I getting myself into?

"I don't know what to say to that."

She stared right into the webcam . . . and my face.

"Did it excite you?" she asked.

Hmm. To be honest, I had never considered the erotic possibilities of my own dismemberment. I find no pleasure in pain, nor have I ever found rendered flesh to be any kind of sexual stimulation, even in fantasy. My arousals seem to be much more catholic than that. Suddenly I felt square and prudish, but I didn't want to appear so to this odd young woman.

"Um," I began wittily, "not at the time."

She seemed disappointed, which in turn disappointed *me*. I didn't want to let her down.

"Oh" was her succinct reply.

There was more pounding on the front door, but I wasn't home.

"Are you alone?" she asked me.

"Oh, yeah."

"Do you live by yourself?"

"I do. How about you?"

"All alone." Another long pause, then, "Are you lonely?"

It took me by surprise. A heavy, rotting ball of isolation started to expand within my chest, and I felt myself sinking under its weight. My mouth worked, but no words came out. Embarrassed, I could feel my eyes inexplicably filling with unspilled sadness. Lonely? Was I lonely? I hadn't noticed . . . until now. Her face, calm in repose, watched me without judgment, and I shrank in embarrassment under her gaze. She waited patiently for my reply, and it became clear that I could tell her the truth.

"I guess maybe I am."

She nodded. "Me too."

It wasn't possible that this beautiful, soft-spoken young woman could ever be allowed loneliness, and I told her so.

"The world is crowded," she replied, "but I don't walk among them."

I knew how she felt, and she did not require an answer.

"Show me your hand," she said.

I held it up to the camera.

"Can you take off the bandage?"

"You sure?"

"I'm sure."

Caught in her hungry gaze, suddenly and inexplicably sprouting an erection hiding beneath the desk, I slowly unwrapped my hand, where the wound gaped, red and raw. She gasped.

"Does it hurt?"

"Not so much."

"Hold it closer."

Her breathing went deeper, and so did mine. I could feel my blood coursing hotly through my body, pulsing with an accelerating beat. She leaned closer.

"I wish I could kiss it better."

My throat choked with emotion, and it took a moment before I could reply, "So do I." And I did.

More pounding on the door by my adoring public.

"Will you do it again tonight?" she asked.

I nodded. "That's the deal. You wouldn't believe how many people have paid for me to do it."

"Yes, I would."

"Are you one of them?" She nodded and smiled, revealing a slightly crooked canine that made her even sexier . . . despite her bloodlust.

"I didn't think it was real. But it was worth the gamble."

The doorbell kept ringing and voices kept piercing the thin walls and windows of my Sherman Oaks chalet. E-mails and IMs kept filling the background of my computer screen. Even my silent cell phone kept up a vibratory boogie over on the counter. I was under siege.

"What's all that noise?"

I sighed. "I guess I've become very popular since last night."

"Is there a crowd there?"

"Just turn on your television; I seem to be all over the place." I spotted a videocamera peering between a gap in the curtains and rushed over to pull it shut.

"I don't have a television," she told me.

I liked her even more. She was oblivious to the expendable fruits of my labors. She had no idea that I had settled for a grasp that far exceeded my reach.

"Well, it seems to be time for a personal crucifixion. They're all out there begging for it."

She started to speak, then backed off a moment.

"What?"

She hesitated again, then continued. "If you want to get away from them, you can always come here."

As the cry for my literal blood ratcheted up in the background, I considered her generous offer.

"Really?"

"Really."

I looked at her peaceful, welcoming visage, and realized I'd never seen anyone with gold eyes before.

I needed to hide.

It didn't take long to ditch the hounds of journalism, and within half an hour I felt free of their slavering jaws as the Beemer sped northward up the Ventura Freeway. Fish-scale clouds domed the browning San Fernando Valley, but they had thinned into a gleaming blue by the time I'd passed through Moorpark. As I cleared the final mountain that announced the citrus farms of the Ojai Valley in a dramatic opening-act reveal, I was stunned at how a ninety-minute drive could change the world so dramatically.

The car's GPS led me through the tranquil little Old California farming town, now best known for its spas and weekend getaways, even while being hemmed in by endless groves of oranges. I passed through the two blocks of downtown, passed a dry but restful old cemetery, and wended my way around the outdoor ramshackle used stacks of Bart's Books, eventually winding up a dirt road to a tiny little Craftsman bungalow, removed from its neighbors. Giant valley oaks cast a canopy of cool shade, their papery leaves rustling a welcome in the breeze. As the tires spat gravel and I coasted to a stop, a silhouette revealed itself behind the shutters.

My heart pounded a military tattoo as I cleared my throat and made my way to the door, not knowing exactly what to expect. I popped the trunk, climbed out of the car, and hefted my iMac to the door. She met me there, and we stood facing one another through the rusty screen door for a wordless eternity. Her oddly lovely face was unmapped by experience, smooth as a ten-year-old's, a translucence seemingly never kissed by sun. Her face was framed in a bob of auburn hair, and her astonishing golden eyes were wide in expectation and glinting in the sun. She was tiny, much smaller than I'd expected: barely five feet. She wore jeans and a loose white cotton blouse under a sort of shawl, as simple and as unadorned as her face. But she was luscious, and her visage soon bloomed into a convivial smile as she held her arms under the shawl to ward off the chill.

"You made good time," she said as she pushed open the screen with a creak.

I stepped into the cool time warp of her home and felt embraced by it. It was furnished mostly in Stickley—or very good copies. The burnished old Mission Oak style suited the house, the setting, and its occupant. It felt untrammeled by the present, save for the modest computer sitting in the corner, out of place on the old desk.

"Where should I put this?" I asked, hugging the iMac.

Limping slightly, she led me to the dining room table, and I set it down. There were no lights on inside; the house was illuminated only by the sunlight filtering through the oaks and the open windows. "Do you want something to drink?"

"What have you got?"

I watched her go into the kitchen and open the fridge.

"I've got water, um, beer, iced tea, Diet Coke."

Beer sounded good, and she pointed me into the living room while she poured the Michelobs. I glimpsed into the bedroom on the way back, noticing a tidy and comfy lived-in quality as I passed. The bed was made, and there was silent-scream art on the walls of a darker nature than you would expect from that soft, sweet face. I sat on the overstuffed couch and took it all in. The place had a history, permanence, something that I lacked. I was a loose end, at sea in a riptide.

She walked into the room, the tray of beers on one hand, and I stood to take it from her, settling back on the couch once she sat. I was trying to understand her, loving the breadcrumb clues she offered.

"Thanks for letting me come up here," I told her.

"Thanks for sharing it with me," she replied.

"Why did you contact me?" As much as I appreciated it, I still didn't understand.

"Because you did something bold and brave. And because I thought I recognized someone of a like mind, and I don't see many of those. Was I wrong?"

"I hope not."

With that, I reached tentatively to take her hand, and she let me. But I was greedy; I wanted both. So I reached with the right hand as well, and her breath caught in her throat. She stared into my eyes, searching, before she wordlessly drew her left arm from under the shawl. It ended halfway between elbow and wrist. I was only beginning to understand the erotic charge coursing through me. Gingerly, I reached out, knowing she wanted me to, and touched the end of her arm, held it gently in my hand. I wanted to kiss it.

My voice broke as I asked, "Did you have an accident?"

"Not exactly," she replied.

"How did it happen?"

She scrutinized me again before deciding to tell.

"I work in a print shop. I was cutting and binding a big job, and as I watched the guillotine hacking off blocks of paper, over and over and over, it sort of cast a spell on me. It was so hypnotic. It kept cutting, chopping as new stacks of paper were fed into it, and it just drew me closer and closer into it." She looked at me, deciding whether or not it was safe to go on. It was. She gripped my hand tighter. "I don't know, I just couldn't keep myself from feeding it. Before I knew it, I'd shoved my hand in and pulled away what was left of my arm, spurting blood all over the piles of paper. My life was all over the book."

She looked at me for a reaction, and I stared back in bewilderment.

"Did it hurt?" I asked her.

"Maybe. But it made me come."

When she said it, I almost did the same. I was raging underneath my jeans. She dropped her single hand into my lap, knowing what was going on down there. I leaned in to kiss her, and she hungrily sucked on my tongue.

I carried her into the tiny bedroom; she barely weighed anything. She was irresistibly petite, and her erotic appetite was completely at odds with her gentle demeanor. As we kissed, her eyes rolled back in her head, and her cries as her body became drenched in sweat were guttural, uninhibited, downright feral. When I laid her on the bed, she wouldn't let me stand and look at her; she pulled me down into the bed with her and feverishly unbuttoned my shirt, willing me to do the same to her. I was happy to oblige.

Her skin was alabaster-new everywhere, practically aglow, as if lit from beneath. When I removed her blouse, the flesh beneath was almost as white as the fabric. She took my hand in hers, bringing it to her mouth, sucking on each of the fingers before settling on the new, raw wound. The wet heat of her mouth was as soothing as it was exciting.

I unfastened her pants, and she eagerly raised her hips to accommodate their removal. They caught as I'd drawn them halfway down, and I struggled with them to pull them all the way off as her breaths came hot and rapid. They had hung up on the straps of her prosthesis. Her leg below the knee was rubber and steel.

When she said "Take it off," I knew what she meant, and removed the artificial limb. Repelled yet hopelessly drawn to it like a moth to light, I kissed and tasted its fleshy sweetness. When I finally entered her, I did not last long.

I woke to darkness as an old mantel clock chimed eight times; the day had lost me in post-orgasmic slumber. The spot on the bed next to me was empty but still warm. Moonlight reached in through the window with chilly fingers to touch me, and I felt vulnerable, dressed only in gooseflesh. I looked down the hallway to see Sally sitting in the dining room, illuminated by the cool light of the iMac. She had set it up while I slept. I slipped out of the bed and into my jeans.

"I didn't want to wake you," she said, and I was grateful for the rest. "I hope you don't mind me setting it up; it was getting late." I thanked her and sat next to her to sign on. She turned away while I entered the appropriate passwords to prepare for tonight's performance. Once that business was attended to, she kissed me, running her tongue under my lips and over my teeth, fully waking me before watching me prepare for the night.

There were no more free samples on TylersThirdAct.com on Night Two. This was now an exclusive club for paid visitors only. Over three thousand of them by now. I could tell that Sally was impressed, but she did not speak as I opened a bag and set up the accoutrements of my public dismemberment: the bowl, the hypo, the anesthetic, the silver tools, the Foreman Grill, the white satin pillow. As they lay out in strict anal-retentive order, my hands began to shake again, and I turned to look up at her over my shoulder.

"Beautiful," she sighed.

"Okay if I take a shower?" I asked, and she nodded.

So I did, shivering and convulsing as the shower washed the slime of my life down the drain. I vomited a thin, liquid gruel of my sins; that's all that was left inside me. And now it had been cast out like a wicked demon.

When I had completed my *toilette*, I returned to the iMac, Sally, and my future. It was close to nine now: one hour from the next chapter.

"You look beautiful," Sally told me, meaning it.

No. She was the beautiful one; all I could do was stare at her, take her in, worship her. If she thought I was beautiful, that made me happy. But I saw innocent, vulnerable beauty sitting before me, tiny and unprotected, and my heart sprung a leak. I took her face in my hands and kissed her, lovingly and lustlessly, gently pressing my coarse, stubbled cheek against the cream of hers.

"What will you remove tonight?" she asked me.

"I—I was thinking of another finger," I stammered.

"Aren't you . . ." She stopped.

"Go ahead," I said. "Aren't I what?"

"Just . . . aren't you afraid of repetition? I mean, were you planning to just do a finger at a time, then maybe your toes?"

"Um . . . kinda, yeah." Was there something wrong with that?

"I think your audience wants some, well, *escalation*. You don't want to lose their interest."

Escalation. For a moment, she sounded like a network executive. But I understood immediately that she was right.

"Like an ear?"

She took my hand in hers.

"Like a hand." She kissed it and looked up into my eyes.

"A hand." I swallowed. There was no turning back now. I had set my course of action, had outlined my final act, and committed to its fulfillment. I had made a contract with myself.

It was quarter after nine. The clock on the wall ticked away the seconds ominously, stealthily, and I could swear that the speed accelerated. But that was probably just my heart.

"And after the hand?"

"Let's think about after," she said, "after the hand."

"You're right," I told her, and she smiled, her golden eyes igniting. She kissed me deeply and at length.

"I don't know if I have the right tools," I said.

Her face still aglow, she said, "I do." I didn't doubt her. She left the room and returned with an oversized paper cutter. She set it gently on the table in front of the iMac and opened its heavy steel jaws. They gleamed in anticipation. I reached over and slammed the guillotine shut, and the hungry *shing* of stainless steel caressing itself sang me a lullaby.

I looked at the computer screen and saw e-mails and last-minute subscribers piling up. I turned to the clock and saw that it was 9:35.

"Well, what do you think?" she asked.

My soul and I had filed for divorce. I had sought resignation from the planet, solitary and insignificant, a single card misfiled among the millions. I looked into the eager eyes of another outcast, tiny and getting tinier. My worth came only in my diminution and eventual demise. So far, my audience had spent close to half a million dollars to watch my destruction, to witness a self-immolating soul cease to be. I found company, romance, and solace in the act of dismemberment, elements that had eluded me in life but burgeoned in the compressed time left.

"I think yes."

I saw her eyes fill with joyful tears and welcomed her approval as she hugged me tight. I began to tremble again, utterly exposed and at her mercy. She pulled away and looked at me, holding a question behind her eyes as I quaked.

"What is it?" I asked.

"Do you want me to make the cut?" I could tell that was what she wanted; maybe it was what I wanted as well. When I nodded, the spasm within my body settled and calmed. I was truly in her hands.

"We'd better get ready," she said. The clock's synchronous symphony continued.

As practiced as a nurse, she injected the Lidocaine all around my wrist. I could feel the tingle as it began to take effect. She put away the needle and massaged my arm, and I absorbed her heat.

"You got any Jack Daniel's?" She had some Maker's Mark, and I made do. As its burn was absorbed into my veins, I calmed even more. The seconds on the clock pounded ferociously by, a telltale heart counting down. Just minutes until showtime. She sat me in a chair right in front of the iMac and took her place on a chair just out of the camera's range. Just before ten, she slipped on a simple, black Halloween mask.

"You ready?" she asked.

I was.

I turned on the webcam and faced the camera. Another three hundred paid subscribers had come online in the last few minutes, and their number kept ticking right up until ten.

I held my hands up to the camera, like a magician about to do a trick. Sally swabbed around my wrist with alcohol. I lay my sleeping arm on top of the paper cutter, and she helped me get it into position. The gleaming blade sparkled in wait. I tilted the screen of the computer so that the camera held my arm in a perfect frame. Then Sally took hold of the blade's handle and, before I had a chance to object, slammed it down. My hand dropped to the satin pillow like a slaughtered starfish.

I jammed the stump of my wrist into the Foreman Grill and passed out.

It's a hoary writer's device to have the lead character lose consciousness and awaken to a new plot development with the passage of time. It's cheap but effective, and I confess to adopting it numerous times, even within this account. Including now. As I had no idea of all the events that transpired during my disconnection from consciousness, all I can convey is my awakening, and the overwhelming aroma that accompanied it. It was the heady, meaty scent of cooking flesh.

My body was bent in an awkward, uncomfortable position, lying on a blanket that covered a hard metal surface. I opened my eyes and waited for them to focus, forgetting momentarily where I was. It was immediately apparent that I was not in my Sherman Oaks apartment. I was in Sally's house, of course, but in a rusting metal enclosure. It was a cage of thick iron bars, barely four feet square. My head was muzzy and clouded, my vision tentative, my body in varying levels of discomfort. Then I realized that my mouth felt dead and swollen inside; there was merely a stump where my tongue used to lie.

I lifted my head to the direction of the kitchen, where a pot sputtered on the stove, delivering its beckoning bouquet. There were voices. I turned to see that Sally had company. Half a dozen visitors were seated around her dining table, each behind an elaborate place setting. Though they were of varying physical types—corpulent, slender, tall, diminutive, and of varying shades and ethnicity—they shared this trait: all were lacking in various body parts. Their flesh houses had been hacked away.

When Sally entered the room, carrying a steaming platter of meat on her single hand, she looked in surprise and delight to see that I was awake. When she said "Good morning," all eyes were on me, and backed me into a corner of my cage. It was then that I recognized some of them: one was Daniel Power, VP of dramatic programming at NBC; another was Carolyn Pfenster from Turner; a third was some low-level development guy from Universal, his name long forgotten after a failed pitch meeting last year. The others were unfamiliar to me.

Then I looked down to see that, aside from sitting naked before them, I was missing more than a hand. An entire leg had been removed as I slept, making my shrunken, dangling privates merely my second leg.

My stomach growled.

"Are you hungry?" Sally asked me. Everyone at the table answered in the affirmative, not realizing the question was not meant for them. I shook my head, denying the starvation that ravished me. I could not cry out for help.

The repast on the table before the gathered group was complete now. There may have been vegetables on the table, but I didn't see them. All I could see was Filet of Sparrow laid out in mouth-watering fashion, and the group of diners tucked in to their delectable meal with relish. This show was no longer my own, I realized; the series I had created chronicling my own demise had been taken over; I'd been replaced as the showrunner. Tyler's Third Act now ran on a new network, co-opted by the new owners and relegated to their own website.

Sally got up from the table with a dish and kneeled before me, just inches from the other side of the bars. Through an opening at the bottom of the cage, she slid in a small plate. My disembodied hand lay there like a pink tarantula, tender meat barely clinging to the bones. "Go ahead," Sally urged me. "It's really good." Yeah, I thought. And so good for me. I couldn't eat it.

That was two weeks ago. Needless to say, I have developed a taste for human flesh, or I would not be here today. Well, what's left of me, anyway. My limbs are gone, and just about everything else. Nothing else could be removed without it being the end of my life; I look like home plate.

They say that it's not how you die that matters, but how you live. I beg to differ. As someone whose life was lived in anonymous mediocrity, my impending death was all that was unique about me. Tonight will be my final dinner party at Sally's. The only pain is in my heart, not my body. Existence is highly overrated. I will not miss it. And if your subscription is paid up, you will join me in my bon voyage party. Sally has gently bathed and groomed me for the wrap-up of my third act, and the webcam is about to be activated. I hope you'll join me for this very special episode before I fade to black and the commercials run.

"Though Thy Lips Are Pale"

Maria Alexander

For youth is youth, and time will have it so,
And though thy lips are pale, and thine eyes wet
Farewell, thou must forget.
—"Good-Bye" by Anonymous, fifteenth-century France

Painful sunlight, cold air blasting between my raw lips. My head lolls forward wearily, the bells of Prime clanging faintly from the abbey. Men in ivory belts and mail coats *shing shing shing* from horse to chateau, squires scuttling like brown spiders behind their dirty gold spurs. Gripping the prayer book tucked in my muff, I am wondering which horse's back holds my dowry. My thousands, our salvation. My life is not where I stand but strapped to a beast in a precious coffer I have never seen. . . .

Three days ago my virginity was but a shadow that would darken another cloister wall. How swiftly this change of fortune visited me. I never dreamed I would be betrothed but assumed I would remain a wilting maid my whole life. My sisters were married, but I was told there was nothing left for me. Perhaps I misunderstood. I sift through every handful of spilt words these last months, but I remember nothing except the endless procession of ministers, priests, and manor lords come to counsel my father on spoiled crops, uprisings, and political strife as he remains loyal to Paris. I do not recall hearing of a marriage contract, or who the visitors might have been who would bring the bride price. Then three nights ago, Mother's proclamation of betrothal came to me in my bedchambers like the Angel's annunciation to the Virgin. I am to wed the son of a duke in the Duchy of Normandy.

I have only thirteen Yuletides.

As Mother and I walk into the weak light of morning, my companions weep piteously from the chateau gate. One secretes a small bottle of rose, cardamom, and cumin in a silk handkerchief as a parting gift. We had whispered excitedly about the marriage: *Would I run a big household? Would I have lots of children? Is my betrothed handsome?* My friends assured me that with my flaxen hair and azure eyes I was pretty enough to love. And I believed them. For a moment, at least.

Mother sees my distress as I leave my companions, and places a hand on my cheek, withering resignation in her touch. "Worry not," she says. "In your trousseau are great swaths of Italian damask that are blue as robins' eggs, linen fair as fresh cream, velvet black as a murder's wings, and fine woolens to fend off the damp chill of Normandy."

I do not recall seeing these fabrics in my trousseau, much less the armoire that holds them. Only the carefully wrapped packs of heavily salted fish and pork, the bulky sacks of *trancheor* loaves, jugs of cider, dried cheese rinds, and other rations. Far more than needed for four days' travel. I suppose one cannot underestimate the appetites of men.

Wrinkled red faces peer from the kitchen. Breezes nuzzle the beech leaves overhead as I am lifted into the gaily colored cart and seated amongst plentiful furs, which I gather around me. I find some toiletries and a few small bundles of rations buried in the furs. It is eerily quiet. No saltarellos, singers, or noisemakers to celebrate my fortune and wish me well.

"Where are the men who serve my betrothed?" I ask Mother. "Why do they not retrieve me as they did my sisters?"

"We must hurry," she says and withdraws her regard. I fall voiceless.

Leaves crackling beneath their feet, the men in ivory belts brandish their swords, swear oaths to great angels, and troth fealty to my mother's amaranthine beauty. My heart floats like cobwebs on a breeze when I hear such words. I sit motionless, suspended in the rapture of their praise for Mother's spiritual and physical perfections. Then they mount their horses with a shout, heraldry held aloft. The horses *clop clop clop* and we move away from the chateau.

I brush away the silt of confusion. I am excited to one day soon have the service of such fine warriors who speak words of admiration, to one day inspire the good deeds and thoughts of a man who fights for both me and mild Mother Mary. One day soon, I will be the one protected and honored. (Then again, the wedding might be some years from now. No one can say.) In the meantime, I can write letters to my mother and sisters, and I love my books. Surely I can have more of those too.

After some distance, I gather my courage and skirts to crawl forward to the curtains. I part them on the far left side to reveal the patchwork *bocage* of Bretagne passing behind us. The black hedges of oak quilt the borders between great squares of dark verdant grasses dotted with ashy broom bushes and the feathery heads of heather wearing tiny jewels of dew. My tongue curls over my lips as if to taste the succulent vegetation. Then the sour stench of the horses worms into the feast as one canters up to my cart. The squire runs alongside to catch up. The man riding the horse is layered in chain mail and a bright red poplin tunic swathed at the waist with an ivory belt. I am frightened by the breadth of his meaty jaw, the cruel squint of his eyes, and the faded mulberry scar ripping the bridge of his nose. A thin veil of benevolence spreads over his otherwise dark face as he speaks to me. "Hail, little one. It goes well?"

I nod.

"You are sick from the cart, no?"

I shake my head.

He raises his head to speak to the others. "Hitch a cart to this one! She is strong as an ox!"

My stomach turns sickeningly with embarrassment as they laugh. I let the curtain close and fall back into darkness. The warriors wheedle me to come out again, but instead I curl up on the furs and sleep until hunger burns all the way into my mouth. My eyes grow accustomed to the darkness. Small blades of light slash through the swaying curtains from the other end of the cart. I fumble for a small bundle of food and devour my rugged, salty *déjeuner* like a starved beggar. The thick, painful lump in my stomach afterward reminds me that for a few days I will have to endure poor foods.

The cart stops once for a brief rest as a magpie harshly chirps *areprepreprep* in the gray branches with yellowish leaves. An ill omen, but also a warning of armed men nearby. Who is he warning of our presence? After emptying my chamber pot over the open lip, I cautiously slide out of the cart and visit the trail. It seems so broken already, as if we were never on a solid road at all. The men in chain mail relieve themselves, murmuring quietly to one another. Their cheeks turn ashen in the mottled light, eyes widening, lips wet with argument. Are they afraid? They cannot possibly be afraid, they who have jousted for Mother. They who have killed infidels, Englishmen, perhaps even brethren. They who have one another. They are never alone. Like me.

"Let us go, little one!" the frightening man calls to me, wincing as his squire helps him into his saddle. A handsome man helps me scramble back into the cart ("Hup!"), where I hide like a field mouse in the folds of fur. I have never been out of the chateau for more than a few hours. I grow more nervous by the moment, as if evil spirits are stitching back and forth through my skin, around my bones and fingers.

As we settle down for night, the darkness ladles generous spoonfuls of dread on my skin. The men eat salted fish and drink weak beer with sober looks that skitter loosely around us into the darkness beyond. I cannot understand why they are fasting. It is neither Lent, nor Advent, nor any holy day. Later in my cart's bed, I shiver from the wolves howling as they prowl sheep fields in the distance. Every small crunch of twig and stone under the men's feet makes me feel vulnerable to danger rather than protected. A thick heat chokes my nose and mouth as small sobs swell from my stomach. The rummy musk of dead animal skins fills my head as I inhale small fistfuls of air. I clasp the little prayer book against my chest, wordlessly repeating the prayers to The Virgin until sleep overtakes me sometime just before dawn.

The cart has been moving for some time, it seems, when I finally awaken to the sound of my own rapid, even breathing. Something feels profoundly different about the air beyond the cart's curtains. A breeze swoops in to bite my nose with a frosty beak. My entire body aches by degrees, my neck and shoulders crying loudest when I shrug them from my bedding. I gather my skirt to crawl to the cart's end, and as the cart wobbles, I scrape my knees.

This time when I draw back the curtains, the murky, crippled fingers of fir trees grasp at us from all sides. The soldiers sit bolt upright in their saddles, grizzled faces sweating, eyes fixed on the ominous gaps between the trees. No one notices that I lean far from the cart, twisting upward to see the unbroken canopy of ancient birch limbs whose gnarled, hairy branches strangle one another for the retreating sunlight. The corpselike bark of the trunks contrasts starkly against the somber pines. The damp ground is clotted with rotting leaves that cling to the horses' hooves as they stomp onward in a death march. A squire slips in the damp every moment or so, then scrambles to get his footing as if a cadaver's hand might burst through the forest floor to seize his ankle.

I begin to imagine the most terrible things lurking in the darkness of the trees. Filthy naked things with black eyes, bloated bellies, and cracked claws. This place feels cursed with its silence and shadows.

"Where are we?" I dare whisper.

The frightening soldier glances at me in a panic, as if by speaking I had broken an oath. Then, a riot of murmurs breaks out from the forest growth and a wind hurtles past us as if chased by the Devil. . . .

I know exactly where we tread.

We are in the heart of Paimpont, the hopeless woods where lovers are turned to stone by heartbroken witches, and hapless travelers wander into labyrinths to be devoured by godless monsters.

The air blurs as another layer of darkness settles on the narrow path, growing ever more bumpy with pallid tree roots that writhe up through the dirt. I fall back on my side as the cart jerks and rocks, bruising my shoulder. Terror drums in my chest as I try to imagine why we have come so far west. To loathsome Paimpont. I have slept so much that I did not notice we have been following the sun. *Prince Jesus,* I pray silently. *Please take pity on me. I pray that Hell gain no mastery over me, a virgin.*

Eventually the cart rolls to a stop. I hear the general noise of camp being set for the night along with the smaller noises of twilight twittering in the surrounding undergrowth. An argument breaks out amongst the men as to who will forage for firewood. They fight as if one had been asked to sacrifice his squire. The frightening man says that they are to search together and not to roam far from the camp. To watch each other. One of the horses already carries bundles of wood from our last camp.

The frightening soldier builds a small fire from it as the squires disperse. "Come out, little one," he orders.

Wrapped tightly in my cloak, prayer book tucked in my muff, I shuffle to the cart's opening and draw back the curtains. The brisk air pinches my cheeks. I hear no wildlife, no insects. The solemn movements of the men underscore the darkness of this place. The crackling of brush under the squires' feet echoes loudly, like the sound of scourges on a prisoner's back.

"Are you hungry?"

Offered pork and bread by the frightening man, I shake my head. The men sit around the low fire and eat salted fish again. I want to ask them why they fast when there is no holy day. No reason to discipline themselves this way. Perhaps I am wrong. The days have turned around in my head like spinning leaves as they fall from the gusts of change. Instead I read from my prayer book by the fire's light, ignoring the anxious stares I draw from the men as they gulp weak beer.

Twilight dwindles to obscurity. I notice a breach in the crowded tree trunks that leads to a clearing of sweet grasses enclosed by hunched oak trees. Only the densest of shadows flickers in the grove from our firelight. I watch the dancing shadows, a *carole* of bleak brush strokes on the fickle canvas of light. I am startled to find the soldiers have surrounded me from behind. They carry torches, a polished pewter urn of water, blankets of bleached poplin . . .

I shrink from their smudged, haunted faces. "What is this?"

"Your father is in grave danger," the frightening man says. "There is something you must do for him. It is the only thing that can save him."

My father is not ill that I know, but he is in considerable danger from threats of war and all the troubles of nobility. "I cannot imagine what you mean for me," I say. "I am just a girl. What can I do for my father but marry well and have a son?"

His big calloused hands grasp my shoulders, turning me toward the clearing. He stoops to speak into my ear, gripping me firmly. "It is a simple thing. You must sit there, in the grove, tonight until the wee hours."

"No!" I cry out, digging my heels into the damp earth, wedging them against a clump of roots. "I beg you, sir! Not in the wood!"

He pushes me forward as I lean back against him, shaking my head desperately. "*No! I beg you! No! No!*" I sob uncontrollably as he lifts me, his scarred hands easily overpowering me as he carries me into the clearing. I am just a rag doll to him. My feet kick backward against his shins, but my heels painfully strike his metal guards.

As we enter the clearing the other soldiers chant a monk's prayer while they spread the white poplin blankets on the grass under the bleeding smoke of the torches. They circle the blankets three times, then set the pewter urn of water to one side and stab a torch in the ground on the other. I sag in my captor's hands to resist him. "We are watching you carefully, little one. Nothing will happen to you."

Rimy tears streak my cheeks as I turn up my face to the distant heavens. So I must sit in the cursed woods. Alone. What would my family say?

What would my betrothed say?

"But why must I do this?"

"That," he says, turning me toward the urn, "is holy water. And that," he says, turning me toward the torch, "is made of wood from Jerusalem. More than that, I cannot say."

The frightening man sets me down on the blankets, and I slouch with misery, listening to their retreating footsteps. The torch awakens the shadowy dancers against the naked trees. They resume their grotesque dance around me with macabre limbs capering in the smoke. I bury my eyes in my muff, dampening the fur heavily with sobs of fear. I rub my nose in the fur and pull out my prayer book, hands trembling as I leaf open to my favorite prayer. I read aloud.

I sit here for some hours, reading the prayers over and over. My tears dry as I pray. There is no danger for me here. I sigh, set the prayer book open on the blanket. The poplin is unspeakably soft, a delicate weave of pure threads. I am wondering if they have taken this from my trousseau when something rustles beyond the staggering gambol of the shadow dancers. I look up expectantly. Perhaps my strange vigil is ended and the men are coming for me—

Another hiss as something steps through the overgrowth.

The sloping snout of a pale beast nods between the trunks of the clearing. The creature bares its teeth viciously, swiping a snowy hoof across the grasses in challenge. It tilts its wooly head to examine me for a heartbeat. I stop breathing as it lopes toward me like a broken apostle with a holy message. Tears of awe and disbelief flood my face as it brandishes the blanching steeple from its forehead. It raises its head for a moment as if to sniff the air, wan lips trembling. Its sallow eyes glisten with distrust and heartache.

There is nothing in the world for me but this feral miracle. I hold up my open hand to it, as if offering a horse a turnip. Cautiously it sniffs at the pewter urn, laps the water noisily, then paces around the white poplin blankets as it turns an eye to the torch. I admire the supple neck when the snout swings about to lick my palm. I shudder as the rough tongue sweeps my delicate skin with broad, leonine strokes. The back legs fold beneath it, and with breathless grace it rests its muscular, powerful jaw on my lap. I tentatively stroke the wiry alabaster mane. I notice with no little horror that the ridges of the blanching steeple are stained with blood. Its ears flicker contentedly, and its breath rumbles like a weary horse, yet something deadly and brutish pulses beneath that waxy pelt. The blood in my hands throbs faintly in response.

The sharp whistle of arrows breaks our communion. I scream, throwing my hands over my head. The men have hidden themselves up in the trees and are shooting nets at the beast as it suddenly rears up to meet the challenge. Tangled but not tamed, the creature thrashes at the heavy mesh, slicing it cleanly in places without even a fray. More men rush the trapped beast with their swords but are confounded by the ghastly maw and threatening stance. It leans back on its haunches, squints its sallow eyes, and howls like a damned thing as it wags its frightful jaw. The cries shake some of the weaker men to their knees, ivory belts dangling on the damp ground.

But not the frightening man and his closest companions. They lunge toward the creature with massive swords drawn, slashing at it to drive it backward. Another volley of arrows sails earthward, pinning another net over the faltering creature. Its eyes begin to fade, to blink like a housecat by a fire. A foreleg bends beneath it awkwardly; a pink froth spatters the wan mouth. The urn is knocked to the ground, the water surging over the gleaming lip to soak the forest floor. I then realize angrily that the "holy water" was poisoned with some kind of herb to make the creature succumb to the assault.

With mounting anguish, I watch the creature fall prey to the trap. My miracle bound by the cruelty of ordinary men. Dreams, desires . . . everything innocent and simple flees from my girlish thoughts during the struggle until the creature's jaw dips against its breast from the poison and it sleeps. The men quickly bind its legs and fit an odd harness over the sloping snout that grips the neck in a helpless position. The supple neck arcs forward, anchored to the forelocks.

They spend some time examining the creature, as one fusses over flowers in the garden. Each expresses his admiration for the beast's courage and fighting spirit, not to mention its strange anatomy. "But will the duke kill it?" one man asks.

"The beast is a marvel. It should be seen," another says. He was one whose knees weakened at the howls.

"Perhaps," the frightening man responds. "The horn alone is of immense magical value—or so I am told. Enough to save the Duchy of Bretagne for certain. And to have the whole beast, alive . . ." He hesitates, thinking. "We will go down in legend like our forefathers if we keep it alive for now. Like Arthur and Gawain. And the duke will want the honor of killing the wretched thing for whatever part he wishes."

"Legends!" the handsome man cries. "We celebrate!"

They haul the drowsy beast closer to the periphery of the campsite. Soon, meat is simmering in pots and copious amounts of wine are spilling down gullets. I am not offered anything, nor am I spoken to for any matter. As they brag about the capture, wallowing excessively in glory, the men do not acknowledge me or my part in the treachery against magic itself. They strip off their armor, empty their boots of rocks. I cannot take my eyes off the pitiful beast in its bonds whilst they feast and drink themselves into oblivion.

Legends? Braggarts and bastards, all of them.

I crawl into the obscurity of my cart and throw the furs around me. I cannot cry. I must think of a way to help the beast before they take me to Normandy. And that is when I hear them:

"And what do we do with the girl?" asks one soldier drunkenly.

"We drop her . . . at the nearettthhh . . . nunnery," another responds. "As her father ordered."

They discuss the elaborate charade, how I could not know the purpose of the expedition or else it would surely fail. I had to be deceived. The betrayal cuts me to the quick.

"Well," announces the frightening man. The ground crunches under his boots as he stands from the campfire. "Since she is forfeit to the nuns . . ."

I cannot imagine what elicits the boisterous laughs that follow, but his heavy steps approach my cart. He tears aside the curtains, his apish shape terrifying in the outline of the fire's light under the arc of the cart cover. The cart dips from his weight as he climbs inside. A smell wafts into the air, musky and sweaty. Vinegary. At first I'm stunned with bewilderment, but soon fiery terror swells from the pit of my stomach and my throat enflames with hoarse screams. As easily as he clasped my shoulders to carry me into the clearing, he pins me to the furs and pulls up my skirts, his thick knees wedging my frail legs apart. I panic, arching my body to pull back my hips. My virginity is exposed to his threatening heat. Sensitive. Delicate. That slight part of me that is worth anything. As I squirm against his iron grip, his hand slams against the side of my head. An explosion behind my eyes. I fall limp. He prods the lips of my tiny opening with the naked end of his bloated, stinking penis.

"Nice and small," he says gruffly. "Just the way I like it."

He forces his manhood into my tiny opening, ripping the delicate skin. Agony floods between my legs at that tender nexus, his first thrust inside burning like a brand on sheep flesh. My narrow opening resists his passage, yet he thrusts up into me again and again, beating my womb like a fist. Nausea blooms in my belly when he removes himself. I feel the sickening dribble against my savaged virginity, the bitter stench of his seed mingling with my blood as it stripes my inner thigh.

Fire licks my sex with disabling anguish. My thighs and stomach are bruised, as is every place he has touched me. . . .

But as soon as he descends from the cart, another enters.

And then another.

I lose consciousness during, between. There are so many.

A squire is egged on by his master, but he takes one look at me, shakes his head, and drops the curtain.

By the time they have all fallen asleep by the fire, the furs of the cart soak with the grisly fluids of my womb and the rancid pus of their violence. My hair has been pulled out and strews the floor like bits of flax. My abdomen throbs so badly I cannot sit up without feeling knives cutting me inside, slicing upward from my bleeding opening. My small tits are ripped. Bitten. Blackened with teeth marks. My left wrist dangles broken, encircled by a hot cuff of pain. I cannot move because the pain has clasped its hands around my head. It shouts in my ear that I have been mortally wounded.

Still, the physical torment is nary a thing compared to the

overwhelming disgust that consumes me. I try to flee the oppressive feelings of hopelessness by imagining myself at home with my companions, at my mother's side, or even in the sanctuary of a nunnery, but the betrayal of my family leaves a gorge in my memory where any good thought once dwelt. I start to pray and realize that the greatest betrayal was from Him who should protect little girls from treachery. We who have so little, who need so much . . .

I am alone. And I want to die.

A rising mistral of hatred stirs in the gorge where my fond memories once dwelt, fanning the winking embers of my will to live, blowing them to a spiraling flame of fury. The words come, bidden by hatred.

Do you want to kill your mother?

Yes, I want to kill my mother.

Do you want to kill your father?

Yes, I want to kill my father.

Do you want to kill the men who did this?

Yes, I want to kill the men who did this. All of them.

Though hatred scalds my veins, I cannot kill those responsible. I am too weak. Too small. My father, my mother. Even the men sleeping around the fire would suffer little at my hand. But there is one thing that I could kill that would hurt them all very, very much. . . .

My limbs quiver uncontrollably as I attempt to sit up. I imagine my eyes blackening, my belly swelling, my nails cracking as I wriggle inch by excruciating inch toward the lip of the cart. My lost hair sticks to my hands as I push myself along the wooden slats. Although I shiver, I feel no chill on my naked skin. Only the feverish embrace of ill intent.

I roll over the lip and hit the soggy ground. Stunned, I lie there, and my eyes open greedily for the slightest noise from the camp. I hear nothing but the labored breathing of evil men. My thighs quiver with agony as I draw my legs under me. I raise my head to scan the fireside. By the remains of the victory feast, a knife lies slick with spit and fat. Shaking, I stand. Stones and twigs gouge my tender soles as I stumble around the braggarts, liars, and rapists. Those devils who swear to angels. With my good hand, I close my fingers around the wooden handle of the knife.

To think they feared things of the wood.

Gripping the knife, I hobble toward the object of my revenge. The creature, pitifully bound in the odd harness, winks at me drowsily. She—for I have determined it is a she—raises her sloping snout as far as she can to salute my staggering approach. As I raise the knife above my head for the strike at her exposed neck, I am overcome with pity for her, and my arm falls to my side. How can I hurt something as innocent and vulnerable as I once was? How can I take away the life that spoke so clearly to my own? I cannot, I realize, and the knife hangs feebly in my weak fingers.

Then the creature bows its head, turning it to further expose its graceful neck. Those deadly and brutish pulses that throb beneath that waxy pelt . . . It offers those pulses to me with such unspeakable dignity that I begin to weep. They say that weeping keeps away the Devil, but I place my hand on the warm pelt and watch the wan lips tremble once again. She knows she will die, one way or the other. The blood in my knife hand—in my entire body—again boldly throbs in desperate response to those brutish pulses. *No one is served by love. No one—*

I mercilessly thrust the blade into the creature's neck with all my hatred. All my despair. All the worthless joy of a little girl who lives in this nightmare of a world. Everything of any strength that I can imagine, I sink into that fateful strike as the creature lies perfectly still for the sacrifice.

From the wound gushes a wellspring of cloying, blackened gore. The creature twitches in gentle death throes against its harness and ropes. I withdraw the knife, which releases ripe droplets one after another in an inky torrent. Mesmerized by the rhythm of the drops, I hold my fingers under the flow and smear the gore between my thumb and forefingers. Like the starlight from a bare winter sky, the blood scintillates with mystery and unholy power. I ghoulishly press my hands to the wound as I revel in it. The sticky fluid quickly coats my hands in a lather that penetrates my fingertips with raw power. I eagerly touch a viscous fingertip to my tongue to taste the surge of triumph in my mouth. The everlasting tingles against my teeth even as I withdraw my finger.

I breathe faster, more excited.

I cup my hand under the droplets until they pool darkly in my palm. I then gingerly part my frail legs, reach up between, and anoint the raging wounds of my sex with this handful of unholy blood.

Starlight and nightfall. Flaxen strands and chalky steeples. Bells peal through the canopy of the cursed wood as I collapse, crippled by the stretching of my bones until they splinter deafeningly and fold back upon themselves. My limbs in front lengthen, hands hardening into sharp stumps. My fair skin erupts in feral snowy hairs. When I try to scream, my high-pitched voice hollows to a hoarse bellow. Azure tears roll down my pale cheeks, the color leaching from my stinging pupils. An eruption behind my eyes forces them tightly closed as something gashes my forehead from within with blinding force. . . .

The men stir from sleep at the fire. They gasp in outrage and confusion.

I lean back on my haunches, squint my sallow eyes, and howl as I wag my frightful jaw. And before any a one can lift a sword, I plunge at a full gallop between the trees into the arms of this blackest fairy night.

Because there, you—and I do mean *you*—will never catch me again

The Slow Haunting
John R. Little

"You didn't kill me, Timmy."

"Don't call me Timmy. You know that. It's Tim . . . but I *did* kill you."

"It was an accident."

"Why are you here?"

"You know."

"I can't see you. Turn on the light."

"Can't do that. I can't touch anything. My fingers go right through. It's pretty weird."

"Does it hurt?"

"No."

"Why aren't you in heaven?"

"You know."

"I'm turning the light on."

Tim climbed out from under the covers and walked to his bedroom door. He blinked as he snapped the light on. He hadn't been sure where Dennis was. His voice seemed to come from everywhere.

"Here," said Dennis. "Right where I belong."

Tim looked up at the top bunk bed, and sure enough, there he was. He looked the same as he always did, sitting cross-legged in the middle of the mattress, arms back as if supporting himself.

Would that work if he can't touch anything?

Looking at Dennis was like looking in the mirror. Same dirty-blond hair, same round face and blue eyes, same small mole on the right cheek.

Dennis smiled. "You don't seem surprised to see me."

"I never felt you leave."

Dennis floated down to the rug and stood face to face with his identical twin. "We've been together since we were born. Can't change that now."

Tim moved to hug Dennis, but his arms fell through thin air and he jumped back in surprise.

"You look real."

"I am real. To you. But things work differently now."

"How long can you stay?"

"As long as you want me, Timmy."

"It's Tim."

Three months earlier, Timmy's mom had sat on his bed, beside him.

"Timmy? It's time to get up."

She swept the hair out of his eyes and touched his cheek.

"We all miss him, but we have to carry on. Today's the big birthday for you. Moving your age into double digits. It'd be a good time to—"

"He would have been ten too."

"Yes, and we'll always remember him on your birthday. And on Christmas and on summer holidays, when you two would be out throwing your baseball around, and on the first day of school, and on every other day of the year."

"It's my fault."

"Don't ever say that, Timmy. We know it was an accident. You were both curious about the gun. We should never have had it in the house."

Her eyes watered, but she kept her voice firm, not wanting to cry again in front of him. "If it's anybody's fault, it's mine. I should have told your father to take the gun with him when he left."

Silence covered the room like a blanket of snow. She heard the tick-tock of the Spider-Man wall clock and the swoosh of a car as it drove through the wet streets outside.

"Timmy?"

"I think I should be called Tim now."

"Okay."

"We stopped calling him Denny last year. I should have done the same. Timmy is for little kids."

She saw a forced smile on his face and stood back so he could climb out of bed. The frame creaked. The noise had never bothered her before, but without the constant chatter between the two boys, every sound seemed out of place.

Tim didn't play any baseball that summer or any of the summers following. Eleven years old . . . twelve . . . thirteen . . . Somehow it wouldn't be the same. The twins had played ball together since they got their first T-ball set when they were five. They graduated to Coach Pitch at seven and spent most of their waking time in summers playing.

But now Dennis wasn't there to catch Tim's pitches, and Tim couldn't be Dennis's fielder when he hit fungos in the park.

Their fifteenth birthday was on March 15.

"Beware the Ides of March, Timmy," whispered Dennis just before daylight.

"You say that every year."

Dennis didn't answer for a few moments. Tim yawned and rubbed his eyes, waiting for a bit of sunlight to start the day.

"Let's play some baseball this year."

"You can't play."

"Sure I can. I'll have just as much fun as you will."

Dennis had aged along with Tim. They were still mirror images.

That Saturday in late May, Tim picked up his glove, went to the ball field, and joined a pickup game. He played second base, and standing right beside him was Dennis, as he always was. Dennis wore his own glove and smacked his fist into it as they both set their stance for the batter.

Tim never talked out loud to Dennis when anybody was around, but he could still talk to him in his mind. Maybe that's where Dennis talked too. Tim never really understood how it all worked that he could hear Dennis, but nobody else could see or hear him.

In the third inning, the batter smacked a grounder up the middle. It was bouncing between Tim and Dennis, and both of them moved to the middle to try to get the ball. It went right through Dennis's mitt and into Tim's. Things like that still surprised him, and he dropped the ball.

"Darn."

"Don't worry," Dennis said. "You still stopped it from going to the outfield."

At the end of the game Tim asked Dennis, without moving his mouth, "How'd you get the glove?"

His twin shrugged. "I get whatever I need. That's just the way it works."

They walked side by side down the street toward home. They ducked into a 7-Eleven, and Tim bought a Coke. He knew Dennis would find a way to have one in his hand when he next looked.

The sun was hot, but Tim didn't feel like rushing home. Burbank might have hot weather, but it was nothing like the heat in their apartment. Mom always promised to find a bigger place with air conditioning, but it never worked out. She worked in a nearby bookstore, but money was always tight since Dad left.

The boys walked through Valley Park and found a cool spot sitting at the base of a shade tree. They drank their Cokes and watched people walk by.

"You ever wish things were different?" asked Tim.

Dennis had never hesitated in answering Tim, so he was surprised that he didn't hear the answer rumble around his head.

"Dennis?"

"Oh, well, sure. I wish I was still alive. Who wouldn't?"

"It was an accident."

Again Dennis didn't reply. He just finished his Coke and then tossed the empty can into the air. It disappeared.

"You know that, right?"

"Yeah, Timmy. I know what happened."

"It's Tim."

"You need to ask Lisa out."

"What?"

"She's just waiting for you to ask. I listened to her talk to that new girl the other day. You know, the fat thing. Lisa told her you're cute."

"What?"

"Just trust me. Lisa's hot. Ask her to a movie or something. We'll all like that."

Tim didn't know what to say. *Lisa?* Did Dennis really hear her say something?

But then, why not? A bunch of other kids were dating. He picked up his glove and smacked it.

"We should get home. Mom's making macaroni casserole."

"Again."

"Again."

The next day, Tim saw Lisa at the water fountain outside homeroom. She was wearing a light blue skirt that showed her long legs. To avoid staring at them, he wondered what it would be like to touch her dark, curly hair.

"Go on."

Tim moved a step closer but froze when Lisa finished her drink and looked up at him. When she smiled, it felt like his guts were going to fall out.

"Hi," she said.

"Hi."

"Did you want some water?"

"Jesus, Timmy, just ask her."

"Keep quiet."

He nodded to Lisa. "Hot day." He started to turn the water on, and when he was looking down, he asked, "Would you like to go to a movie sometime? Or something?"

A million years passed in silence. The water ran down the drain while he watched with a parched throat.

"Sure," she said. "That sounds like fun."

Six weeks later, she kissed him. They were holding hands and walking home after the last day of school. She stopped walking, turned to him, and out of the blue leaned to him and kissed him.

"Wow, that was nice," he said when she pulled back.

For once, Dennis kept quiet.

That night, Tim woke in the middle of the night. He'd dreamed of Lisa again, and he had a huge erection. He wasn't surprised. He often woke this way after dreaming of her, and he started to stroke himself, thinking of the day when they would be together. He knew it would happen one day, thought she wanted it as much as he did, but he also knew he was too afraid of screwing things up to try anything.

He thought of feeling her boobs and touching her between her legs, wanting her to touch him as he was doing to himself.

"You should move faster with her."

Tim jumped and pulled his hand back. He pulled the blanket back on top of him that he'd moved aside earlier. "Jesus, you shouldn't be spying on me."

"You know she wants you to."

"Shut up."

"I see it in her eyes."

"What do you know? You died five years ago. You never had a girlfriend. You don't have a clue what it feels like."

Silence filled the room, and Tim felt terrible. He'd never wanted to bring up Dennis's death. His erection wilted away.

"Dennis? I'm sorry. I shouldn't have said that."

Still nothing. Tim climbed out of bed and flipped the light on. The top bunk was empty.

In the years since Dennis was killed, they'd lived together with their secret friendship. The bond between them was stronger than between any other friends Tim knew of, and he would never endanger it.

"Dennis? Come back. Please."

He pulled out the chair from his desk and sat, staring at the bunk beds. After a moment, he noticed the tick-tock of the clock and glanced at it—4:42 a.m.

The gun was supposed to have been locked up in the cabinet near the bathroom, but the whole apartment had been turned upside down. Dad was leaving, and neither Tim nor Dennis knew why. Mom spent all her time in her bedroom crying. She only came out to go to work, and when she arrived back home, she brought fast food for the twins' dinner. For two weeks, they lived on burgers, pizza, tacos, and wings.

Then Mom started to be okay. She never did talk about why Dad left, and he never came to visit them. Tim only saw him the one time, at Dennis's funeral. Even then, they didn't even find a way to say "hi" to each other. Dad sat at the back of the church with a woman Tim didn't recognize.

The cabinet wasn't locked.

It must have been due to the rush of Dad moving out. He'd been grabbing things all over the place, throwing them inside two ratty suitcases, glaring at the boys, and yelling at Mom, who yelled right back.

The twins mostly tried to sit on the couch, holding hands, hoping the fight would just end.

Dad yelled one more time at Mom, and then he stormed out and slammed the door. After crying for an hour, Mom washed her face and left too. Tim knew she was going to the bar down the street. He hoped Dad would be there, too, but that seemed like a slim possibility.

"What a mess."

"Yeah."

There were clothes scattered through the apartment, some Dad's, some Mom's, and even some of the boys'. They picked up their own clothes and took them to their room. There was broken glass in the kitchen, and papers covered much of the hall floor.

"I think they're bills or something," said Dennis.

"Hey, look."

The cabinet door was ajar. Through the glass window, they could see the gun.

"Wow. I'll get it," Dennis said as he swung the door open and grabbed the gun.

"Let me have it. I saw it first!"

"No, I've got to—"

"Damnit, Dennis, you can't have everything and—"

Tim pulled his mind back from that awful day and focused again on the top bunk.

For the first time in his life, he felt alone. The invisible elastic band that always connected him to Dennis had snapped, and he was adrift, as if sailing off on a lifeboat by himself.

He opened the top drawer of his desk and pulled out his scrapbook. Inside were photos of him and Dennis, several from the last year before the accident. He touched Dennis's pictures and tried to smile, but nothing felt right.

Tears fell down his cheeks. He blew his nose and wiped his face before flicking the light back off and heading back under the covers. All thoughts of Lisa were gone. He just replayed memories of Dennis and himself in his mind for about thirty minutes. Finally he drifted off to sleep.

"Hey, sleepyhead. Time to wake up."

"Dennis?"

"Who else?"

"You're back!"

"I couldn't stay away. I missed you."

Tim stood beside the bed and stared up at Dennis. "It's Saturday. Wanna hit a movie this aft?"

"Sure."

Tim got dressed and they went down for breakfast. As always, Dennis paced around the kitchen and living room, waiting for Tim to eat his cereal. Mom read the newspaper and drank a black coffee.

"You should try a coffee sometime," called Dennis. "We're getting old enough."

Tim shrugged and answered silently, "Doesn't smell very good."

"Lisa'll like you better. Make you look grown up."

He finished off the Rice Krispies and rinsed his bowl in the sink.

"She wants you to grow up faster. Wants you to fuck her."

"What did you say?"

"Tim?" Mom looked over at him. "I didn't say anything."

"No, it's okay. Sorry, Mom. I was just . . ."

"Talking to Dennis again? I thought you'd stopped that."

Dennis started laughing.

"Do you ever feel that he's still here?" asked Tim.

Mom put her paper down. Dennis stared at her and then back to Tim.

"I feel him every day. I'll always have him."

"Bullshit," Dennis said. "She's got nothing."

"Yeah," said Tim. "It just feels like he's right beside us sometimes." He looked over at Dennis, who now was wearing his spring jacket.

"Oh, aren't you the funny one."

"We'll never forget him." Mom picked up her paper again.

Tim grabbed a lacrosse ball and his baseball glove and walked over to the schoolyard. The back of the school was solid, no windows, and he tossed the ball at the wall. It bounced back just as hard as he threw it, and it smacked hard into his mitt.

For thirty minutes, Tim threw the ball over and over. Dennis dodged in front of him, trying to block Tim's view. The normal game they played.

"I meant it," Dennis said. "She wants to fuck you."

"Don't say that. She's nice. She wouldn't talk like that."

"Sez you. Just go for it. She's waiting for you to find a way."

The next day, Tim met Lisa in the afternoon and suggested they go for a walk through the woods in the park. Almost nobody ever did that, because there weren't any normal walking paths. You had to pick your way among thick trees.

As they moved into the forested area, Tim clenched his mouth and took hold of Lisa's hand. She didn't shake him off, just smiled.

"That's nice," she said.

"See," said Dennis. "Told ya."

They found a clearing in the middle of the woods, sat down, and talked about school. They laughed, and Dennis just watched. At one point he rolled his hand in a circle. *Get a move on.*

During a lull in the talk, Tim leaned over and kissed Lisa. They kissed for a long time, and Tim felt unbelievable. Lisa placed her hands behind his head, and he tried to copy her.

Go for it.

She was driving him crazy, and that gave him courage. He moved his hand under the front of her T-shirt and lifted up to cup her breast. He couldn't believe he had the nerve to do it.

"Hey!" Lisa slapped his arm away. "What do you think you're doing?"

"I—I thought . . ."

"I'm not that kind of girl. Besides, we're only fifteen, for God's sake. I thought you liked me."

"I do. I *really* like you."

She stood up and crossed her arms. "I'm going home."

"I'm sorry."

"You can come with me if you want or you can stay, but I'm going."

He rushed to keep up with her as they headed back out through the trees to the street.

"Lisa, I'm really sorry. I was just being stupid."

She slowed her walk a bit and looked at him. "C'mon, let's get home."

Dennis laughed on the way out of the woods and all the way home.

Later, Tim asked him, "Why'd you lie to me?"

"Just trying to help. I thought she wanted it."

"You said you *knew.*"

"Yeah, well. I was wrong. But at least you got to feel her boob."

Lisa and Tim were eighteen when they made love for the first time. It happened in the back of Tim's ten-year-old, secondhand Taurus, and this time it was Lisa who engineered things.

Dennis sat in the front seat and didn't make a sound.

They were twenty-one when they got married. Dennis was Tim's unofficial best man, standing right there along with the rest of the wedding party. He wore a matching tuxedo.

Lisa's parents were happy to splurge for a huge ceremony. "As long as you understand we won't pay for another one," her father whispered to her that morning. "So make this work."

Tim's dad wasn't invited.

Lisa's father walked her down the aisle. She was the most beautiful bride in the world, and even after all these years, Tim couldn't believe how lucky he was to be with her.

Every day is devoted to you, my love. He would never tell Dennis, but for the first time ever, Dennis was not the closest person to him and never would be again.

Tim's voice cracked when he said, "I do." His hand shook as he slipped the ring onto her finger, not caring one whit that he'd be paying for the diamond for the next three years. She was worth every penny.

Through their courtship, they'd talked about everything to do with their future. Career aspirations, kids, houses, even what they wanted to do when they retired, though that was an unimaginable time in the distant future. She wanted to be *sure* he was the right man for her.

Their entire lives were mapped away in her mind, and he loved her all the more for it.

Dennis helped answer all Lisa's questions, which was fine with Tim. After all, they were one, and what mattered to Dennis mattered to Tim. Sometimes he just figured it out faster.

The newlyweds wanted three children, spaced over eight years. Not too close together, not too far apart. They planned to conceive their first child a year after their marriage.

Sixteen months passed.

"Tim? Look!"

She held the little plastic stick up to his face. "Positive!"

"Hey!"

He picked her up and twirled her around their apartment. When he put her back down, he stared at the test. "You're sure?"

"Well, these things are never a hundred percent, but I'm as sure as I can be."

"Get her a glass of wine to celebrate," called Dennis. "Piss her up!"

Tim ignored him. "We need to get you to the doctor to double check."

They kissed. The elastic bond between Tim and Dennis was definitely weakening as the bond grew stronger with his own family.

Seven months later, Lisa delivered a perfect set of identical twin girls. They named them Patricia and Denise.

Patricia was Lisa's mother's name. Tim said he wanted to name their other daughter Denise, to honor his long-dead brother. Lisa thought that odd, but she liked the sound of the name.

"Denise is the pretty one," said Dennis. "Of course."

Tim laughed. "Just like I'm the more handsome of us."

Dennis spoke more somberly, "I feel like I'm their father as much as you."

Tim just nodded and smiled. *Not a fucking chance,* he thought.

Having his brother's ghost around was second nature, and he could always carry on separate conversations with him and with Lisa whenever he needed to. Some things, though, were better left unsaid.

Lisa never suspected he was talking to a dead man.

Tim couldn't have imagined how his life would change after the girls were born. They became his first thought every morning and his last thought at night. He held them in his arms every evening, waiting for them to fall asleep. And when they learned to smile, he knew he was totally sunk. His whole life was devoted to the girls.

Lisa didn't mind. She never felt ignored or neglected, and she appreciated all the time Tim spent taking care of them. It gave her a chance to escape after being with them all day while Tim was at work.

Even Dennis didn't mind. He seemed to love the girls just as much as Tim.

"I wish I could hold them," he said one night.

Lisa was out picking up a couple of groceries, so Tim talked out loud. "We're awfully lucky. Everyone says so."

Dennis reached his hand to Denise and pretended to pat her hair. Tim thought he felt more involved in the family when he acted out like this.

"Just don't leave any guns around," Dennis whispered.

Tim didn't answer. He was shocked that Dennis would even bring up such a possibility.

They heard Lisa's car door slam, and the ghost pulled his hand back, as if he'd been caught doing something he shouldn't.

Tim automatically switched to talking to Dennis in his mind. "I wish she'd met you when you were alive."

"Well, she kinda did, since we're identical, right down to the last cell."

"We only look the same. We don't think the same at all."

Dennis shrugged and floated to the other side of the room, knowing Lisa would rush in and sit down where he'd been sitting.

"No, we don't," he said after a moment.

By the time the girls hit their ninth birthday, Lisa's long-term plan for their lives was scattered to the winds. They never conceived another child and probably never would. Neither of them wanted to go to the doctor to see whose plumbing was at fault. They were happy with Denise and Patricia.

The bigger house she had hoped for didn't work out either. Living in Burbank wasn't cheap, and they'd only been able to afford to rent a basement apartment. Both of them worked full time, she in the local Starbucks, and he at an auto body shop. They weren't rich, and sometimes he wondered about the endgame of Lisa's plan: retirement. He'd already passed his thirty-first birthday, and he could see tiny tufts of gray hair on the back of Dennis's head. He refused to look that closely in the mirror, but he knew what he'd see.

"Hard to believe it's their birthday again," said Dennis. He'd been missing for the past half hour, which had worried Tim.

"Where've you been?"

"Just reminiscing."

"What do you mean?"

"Sometimes, I just get sad." He walked to the window and looked outside. "Do you ever think about that day?"

Tim moved to stand beside him. The girls were in their room, napping, and Lisa was out picking up party supplies. It was still a few hours until the guests arrived.

"Sure. I still think of it all the time."

"We were nine. Just like Denise."

"And Patricia. Why do you always leave her out?"

"You shouldn't have tried to grab the gun."

Tim took a long breath and watched a car roll down the street.

"It was an accident."

Dennis said, "It's hot. I'm going to open the window."

And he did.

Tim took a step backward. *What the fuck?*

His first thought was that he'd just had some kind of daydream—imagined what he'd seen. But, no. He replayed it in his mind. Dennis had leaned down and turned the rusty lever at the top of the window, lifting the screen and pushing the window open.

"You can't do that."

"Apparently I can."

"What the fuck's going on, Dennis? How long have you been able to do that?"

Dennis stared at him. "Since you fucking well killed me." He took a step toward Tim, who stumbled back and found himself in his easy chair.

"You can touch things. Why wouldn't you tell me?"

"Let me show you something," Dennis said. He moved to Tim and grabbed his left arm.

"Jesus, what are you doing?"

Dennis's fingernails were sharp. He scratched deep into Tim's arm, leaving three bright scars.

Tim stared, speechless.

"You *killed* me."

"It was a fucking accident, and you goddamn well know it."

"I remember the pain. I didn't die right away. Remember that? You shot me in the gut."

Dennis lifted his T-shirt and rubbed his stomach and chest.

"You burst my left lung, and fragments of the bullet bounced around everywhere. My heart started to leak, and I couldn't get enough breath. I guess Mom never bothered you with all the gruesome details."

Tim couldn't say anything.

"You don't remember? I suppose you don't remember me drowning in my own blood, spitting up painful red vomit and looking at you for help. And I'm sure you don't remember how you just froze, didn't move a muscle to help, didn't call nine-one-one, didn't do a godammned thing."

"I was only a little kid."

"A little murderer, you mean."

"You always told me you couldn't touch things."

"I lied."

"What's going on? Why are you doing this?"

"Because it's Denise's ninth birthday. She's lived as long as I did, and that's long enough."

Tim stood up. "You touch her and I'll—"

Dennis laughed. "What? You'll kill me?"

"It's time for you to go."

"Actually, on that, I agree. I've just been waiting for today. Waiting a long time. I've already killed her. That's where I was earlier."

"You shit. I don't believe you."

Tim pushed past Dennis to go toward the kids' room, but Dennis grabbed him. He had more strength than seemed possible, and he used it to throw Tim down into his chair.

"And I called the police to confess. They should be here any minute."

"They wouldn't be able to hear you . . ."

"Sure, they heard me. Probably recorded me. And my voice is identical to yours."

"Let me get to her."

Again he stood, and again Dennis threw him down, rougher this time.

In the distance, Tim heard a siren, and in his heart he knew that Dennis was telling the truth, that Denise was dead.

"How did you . . . ?"

"I strangled her. She was sleeping and I used every ounce of my strength to squeeze the life out of her. She tried to fight, but there wasn't much she could do. She didn't understand why her daddy was doing that."

Tears rolled down Tim's face.

"They'll find my DNA on the skin beneath her fingernails. Defensive wounds. Just for good measure I spat in her face."

Tim closed his eyes and lowered his face into his hands.

"Of course, the DNA they find will match yours. We're identical twins, after all. Even our scratches match."

Dennis rolled up his sleeve to show identical scars to those he'd given Tim.

The sirens screamed as two patrol cars pulled up in front of the house.

"Open up!"

"Not yet, brother." Dennis kept Tim a prisoner in his seat.

After a moment, the police broke down the door and found Tim alone in his living room, staring with guilt into his hands.

Food of the Gods

Simon R. Green

We are what we eat. No. Wait. That's not quite right.

I wake up, and I don't know where I am. Red room, red room, dark shadows all around and a single bare red bulb, swinging back and forth, coating the room with bloody light. I'm sitting on the floor with my back pressed against the wall, and I can't seem to remember how I got here. And set on the floor before me, like a gift or an offering, on a plain white china plate, is a severed human head.

I'm sure I know the face, but I can't put a name to it.

I can't think clearly. Something's wrong. Something has happened, something important, but I can't think what. And the severed head stares at me accusingly, as though this is all my fault. I can't seem to look away from the head, but there isn't much else to look at. Bare walls, bare floor boards, a single closed door just to my left. And the blood-red light rising and falling as the bulb swings slowly back and forth. I don't want to be here. This is a bad place. How did I end up in a place like this?

The name's James Eddow. Reporter. Investigative reporter, for one of the dailies. Feeding the public appetite for all the things it's not supposed to know. I went looking for a story—and I think I found one. Yes, I remember. There were rumors of a man who ate only the finest food, prepared in the finest ways. A man who wouldn't lower himself to eat the kinds of things other people eat. The Epicure. He lived in the shadows, avoiding all publicity, but everyone who mattered had heard of him, and it was said . . . that if you could find him, and if you could convince him you were worthy, he would make you the greatest meal of your life. Food to die for.

It had been a long time since I'd handed in a really good story. My editor was getting impatient. I needed something new, something now, something really tasty. So I went looking for the Epicure.

I went walking through the night side of the city, buying drinks for familiar faces in bars and clubs and members-only establishments, talking casually with people in the know, dropping a little folding money here and there, and finally found myself a native guide. Mister Fetch. There's always someone like him, in every scene. The facilitator, always happy to put like-minded souls together, at entirely reasonable rates. He can lay his hands on anything, or knows someone who can, and he knew the Epicure, oh yes, though he gave me the strangest look when I said I just had to meet him. Actually had the nerve to turn up his nose and tell me to run along home. That I didn't know what I was getting into. But money talks, in a loud and persuasive voice, and Mister Fetch put aside his scruples, just for me.

Why can't I move? I don't feel drugged, or paralyzed. But I just sit here with my hands folded neatly in my lap while the face on the severed head stares sadly back at me. I know that face. I'm sure I do. Why am I not shocked, or horrified? Why can't I look away? I know that face. The name's on the tip of my tongue.

Mister Fetch took me to a faded hole-in-the-wall restaurant in the shabbier end of the city. No one looked at us as we marched through the dining area. The diners concentrated on their meals while the waiters stared into space. A door at the back led through into an entirely ordinary kitchen, and there, sitting at an empty table, was the Epicure. Not much to look at. Average size, average face. Fever-bright eyes. His presence seemed to fill the whole kitchen. He smiled at me and gestured for me to sit down opposite him. Mister Fetch couldn't wait to get his money and depart at speed. He wouldn't even look at the

Epicure.

The great man looked me over, nodded slowly, and immediately identified me as a journalist. I just nodded. This wasn't the kind of man you could lie to. He laughed, briefly, and then started talking before I'd even got my tape recorder set up. As though he'd been waiting for someone he could tell his story to. Someone who'd appreciate it.

"I can smell the hunger on you," he said in his soft, rich voice.

"Tell me," I said. "Tell me everything."

"I eat only the finest food," said the Epicure, "made from the finest ingredients. The food of the gods. I have a meal waiting, already prepared. Would you care to join me?"

"Of course," I said. "I'd be honored."

It was excellent. Delicious. Good beyond words. I asked him what was in it, and he smiled a slow, satisfied smile.

"The last journalist who came looking for me."

I was too angry, too disappointed, to be shocked. I laughed right in his face.

"That's it? That's your great secret? You claim you're a cannibal?"

"Oh no," he said. "There's far more to it than that."

Still sitting in the red room. Still staring at the neatly severed head. There's a sense of threat in the room now, a feeling of menace and imminent danger. I've got to get out of here before something bad happens. But still I don't move, or rather, it's more that somehow I don't want to move. Something bad, something really bad, has already happened. Have I . . . done something bad?

Memories surge through me, jumbled, flaring up in bright splashes of good times and bad—a rushing kaleidoscope of my past, my life.

I remember being young, and small, and rolling down endless grassy slopes, with the smell of grass and earth and trees almost unbearably rich in my head. The sun was so bright, the air so warm on my bare arms and legs, comforting as my mother's arms. I remember walking along a sandy beach with Emily's arm thrust possessively through mine, both of us smiling and laughing and telling each other things we'd never told anyone before. To be young and in love, happiness building and building inside me till I thought I'd explode through sheer joy. And then . . .

I remembered Emily walking away from me, her shoulders hunched against the cold night air, and the pleas I was yelling after her. I'd tried to talk to her, but she wouldn't listen, her reasons just excuses to justify a decision she'd already made. I remembered standing at my parents' grave after the car accident, feeling a cold empty numbness that was worse than tears.

And the worst memory of all: realizing long before my editor told me that I just wasn't good enough to be the kind of reporter I wanted to be.

Memories, memories, good and bad and everything in between, things I hadn't let myself think of in years, rushing by me faster and faster, sharp and vivid and yet somehow strangely distant.

The Epicure continued eating as he lectured me on traditional cannibal beliefs. How certain ancient peoples believed that eating a brave man's heart would give you courage, or eating a big man's muscles would make you strong. How recent medical science had both proved and extended these beliefs. Take a planarian worm and teach it to run a maze. Then chop up the worm and feed it to other planarian worms. And they will run the maze perfectly, even though they've never seen it before. Meat is memory. Eat a man's mind, and you can gain access to all his most precious memories. For a while.

He laughed then, as the drug he'd put in my food finally took effect, and I lost consciousness.

I finally recognize the face on the severed head. Of course I know that face. It's mine. Because I'm not who I think I am. I'm somebody else, remembering me. The Epicure doesn't care about the meat; he eats minds so he can savour the memories. All my most precious moments, all my triumphs and despairs, all the things that have made me who I am . . . reduced to a meal, to satisfying another man's appetite. I want to cry about what I've lost, at what has been taken from me, but they aren't my eyes. Already my memories are fading, my thoughts are fading, as he comes rising up inside me like a great shark in some bloody sea, eating up what's left of me so he can be himself again.

There's a rich, happy, satisfied smile on my lips.

You are who you eat. But not for long.

Do Sunflowers Have a Fragrance?

Del James

When the doorbell rang, Chloe's pulse immediately accelerated into a higher gear. The thumping in her chest reverberated up to her ears. A light surge of sweat seeped out from her pores.

Her posture turning rigid, she sensed she might be overreacting, but after everything she'd been through, defensiveness shaped her outlook. It wasn't who she wanted to be. In fact the exact opposite held true, but in order to regain control of her life she needed to make certain changes. For starters, she couldn't be so anxious and jumpy every time someone knocked on the door.

Buzz. Buzz.

This wouldn't be the first time Dieter showed up unannounced. No matter how many times she asked him not to "just stop by," her requests fell upon deaf ears. Even after changing the locks, nothing she said or did mattered. Threats of a restraining order brought laughter. *He laughed at her.* Condescending, empowered laughter that bellowed with entitlement. Laughter worse than any of the cruel words he hurled at her.

Really now, what could she do to stop him from doing whatever the hell he damn well pleased?

Didn't she understand that he loved her?

He *loved* her.

Dieter seemed hell bent on making sure Chloe knew he was still in love with her. Over and over and over. So many times, in fact, that he often filled up the voice mail on her cell phone. Deleting them only freed up more space for his next tirade.

When Dieter wanted to induce sympathy by trying to make her feel guilty for no longer wanting him, he uttered in soft tones. Sometimes he used a jovial timbre, hoping to break her down with playful humor and not-so-subtle innuendo. If he got frustrated, he unleashed unmistakable harshness and then later called back to apologize for losing his cool. Chloe knew all these voices. She heard them in her sleep.

A voice from the past.

Dieter presented an explanation for everything, a visionary plan to make things better between them. Answers for their endless array of problems. He tried and tried and tried to scramble together oral pieces of an emotional puzzle in hopes that something came together. What he failed to acknowledge was that Chloe didn't care to hear his perspective anymore. Rust corroded the solution like cancer upon her soul.

Looking out through a window with steel security bars protecting her from burglars, she saw thousands of tiny lights illuminating the city. Even more magnificent, the soft moonlight beaming down reminded her that a world of possibility existed beyond Dieter's reach. Then something flew past the living room window. A crow, a bat, it didn't matter. That movement snapped her out of the momentary trance.

Someone was at her door.

It could be anyone. Wasn't very late, just after sundown. *Maybe a friend dropped by? Maybe it was someone she actually wanted to see?* She made friends easily and constantly received invitations to go out. Maybe the person ringing her bell could take her thoughts off Dieter? That would be a great way of spending the evening.

Chloe wasn't much for makeup. She didn't need it. Face angular, cheekbones pronounced, her alabaster tone was something other women strived for. Without giving it any thought, she shaped her silky raven mane with long fingernails. The dull points glided through as well as any expensive brush.

As she cautiously approached the door, each step became a minor victory. She was not afraid. Well, not so afraid that she felt paralyzed. Apprehensive, yes. The unease filling her stomach signaled a warning she knew not to ignore. Tension infiltrated tight muscles. Without realizing it, she balled her fingers into fists.

"Who is it?"

"Delivery . . . flowers."

Sent by a man who wouldn't take no for an answer.

"Just leave them by the door."

"You have to sign for them."

Her breathing went from reflexive to strained as she slowly opened the door. This was yet another thing Dieter forced her to do against her will. Chloe didn't want to open the door. She didn't want to sign for anything. Didn't want the fucking flowers, but here they were inside her apartment, invading her personal space.

Did sunflowers have a scent? People had debated this point for many years without ever reaching a definitive conclusion. Of course they had some sort of plant smell, but was that a true flower fragrance? And if they didn't have a scent, then how ironic was it that one of the brightest of all flowers could be so bland?

The phone rang.

Ring.

Ring.

Ring.

Ring.

Ring.

No need to answer. She knew who was calling.

"Hi, this is Chloe and I can't answer the phone right now. Please leave a message after the tone."

Beeeep.

"Hey hi, this is Dieter. I was just thinking about you. About us. Uh, I called your cell phone but you didn't pick up. . . . Um, uh, I hope you like the flowers. . . . You know what today is, right? Today is the anniversary of that time we drank together up in the mountains, and even though sunflowers really aren't regional to the mountains, I know they're your favorites. Anyway, gimme a call when you get a chance. I look forward to hearing your voice."

The apartment fell silent, but Dieter's presence loomed like lecherous eyes peering in through her window. No matter how politely she asked, no matter how firmly she insisted, no matter how much distance she put between them, he never stopped his relentless pursuit. Regardless of where she went or who she was with, Chloe always felt the need to look over her shoulder. It didn't matter how much time had passed since they'd split up; Dieter could not comprehend that she was no longer interested.

Barring a leap year, if there were 365 days per year, and since he dialed at least eight times a night, he averaged over 2,900 phone messages. Probably typed in as many texts. When she thought about it—and well, when didn't she—the math was astonishing. The invading volume of his overwhelming obsession probably would have crushed a weaker woman into submission.

No amount of imported vodka or painkillers made the tension disappear. Sometimes she felt close to free, but those moments proved fleeting. Chloe knew better than to get too caught up in her own escape because Dieter would eventually show up and ruin the moment. In one form or another, he always appeared.

Just like tonight.

Eyes alight with contempt, she stared at the bouquet resting on the counter. Coming from anyone else, flowers would have been a sweet gesture, but Chloe understood that he wanted her to let down her guard so that he could pounce. Any gesture of appreciation or gratitude inevitably got used against her.

Examining the yellow heads with spiraling disc florets that mature into seeds, she saw that each sunflower was actually many flowers sitting on a common receptacle. Each one was a completely separate flower with a separate reproductive system. Growers could yield thousands of flowers and thousands of seeds from one crop of these big-headed sunflowers.

Who could have imagined that something as pretty as flowers would be used as a weapon? Harmless, innocuous sunflowers. But there was never anything innocent about Dieter's intentions. Everything he said or did served a purpose.

Trapped in the definition, following the brush stokes from retinas to reality, stood the motive. In the center of the yellow visitors, a plastic stick held a small card. Did she really think he was going to send flowers without a card?

Might as well get it over with. That became her approach to most things involving Dieter. Answering the phone, replying to an e-mail or instant message. She could only avoid and avoid and avoid for so long—weeks and months—but eventually he wore her down to the point where she felt compelled to reply. To ask him to go away again. To tell him she did not want him calling or harassing her or "accidentally" showing up at the same restaurants she frequented. She did not need his help with anything, and no, she didn't miss his face.

Chloe opened the tiny envelope.

No one will ever love you the way I do.

Ring.

Ring.

Ring.

Ring.

Ring.

The answering machine made its outgoing announcement and then beeped.

"Hey babe, it's me again. I just called the florist and they said they delivered the sunflowers. I hope you like them. Uh, um, what are you doing later? Are you hungry? How would you feel about letting me take you to your favorite restaurant? Or any restaurant that serves food and drinks. I could really use a glass of wine and some conversation. Or if you're not hungry now, how about tomorrow? I know you love eggs Benedict, and there's this quaint little place that's open all night and they make the absolute best eggs Benedict around, and you're the best so the best should only have the best and uh . . . I hope you liked the flowers. Call me, okay?"

Her focus shifted from the answering machine back to the bouquet.

As she absorbed every intricate detail, the sunflowers seemed to be mocking her. After stepping closer, she removed one of the flowers from the vase. Healthy, damp, and recently cut, the center felt sticky. Her slender thumb and forefinger grabbing the soft yellow head, she snapped it off in a botanic decapitation.

Ring.

Ring.

Ring.

Ring.

Ring. "Hi, this is Chloe and I can't answer the phone right now. Please leave a message after the tone."

Beeeep.

"Okay Chloe look, I'm about to give up for the evening but not quite yet because I am going to do everything in my power to win you over and be your lover and have the relationship I know that you can only have with me and I can only have with you. Believe me, in light of everything, I am more nervous about seeing you than you could ever be, but I miss your touch, your labored breathing, and falling asleep next to you. I yearn to feel your lips pressed against mine. Mostly, I would love to feel some of that resistance escape your beautiful body with that first much-needed nibble. I would love to see you, and while I don't mean only tonight, we can take it one day at a time if you want. You are the only one I have ever truly wanted to be with or give myself to so completely. What do you want, blood? Let me prove to you how much I can do to make you happy and make you fall back in love with me."

"Please, Dieter, just shut the fuck up."

But he didn't. There was room to leave more of a message.

"I don't know what I did to kill the passion or desire in you. You turn your back on me in part because I tell you that you are the one, my one true love, and that I want to be with—"

The machine cut him off. That didn't matter. He kept her number on speed dial.

Ring.

Ring.

Ring.

Ring.

Ring. "Hi, this is Chloe and I can't answer the phone right now. Please leave a message after the tone."

Beeeep.

"Hey, it's me again. Your machine cut me off, but don't worry, this is the last time I'll be calling tonight. I used to think being with you was my future, but being in love with you and wanting to be with you is an exercise in futility. I really won't bother you anymore tonight. Enjoy our wine-tasting anniversary and the flowers. I thought it would always be like that, and it truly makes me depressed to think that it may not be . . . I think the worst thing I could have done to try to be with you forever was tell you how much I wanted it and how happy you make me. How much I love you . . . My life must really be meaningless if all I want to do is spend it with you. Enjoy your life and all your beautiful friends and dates. It must be so much more wonderful to be incomplete than it was when I thought we were happy together . . . Um, why don't you want to see me and talk to me and make me feel better? I don't understand you! I would rather talk to you and hear your voice and look in your eyes instead of leaving all these stupid messages, but I suppose you feel so guilty and upset about turning your back on me that now I can't even have that. You won't even pick up your phone to tell me thanks for the flowers!"

"*Damn you and the flowers!*" she screamed, picking up the vase and hurling it as hard as she could. The flowers exploded in a violent burst of noise and color. The wet, white wall resembled a fresh wound, and shards of glass and strewn sunflowers littered the hardwood floor.

A grin formed on her pale face.

Destruction always brought about a sense of liberation. After she slashed a painting, her vibrant green eyes brimmed with joy. Ripping up exquisite garments proved to be yet another thrill. Petty perhaps, but satisfying. He tried suffocating her with his relentless pursuit, so she took revenge on the trinkets he bought for her.

As she stared at the mess on the floor, a mess that she would have to clean up, her thoughts drifted. *How dare he claim to adore her?* Love did not feel like this! Love had nothing in common with the way he made her feel. There was no malaise attached to passion. No dreadful enslavement with amour. His interpretation of what he thought defined love and the actual meaning bound very different books.

Ripping his pages out had never been her intention. A long, long time ago they had shared something special. She could respect those nights and honor their memory if only he would do the same. The past echoed in the past and should stay there. Yesterday offered nothing for tomorrow.

Regaining control over her emotions, Chloe silently acknowledged that this situation was no longer about love. Maybe at one point it had been. Maybe originally it had been an issue of the heart, but that issue had gotten lost in the mania. He didn't truly love her; if he did, he wouldn't behave in such a subjugating manner. *This wasn't love.* This boiled down to getting in the final word. About his ego. About his hubris and not losing. Dieter wasn't some forlorn romantic pining away over his one true love. He embodied a selfish egomaniac who refused to be refused. He had proven to be a relentless manipulator, a bloodsucking negotiator who would haunt her until the end of time.

Chloe couldn't quite pinpoint when this had all begun. Seemed like forever and a day. No matter where she went or what she did to try to lose him, Dieter always lurked, trying to claw his way back into her heart. This had started way before the Internet replaced television and e-mail replaced letter writing. Before the cell phone replaced the rotary phone.

Before the telephone, actually.

Cursed by fate, their destinies had intertwined for as long as she could remember. Not just decades—those were a mere drop in the bucket. Fads and trends occurred during certain decades. What she had enjoyed most about the fifties were the fantastic American cars, while the sixties brought music of revolution. Fads were fun and fleeting, but only after the passing of several centuries could a person really gain perspective.

Change was a necessary part of evolution. Machine tools, neoclassicism, the steam engine, the cotton gin, famine, agriculture, photography, medical advancements, impressionism, gas lighting, perfume, the Great Depression, dental floss, Prohibition, world wars, the splitting of the atom, antibiotics, surrealism, the Civil Rights Movement, space travel, the Cuban missile crisis, women's liberation, Les Paul guitars, oil, biohazards, microwaves, high-heel shoes, the fall of communism, Acquired Immune Deficiency Syndrome, Chernobyl, high-definition TV, Tiananmen Square, Victoria's Secret, laptop computers, the World Trade Center, and the iPhone had all helped shape the course of history. Helped alter the way the world operated. When she wasn't trying to shake Dieter, Chloe had witnessed these marvels and countless others with her own two eyes.

Seeing the Spanish, Chinese, and Ottoman empires crumble, the dissolving of Holy Roman Empire, and the collapse of the Mughal Empire made the presidencies of Richard Nixon or either Bush seem brief thundershowers of greed and corruption. Litter upon the sands of time. The oppression once ranking women and blacks as inferior to men, a condition that most people today could not fathom, offered hope that maybe one day those same blinds would be removed from society's perspective on homosexuals. The nature of sin and the Puritan conscience that once dominated these shores giving way to a black president and condoms being sold from vending machines in public bathrooms presented genuine change.

Unfortunately, Dieter would never change unless Chloe did something drastic. She had tried and tried and tried to get through to him. She had tried going her own way and giving him his space, but no matter where she traveled, he followed. It didn't matter if she hid in Berlin, Helsinki, Paris, Calcutta, London, or the City of Lost Angels, somehow he eventually located her.

Ring.

Ring.

Ring.

Ring.

Ring. "Hi, this is Chloe and I can't answer the phone right now. Please leave a message after the tone."

"Hey, you know after everything I've done for you, the least you could do is show me a little bit of respect and answer the damn phone when I call. It wouldn't kill you to be considerate of someone other than yourself. I'm just trying to be civil here. I'm reaching out. I've reached out across the world in hopes that you'll take my hand. Please, I never wanted anyone other than you. Never will, but we are back to you saying no to everything I try to do. I miss the girl you used to be. I miss the taste of . . . I miss that look in your eyes. I miss the divine sound of your voice. Baby, please, please, please just talk to me. I'm asking you to talk to me. If not tonight, then soon. I can wait. I will wait forever. Chloe, just talk to me . . . I love you."

A long sigh, not of frustration but inevitability, fluttered through her lips. Then there was silence. Then footsteps.

She tread softly into the kitchen. No matter how long she'd existed in the shadows of civilization, whenever she took residence inside a condominium or an apartment, Chloe always reserved one drawer in the kitchen to store her tools. Measuring tape, vise grips, screws, adjustable wrench.

Searching for another implement, her fingers pushed aside a hammer and screwdriver.

Spiking was so customary. Romantic even. The penetration and unification. The spurting of crimson that signifies the end for a vampire. The looking into one another's eyes one last time. There was no way she would allow Dieter's final moment to be something so intimate. After everything she'd endured, spiking came across as too kind an act.

No matter how many centuries had passed since Dieter transformed her from an unsuspecting victim into an immortal, he never gave any consideration to what she might be experiencing. Regardless of how many times she screamed that he could not come in, and no matter how firm she stood in her position of unavailability, he never listened. All her pursuer cared about was wearing her down, winning his quest to have her, and claiming the prize. As far back as she could recall she had tried explaining how she felt, but that didn't matter to an intrusive bastard who refused to listen to reason. And now, thanks to a batch of unwanted sunflowers, Chloe had attained the clarity she so desperately sought.

Her fingertips gently rubbing back and forth against a sharp edge, she wondered how much resistance his soft flesh would offer. If spiking could be viewed as traditional and romantic, then maybe a slow decapitation with a serrated blade might finally drive home the fact that she did not love him. And even if Dieter didn't die with that understanding, at least now he would finally stop calling.

She removed a hacksaw from the drawer.

It was well balanced and lethal, and the metal handle rested comfortably in her grip. Holding on tightly, she felt a reassuring rush of power travel from the deadly implement into her hand and then up into her body. Whether that sensation was real or purely symbolic did not matter. A slight grin formed on her lips as she began preparing for what she was about to do next.

Chloe needed to thank Dieter for the flowers.

The Wandering Unholy

Victor Salva

Stenecker watched the falling snow out the window of his sedan and thought of something his mother had told him long ago when he was a child. "It is the dust of the angels," she had once said, and he could never look at a snowfall without thinking of this. And as his caravan jostled down the shallow ravine that passed for a road, Stenecker dozed off and drifted back to the small house he had grown up in, with the snow on the windowsill and the warmth of the kitchen where his mother was always baking bread. . . .

The sedan hit a sharp crag that jolted him back to reality.

"Forgive me, Herr Field Marshal." His driver stared at him from the rearview mirror. "I think this road was meant for something other than automobiles." Stenecker looked at the boy's face and remembered back when he, too, had looked like Hans: young, handsome, blue-eyed, and vital. The picture of Hitler's ideal soldier.

The sedan rolled to a stop, and Stenecker looked ahead at the large covered truck and its platoon of soldiers. Major Grunwald hopped from the cab and strode through the snow toward him. Stenecker rolled down a window as Grunwald's oddly square head leaned in. Mist blossomed at his lips with each word. "We might be getting close, Herr

Field Marshal."

"We're looking for a cross," Stenecker told him, "a large one. Take two men and make certain the pass is clear."

Grunwald waved two fingers in the air and Gunnery Sergeant Kimmel climbed out the back of the truck with two of the soldiers. "Clear the pass," Grunwald told them. "And remember, the white of the snow makes you easy targets."

Kimmel and his men had rounded two bends of banked snow- and ice-capped trees when one of the soldiers whispered through chattering teeth. "What exactly are we looking for out here, Sergeant?"

"For soldiers who use their eyes and not their mouths," Kimmel snapped back. "Stay quiet!"

A sound to the left of them.

They hit the ground hard, rifles leveled at a bank of snow some yards away. When the sound came again, it was with the strange sight of the snow shifting and churning as if something were under it. Something large and working its way toward the surface.

A hand jutted from the ice, and they almost fired. It clutched at the cold air as if it might scoop up oxygen, and Kimmel and his men bellied toward it. A head emerged then—white and frosted over like the rocks and trees around them.

Kimmel's mouth dropped open at the sight. The eyes looked frozen shut, and as a shoulder broke through the ice, the coat it wore bore stripes. "This man is a German officer!" Kimmel launched to his feet and barreled toward him. And halted abruptly when the frozen man's head dropped back and his eyes popped open. You could hear the sound they made, the lids were so brittle, and the eyeballs themselves had a nightmare aspect, as they had frosted over completely.

Kimmel's throat tightened, and he could barely get out words ". . . What in the name of the Führer?"

And the snow beneath that frozen head erupted with gunfire.

The officer was shooting! Lurching up, waist deep in the snow, his semiautomatic cut down Kimmel's soldiers as the gunnery sergeant flailed back and returned fire. The truck's soldiers spilled out as Kimmel's own rifle obliterated the snowbound officer. But there was more snow moving now, all around him.

To his left, another bank erupted, and two more on the bank opposite, all with frozen hands, fingers splaying in the icy air. Beyond those, the snow exploded again as another soldier erupted from the powdered earth, firing in all directions.

Using the truck as cover, the Nazi ranks fired back and Kimmel spun around, crashing to the snow to find his own cover as the ice soldiers held their position and their guns blazed.

Soldiers at the truck split off and charged down the ravine, ripping off shots as they moved. Anchored in the ice, their element of surprise gone, the snowbound assassins were easy targets, and they finally dropped and buckled under the barrage of return fire.

Kimmel pulled himself to his feet. In the new stillness, neither he nor any other approaching soldier could fathom what had happened. A young soldier met Kimmel's eyes. "Where did they come from?"

But something was already springing out of the snow behind him. The boy's breath was cut short by a terrible slicing sound, and his eyes went wide. Their gaze dropped to the frozen bayonet sticking out of his sternum. His last breath visibly drifted into the air as he slid off the blade to reveal his icy executioner.

Sergeant Kimmel swung his pistol up and picked him off with a single shot to the head. He dropped to the snow with the sound of ringing metal as the fatal shot punctured the soldier's helmet.

Now Field Marshal Stenecker strode toward them from the sedan. His look betrayed nothing as he took silent inventory of the frozen carnage all around them.

"They look like they're blind!" Major Grunwald sputtered. "How could they fire a rifle?"

"Not blind, their eyes are frozen over." Kimmel could barely find his voice.

"This man has an Iron Cross! He was decorated!" Grunwald jabbed a finger at a frozen corpse. "These are all German soldiers—why in the fires of Hell would they be shooting at us?!"

Kimmel called out and they rushed to the frozen soldier with the bayonet. "I took him down with a single shot to the head." He pointed to the hole between the soldier's frosted eyes.

"Not a drop of blood," Grunwald whispered. "These men are iced to the bone. . . ."

"Not just that, Major, look! He's already been shot!" Kimmel became more unglued as he pointed to an iced-over wound in the soldier's neck. "And more than once!" Kimmel brushed snow off an old chest wound that had ripped the soldier's frosty uniform.

"What are you saying?" Stenecker asked calmly.

Then Kimmel saw something across the ravine that paled him even further. He scrambled to the officer who had first clawed out of the ice. The man was still waist deep in a snowbank, and Kimmel reached down and yanked him out by the arm.

The officer was only half a man. He ended just below his frozen waist.

"These men were not only buried in the snow." Kimmel dropped him back into the ice. "They were dead when they attacked us."

The wind whistled as the snow fell and the men surveyed the countryside.

Only Stenecker showed no horror. "Moving forward with eyes sharp, gentlemen," he said at last without emotion. "We have come to the right place."

Greystone Abbey had the aspect of a gigantic stone box carved into the rocky mountainside. A massive granite cross centered the battlements over the mammoth gates, collecting snow as the caravan pulled up and Major Grunwald and Sergeant Kimmel moved out into the bracing cold.

"This is a convent?" Kimmel asked, staring up at the ugly stone cross. "It looks more like a fortress." He reached out to an oversized bell at one of the hefty rusted hinges on the fortress's high walls.

"Do not ring that bell, Sergeant," Stenecker's voice cut through the wind. He stood at the front of his sedan, young Hans at his side. "Do nothing they would expect."

Kimmel lifted a large megaphone he had brought and took a breath, but before a word could be uttered, the ground began to rumble, and so deeply that they could feel it through the soles of their boots.

The great gates to the abbey were parting. Opening to reveal a vast courtyard covered in snow. Grunwald's command brought the platoon off the truck, and they raced past the field marshal and dropped to one knee, aiming at the hulking stone palace the courtyard presented.

The falling snow disguised the abbey's lower dimensions, including a long granite staircase that rose to a high outer balcony: one that was already filling with a strange procession of thick black shawls and strings of heavy rosary beads that rattled and rolled across large oval collars of starched white.

Collecting flakes of snow, each of the assembling wore a tall black headdress as the faces beneath them stared down with a grimness as stony as the granite they stood on. The oldest, a small withered-looking woman of considerable age, took a half step forward as her voice carried across the frozen cobblestones below. "Can we be of service to you?"

Major Grunwald's square jaw tightened as he shouted up at them, "We will ask the questions, Sister. This is, we presume, Greystone Abbey?"

The old woman's hands twitched with palsy as she wrapped her gnarled fingers nervously around her rosary and bowed her head in the affirmative.

"I am Major Hermann Grunwald and this is Sergeant Kimmel." He nodded back to the caravan. "We are twenty in number and we will need rooms for sleep and hot water to bathe. You will also supply food and drink for us."

The old nun's voice quivered and she had to clear her throat. "We can make you as comfortable as we are able, Herr Major, but you might find us lacking in some of the amenities of the modern world."

"Do as the major says," a voice said from behind the assembled sisters. Both nuns and Nazis turned to see a tall woman stepping onto the balcony as the others parted to put her at its center. Even at seventy, her strength and power were evident. "You must forgive Sister Mary Ruth," the woman said, bowing apologetically. "She is young and has yet to learn the ways of the order."

Kimmel and Grunwald stared at Sister Mary Ruth. *Young?* She looked as if she were at Death's door. . . .

"And what order is that, specifically, Sister?" Stenecker's voice cut across the windy plaza.

Grunwald moved aside and said, "May I introduce Field Marshal Stenecker."

The tall woman bowed again. "We are the sisters of St. Ignatius, Herr Stenecker. The order has been here for more than two centuries now."

"And during that time, have you always been in the practice of insulting your masters by looking down on them?" Stenecker's eyes narrowed.

"We meant no disrespect—"

"Come down this instant!" Stenecker's words were clipped and cutting. Led by their imposing mistress, the nuns started a quiet descent down the stone steps. "We stay on the parapet for our own protection, Herr Stenecker—"

"*Field Marshal* Stenecker," he snapped.

She stepped to the courtyard floor and again bowed her head. "I am Sister O'Cyrus. Mother superior of the abbey."

"No," he said sharply, "your title is not recognized by the Führer. Therefore it would be equally insulting to refer to you as 'superior' in any way. You are, in the eyes of the Reich, superior to no one, Sister." He didn't hide his quiet joy in demoting her.

Mother O'Cyrus showed no indignation. There was something behind those eyes, something being masked by that stoic face, but it wasn't anger. And Stenecker did not like it. He did not like that his presence left these old women so seemingly undisturbed. He suddenly turned to all of them and hissed, "Heil Hitler."

He waited a moment, then stabbed his arm into the air. "I said, Heil

Hitler!" The nuns bowed their heads and Stenecker turned to the mother superior. "I will say it once again, and only once. Heil Hitler, Sister . . ."

She stared at him before she lifted her arm. Her words were soft in the whistling snowfall. "Heil Hitler, Field Marshal Stenecker."

"All of you!" Stenecker swung around and grabbed Sister Mary Ruth by her tremulous arm and jerked her forward as he would a disobedient child.

The nuns all raised their arms now, Sister Mary Ruth's shaking with palsy as they gave a somber, joyless salute to the Führer. Stenecker moved back to Mother O'Cyrus and leaned in so close he could smell the dampness of her woolen shawl. "You said you stay on the parapet for your own protection, Sister. Protection from what?"

"You have entered a very dark and strange country, Herr Field Marshal," Mother O'Cyrus replied.

"Have we?"

"Beyond your darkest dreams," she said quietly.

He leaned even closer and studied her with a quiet menace. His words billowed mist into the icy air. "I doubt you could fathom the darkness of my dreams, Sister." He looked back at the massive gates and the mountains beyond them. "And if there is so much to be wary of here, then why, in fact, did you open the gates?"

Mother O'Cyrus looked up slowly as if she were going to answer. But she didn't.

The vast dining hall was flanked by two enormous archways, each sentried by Stenecker's soldiers, guns at the ready, suspiciously eyeing the sisters who worked to clear the long table where the platoon was finishing their meal. The men's voices echoed to the high rafters and found their way down again to the second table, closer to the fireplace, where logs snapped and popped and warmed the field marshal, Kimmel, and Grunwald as they ate.

Hanging high above them was a long blue banner with large Latin words embroidered in gold. *Abyssus abyssum invocat.*

"What does that say, Sister?" Major Grunwald nodded to a small, skeletal sister who was collecting their dishes. The tiny woman lifted her eyes and studied the banner as if she couldn't remember.

"Hell calls Hell," Sister Mary Ruth answered for her, "is the literal translation, Major."

"A Latin warning that one misstep leads to another," Kimmel added.

He felt a vibration move across the table. He saw his wine goblet rattle beside his fork and studied it a moment before turning away.

A sharp scrape turned him back.

The other officers now stared as well. "My wine," Kimmel said, "did you see? It moved. It moved by an inch. . . ."

He looked over at Stenecker, who calmly spoke while picking his teeth. "What's the matter, Herr Kimmel? Are you letting your imagination get the best of you?"

The gunnery sergeant lifted his eyes to the rafters. "I am wondering what other black magic we have walked into here. I am remembering dead soldiers attacking us in the snow."

Stenecker stared past his toothpick at him. No one had mentioned the events of this morning, and now suddenly all were thinking about it again. "Do you know what we are talking about?" Stenecker narrowed his eyes at Sister Mary Ruth. The old woman reached down with a palsied hand and took his plate. He grabbed her gnarled fingers forcefully. She dropped the dish and it clattered back to the tabletop. "I asked you a question."

She looked at him with milky gray eyes as he gripped her tighter. "These things in the snow that once were men? Do you know what they are?"

"The wandering unholy." Mother O'Cyrus's voice echoed from a distant archway. Her words turned every Nazi head in the room. "That is what we call them."

"You seem strangely untroubled by their presence." Stenecker released Sister Mary Ruth and pushed his plate toward her.

"We have been in these mountains many years now." Mother O'Cyrus moved toward him. "We have seen many things that might trouble those who have not."

"Does it not challenge your beliefs, Sister, to have these 'unholy,' as you call them, walking about?"

"You would be surprised, Herr Field Marshal, at the kinds of creatures wandering the woods these days."

A sudden silence, and then Stenecker smiled at her note of irony. He stood and encouraged the smiles of those around him—and then backhanded the mother superior viciously.

Even the officers were taken by surprise. The old woman reeled and almost fell to the floor. Stenecker's whispered voice again was laced with menace: "Watch your tongue, Sister, if you would like to keep it."

Mother O'Cyrus did not look up. Her hand went to her lip as she kept her head bowed and said softly, "Perhaps you misunderstood my meaning."

"Or understood it perfectly. I am sure you are aware, the Führer has nothing but contempt for your Christianity." She found the strength to look at him then. He added, "The greatest setback in the history of Man, to use his exact appraisal. The most severe blow mankind has ever endured."

"We are aware the Führer has other allegiances, gentlemen," Mother O'Cyrus said, leveling her look at Stenecker.

"Then you might also be able to guess the focus of our mission."

"You would do me a great kindness by telling me."

"You have a necromancer here, Sister," Stenecker announced. "We know this now."

The mother superior narrowed her eyes. "I am not even certain I understand the meaning of this word—"

Stenecker grabbed her by the throat, and her large white collar bent as he pulled her to him. "I will break your neck with my bare hands, old woman, if you lie to me again. Did you think we could be stopped by a few frozen corpses this creature might throw in our way?" He searched her eyes for fear and again could find little. "You have a necromancer. Either here, within these walls, or you know where this creature dwells."

He released her and she brought a hand to her throat.

"If a necromancer is someone who can raise the dead, Herr Field Marshal, in my belief, there is only one man capable of this—"

Stenecker swung his pistol from his holster and pointed it directly at her. "If you think, even for a moment, that I will leave this place without taking with me what I have been sent to retrieve, then you underestimate my resolve." He took a step closer, until the barrel of the Luger rested upon the creases of her forehead, "Do you admit you know of this creature?"

Mother O'Cyrus nodded without meeting his eyes, and Stenecker nodded back. "You will take me to him."

"To *her*, Herr Field Marshal."

She met his look then, and a wave of panic rushed over him. Grunwald and Kimmel lurched up from their seats to draw their pistols. "No," Mother O'Cyrus said softly, "it is not I." Stenecker lowered his gun, and Kimmel and Grunwald poorly masked their relief.

"It is the sister who began this order. Our mother foundress."

"You told us the order had been founded over two centuries ago."

Mother O'Cyrus nodded, and Stenecker's pistol raised again. "You want us to believe that this woman is over two hundred years old and still living?"

"She has many powers the Lord has seen fit to give her. One is longevity beyond human boundaries."

"And she is your necromancer?" Stenecker's words brought the hall to a sudden silence. Only the popping of the logs in the fire punctuated his next inquiry. "Answer me! She then is your necromancer?"

Mother O'Cyrus stared back in silent confirmation.

"You will take us to her." His voice became hushed and full of purpose. "Now."

The long stone hall was lined with cruel-looking iron-pronged candleholders, all of them empty, making the fire from the sisters' candelabras the only light for Stenecker, his officers, and six armed soldiers as they were led into the abbey's lower chambers.

Major Grunwald, at the rear of the procession, watched the squarish shape of his head, its shadow cast by the candlelight growing and shrinking as it glided down the wall next to him until he could clearly make out two small points, jutting out just above his ears. He looked to the soldiers moving between them, deciding it was the upturned barrels of their rifles that added this sinister affectation.

"There are no lights in this part of the abbey, Sister?" Kimmel inquired.

"Not for the mother foundress," Mother O'Cyrus called back to him and then met Stenecker's suspicious stare. "She takes great exception to light."

"Why do you keep her so isolated?"

"She is, with all due respect to her, frightening to the other sisters, Herr Field Marshal." Her admission made the officers exchange glances. She saw this and said, "Make no mistake, she is a gift from God. The Sisters of St. Ignatius were created solely to watch over her. We have done this now for many decades."

Stenecker was getting uneasy. They were moving farther from the dining hall and deeper into the ancient convent. "I warn you, old woman, if you think you might lead us into a trap, any action taken by you or your gaggle of old geese will be met with the most severe opposition."

"With my most sincere apologies, Herr Field Marshal, it is I who must warn you." She came to the end of the hall and slid her candelabra onto iron prongs beside a set of substantial double doors. "There was a time when the mother foundress would commune with deceased saints to answer questions of papal importance—"

Stenecker cut her off abruptly. "And why our intelligence reports back to us that His Holiness, your pope, makes great use of this creature."

"But she has grown over the years," she cautioned. "And her powers have grown with her, powers no longer restricted to her communiqués with the dead." Her words were cut short as Stenecker pushed her toward the doors. "You asked us why we opened the gates for you? It takes twelve of us to open the courtyard gates, and they can only be opened manually." She looked past Stenecker at all of them now. "We did not open them, gentlemen. The mother foundress did."

Stenecker was having none of it. "Then why did we not see her there?"

"Because—" The nun spoke, then hesitated. The sudden silence was as unnerving as her next words.

"She does not need to be in the courtyard to open the gate."

"I have heard enough talk, Sister. Open this door," Stenecker ordered.

"The men in the snow who attacked you? We did not send them to stop you!" She turned to him as he tried to reach out and pull the iron handles. The doors were locked, and her words became a cutting whisper. "We did not even know you were coming."

"Unlock the door, Sister."

"*She* knew. The mother foundress. She pulled them out of the snow where they had died and she sent them to stop you!"

For the first time, Stenecker could see fear in her eyes. And not because of him.

It was because of what lay beyond that door.

This troubled him, and though he would never betray this, he turned and pushed back through his men to young Hans, whispering in his ear, "Go back to the dining hall. Find Gerhard and tell him to radio our position. Tell him we may need more men."

Stenecker grabbed the candelabra from Sister Mary Ruth and gave it to him. Hans and his flame retreated and were swallowed by the cavernous hall as Stenecker strode back to Mother O'Cyrus. "Open this door."

"There is a protocol for communicating with her," she said.

Stenecker turned to five of his six soldiers. "If anyone comes down this hall, shoot them." Then he nodded to the sixth. "You, draw your pistol and stay at our flank."

"You would be doing yourself a great kindness to allow me to facilitate the conversation," Mother O'Cyrus said as she slid a key into the lock. He pushed her aside and turned the key himself. An ancient tumbler turned, and Stenecker grabbed the large iron handles and pulled. The rusty hinges squealed like a dying pig as the doors swung open onto a vast darkness.

Moonlight streaked in from high rectangular windows and silhouetted a mountainous shadow some yards away. Stenecker grabbed the mother superior's candelabra and took several steps toward it, just enough to see the enormity of what sat in the center of this room.

The mother foundress was not only centuries old, she was massive.

She was perhaps three times as large as any human being, an insanely obese woman, slumped and motionless in the largest wooden chair Stenecker had ever seen. The soldiers all stared in puzzlement. The woman's great, shadowed head was bowed in sleep, and thick gray strings of hair hung from it like some oversized mop in need of wringing out. Her guttural snore marked the rise and fall of her enormous shoulders, stooped with the weight of the thick and rusted chains that anchored her to the floor.

For a moment Stenecker could not find his voice. "Why is she chained?"

"She has, on occasion, attacked . . . some of the sisters," Mother O'Cyrus whispered back.

"Surely she cannot move."

"She bites them, Herr Stenecker, when they get close enough to feed or wash her."

"She is mad?"

O'Cyrus recited a line of Latin and then translated: "God's beautiful abomination." The stunned officers moved deeper into the room, trying to confirm this human impossibility.

"Wake her," Stenecker said.

"She is never asleep."

"Prove to me this old sow is your necromancer," Stenecker hissed, "and that you do not think to make fools of us!"

"You have seen her powers," Mother O'Cyrus insisted.

"I said prove this is the creature we seek! Tell her we wish to speak to her!"

"She hears everything we are saying, Herr Field Marshal, believe this. And she does only what she wishes. She will not perform like a monkey on a chain."

"She is already on a chain, sister!" He glared at her. "And if what she does will be exclusively her choice, then she can choose to speak to me or watch the rest of you die. Sergeant Kimmel, take your pistol out and shoot that old one."

Kimmel looked back at him.

"Do it!" Stenecker barked.

The gunnery sergeant raised his Luger and aimed it at Sister Mary Ruth. He saw her hands shaking uncontrollably and swung his aim at another. "Which old one, Herr Field Marshal?"

"Any of them, you idiot!"

"I would not do that, Herr Stenecker," Mother O'Cyrus cautioned. "The mother foundress likes to teach. Especially the commandments."

"Shoot any of them!" Stenecker shouted, and Kimmel swung back to Sister Mary Ruth and fired point blank at the old woman—but his own chest exploded with the shot. The gunnery sergeant went wide-eyed and clutched at his wound as he saw his weapon's smoking and shredded metal. *The bullet had fired out the back of the gun!*

As he crashed to the floor, Kimmel heard Mother O'Cyrus's voice: "Do unto others, Herr Field Marshal—"

Major Grunwald stepped up, aimed his own pistol directly at Sister Mary Ruth's forehead, and pulled the trigger. The bullet ripped into Grunwald's own head, and he flailed back and slammed into the wall.

"—as you would have them do unto you." The mother superior bowed her head.

Stenecker whipped around and aimed his Luger directly at her. She didn't even raise her head, just said softly, "I would most strongly dissuade you from that."

The field marshal slowly lowered his weapon as a sound began to fill the room, a deep churning as if from some ancient, titanic machine.

The mother foundress was laughing.

A sound so low and guttural, it surely came from the belly of some mammoth beast. Her shoulders quaked, and her chains clattered, and her great head lifted, drifting through a slash of light. She was more of a nightmare than he could ever have imagined. Her ancient visage was so severely ravaged by time and gluttony, she had the aspect of some grotesque apple doll. The folds and creases of her withered flesh were so heavy and so deep in her face, they eclipsed her eyes as if she had none

"How horrible it must be"—Stenecker thought Mother O'Cyrus was talking about the hideous thing chained to the chair—"to find that your power came only from a gun, a gun that now will only shoot you."

"You are a great hypocrite, Sister!" Stenecker spat back. "Thou shalt not kill! Have you never heard of this?! You are breaking your own commandments!"

The mother foundress laughed so hard that her great heft seesawed in the chair. Stenecker felt it right through his boots.

"Are you finding religion, Herr Field Marshal?" The room rocked suddenly as if it struck by a mortar shell. It rattled the doors as Stenecker rushed to throw them open.

The dark hall was lined with the bodies of floating soldiers.

The field marshall thrust his candelabra forward, and its orange light caught their rifles as they clattered to the floor beneath feet that no longer touched the ground.

These men weren't floating—*they were impaled!*

Each was on one of the iron candleholders that lined the walls, as if all of the soldiers had been lifted in unison and then slammed against the upturned spikes—left to hang there like grisly ornaments.

Stenecker rushed to the nearest one, whose mouth opened but only sputtered blood. The field marshal barely glimpsed the glistening mass that slipped off the metal spike. It was the soldier's liver. It had been pushed out and dropped neatly between Stenecker's boots.

A gentle whisper wafted into the hall: "It gave us no joy, Herr Stenecker, no joy at all"—it was Mother O'Cyrus, stepping from the dark room into the hallway—"to know that the moment she opened the gates, none of you would be leaving."

The Field Marshall stared back as the color ran from his face. "We shall see about that!" His pistol came up again—a reflex. Then he remembered he couldn't fire, and in desperation he sought out his only remaining ally, the sixth sentry: a soldier who, like him, was the color of a sheet.

Stenecker raced down the hall with him, a move that sent the mother foundress wailing, lurching up from her great wooden throne back in the shadows and straining the heavy chains. One of them snapped as if it were twine, and a long piece of it flew like shrapnel across the room toward the doors.

A terrible sound whirled Stenecker around: he saw the soldier lurch to a halt as if he had been stabbed in the back. His mouth opened, but he never spoke. The length of chain dangled out of his stomach like a rusty umbilical cord—and in the instant he clutched it, *it yanked him back like he was a fish on a line.*

He ran screaming past the nuns and disappeared into the dark mouth of the mother foundress's room. The sisters did not look back; they simply bowed their heads, and while Stenecker watched, made the sign of the cross.

The field marshal was no longer masking his terror. He raced away so fast that his candles snuffed out, leaving him to sprint madly through the dark in the desperate hope that it would deliver him back to the lights and fire of the dining hall. He was breathless by the time he staggered through the archway and was met by young Hans. "We have radioed, Herr Field Marshal! They are sending more men!"

Stenecker grabbed him and swung him around. "Run!" He pushed him toward the doors far across the room. "All of you!" The room full of soldiers looked back in utter confusion. "We are leaving this instant!"

"The mother foundress would never allow that," Mother O'Cyrus said, casting a long, dark shadow as she stepped into the hall with the sisters gathering behind her.

"She is a devil!" Stenecker pointed at her rabidly. "She is a demon and you are at her mercy!" The vast chamber rocked as if it objected to this remark; the floor erupted, hit by an invisible force that blasted several soldiers off their feet. One slid all the way down the long dining table, screaming at its end as he pitched into space. He smashed into the roaring fireplace, striking it so hard that a blast of sparks and cinders flew out like fireworks.

Others who found themselves airborne were equally unlucky: they struck the walls and left gruesome trails of gore as they slid to the floor.

Stenecker could muster only a coarse whisper. "Run for your lives. . . ."

He started a frantic exodus across the hall as it trembled up to its highest rafters.

"How can you pretend that she is something holy?" Stenecker screamed across the room as he ran. "She is pure evil, Sister, and you know this! She is as far from God as any one thing has ever been!"

A rafter splintered and the long blue banner embroidered with Latin came loose. Its metal pole, still tethered to a heavy rope, fell. Stenecker saw it descending and ran, certain he was its target. He pushed madly ahead of the terrified exodus as the long metal rod swung down in a graceful arc and pierced three retreating soldiers at once. Like a mammoth needle and thread, the pole pulled the rope through them, sewing them together before it found Stenecker and staked him to the wall.

Hans charged toward him as the field marshal wailed. The boy struggled to wrestle the pole out of his lower shoulder: first by pulling madly, and finally by sliding back the others who were skewered on it as well.

They collapsed to the floor, the rope still laced through their wounds like some grisly human necklace.

The pole finally slid out of Stenecker and he howled in pain. Hans pulled him toward their escape, and Stenecker staggered ahead as he found ire enough to bellow back at Mother O'Cyrus, "You crazy old bitch! Don't you see? She is an abomination! You are in service to a monster!"

He was already gone when Mother O'Cyrus replied, "Heil Hitler, Herr Field Marshal."

Stenecker almost tumbled down the long descent of stone steps from the abbey. His men ran with him—the ones who weren't pitched over the parapet by a force unseen that he now understood was the mother foundress, still in a tantrum deep inside the granite walls of her chamber.

He could hear the men raining down the stairs past him and hitting the frozen cobblestones far below. Their skulls cracked and their bones snapped. Stenecker jumped from the steps at the first survivable elevation and staggered to his feet, his shoulder throbbing and his right arm useless as he raced with young Hans toward his sedan. He stopped abruptly with the others.

The massive gates were closed.

Shut tight as a tomb as the moonlit snow fell past them. Stenecker grabbed his men and threw them forward. "On the gates! Everyone!" They charged forward and were struggling to achieve a unified grip when the earth beneath their boots rumbled and shook and the gargantuan doors began parting without their help.

Stenecker stood breathless, peering at the first increment of moonlit countryside revealed. But as the gates swung wider, they presented an even more heartening sight, one that filled the men with joy and brought a cheer from young Hans.

A full German platoon stood out in the snow just beyond the gates.

When they saw Stenecker and his men, they raised their arms in a perfect salute.

"They came! They came, Herr Field Marshal!" young Hans cried out, and he raced toward them as his boots spit up snow.

The field marshal pointed behind him, but words failed as he tried to explain to his rescuers what horrors lay up the dark, stone steps of Greystone Abbey. Instead he could only laugh as he moved forward. Or was he crying? Or were the sounds he made more like a madman singing in the wind?

Whatever they were, they were cut short as the platoon opened fire on him.

In a flash of blinding light and angry sound, Stenecker felt his body being torn into. A terrible burn rushed down his torso and took the power from his legs. He crashed to his knees.

He saw young Hans's beautiful face as it met a spray of gunfire. It belched out blood from a gaping mouth, a split nose, and an eye socket suddenly missing its globe. The young lad pitched into the snow, and every man around him was cut down as quickly.

Stenecker struggled to stay up and saw that their executioners were more of the frozen Nazi dead, their eyes frosted white, helmets dusted with snow, and flesh the sickly ash-gray of the no longer breathing.

The field marshal was the last to close his eyes. He stayed alive long enough to watch the snow falling past the parapet. "It is the dust of the angels," he could hear his mother telling him from somewhere. But the only figures he could see were dressed in black and filing onto the balcony with Mother O'Cyrus at their center.

They looked more like an army of Grim Reapers than angels, staring down in their dark shawls as they watched Stenecker finally topple lifeless onto the icy cobblestone.

In the eerie quiet of the whistling wind, they made the sign of the cross and then headed back inside. Only Sister Mary Ruth slowed as she heard movement in the snow below. She did not turn—she simply clutched her rosary in her trembling hand and walked away.

She had nightmares enough and did not need the sight of the freshly dead field marshal and his murdered men pulling themselves up from their puddles of blood-red snow and moving out the abbey gates.

The granite cross above them cast a deep, black shadow in the snow they crossed—to join the mother foundress's army of the dead as the great gates of Greystone Abbey swung closed again.

Man with a Canvas Bag

Gary A. Braunbeck

When I was a little boy, there lived on our street—four houses down from my family, to be exact—a man who killed his five-year-old daughter. I can't say "accidentally killed" because for all the years my family knew Earl and Patricia Spencer, Earl spoke of the event (when he spoke at all) as if Cathy's death had been a premeditated act on his part, the culmination of some grand evil scheme, meticulously planned and skillfully executed. He spun the narrative of his crime with such deep conviction that anyone listening would almost believe he *had* deliberately taken her life. Earl needed to believe that we thought him guilty, so we pretended that we did, and that our forgiveness was implicit. It made the truth easier to live with when never a word of it was spoken. It was simpler for Earl to blame himself for Cathy's death than it was for him to accept the probability that we live in a charnel-house universe where everything was, is, and always will be a random fuck-up, including the formation of certain dyssymmetrical protein molecules that arbitrarily gave way to the double helix and—*voilà!*—humankind doing its endless happy dance across the face of this planet.

I was nine years old on the morning Cathy Spencer was killed. American troops were still in Vietnam. Richard Nixon was still president. It was the twenty-ninth of October and every house on either side of North Tenth Street had two things in common:

Halloween jack-o'-lanterns, and autumn leaves raked into neat piles at the curb, or at the foot of driveways, or the base of trees. The air was rich with the afterscents of neighbors' burned leaves from the night before (you were still allowed to burn leaves back then, and, God, how I miss that smell being part of the world). The Kid-Countdown-to-Beggars'-Night clock was ticking so loudly it was all anyone under the age of twelve could hear or wanted to think about.

I was raking leaves in our front yard. I loved raking leaves into a great big pile because then I could take a good running jump into that pile, watch the explosion of autumn colors, and hear that unmistakable dry, scratching whisper only autumn leaves can make as the wind pushes them across a cold sidewalk. Sometimes I'd hide in the pile when I saw one of my friends approaching and then jump out with a monster scream just as they reached our driveway. One of the greatest joys of childhood is that ear-splitting shriek of terror made by your friends when you've successfully scared the living shit out of them.

"Hey, *Tommy*!" shouted Cathy Spencer, jumping up and down and waving her arms like she was trying to signal an airplane. She was dressed in her Wilhemina W. Witchiepoo costume, her favorite character from the *H.R. Pufnstuf* television show. I was an Orson Vulture fan, myself, but only my parents and Cathy knew that.

I waved back at her. "You aren't wearing your nose."

She giggled and rolled her eyes. "Dummy."

"Well, you *aren't* wearing it. But, hey, it looks real good anyway."

Cathy smiled at me and pointed to my ever-growing leaf pile, then to the one at the foot of her parents' driveway. "Lotsa leaves, huh?"

"Uh-huh."

"I still go trick-treating with you?" Her eyes got really wide when she asked this, like I was going to say no. I'd taken her trick-or-treating for the last three years. She was fun to be with on Halloween.

"I don't know," I said. "You *did* forget to put on your nose."

She stuck out her tongue and giggled.

"We'll have the best costumes, you and me."

"Uh-huh. Thank you, Tommy."

"You're welcome."

"There's lotsa leaves." She scooped up a handful and buried her face in them, taking a deep smell. "Pretty." She dropped the leaves, smiled again, then waved as she made her way back toward her front porch. I turned my attention back to the project at hand and doubled my raking speed. I couldn't stop smiling. Cathy had that effect on you. She was sweet, courteous, a little sneaky when she put her mind to it, and everyone's friend. Cathy was also retarded. Back then, it wasn't called Down syndrome, a person wasn't "developmentally disabled," and the term "special needs," as it's known in its current context, didn't even exist. A person like Cathy was retarded, period. It wasn't a contemptuous term—no, for that, you pulled out that old chestnut "mongoloid," a word no one in the neighborhood ever used or *allowed* anyone to use. Though she was five then—almost six, she'd remind you when given the opportunity—Cathy would always be three years old. And like any three-year-old, Cathy could be, as my mom put it, "a little stinker."

When I looked back, Earl Spencer was trotting out the front door, lunch pail in one hand, keys to the bus in the other. Earl's "bus" was actually an extra-large passenger van that held a maximum of twelve people. He drove a route that took him from one end of Granville Street to the other, then into downtown Cedar Hill, where he made a circle around the square before heading back. The Cedar Hill City Council contracted with Earl and three other drivers (each of whom owned his own "bus") to cover the entire city, and while there was decent enough business to keep all four drivers busy year-round, the last two and a half months of every year were a particularly busy time—lots of people doing early Thanksgiving shopping, early Christmas shopping, or making last-minute Halloween candy and decoration runs.

Earl gave me a quick wave as he rounded the front of the bus and climbed in, firing up the engine. Looking at my trusty Superman watch, I realized that he was running about fifteen minutes late. He put the bus in gear, honked his horn as he waved good-bye to Patricia, and backed out of the driveway. Then the pile of leaves at the foot of the Spencer's driveway moved.

Lotsa leaves.

To this day I can't tell you how I knew it was Cathy and not the autumn wind.

"... a little stinker."

I just *knew*, period.

I threw down the rake and ran toward the bus as fast as I could, screaming for Mr. Spencer to stop, Stop *Stop STOP!,* but he either didn't hear me or didn't realize what had happened until he looked in the rearview mirror and saw me standing in the middle of the street, my pants soaked in Cathy's blood because I'd slipped in the heavy wet streaks left by the tires.

I remember the loud *pop!* as the bus backed over the leaves and into the street (he'd run over her head right away, but I didn't know that yet). I remember seeing the great, wide splash of bright red spit up from inside the leaves and spatter the back side of the suddenly too-white bus (and running over her head first, that was a blessing in disguise, wasn't it?). I remember looking down and seeing one of Cathy's arms shudder (involuntary muscle reaction, but at the time I thought she was still alive). I remember looking up and seeing her other arm being dragged by the rear bumper (that proved she was still alive, because she'd grabbed the bumper as if she really were Wilhemina W. Witchiepoo and could stop the bus just by touching it). I slipped in the blood, scrambled to my feet, screamed at Mr. Spencer again—"She's hurt real bad! She's hurt *real bad!*"—and then spun around, dropped to my knees, and began pulling Cathy from the now soaked and half-crushed pile of leaves.

I was later told that it took three people to get my arms loose from her body. I was later told that I tried to put her head back together using the bits of skull and pieces of brain that I could find, and then clumps of bloody leaves and small broken twigs when there was no more skull or brains to be found. I was later told that Earl Spencer stood frozen at the back of his van, howling like a wounded animal. I was told all of these things by my parents, and so I never questioned whether or not they were true.

Since I was the sole witness to what happened, the police talked to me first. I remember that Mom knelt beside me the entire time, holding my hand in hers. I told the police everything that I'd seen, up to the moment I started digging Cathy out of the leaves; from there, I had no concrete memory of events.

"He's in shock," said one of the officers. "We'd better get him to the hospital."

I pointed to the middle of the street.

"What's he doing?" Both Mom and the officer looked, and saw nothing.

"But he's *right there*," I said. "See? That man with the bag?"

Mom shook her head and put her arm around my shoulder. "Hon, there's no man with a bag in the street."

"Okay," said the officer. "He's seeing things. We take him to the hospital *now*."

I turned around, feeling dizzy, and bumped into the gurney carrying the slick black bag that held what was left of Cathy's body. My elbow bumped into it as I stumbled back, and something inside the bag made a thick, wet, slopping sound; it moved just like the pile of leaves. I imagined Cathy's hand inside, trying to find the zipper and open the bag before she drowned in the leakage from her own broken pieces. I watched as her remains were loaded into the coroner's wagon—what all of us kids used to call "the meat wagon," a term that suddenly made me sick—and for some reason, I waved at her and whispered, "Good-bye, Witchiepoo."

I waited for her hand to come out of the bag and wave back.

I still go trick-treating with you?

I guess she was all gone by then.

They gave me some kind of a shot at the hospital that made me feel all sleepy, so I don't remember the drive home or Dad carrying me upstairs and putting me to bed. I came wide awake sometime around four in the morning, and for a few moments wasn't sure where I was, but then I saw my shelf full of Aurora monster models and let out the breath I didn't realize I'd been holding.

I got up, dressed, and put on my shoes. I saw that Mom had put a glass of water on my bedside table, which was good because I was really thirsty. Mom always thought of those things.

I finished the water and walked over to my bedroom window. My bedroom was at the front of the house, so I could see the street. I wanted to see the spot where Cathy had died, and I was going to sneak out if I had to. The street seemed a lot brighter than it usually did at night. I pulled back the curtain and saw the man with the canvas bag walking down the middle of the street. At every house he'd stop and kick through the leaf-piles, looking for . . . I don't what.

But when he got to Cathy's house, he put down his bag—that now glowed this bright kind of silver from deep inside—and began to sort through the leaf pile where Cathy had been hiding. I was surprised that one of our neighbors hadn't gotten rid of that pile yet. I couldn't imagine anyone thinking that Earl and Pat would want to look at it again, not after this morning.

Then I realized that the leaf pile *was* gone; what the man with the canvas bag was sorting through were . . . well . . . *the ghosts* of the leaves, and they gave off a bright silver light. When he got to the inside of the pile, to where Cathy's body had been, there was this soft blue light that was kind of shaped like a human body . . . only one that had been crushed and broken apart and killed.

I must have been really quiet when I went downstairs and unlocked the front door, because Mom, she was a really light sleeper, *anything* woke her up, but I got out of the house without waking her or Dad.

The closer I got to the man with the canvas bag, I saw that even Cathy's blood left a kind of ghost behind; where the street had been slick and dark, there was now a smear of the same light blue that marked the spot where Cathy's body had been. The man with the canvas bag was picking out very small things from the ghost blood, as well as from the gutters across the street. I looked closer, and I could see that there were these little blue pieces—and some that weren't so little—scattered all over the street, even past the point where Mr. Spencer had stopped the bus.

"They never close off the areas for long enough," said the man, still gathering ghost pieces. "They forget that the other cars that come through here afterward might catch the smallest bits in their tires and carry them—ah, here it is!" He held up something that looked like a jagged section of glass, and it was only as I walked closer that I saw it was a piece of skull, only blue.

"Yes," he said to the question I hadn't even asked yet, "even your blood and bones leave ghosts behind."

"Is that what you're doing? Finding the missing pieces?"

He stopped, grinned at me (his grin was kind of sad and scary), and said: "You catch on fast. I knew you were going to be trouble when you spotted me this morning."

I began backing away. "I . . . I won't tell anybody, I swear. *I swear!* P-please don't hurt me."

"*Hurt you?*" he said. "Why would I want to hurt the first person to see me in a while, let alone come over to talk to me?" He found another ghost piece, but I didn't want to see what it was.

"Just so you know," he said to me as he continued about his task, "Cathy didn't feel much pain. I won't lie to you, Tommy, she *did* have one moment of pain and pressure—kind of like when you've got a really bad stuffed-up nose and there's a sneeze coming on and you feel the burst of pain rushing toward the front of your face and for a second or two that pressure is all you can think about. You ever have that feeling?"

I nodded. "When I had the flu last year. It hurt."

"But was it a terrible hurt?"

I though about it. "No, I guess not. Kinda like what you said."

"That's all the pain Cathy felt, just that and nothing more. Everything went bright and she was pulled away before the worst of it happened." He stopped his task and looked at me. "She didn't suffer, is what I'm saying. Do you understand?"

I could feel my throat getting all tight and the snot building up in my nose and my eyes starting to burn. I didn't want to cry. "Yessir," I said. "That's good. She was really sweet. She was gonna go trick-or-treating with me. She was going to go as—" And that was all I got out before the tears and shakes overtook me. I felt so alone, so sad, so helpless and . . . *responsible*. I almost always watched to make sure Cathy went inside, but I had been too busy raking leaves that morning to bother. Maybe if I had, I would have seen her climb into the pile and cover herself up. Maybe if I had—

"*Please* don't do that, Tommy," said the man with a canvas bag. "I mean, go on and cry for the loss of your friend, of course, absolutely— I'd be surprised if you didn't—but don't you *dare* try and blame yourself for what happened."

". . . B-b-but if I'd've . . . if I'd've . . ."

"If you'd have what? Watched her climb into the pile, then you could have warned Mr. Spencer and none of it would have happened? What if you'd had to go to the bathroom before she got into the pile? Would you blame yourself because you were inside doing a Number One instead of out here keeping an eye on her? What if your mom had called you inside for some reason? You'll ruin what's left of your childhood with 'What if . . . ? 'Yes, I can tell some of what you're thinking, not *all* of it, but the loudest parts. And right now your thoughts are pretty damned loud."

I looked up at him and pulled in a deep breath. "I miss her so much already."

"You should. She was a great little girl. Nothing wrong with missing someone you love."

I started to say something in protest, but realized he was right. I'd loved her like she was my own little sister.

"And she knew that, Tommy. She knew that."

I wiped my nose on my shirtsleeve, then wiped my eyes with my hands. "So, is there anything I can do to help?"

"Yes," he said, walking toward me and opening his canvas bag. The silver light was really bright, and I wondered why it wasn't causing people to wake up.

"Only people who can see me can see the ghostlights," he said. "Stop worrying so much."

I looked at the opened bag. "Do you want me to help you gather up more pieces? Or maybe take something out of there?"

He shook his head. "No. But isn't there something you'd like to put in here?"

I stared at him. "I don't have anything."

"Yes, you do. And if you don't put it in here, I can't reassemble Cathy's ghost, and if I can't reassemble her ghost, well . . . no one will remember that she was ever here. Oh, sure, I mean you, your folks, her parents, people in this neighborhood, you'll remember her for a while. But as the years go by and all of you grow older, the memories of her will start to dim, becoming less specific, less important, less necessary, until, at the last, everyone who was alive on this street on this day will die and forget to pass Cathy along to those left behind—those who never had a chance to see her smile, hear that goofy damn giggle, or catch her being sneaky around Christmas or her birthday.

"That may seem like an awful long time to you right now, Tommy, but trust me—it's the blink of an eye. Part of my job is reassembling broken ghosts, but I also have to . . . I have to find the *glue* to use when putting them back together."

"Like with my monster models?"

He considered this for a moment. "Not a bad simile, not bad at all. Yes, like with your monster models."

"I could run back to the house and get my glue and put it in here. It's real good glue, but you gotta watch out if you get it on your fingers, because then it dries kinda fast, and it's smelly and sticky, and . . . and you don't mean *that* kinda glue, do you?"

He grinned again. "You do not fail to surprise, I'll give you that."

I was sore, and thirsty, and tired, and I knew I was going to start crying again. I had no idea what he was talking about, only what he *wasn't* talking about. I walked over to the pile of ghost leaves and looked down at the smoky-blue form that now lay where Cathy's body had been. For a moment I was tempted to kneel down and touch it, only what if my hand went through? Or what if I lost my balance and fell in? Where would I be?

"Do you want to know why it is that my bag is so full and shines so brightly?"

"Yessir."

He knelt beside me, both of us looking into the smoky-blue emptiness inside the ghost leaves.

"I have one of the hardest jobs of all the . . . well, I guess you'd call us janitors. It's my job to gather up the missing pieces of the broken ghosts of children who died too soon. Cancer, starvation, abuse, neglect, terrible, *terrible* accidents like this morning. All of them always leave missing pieces behind. Sometimes—like with Cathy—there are more pieces than usual, but there's always *something* missing. And I have to find it and then put everything back together so that these children will not be forgotten. That's what ghosts really are, Tommy—our forgotten memories given eternal life outside of our minds and hearts. Do you understand?"

"I think so."

He pulled the bag closer to us. "The reason my bag is so full, Tommy, the reason it shines so very brightly, is because it is filled with the broken ghosts of children that I could not put back together. There are broken ghosts in here of children who died hundreds, even *thousands* of years ago. And I can never fix them, so they've been forgotten by everyone except me. Care to guess why I couldn't fix them?"

The tears started coming again, but I was ready, and I managed to keep most of them back. "Because the people you asked for . . . for 'glue,' they said no?"

"That's exactly right. And when they awoke the next morning, I was nothing more to them than some errant wisp of a dream that was forgotten before their feet even hit the floor. And the little ones whose broken ghosts were in my bag, they're trapped in there forever. They don't even have the comfort of knowing that they're not alone. All any of them are aware of is their own isolation, their own loneliness, their own sadness. And each of them remembers the moment of their death in terrible, awful detail. Oh, I can relieve a little of their loneliness from time to time. I can open the bag and pick one and talk to them briefly, but it's not enough. What they suffered during the last moments of their lives follows them even past death. And that *stinks*, Tommy. It stinks on ice.

"Is that what you want for Cathy?"

"Oh, God—*no*. I don't want her to feel all lonely and forgotten. I don't want her to feel like nobody loved her."

"Then give me what I need—or, rather, give me the thing you need to put in here."

"I don't understand. I'm real sorry, but I *don't*."

He looked into my eyes and did not blink. "If you could do it, would you die to bring her back? Did you love your friend that much? That you would give your life to have her back in the world?"

"I don't wanna *die! Please?*"

"Most people don't want to die, Tommy. I'm not asking you to die. I'm asking you if it were possible to bring her back by giving your own life, would you do it?"

"I—"

He held up a finger to silence me. "Before you answer, there's something else you need to know. If you say yes, and you give me that, if you give me that willingness to offer up your life to have Cathy back in the world, you can never make that offer again. Believe it or not, Tommy, there comes a moment in everyone's life when they get the chance to make that offer *once*, and have it accepted, without dying themselves. If you say yes and give me that so that I can put Cathy's ghost back together, you can never make this deal again. Ten, twenty, thirty years from now, you might have a wife, or a child of your own, who is very sick and on the brink of death, and you won't be able to save them because you will have used your one 'Get Out of Jail *Free*' card. This is no small thing I'm asking of you."

"Is this why so many people said no to you and left the broken ghosts in your bag?"

He nodded.

I looked at the smoky-blue form left in place of Cathy's body. "Can I ask you something before I decide?"

"Of course."

"Why does stuff like this have to happen? I mean, what you said, kids who get killed, who die of cancer or starve to death? How come anyone has to be hurt or sad or sick and lonely like that?"

"Look at me, Thomas Franklin Ireland."

I did.

"I'm going to tell you something that I've told maybe, *maybe* four other people in all the thousands of years I've been on the job. Listen carefully.

"There *is* a reason for all of this. We are heading toward something so . . . so incredible, so beautiful, so indescribably wonderful that when it at last happens, everyone will look back at all of the savagery, all of the starvation, all of the brutality and disease and suffering and loneliness and fear and misery, and as one they will say: 'It was worth it. To get *here* to achieve this wondrous thing . . . all of the pain and anguish suffered by every living thing since the beginning of time was *worth it*.'

"I can't tell you what that thing is, Tommy, because I don't know. I didn't get that particular memo. I'm just the janitor."

I wiped my eyes and inhaled a bunch of snot. "She was a really great little girl."

"Yes, yes, she was."

I stood up. "Yes."

For a moment, he looked confused. "Do you mean . . . ?"

"Yes. I would give my life to have her back."

He held the bag toward me. "Then, please, drop it inside."

I looked down and saw that both of my hands were clasped around something that looked like a bluish-silver leaf. I carefully moved my hands until they were over the bag and then let it go. It drifted down as if caught in a gentle breeze, back and forth, back and forth, back and forth, and I felt—though I didn't have the emotional vocabulary to articulate it at the time—I felt something of sadness lifted from my eyes.

"I'll remember her," I said. "I'll make sure everyone will."

"I know that," said the man, pulling on a rope laced through the top of the bag and drawing it closed. "Cathy won't be trapped in here with the others now. You did that. You did a great thing, Tommy. It's too bad you won't ever be able to tell anyone about it."

"Why not?"

That grin one last time. "Do you think they'd *believe* you?"

I shrugged. "Probably not."

"You're quite the kid, Tommy. Maybe we'll meet up again sometime."

"That would be nice."

He pointed back toward my house. "Your dad is going to get up in about five minutes to take a leak, and he's going to look in on you afterward. It would be best if you were in your room when he does."

I turned and looked at my house, then turned back to him. "I'll be real quiet. I was quiet when I left. My mom's a light—"

But he was gone.

I lost my mother to emphysema. I could do nothing to save her.

I lost my father to cancer. I could do nothing to save him.

They both suffered so horribly, and for so long.

I married. We had a little girl. She was born with hydrocephaly and died when the shunt operation didn't work. She was six days old and left this world without even a name. I could do nothing to save her, could offer nothing in exchange for her life.

I lost my wife to suicide five months later. I'd suspected it was coming but could strike no bargain to keep her with me.

I see the man with a canvas bag often: in news footage of a traffic accident, in pictures taken of villages in starving countries, in crime scene photos where a child or several children were killed or tortured or beaten or died of neglect. He's always in the background, waiting for everyone to leave so he can begin putting those broken ghosts back together. I never ask anyone else if they see him there because I know they can't. Once, during a breaking news report about a local man who'd shaken his four-month-old son to death, I actually saw him wave at the camera and mouth the words, "Cathy says hi."

My mother. My father. My daughter. My wife. Any one of them I could have saved had I not . . .

But I could ruin what's left of my life with "Had I Not . . ." or "What if . . . ?"

On those nights when it gets bad, when I hate myself for having been an impulsive child—or think that maybe he'd always *known* what was coming my way and just conned me because *he* couldn't bear the thought of another child's broken ghost being forever trapped in a state of perpetual loneliness within his canvas bag—when there's nothing more I'd like to do than find him again and wrap my hands around his throat and just *squeeze* . . . it's then that I remember what he told me: *We are heading toward something so . . . so incredible, so beautiful, so indescribably wonderful that when it at last happens, everyone will look back at all the savagery, all the starvation, all the disease and suffering and loneliness and fear and misery, and as one will say: 'It was worth it. To get* here *to achieve this wondrous thing . . . all of the pain and anguish suffered by every living thing since the beginning of time was worth it.*

I remember. And wonder if I'll be around to see it happen. I know I won't be, that I'll be long gone and forgotten by then, but on those nights when it gets bad, I remember his words, I remember Cathy's smile, and for a little while, I can forgive myself—at least until morning comes—and I can hope.

Sometimes it helps. Not much, but some.

And I fall asleep with the echoes of thousands of broken ghosts calling out from the bottom of a canvas bag.

Fetch

Chuck Palahniuk

Hank stands with one foot planted a step in front of his other, all his weight balanced on that behind foot. He crouches down on his rear leg, squatting low on that behind leg, his knee bent, his torso, shoulders, and head all twisted and pulled back to the farthest point from the toe of his forward foot. At the moment he exhales, Hank's rear leg explodes straight, that hip flexing to throw his whole body forward. His torso twists to throw one shoulder forward. His shoulder throws his elbow. His elbow throws his wrist. All of that one arm swings in a curve, cracking fast as a bullwhip. His every muscle snaps that one hand forward, and at the point where Hank should fall onto his face, his hand releases the ball. A tennis ball, bright yellow, flying fast as a gunshot, the ball flies until almost disappearing into the blue sky, following a yellow arc as high as the sun.

Hank throws with his entire body, the way a man's supposed to throw. Jenny's Labrador retriever bounds after the tennis ball, a black smear shooting toward the horizon, dodging between the tombstones, then bounding back, tail wagging, and drops the ball at my feet.

How I throw a ball, I only use my fingers. Maybe my wrist, a little—I have skinny wrists. Nobody ever taught me any better, so my throw bounces off the first row of tombstones, ricocheting off a mausoleum, rolling through the grass, and disappearing behind somebody's grave marker while Hank grins at his feet and shakes his head from side to side, saying, "Good throw, loser." From deep down in his chest, Hank hawks a wad and spits a fat throat oyster into the grass between my bare feet.

Jenny's dog only stands there, part black Lab, part stupid, looking at Jenny. Jenny looking at Hank. Hank looking at me and saying, "What're you waiting for, boy, go fetch." Hank jerks his head at where the tennis ball has vanished, lost among the headstones. Hank talks to me the same way Jenny talks to her dog.

Jenny twists a strand of her long hair between the fingers of one hand, looking behind us to where Hank's car sits in the empty parking lot. The sunlight shining through her skirt, no slip underneath, the light outlining her legs all the way up to her panties, she says, "Go ahead. We'll wait. I swear."

Written on the close-up tombstones, no dates come any newer than 1930-something. Just guessing, my throw landed around the 1880s. Hank's throw went all the way back to the stupid Pilgrims on the stupid *Mayflower.*

With my first step, I feel wet against the bottom of my bare foot, some ooze, sticky and still warm. Hank's spit smears under my heel, between my toes, so I drag my foot on the grass to wipe it. Behind me, Jenny laughs while I drag that foot up the slope toward the first row of graves. Bouquets of plastic roses stick in the ground. Little American flags twitch in the breeze. The black Lab runs ahead, sniffing at the dead brown spots in the grass, then adding its piss. The tennis ball isn't behind the row of 1870s graves. Behind the 1860s: more nothing. Names of dead folks stretch away from me in every direction. Beloved husbands. Cherished wives. Adored mothers and fathers. The names stretch as far as I can see, getting pissed on by Jenny's dog; this army of dead folks lies just under the ground.

With my next step, the ground explodes, the mowed grass geysers with landmines of cold water, hosing my jeans and shirt. A booby trap of sheer freezing cold. The underground lawn sprinklers drive sprays of water, blasting my eyes shut, washing my hair flat. Cold water hits from every direction. From behind me comes laughter, Hank and Jenny laughing so **hard** they fall into each other for support, their clothes wet and sticking to Jenny's tits and molded over the shadow of her bush. They fall to the grass, still hugging, and their laughter stops as their wet mouths come together.

Here's the dead pissing back on us. The ice-cold way death can hit you in the noontime of a sunny day just when you'd never expect it.

Jenny's stupid Labrador barks and snaps at a jet of water, biting the sprinkler head next to me. Just as fast, the automatic sprinklers drop back into the ground. My T-shirt drips. Water runs down my face from the soaked mop of my hair. Sopping wet, my jeans feel stiff and heavy as concrete.

Not two graves away, the ball sits behind a tombstone. Pointing my finger, I tell the dog, "Fetch," and he runs over, sniffs the tennis ball, growls at it, then runs back without it. Walking over, I pick up the yellow fuzz, wet from the sprinklers. Stupid dog.

When I turn to throw the ball back to Jenny, the grass sloping down below me is empty. Beyond that, the parking lot spreads, empty. No Hank or Jenny. No car. All that's left is a puddle of black oil dripped out of Hank's engine pan and two trails of their wet footprints walking out and stopping where the car was parked.

In one huge throw, every skinny muscle the length of my arm whips, heaving the ball downhill to the spot where Hank's spit wet the grass. I tell the dog, "Fetch," and it only looks at me. Still dragging one foot, I start back downhill, until my toes feel warm again. This time, dog piss. Where I stand, the grass feels coarse. Dead. When I look up, the ball sits next to me, as if it's rolled uphill. Where I can see, the cemetery looks empty except for thousands of names carved in stone.

Throwing the ball, again, down the long slope, I tell the dog, "Fetch." The dog just looks at me, but in the distance the ball rolls closer and closer. Returning to me. Rolling up the slope. Defying gravity. Rolling uphill.

One of my feet is burning, the scratches and bunions of my bare foot stinging with dog piss. My other foot, the toes are webbed with Hank's foaming, gray spit. My shoes: in the backseat of his car. Gone. Me, dumped here to babysit her stupid pooch while Jenny's run off.

Walking back through the graves, I drag one foot to wipe it clean on the grass. With the next step, I drag the other foot. Dragging each foot, I leave a trail of flattened skid marks in the lawn all the way to the empty parking lot.

This tennis ball—now the dog won't go near it. In the parking lot, I stand next to the pool of dripped crankcase oil, and I throw the ball, again, chucking it hard as I'm able. The ball rolls back, spiraling around me, forcing me to keep turning to watch it, the yellow ball circling me until my head's spinning, dizzy. When the ball stops at my foot, I throw it again. Rolling back to me, this time the ball takes a detour, rolling against the grade, breaking that Law of Gravity. The ball circles in the pool of Hank's crankcase oil, soaking up the black muck. Stained black, the tennis ball rolls within kicking distance of my bare foot. Looping, jumping, doubling back on itself, the ball leaves a trail of black across the gray concrete; then it stops. A black tennis ball, round as the period at the end of a sentence. A dot at the bottom of an exclamation point.

The stupid black Lab shakes, too close, spraying me with dog water from its sopping fur. The stink of wet dog and spatters of mud stick everywhere on my jeans and T-shirt.

The ball's oily, black trail forms letters, those letters spelling words across the concrete parking lot, writing the sentence: "Please help me!"

The ball returns to the puddle of engine oil, soaking its fuzz with black, then rolling, writing in big, loopy handwriting: "We need to rescue her."

As I reach to pick it up, just squatting down to grab the tennis ball, it bounces a few steps away. I take a step, and the ball bounces again, reaching the edge of the parking lot. As I follow, it bounces, coming to a complete stop as if glued to the road, leading me out of the cemetery. I follow, the blacktop burning hot and sharp under my bare feet, hopping from one foot to the other. The ball leads, bouncing a row of black dots down the road ahead of me like the twin tracks of Jenny and Hank's footprints, leading nowhere. The black Lab follows. A sheriff's patrol car cruises past, not slowing. At the stop sign where the cemetery road meets the county road, the ball stops, waiting for me to catch up.

With each bounce, it leaves less oil. Me, I'm not feeling much, I'm so pulled forward by this vision of the impossible. The ball stops bouncing, stuck in one spot now. A car trails us, crawling along at the same speed. The horn honks, and I turn to see Hank behind the wheel; Jenny sits beside him in the front seat. Rolling down the shotgun window, Jenny leans her head out, her long hair hanging down the outside of the car door, and she says, "Are you crazy? Are you high?" With one arm, Jenny reaches into the backseat, then reaches out the car window, holding my shoes in her hand. She says, "For crying out loud, just look at your feet. . . ."

With each step, my raw feet leave behind a little more red—blood— my footprints stamped in blood on the pavement, marking my path all the way from the cemetery parking lot. Stopped in this one spot, I'm standing in a puddle of my own red juice, not feeling the sharp gravel and broken glass on the roadside.

One bounce ahead of me, the tennis ball waits.

Sitting behind the steering wheel, Hank twists one shoulder backward, hooking his arm over the seat back and pinching the tab of the door lock between two fingers. Pulling up the tab, he reaches down and yanks the handle to throw open the door, saying, "Get in the car." He says, "Get in the fucking car, *now*."

Jenny swings her hand, dropping my tennis shoes so they fly halfway to where I stand, flapping down in the roadside gravel. Their tongues and laces hang out, tangled.

Standing here, my feet dark as hooves or church shoes, so coated with dried blood and dust, all I can do is point at the dirty tennis ball . . . fat, black houseflies circling me . . . except the ball only sits there, not moving, not leading me anywhere, stopped along the edge of the blacktop where the pigweeds grow.

Hank punches the middle of his steering wheel, blasting me with a gigantic honk. A second honk comes so loud it echoes back from the nowhere over the horizon. All the flat sugar beet fields, the crops all around me and their car, filled with Hank's loud horn. Under the car hood the engine revs, the pushrods banging and cams knocking, and

Jenny leans out her shotgun window, saying, "Don't make him pissed off." She says, "Just get in the car."

A flash of black jumps past my legs, and the stupid Labrador jumps in the door Hank holds open. With his twisted-around arm, Hank yanks the door shut and cranks the steering wheel hard to one side. Flipping a big U-turn, his beater car tears off. Gravel rattling inside the wheel wells. Jenny's one hand still trailing out her open window. After them, Hank's tires leave twin smoking tracks of burned rubber. That stink.

Watching them go, I bend over to pick up my shoes. It's right then when—pock—something slams into the back of my head. Rubbing my scalp with one hand, I turn to look at what hit me, and already the stupid tennis ball is on the move, bouncing down the road in the opposite direction from Hank's car.

Kneeling down, knotting my shoes, I yell, "Wait!" Only the ball keeps going.

Running after it, I yell, "Hold up!" And the ball keeps bouncing, bouncing, big jumps right in line with the road. At the stop sign for Fisher Road, mid-jump, at the highest point in one bounce, the ball cuts to the right. Turning the corner in midair, and bouncing down Fisher, me still trucking along behind. Down Fisher, past the junkyard where it turns into Millers Road, there the ball turns left onto Turner Road and starts going upriver, parallel to the bank of Skinners Creek. Staying out of the trees, the oil-soaked, dust-packed tennis ball really flies along, puffing up a little cloud of dirt every time it smacks down in the road.

Where two old wheel ruts leave the road and run through the weeds, the ball turns right, rolling now. The ball rolls along the dried mud of one rut, swerving to go around the worst puddles and potholes. My shoelaces dangle and whip against my ankles. Me panting, shuffling along after the ball, losing sight of it in the tall grass. Catching sight of it when it bounces, bouncing in one place until I find it there. I follow, and the houseflies follow me. Then, rolling along the rut, the ball leads me into the cottonwood trees that grow along the creekside.

Nobody's standing in line to give me any scholarship. Not after my three big fat D grades Mr. Lockard handed me in algebra, geometry, and physics. But I'm almost sure no ball should be able to roll uphill, not forever. No tennis ball can stop perfectly still in one place, then start up bouncing off by itself. It's an impossibility, how this ball comes flying out of nowhere, socking me in the forehead to grab my attention any time I even look away.

One step into the trees, I need to stop and let my eyes adjust. Just that one little wait, and—pow—I have dirty tennis ball stamped on my face. My forehead feeling greasy and smelling like motor oil. Both my hands raise up by reflex, swatting at air the way you'd fight off a hornet too fast to see. I'm waving away nothing but air, and the tennis ball is already jumping out ahead of me, the thumping, thudding sound going off through the woods.

Going all the way to the creek bank, the ball leaps out ahead, then stops. In the mud between two forked roots of a cottonwood tree, it rolls to a standstill. As I catch up, it makes a little bounce, not knee high. It makes a second bounce, this time waist high. The ball bounces shoulder high, head high, always landing in the same exact spot, and with every landing it pushes itself deeper into the mud. Bouncing higher than I could reach, up around the leaves of the tree, the ball clears away a little hole, there, between the roots.

The sounds of birds, the magpies, stop. Silence. No mosquitoes or buzz of deer flies. Nothing makes any sound except this ball and my heartbeat in my chest. Both thudding faster and faster.

Another bounce, and the ball clinks against metal. Not a sharp sound, more a clank, like hitting a home run off the gutter of old Mr. Lloyd's house, or skipping a rock off the roof of a car parked on Lovers Lane. The ball hits dirt, hard as if it's pulled with a magnet, stops, and rolls to one side. And deep in the hole it's dug, a little brass shines out. The metal of something buried. The brass lid of a canning jar, printed Mason, same as your mom would put up tomatoes in for the winter.

No ball has to tell me more. I dig, my hands clawing away the mud, my fingers slippery around the buried glass outsides of the jar. The tennis ball waiting, I kneel there and pull this dirty jar out from the sucking mud, big around as a blue-ribbon turnip. The glass so smeared with mud I can't see what feels so heavy inside.

Using spit, spit and my T-shirt still wet from the graveyard sprinklers, I wipe. The lid stuck on, tight, swollen with rust and crud. I spit and wipe until something gold is looking back from inside the glass: gold coins, showing the heads of dead presidents and flying eagles. The same as you'd find if you followed a stupid leprechaun to the base of a rainbow—if you believed that crap—here's a quart jar filled with gold coins packed so tight together they don't rattle. They don't roll. All they do is shine as bright as the alloy wheels I'm going to buy to blow Hank's crap-burner car off the road. Bright as the diamond ring I'll take Jenny to buy at the Crossroad Mall. Right here in my two hands— and, pow.

The bright gold replaced with shooting stars. The smell of motor oil.

The next smell, my own nose collapsed and filling with blood. Busted.

The tennis ball blasts against my face, bouncing angry as a hornet. Slugging me, the ball flies in my face while I fight it back with the heavy jar, shielding my eyes, my arm muscles burning from the gold's weight. Blood runs down from my nose, sputtered out by my yelling. Twisting one foot in the slick mud, I launch over the creek bank. Same as Cub Scouts teaches you to do in a wasp attack, I splash into the water and wade out to over my head.

From underwater, between me and the sky, the ball floats on the surface of the creek. Waiting. The heavy jar of gold coins holds me tight to the rocks on the creek bed, but rolling it along, my chest full of my breath, I work my way upstream. The current carries the tennis ball downstream while the gold anchors me, cut off from the sun and air. Working my way into the shallows, the moment my breath gives out and the ball's nowhere to be seen, I pop my head up for a gasp. One big breath and I duck back under. The ball's floating, bobbing, maybe a half mile downstream, hard to tell because it looks so oily black on the deep water, but the ball's following the trail of my nose blood, tracking me in the direction of the current.

When my new air gives out, I stand up half out of the water and wade to shore, hauling the gold and making as little splash and noise as possible. Sniffing the blood back up my busted nose. One look backward over my shoulder, and already the ball's swimming, slow as a paddling mallard, against the current, coming after me.

Another Sir Isaac Newton impossibility.

With both my arms wrapped around that jar full of gold, I scramble up the creekside, the water squishing in my shoes, and I take off running through the woods.

With my every running step, mud slides under my shoes. The jar swings me sideways, almost off balance, spinning me when I jerk too far the other way. My chest aches, my ribcage feels caved in. With every landing I just about fall on my face, grabbing the jar so tight that if I fell, the glass would bust and stab straight into my eyes and heart. I'd bleed right to death, slipped here facedown in a puddle of mud and gold and broken glass. From behind, the tennis ball shoots through the leaves, snapping twigs and branches, whistling the same whiz-bang noise as a bullet ripping through the Vietnam jungle next to somebody's head in some television war movie.

Maybe one good bounce before the ball catches me, I duck low. There, the rotted trunk of a cottonwood has busted and fallen, and I stuff the heavy jar deep into the boggy center of the roots, the mud cave where the tree's pulled out from the ground on one side. The gold, my gold, hidden. The ball probably doesn't see because it keeps after me as I run faster, jumping and crashing my way through blackberry vines and saplings, stomping up sprays of muddy water until I hit the gravel of Turner Road. My shoes chew up the gravel, my every long jump shakes the water from my clothes. The cemetery sprinkler water replaced by dog piss replaced by Skinners Creek replaced by me sweating, the legs of my jeans rub me, the denim stiff with stuck-on dust. Me, panting so hard I'm ready to blow both lungs out my mouth, turned inside-out, my innards puked out like pink bubble-gum bubbles.

Midway between one running step and the next, the moment both my legs are stretched out, one in front and the other in back of me, in midair, something slams me in the back. Stumbling forward, I recover, but this something smacks me again, square in my backbone between my shoulder blades. Just as hard, arching my back, something hits me, a third go-round. It hits the back of my head, hard as a foul ball or a bunt in softball. Fast as a line drive fresh off the sweet spot of a Louisville Slugger, slamming you dead-on, this something hits me another time. The stink of crankcase oil. Shooting stars and comets swimming in my eyes, I pitch forward, still on my feet, running full tilt.

I'm winded, sucking air, and blinded with sweat; my feet tangle together, the something wings me one more time, beaning the top of my skull, and I go down. The bare skin of my elbows plow the gravel. My knees and face dive into the dust of my landing. My teeth grit together with the dirt in my mouth, and my eyes squeeze shut. The mystery something punches my ribs, slugs my kidneys as I squirm on the road. This something bounces, hard, to break my arms. It keeps bouncing, piledriving its massive impact, drilling me in my gut, slugging my ears while I curl tight to protect my nuts.

Past the moment I could still walk back and show the ball where the gold's hidden, almost to the total black of being knocked out, I'm pounded. Beat on. Until a gigantic honk wakes me up. A second honk saves me, so loud it echoes back from the nowhere over the horizon, all the bottomland cottonwoods and tall weeds all around me filled with Hank's loud car horn. Hank's whitewall tires skid to a stop.

Jenny's voice says, "Don't make him pissed off." She says, "Just get in the car."

I pop open my eyes, glued with blood and dust, and the ball just sits next to me in the road. Hank's pulled up, idling his engine. Under the car hood the engine revs, the pushrods banging and cams knocking.

Looking up at Jenny, I spit blood. Pink drool leaks out, running down my chin, and my tongue can feel my chipped teeth. One eye almost swelled shut, I say, "Jenny?" I say, "Will you marry me?"

The filthy tennis ball, waiting. Jenny's dog, panting in the backseat of the car. The jar filled with gold, hidden where only I can find it.

My ears glow hot and raw. My lips split and bleeding, I say, "If I can beat Hank Richardson just one game in tennis, will you marry me?"

Spitting blood, I say, "If I lose, I'll buy you a car. I swear." I say, "Brand-new with electric windows, power steering, a stereo, the works . . ."

The tennis ball sits, nested in the gravel, listening. Behind his steering wheel, Hank shakes his head side to side. "Deal," Hank says. "Hell, yeah, she'll marry you."

Sitting shotgun, her face framed in the car window, Jenny says, "It's your funeral." She says, "Now climb in."

Getting to my feet, standing, I stoop over and grab the tennis ball. For now, just something rubber filled with air. Not alive, in my hand the ball just feels wet with the creek water, soft with a layer of gravel dust. We drive to the tennis courts behind the high school, where nobody plays and the white lines look faded. The chain-link fences flake red rust, they were built so long ago. Weeds grow through the cracked concrete, and the tennis net sags in the middle.

Jenny flips a quarter, and Hanks gets to serve first.

His racquet whacks the ball, faster than I can see, into a corner where I could never reach, and Hank gets the first point. The same with his second point. The same with the whole first game.

When the serve comes to me, I hold the tennis ball close by my lips and whisper my deal. My bargain. If the ball helps me win the match— to win Jenny—I'll help with the gold. But if I lose to Hank, it can pound me dead and I'll never tell where the gold is hidden.

"Serve, already!" Hank yells. He says, "Stop kissing the damned ball . . . ."

My first serve drills Hank, ka-pow, in his nuts. My second takes out his left eye. Hank returns my third serve, fast and low, but the tennis ball slows to almost a stop and bounces right in front of me. With my every serve, the ball flies faster than I could ever hit it and knocks another tooth out of Hank's stupid mouth. Any returns, the ball swerves to me, slows, and bounces where I can hit it back.

No surprise, but I win.

Even crippled as I look, Hank looks worse, his eyes almost swollen shut. His knuckles puffed up and scabbed over. Hank's limping from so many drives straight to his crotch. Jenny helps him lie down in the backseat of his car so she can drive him home.

I tell her, "Even if I won, you don't have to go out with me. . . ."

And Jenny says, "Good."

I ask if it would make any difference if I was rich. Really super rich.

And Jenny says, "Are you?"

Sitting alone on the cracked tennis court, the ball looks red, stained with Hank's blood. It rolls, making looping blood-red handwriting that reads, "Forget her."

I wait and wait, then shake my head. "No. I'm not rich."

After they drive away, I pick up the tennis ball and head back toward Skinners Creek. From under the roots of the downed cottonwood tree, I lift out the Mason jar heavy with gold coins. Carrying the jar, I drop the ball. As it rolls away, I follow. Rolling uphill, violating every law of gravity, the ball rolls all afternoon. Rolling through weeds and sand, the ball rolls into the twilight. All this time, I follow behind, lugging that jar of gold treasure. Down Turner Road, down Millers Road, north along the old highway, then westbound along dirt roads with no name.

A bump rides the horizon, the sun setting behind it. As we get closer, the bump grows into a lump. A shack. From closer up, the shack is a house sitting in a nest of paint curls peeled off its wood by the weather and fallen to make a ring around its brick foundation. The same way dead skin peels off a sunburn. The bare wood siding curves and warps. On the roof, the tarpaper shingles buckle and ripple. Stapled to the front door, a sheet of yellow-color paper says, "Condemned."

The yellow paper, turned more yellow by the sunset. The gold in the Mason jar, shining even deeper gold in the yellow light.

The tennis ball rolls up the road, up the dirt driveway. It bounces up the brick steps, hitting the front door with a hollow sound. Bouncing off the porch, the ball beats the door again. From inside the house come footsteps, creaking and echoing on bare wood. From behind the closed door, the "Condemned" sign, a voice says, "Hello?"

A witch voice, cracked and brittle as the warped wood siding. A voice faint as the faded colors of paint flaked on the ground.

I knock, saying, "I have a delivery, I think. . . ."

The jar of gold, stretching my arm muscles into thin wire, into my bones almost breaking.

The tennis ball bounces off the door, again, beating one drumbeat.

The witch's voice says, "Go away, please."

The ball bounces against the wood door, only now the sound is metal. A clack of metal. A clank. Across the bottom of the door stretches a slot framed in gold-colored metal with the word "Letters" written under it.

Crouching down, then kneeling, I unscrew the Mason jar. Twisting off the cap, I put the lip of the jar against the "Letters" slot and tip the jar, shaking it to loosen up the coins inside. Kneeling there on the front porch, I pour the gold through the slot in the door. The coins rattle and ring, tumbling inside and rolling across the bare floor. A jackpot spilling out where I can't see. When the glass jar is empty, I leave it on the porch and start down the steps. Behind me, the doorknob pops, the snap of a lock turning, a deadbolt sliding open. The hinges creak, and a crack of inside darkness appears along one edge of the frame.

From that inside darkness, the witch voice says, "My husband's coin collection . . ."

The tennis ball, sticky with Hank's blood, coated with dirt, rolls along at my heels, following me the way Jenny's dog follows her. Tagging along the way I used to follow Jenny.

The witch voice says, "How did you find them?"

From the porch, the voice says, "Did you know my husband?"

The voice shouts, "Who are you?"

But me, I only keep walking away.

The Architect of Snow

David Morrell

On the first Monday in October, Samuel Carver, who was seventy-two and suddenly unemployed, stepped in front of a fast-moving bus. Carver was an editor for Edwin March & Sons, until recently one of the last privately owned publishing houses in New York.

"To describe Carver as an editor is an understatement," I said in his eulogy. Having indirectly caused his death, March & Sons, now a division of Gladstone International, sent me to represent the company at his funeral. "He was a legend. To find someone with his reputation, you need to go back to the nineteen-twenties, to Maxwell Perkins and his relationships with Ernest Hemingway, F. Scott Fitzgerald, and Thomas Wolfe. It was Perkins who massaged Hemingway's ego, helped Fitzgerald recover from hangovers, and realized that the two feet of manuscript Wolfe lugged into his office could be divided into several novels."

Standing next to Carver's coffin at the front of a Presbyterian church in lower Manhattan, I counted ten mourners. "Carver followed that example," I went on. "For much of the past five decades, he discovered an amazing number of major authors. He nurtured them through writer's block and discouraging reviews. He lent them money.

He promoted them tirelessly. He made them realize the scope of their creative powers. R. J. Wentworth's classic about childhood and stolen innocence, *The Sand Castle*. Carol Fabin's verse novel, *Wagon Mound*. Roger Kilpatrick's Vietnam war novel, *The Disinherited*. Eventual recipients of Pulitzer Prizes, these were buried in piles of unsolicited manuscripts that Carver loved to search through."

Ten mourners. Many of the authors Carver had championed were dead. Others had progressed to huge advances at bigger publishers and seemed to have forgotten their debt to him. A few retired editors paid their respects. *Publishers Weekly* sent someone who took a few notes. Carver's wife had died seven years earlier. They didn't have children. The church echoed coldly. So much for being a legend.

The official explanation was that Carver stumbled in front of the bus, but I had no doubt he committed suicide. Despite my praise about the past five decades, he hadn't been a creative presence since his wife's death. Age, ill health, and grief wore him down. At the same time, the book business changed so drastically that his instincts didn't fit. He was a lover of long shots, with the patience to give talent a chance to develop. But in the profit-obsessed climate of modern publishing, manuscripts needed to survive the focus groups of the marketing department. If the books weren't trendy and easily promotable, they didn't get accepted. For the past seven years, George March, the grandson of the company's founder, had loyally postponed forcing Carver into retirement, paying him a token amount to come to the office two days a week. The elderly gentleman had a desk in a corner where he studied unsolicited manuscripts and read newspapers. He also functioned as a corporate memory, although it was hard to imagine how stories about the good old days could help an editor survive in contemporary publishing. Not that it mattered—I was one of the few who asked him anything.

Eventually, March & Sons succumbed to a conglomerate. Gladstone International hoped to strengthen its film-and-broadcast division by acquiring a publisher and ordering it to focus on novels suited for movies and TV series. The trade buzzword for this is "synergy." As usually happens when a conglomerate takes over a business, the first thing the new owner did was downsize the staff, and Carver was an obvious target for elimination. Maybe he had felt that his former contributions made him immune. That would account for his stunned reaction when he came to work that Monday morning and got the bad news.

"What am I going to do?" I heard the old man murmur. His liver-spotted hands shook as he packed framed photographs into a flimsy box. "How will I manage? How will I fill the time?" Evidently, he decided that he wouldn't. The box in one hand, his umbrella in the other, he went outside and let the bus solve his problems.

Because Carver and I seemed to be friends, the new CEO put me in charge of whatever projects Carver was trying to develop. Mostly, that meant sending a few polite rejection letters. Also, I removed some items Carver forgot in his desk drawer: cough drops, chewing gum, and a packet of Kleenex.

"Mr. Neal?"

"Mmmm?" I glanced up from one of the hundreds of e-mails I received each day.

My assistant stood in my office doorway. His black turtleneck and sports coat gave him the appearance of authority. Young, tall, thin, and ambitious, he held a book mailer.

"This arrived for Mr. Carver. No return address. Should I handle it for you?"

In theory, it was an innocent suggestion. But in the new corporate climate, I doubted there was any such thing as an innocent suggestion. When my assistant offered to take one of my duties, I wondered if it was the first step in assuming *all* of my duties. After Carver was fired, three other editors, each over fifty, got termination notices. I'm forty-six. Mr. Carver. Mr. Neal. I often asked my assistant to call me Tom. He never complied. "Mister" isn't only a term of respect—it's also a way of depersonalizing the competition.

"Thanks, but I'll take care of it."

Determined to stake out my territory, I carried the package home. But I forgot about it until Sunday afternoon after I had worked through several gut-busting boxes of submissions that included two serial-killer novels and a romantic saga about California's wine country. The time-demanding tyranny of those manuscripts is one reason my wife had moved out years earlier. She said she lived as if she were single, so she might as well *be* single. Most days, I don't blame her.

A Yankees game was on television. I opened a beer, noticed the package on a side table, and decided to flip though its contents during commercials. When I tore it open, I found a manuscript. It was typed. Double-spaced in professional format. With unsolicited manuscripts, you can't count on that. It didn't reek of cigarette smoke or food odors, and that, too, was encouraging. Still, I was bothered not to find an introductory letter and return postage.

The manuscript didn't have the uniform typeface that word processors and printers create. Some letters were faint, others dark. Some were slightly above or below others. The author had actually put this through a typewriter, I realized in amazement. It was a novel called *The Architecture of Snow*. An evocative title, I decided, although the marketing department would claim that bookstore clerks would mistakenly put it in the arts-and-architecture section. The writer's name was Peter Thomas. Bland. The marketing department preferred last names that had easily remembered concrete nouns like "King," "Bond," or "Steele."

With zero expectation, I started to read. Hardly any time seemed to pass before the baseball game ended. My beer glass was empty, but I didn't remember drinking its contents. Surprised, I noticed the darkness outside my apartment's windows. I glanced at my watch. Ten o'clock? Another fifty pages to go. Eager to proceed, I made a sandwich, opened another beer, shut off the TV, and finished one of the best novels I'd read in years.

You dream about something like that. An absolutely perfect manuscript. Nothing to correct. Just a wonderful combination of hypnotic tone, powerful emotion, palpable vividness, beautiful sentences, and characters you never want to leave. The story was about a ten-year-old boy living alone with his divorced father on a farm in Vermont. In the middle of January, a blizzard hits the area. It knocks down electricity and telephone lines. It disables cell phone relays. It blocks roads and imprisons the boy and his father.

"The father starts throwing up," I told the marketing/editorial committee. "He gets a high fever. His lower right abdomen's in terrific pain. There's a medical book in the house, and it doesn't take them long to realize the father has appendicitis. But they can't telephone for help, and the father's too sick to drive. Even if he could, his truck would never get through the massive drifts. Meanwhile, with the power off, their furnace doesn't work. The temperature in the house drops to zero. When the boy isn't trying to do something for his father, he works to keep a fire going in the living room, where they retreat. Plus, the animals in the barn need food, the cows need milking. The boy has to struggle through the storm to reach the barn and keep them alive. With the pipes frozen, he can't get water from the well. He melts snow in pots near the fire. He heats canned soup for his dad, but the man's too sick to keep it down. Finally, the boy hears a snowplow on a nearby road. In desperation, he dresses as warmly as he can. He fights through drifts to try to reach the road."

"So basically it's a young adult book," the head of marketing interrupted without enthusiasm. Young adult is trade jargon for kid's story.

"A child might read it as an adventure, but an adult will see far more than that," I explained. "The emotions carry a world of meaning."

"Does the boy save the father?" the new CEO asked. He came from Gladstone's broadcast division.

"Nearly dying in the process."

"Well, at least it isn't a downer." The head of marketing shook his head from side to side. "A couple of days on a farm in a storm. Feels small. The book chains want global threats and international conspiracies."

"I promise—on the page, those few days feel huge. The ten-year-old becomes the father. The sick father becomes the son. At first, the boy's overwhelmed. Then he manages almost superhuman efforts."

"Child in jeopardy. The book won't appeal to women. What's the title mean?"

"The epigraph indicates that *The Architecture of Snow* is a quote from an Emerson poem about how everything in life is connected as if covered by snow."

The CEO sounded doubtful. "Has anybody heard of the author?"

"No."

"A first novel. A small subject. It'll be hard to persuade the book chains to support it. I don't see movie potential. Send the usual rejection letter."

"Can't," I said, risking my job. "The author didn't give a return address."

"A typical amateur."

"I don't think so." I paused, about to take the biggest risk of my career. But if my suspicion was correct, I no longer needed to worry about my job. "The book's beautifully, powerfully written. It has a distinctive, hypnotic rhythm. The punctuation's distinctive also: an unusual use of dashes and italics. A father and a son. Lost innocence. The book's style and theme are synonymous with . . ." I took the chance. "They remind me of R. J. Wentworth."

The CEO thought a moment. "*The Sand Castle?*"

"We've sold eight million copies so far, a hundred thousand paperbacks to colleges this year alone."

"You're suggesting someone imitated his style?"

"Not at all."

"Then . . . ?"

"I don't believe it's an imitation. I think Peter Thomas *is* R. J. Wentworth."

The room became so quiet, I heard traffic outside.

"But isn't Wentworth *dead?*" a marketer asked. "Wasn't he killed in a car accident in the sixties?"

"Not exactly."

October 15, 1961. Three disasters happened simultaneously. A movie based on one of Wentworth's short stories premiered that month. The story was called "The Fortune Teller," but the studio changed the title to *A Valentine for Two*. It also added a couple of songs. Those changes confirmed Wentworth's suspicions about Hollywood. The only reason he sold the rights to the short story was that every producer was begging for *The Sand Castle* and he decided to use "The Fortune Teller" as a test case. He lived with his wife and two sons in Connecticut. The family begged him to drive them into Manhattan for the premiere, to see how truly bad the film was and laugh it off. En route, rain turned to sleet. The car flipped off the road. Wentworth's wife and two sons were killed.

The film was more dreadful than anyone imagined. The story's New England setting became a cruise ship. A teenage idol played the main character—originally a college professor but now a dance instructor. Every review was scathing. Nearly all of them blamed Wentworth for giving Hollywood the chance to pervert a beloved story. Most critics wrote their attacks in mock Wentworth prose, with his distinctive rhythms and his odd use of dashes and italics.

Meanwhile, his new book, a collection of two novellas, *Opposites Attract*, was published the same day. March & Sons wanted to take advantage of the movie publicity. Of course, when the date was originally chosen, no one could have known how rotten the movie would be. By the time rumors spread, it was too late to change the schedule. Reviewers already had the book in their hands. It was charming. It was entertaining. In many places, it was even meaningful. But it wasn't as magnificent as *The Sand Castle*. Anticipation led to disappointment, which turned to nastiness. Many reviewers crowed that Wentworth wasn't the genius some had reputed him to be. They took another look at *The Sand Castle* and now faulted passages in *it*.

"All on the same day," I told the marketing/editorial committee.

"October 15, 1961. Wentworth blamed everything on himself. His fiction echoes transcendental writers like Thoreau, so it isn't surprising that he followed Thoreau's example and retreated to the countryside— in this case, Vermont, where he bought a house on two acres outside a small town called Tipton. He enclosed the property with a high fence, and that was the end of his public life. But the myth started when *Time* put him on its cover and told as much as it could without being able to interview him. College students began romanticizing his retreat to the countryside: the grieving, guilt-ridden author, father, and husband living in isolation. When the paperback of *Opposites Attract* was published, it became a two-year best seller. More than that, it was suddenly perceived as a minor masterpiece. Not *The Sand Castle*, of course. But far superior to what critics first maintained. With each year of his seclusion, his reputation increased."

"How do you know so much about him?" the head of marketing asked.

"I wrote several essays about him when I was an undergrad at Penn State."

"And you're convinced this is a genuine Wentworth manuscript?"

"One of the tantalizing rumors about him is that, although he never published anything after 1961, he kept writing every day. He implied as much to a high school student who knocked on his gate and actually got an interview with him."

"Those essays you wrote made you an expert? You're confident you can tell the real thing from an imitation?" the CEO asked.

"The book's set in Vermont, where Wentworth retreated. The boy limps from frostbite on his right foot, the same foot Wentworth injured in the accident. But I have another reason to believe it's genuine. Wentworth's editor, the man who discovered him, was Samuel Carver."

"*Carver?*" The CEO leaned forward in surprise. "After more than forty years, Wentworth finally sent his editor a manuscript? Why the pseudonym?"

"I don't have an answer. But the absence of a letter and a return address tells me that the author expected Carver to know how to get in touch with him. I can think of only one author who could take that for granted."

"Jesus," the CEO said, "if we can prove this was written by Wentworth—"

"Every talk show would want him," the head of marketing said. "A legendary hermit coming out of seclusion. A solitary genius ready to tell his story. Larry King would jump at the chance. The *Today* show. *Sixty Minutes*. *Oprah*. My God, *Oprah*. He'd easily make the cover of *Time* again. Maybe *Newsweek*. Maybe both. We'd have a guaranteed number-one best seller."

"Wait a second," a marketer asked. "How *old* is he?"

"Seventy-eight," I answered.

"Maybe he can barely talk. Maybe he'd be useless on *Oprah*."

"That's one of a lot of things you need to find out," the CEO told me. "Track him down. Find out if he wrote this manuscript. Our parent company wants a twenty-percent increase in profits. We won't do that by promoting authors who sell only fifty or a hundred thousand hardbacks. We need a million-seller. I'm meeting the Gladstone executives on Monday. They want to know what progress we're making. It would be fabulous if I could tell them we have Wentworth."

I tried to telephone Wentworth's agent to see if she had contact information. But it turned out that she had died twelve years earlier and that no arrangements had been made for anyone else to represent the author, who wasn't expected to publish again. I called Vermont's telephone directory assistance and learned that Wentworth didn't have a listed phone number. The Author's Guild couldn't help either.

My CEO walked in. "What did he tell you? Does he admit he's the author?"

"I haven't been able to ask him. I can't find a way to contact him."

"This is too important. Show some initiative. Go up there. Knock on his door. Keep knocking until he answers."

I got a map and located Tipton in the southern part of Vermont. Few people live near the town, I discovered. It was hard to reach by plane or train, so the next morning, I rented a car and drove six hours north through Connecticut and Massachusetts.

In mid-October, Vermont's maple-covered hills had glorious colors, although I was too preoccupied to give them full attention. With difficulty—because a crossroads wasn't clearly marked—I reached Tipton (population 5,073) after dark and checked into one of its few motels without getting a look at the town.

At eight the next morning, I stepped from my room and breathed cool, clean air. Rustic buildings lined the main street, mostly white clapboards with high-pitched roofs. A church steeple towered above a square. Calm. Clean. Quiet. Ordered. The contrast with Manhattan was dramatic.

Down the street, a sign read Meg's Pantry. As I passed an antique store, I had the palpable sense of former years. I imagined that, except for satellite dishes and SUVs, Tipton looked the same now as it had a hundred years earlier, perhaps *two* hundred years, that the town was a time capsule. Then I noticed a plaque: Jeremiah Tipton Constructed This Bulding in 1792.

When I opened the door, the smell of coffee, pancakes, eggs, bacon, and hash browns overwhelmed me. A dozen ruddy-faced patrons looked up from their breakfasts. My pale cheeks made me self-conscious, as did my slacks and sports coat. Amid jeans and checkered wool shirts, I obviously wasn't a local. Not that I sensed hostility. A town that earned its income from tourists tolerated strangers.

As they resumed their murmured conversations, I sat at the counter. A gray-haired woman with spectacles came over, gave me a menu, and pulled a notepad from an apron.

"What's the special?" I asked.

"Corned beef and eggs."

Tension ruined my appetite, but I knew I couldn't establish rapport if my bill wasn't high enough for the waitress to expect a good tip. "I'll take it."

"Coffee?"

"You bet. Regular. And orange juice."

When she brought the food, I said, "Town's kind of quiet."

"Gets busy on the weekends. Especially now that the leaves are in color."

When she brought the check, I said, "I'm told there's a writer who lives in the neighborhood. R. J. Wentworth."

Everyone looked at me.

"Wentworth? I don't think I ever heard of him," the waitress said. "Mind you, I'm not a reader."

"You'd love his books," I said. The obvious response to a statement like that is, "Really? What are they about?" But all I received was a guarded look. "Keep the change," I said.

Subtlety not having worked, I went outside and noticed slightly more activity on the street. Some of it wasn't reassuring. A rumpled guy in ragged clothes came out of an alley. He had the vacant look of a druggy.

Other movement caught my attention. A slender man wearing a cap and a windbreaker reached a bookstore across the street, unlocked its door, and went in. When I crossed to it, I saw that most of the volumes in the window had lush covers depicting covered bridges, autumn foliage, or snow-covered slopes, with titles related to Vermont's history and beauty. But one volume, small and plain, was a history of Tipton. I tried the door and found it was locked.

Through the window, I saw the slender man take off his windbreaker. His cap was already off, revealing thin hair. He turned toward the rattling doorknob and shook his head, motioning courteously for me to leave. When I pretended to be confused, he walked over and unlocked the door.

"I'm not open yet. Can you come back in an hour?"

"Sure. I want to buy that book in the window—the history of Tipton."

That caught his attention. "You've got excellent taste. Come in."

An overhead bell rang when he opened the door wider. The store was filled with pleasant mustiness. He tugged a pen from his shirt pocket. "I'll autograph it for you."

"You're the author?"

"Guilty."

I looked at the cover. *Tales of Historic Tipton* by Jonathan Wade. "I'm from New York. An editor for March and Sons. It's always a pleasure to meet an author."

"You're here to see the colors?" Wade asked.

"A little pleasure with business." I handed him fifteen dollars for the book.

"Business?"

"An author lives around here."

"Oh?"

"R. J. Wentworth."

"Oh?"

"I need to speak to him."

"Couldn't you just write him a letter?"

"I don't have his address."

"I see." Wade pointed at the book in my hands. "And you thought perhaps the address is in *there*?"

"The thought crossed my mind."

"You won't find it. Still want to buy the book?"

"Absolutely. I love history, and when I meet an author, I'm always curious to see how he writes."

"Not with the brilliance of R. J. Wentworth, I regret to say. We used to get people asking about him all the time. Thirty years ago, my father had a thriving business, selling Wentworth's books to people who asked about him. In fact, without Wentworth, he wouldn't have made a living. Nor would anybody else in town, for that matter. Tipton would have dried up if not for the tourists Wentworth attracted."

"But not anymore?"

"His fans got old, I guess, and people don't read much these days."

"So a waitress across the street told me."

"This town owes him a lot, even if he didn't mean to do us a favor. In these parts, if you're not born here, you're always an outsider. But after more than forty years of living here, he's definitely one of us. You won't find anybody who'll tell you where he is. I wouldn't be able to look him in the eyes if I violated his privacy."

"In the eyes?" I asked in amazement. "You mean you've spoken with him?"

"Despite Bob's reputation for being a hermit, he isn't antisocial."

"'Bob'?" I asked in greater amazement. The familiarity sounded almost profane.

"His first name is Robert, after all. He insists on being called Bob. He comes into town on occasion. Buys books. Eats at the Pantry. Gets a haircut. Watches a baseball game at the tavern down the street."

I continued to be astounded.

"Not often and certainly never on a weekend during peak tourist season," Wade said. "He picks times when he knows he can move around without being bothered."

"Even at his age?"

"You'd be surprised."

"But what's he like?"

"Polite. Considerate. He doesn't make assumptions about himself. What I mostly notice is how clear his eyes are. You've read his work?"

"Many times."

"Then you know how much it's influenced by transcendentalism. He's like Thoreau. Calm. Still. Reflective. It's soothing to be around him."

"But you won't help me meet him?"

"Definitely not."

"Could you at least phone him and try to arrange a meeting?"

"Can't."

"I understand."

"I'm not sure you do. I literally can't. Bob doesn't have a telephone. And I'm not about to knock on his door. Why do you need to talk to him?"

I told Wade about the manuscript. "I think it's his work, but it doesn't have his name on it." I added the detail that I hoped would make Wade cooperate. "It was addressed to his editor. But unfortunately, his editor died recently. They were friends. I wonder if he's been told."

"I only have your word that you're an editor."

"Here's my business card."

"Twenty years ago, a man showed me a business card, claiming he worked in the White House. He said the President wanted to give Bob an award, but he turned out to be an assistant to a Hollywood producer who wanted the movie rights for *The Sand Castle*."

"What harm would it do to put a note in his mailbox?"

"I've never intruded on him. I'm not about to start now."

Outside, a pickup truck rattled past. A few more locals appeared on the sidewalk. Another rumpled guy came out of an alley. A half-block to my right, a Jeep was parked outside an office marked Tipton Realty. I walked over and pretended to admire a display of properties for sale: farms, cabins, and historic-looking homes.

When I stepped inside, the hardwood floor creaked. The smell of furniture polish reminded me of my grandmother's house.

At an antique desk, an attractive red-haired woman looked up from a computer screen. "May I help you?" Her voice was pleasant.

"I was wondering if you had a map of the roads around here. My Vermont map doesn't provide much detail."

"Looking for property?"

"Don't know yet. As you can probably tell, I'm not from around here. But the scenery's so magnificent, I thought I might drive around and see if anything appeals to me."

"A weekend place to live?"

"Something like that."

"You're from New York, right?"

"It's that obvious?"

"I meet a lot of people passing through. I'm a good judge of accents. New York's a little far to have a weekend place here."

"I'm not sure it would be just for weekends. I'm a book editor. But I've given some thought to writing a novel."

This attracted her interest.

"I hear the location has inspired other writers," I said. "Doesn't John Irving live in Vermont?"

"And David Mamet and Grace Paley."

"And R. J. Wentworth," I said. "Doesn't he live around here?"

Her expression became guarded.

"Great writer," I said.

Her tone was now curt. "You'll find maps on that table."

As I walked to my car, I thought that the CIA or the mafia ought to send their recruits for training in Tipton. The townspeople knew how to keep secrets. I chose north, driving along brilliantly wooded back roads. The fragrance of the falling leaves was powerful, reminding me of my boyhood on Long Island, of helping my father rake the yard. He burned the leaves in a fallow vegetable garden behind our house. He always let me strike the match. He died from a heart attack when I was twelve.

I turned up a dirt road, passed a cabin, reached a wall of trees, and went back to the main road. Farther along, I turned up another dirt road, passed *two* cabins, reached a stream that blocked the road, and again went back.

My search wasn't as futile as it seemed. After all, I knew what I was looking for: a high fence that enclosed a couple of acres. The female student who'd been fortunate enough to get an interview with Wentworth years earlier had described the property. The high gate was almost indistinguishable from the fence, she wrote. The mailbox was embedded in the fence and had a hatch on the opposite side so Wentworth didn't need to leave the compound to get his mail. A sign warned No Solicitors.

But nothing in the north sector matched that description. Of course, the student's interview was two decades old. Wentworth might have changed things since then, in which case I was wasting my time. How far away from town would he have wanted to live? I arbitrarily decided that fifteen miles was too far and switched my search to the side roads in the west. More farms and cabins, more falling leaves and wood smoke. By the time I finished the western sector and headed south, the afternoon light was fading.

My cell phone rang.

"Have you found him yet?" my boss demanded.

The reception was so poor, I could barely hear him. When I explained the problems I was having, he interrupted. "Just get it done. If Wentworth wrote this book, remind him his last contract with March and Sons gives us the option on it. There's no way I'm going to let anybody else publish it. Do you have the agreement with you?"

"In my jacket."

"Make sure you get him to sign it."

"He'll want to talk to an agent."

"You told me his agent's dead. Anyway, why does he need an agent? We'll give him whatever he wants. Within reason." The transmission crackled. "This'll go a long way toward proving you're a necessary part of the team." The crackle worsened. "Don't disappoint . . . Call . . . soon . . . find . . ."

With renewed motivation, I searched the southern sector, not giving up until dark. In town, I refilled the gas tank, ready for an early start the next morning. Then I walked along the shadowy main street, noticing For Sale signs on a lot of doors. The financial troubles gave me an idea.

Tipton Realty had its lights on. I knocked.

"Come in," a woman's voice said.

As I entered, I couldn't help noticing my haggard reflection on the door's window.

Again the hardwood floor creaked.

"Busy day?" The same woman sat at the desk. She was about thirty-five. Her lush red hair hung past her shoulders. Her bright green eyes were hard to look away from.

"I saw a lot of beautiful country."

"Did you find him?"

"Find . . .?"

"Bob Wentworth. Everybody in town knows you're looking for him."

I glanced down. "I guess I'd make a poor spy. No, I didn't find him." I held out my hand. "Tom Neal."

She shook it. "Becky Shafer."

"I can't get used to people calling him 'Bob.' I gather you've met him."

"Not as much as other people in Tipton. I'm new."

"Oh?"

"Yeah, I came here only twelve years ago."

I chuckled.

"I drove into town with my artist boyfriend," she said. "We loved the quiet and the scenery. We decided to stay. The boyfriend's long gone, but I'm still a newcomer."

"Sorry about the boyfriend." I noticed she didn't wear a wedding ring.

"No need to be sorry. He turned out to be a creep."

"A lot of that going around." I thought of my CEO.

She gave me a look that made me think she applied the word to me.

"I do have an important reason to see him," I said.

After I told her about the manuscript, she thought a moment. "But why would he use a pseudonym?"

"That's one of many things I'd like to ask him." Thinking of the For Sale signs, I took my chance to propose my idea. "To hear the old-timers tell it, things got crazy here with so many fans wanting to talk to him. You can imagine the effect a new book would create. The publicity. The pent-up demand. This town would attract a lot of fans again. It would be like the excitement of thirty years ago."

I let the temptation sink in.

Becky didn't respond for several moments. Her gaze hardened. "So all I need to do is show you where Bob lives, and in exchange, next year I'll have more business than I can handle?"

"When you put it that way, I guess that's right," I said.

"Gosh, I didn't realize it was so late." She angrily pulled her car keys from her purse. "You'll have to excuse me. I need to go home."

The weathered old Tipton Tavern was presumably the place Wade had told me about, where Wentworth sometimes watched a baseball game. There was indeed a baseball game on the TV, but I was the main interest—the patrons set down their drinks and looked at me. As much as I could tell from recalling the photograph on Wentworth's books (a dark-haired man with soulful eyes), he wasn't in the room.

Heading back to the motel, I didn't go far before I heard wary footsteps behind me. A cold breeze made me shiver as I glanced back toward the shadowy street. The footsteps ended. I resumed walking and again heard stealthy footsteps. My Manhattan instincts took charge. Not quite running, I passed my car and reached the motel. My cold hands fumbled with the room key.

In the night, glass broke outside my room. I phoned the front desk, but no one answered. In the morning, not having slept well, I went out to my car and found the driver's window shattered. A rock lay on the seat. The radio was gone.

The surprised desk clerk told me, "The town constable runs the barbershop."

But the barbershop wasn't open yet. Nor did I find it open after a quick cup of coffee at Meg's Pantry. Determined not to waste time, I swept the broken glass from the seat and drove to the hills east of town. But after a painstaking search, I found nothing that resembled Wentworth's compound.

By then, it was noon. When I got back to town, the barbershop was open. It smelled of aftershave.

"Yes, we've been having incidents lately." The heavyset barber trimmed an elderly man's spindly hair. "A bicycle was stolen. A cabin was broken into."

I took a close look at the man in the chair and decided he wasn't Wentworth.

"Town's changing. Outsiders are hanging around," the barber continued.

I recalled the two druggies I'd seen emerge from an alley the previous day. "What are you going to do about it?"

"Contact the state police. I hoped the problem would go away as the weather got colder."

"Please remember I reported the stolen radio. The rental car agency will contact you." Hoping to catch him off guard, I added, "Where does Bob Wentworth live?"

The barber almost responded. Then he caught himself. "Can't say."

But like a bad poker player, he couldn't repress a glance past me toward the right side of the street.

"Thanks anyway," I said.

I went to the left to avoid suspicion. Then I walked around the block and returned to the main street, out of sight of the barbershop. As I stepped from an alley, I again had the sense that someone was following me, but when I looked back, I seemed alone.

More people were on the sidewalk, many dressed like outsiders, the town finally attracting business as the weekend approached. But the locals paid attention only to me. Trying to look casual, I went into a quilt shop, then continued down the street. Wentworth didn't live on a country road, I now realized with growing excitement. He was in town. But I'd checked all the side streets. In fact, I'd used some of those streets to drive north, west, south, and east. Where was he hiding?

Then I saw it. On my left, a gate blocked a lane between an empty store and a cookie shop. The gate had the same white color as the adjacent buildings. It blended so well that I hadn't noticed it despite having driven past it several times. The blocked lane went past buildings toward the edge of town.

I walked to the end of the street. In a park of brilliant maples, dead leaves crunched under my shoes as I followed a stream. I soon reached a tall fence.

My cell phone rang.

"I hope you've found him," a stern voice said.

"I'm making progress."

"I want more than progress. The Gladstone executives phoned to remind me they expect a better profit picture when I report on Monday. I hinted I'd have major news. Don't let me down. Get Wentworth, or don't come back."

Another gate blocked a lane. It was as high as my shoulders, but I managed to climb over, tearing a button off my sports jacket.

Sunlight cast the shadows of branches. To my left were the backyards of houses. But on my right, the fence stretched on. A crow cawed. Leaves rattled as I came to a door that blended with the fence. A sign warned No Solicitors. A mailbox was recessed into the fence.

When I knocked on the door, the crow stopped cawing. The door shook. I waited, then knocked again, this time harder. The noise echoed in the lane. I knocked a third time.

"Mr. Wentworth?"

Leaves fell.

"Mr. Wentworth? My name's Tom Neal. I work for March and Sons. I need to talk to you about a manuscript we think you sent."

A breeze chilled my face.

I knocked a fourth time, hurting my knuckles. "*Mr. Wentworth?*"

Finally, I took out a pen and a notepad. I thought about writing that Carver was dead, but that seemed a harsh way for Wentworth to get the news. So I gave him the name of the motel and left my cell phone number. Then I remembered that Wentworth didn't have a phone. But if he sometimes left his compound, he could use a phone in town, I concluded. Or he could walk to the motel.

"I'm shoving a note under the gate!"

Back in the park, I sat on a bench and tried to enjoy the view, but the breeze got cooler. After an hour, I climbed back into the lane and returned to Wentworth's gate. A corner of my note remained visible under it.

"Mr. Wentworth, *please*, I need to talk to you! It's important!"

Maybe he's gone for a walk in the woods, I thought. Or maybe he isn't even in town. Hell, he might be in a hospital somewhere.

"Did you find him?"

In the tavern, I looked up from a glass of beer. "No." Strictly speaking, it wasn't a lie.

Becky Shafer stood next to me at the bar. Her green eyes were as hypnotic as they had been on the previous evening. "I saw you walk in here," she said.

"You and everybody else in town."

"I thought about our conversation last night. I came to apologize for being abrupt."

"Hey, I'm from New York, remember? It's impossible to be abrupt to me. Anyway, I can't blame you for trying to protect someone who lives here."

"May I sit down?"

"I welcome the company. Can I buy you a beer?"

"Rye and diet Coke."

"Rye?" I mock shuddered. "I admire an honest drinker."

She laughed as the bartender took my order. "Maybe it *would* be good for the town if Bob published another book. Who knows? It's just that I don't like to feel manipulated."

"I'm so used to being manipulated, it feels normal."

She gave me a questioning look.

"When I first became an editor, all I needed to worry about was helping an author write a good book. But now conglomerates own just about every publisher. They think of books as commodities like laundry detergent. If authors don't sell a quarter million copies, the head office doesn't care about them, and editors who don't find the next blockbuster are taking up space. Every morning, I go to March and Sons wondering if I still work there. What's that line from Joseph Heller? 'Closed doors give me the willies.' Damned right."

"I know what you mean." Becky sipped her drink. "I'm also an attorney." My surprised look made her nod. "Yep. Harvard Law School."

"I'm impressed."

"So was the Boston law firm that hired me. But I couldn't bear how the senior partners pitted us against each other to see who generated the most fees. That's why I ended up here. I don't earn much money, but I sure enjoy waking up each morning."

"I don't hear many people say that."

"Stay here longer. Maybe you'll be able to say it."

Walking back to the motel, I again heard footsteps. As on the previous night, they stopped when I turned toward the shadows. Their echo resumed when I moved on. Thinking of my broken car window, I increased speed. My cell phone rang, but I didn't have time to answer it. Only after I entered my room and locked the door did I listen to the message, hoping it was from Wentworth.

But the voice belonged to my CEO. "You're taking too long," he told me.

"Mr. Wentworth?" At nine the next morning, amid a strong breeze, I pounded on his gate. "It's really important that I talk to you about your manuscript! And Sam Carver! I need to talk to you about *him!*"

I stared at the bottom of the gate. Part of my note still remained visible. A thought from yesterday struck me. Maybe he isn't home. Or maybe—a new thought struck harder—maybe he *is* home. Maybe he's sick. Too sick to come to the gate.

"Mr. Wentworth?" I hammered the gate. "Are you all right?" I tried the knob, but it didn't turn. "Mr. Wentworth, can you hear me? Is anything wrong? *Do you need help?*"

Perhaps there was another way in. Chilled by the strengthening breeze, I returned the way I had come and climbed back into the park. I followed the fence to a corner, then continued along the back, struggling through dense trees and undergrowth.

Indeed, there *was* another way in. Hidden among bushes, a gate shuddered as I pounded. "Mr. Wentworth?" I shoved a branch away and tried the knob, but it, too, wouldn't turn. I rammed my shoulder against the gate, but it held firm. A tree grew next to the fence. I grabbed a branch and pulled myself up. Higher branches acted as steps. Buffeted by the wind, I straddled the fence, squirmed over, dangled, and dropped into a pile of soft leaves.

Immediately, I felt a difference. The wind stopped. Sounds were muted. The air became cushioned, as if a bubble enclosed the property. A buffer of some kind. No doubt, the effect was caused by the tall fence. Or maybe it was because I'd entered sacred territory. As far as I knew, I was one of the few ever to set foot there. Although I breathed quickly, I felt a hush.

Apples hung on trees or lay on the ground amid leaves. A few raspberries remained on bushes. A vegetable garden contained the frost-browned remnants of tomato plants. Pumpkins and acorn squash bulged from vines. Continuing to be enveloped in a hush, I walked along a stone path bordered by rosebushes. Ahead were a gazebo, a cottage, and a smaller building, the latter two made from white clapboard.

"Mr. Wentworth?"

When I rounded the gazebo and headed toward the cottage, I heard a door creak open. A man stepped out. He wore sneakers, jeans, and a sweater. He was slender, with slightly graying hair. He had dark, intense eyes.

But what I noticed most was the pistol in his hand.

"Wait." I jerked up my hands, thinking, My God, he's been living alone for so long, he's lost his mind. He's going to shoot me.

"Walk to the front gate."

"This isn't what it looks like." My chest cramped. "I thought you were ill. I came to see if I can help."

"Stay ahead of me."

"My name's Tom Neal. I knocked on the gate."

"*Move.*"

"I left a note. I'm an editor for March and Sons. Please," I blurted. "I need to talk to you about a manuscript I think you sent us. It was addressed to Sam Carver. He's dead. I took over his duties. That's why—"

"Stop," the man said.

His command made the air feel stiller. Crows cawing, squirrels scampering along branches, leaves falling: everything seemed to halt.

"Sam's dead?" The man frowned, as if the notion was unthinkable.

"A week ago Monday."

Slowly, he lowered the gun. He had Wentworth's sensitive features and soulful eyes. But Wentworth would be in his late seventies, and this man looked twenty years younger, his cheeks aglow.

"Who *are* you?" I asked.

The man rubbed his forehead in shock. "What? Who . . . ? Nobody. Bob's son. He's out of town. I'm watching the house for him."

Bob's son? But that didn't make sense. The child would have been born when Wentworth was around twenty, before he got married, before *The Sand Castle* was published. Later, the furor of interest in Wentworth was so great that it would have been impossible to keep an illegitimate child a secret.

The man continued to look shocked. "What happened to Sam?"

I explained about the firm's new owner and how Carver was fired.

"The way you talk about the bus, are you suggesting . . ."

"I don't think Sam had much to live for. The look on his face when he carried his belongings from the office . . ."

The man seemed to peer at something far away. "Too late."

"What?"

Despondent, he shook his head from side to side. "The gate self-locks. Let yourself out."

As he turned toward the cottage, he limped.

"You're not Wentworth's son."

He paused.

"The limp's from your accident. You're R. J. Wentworth. You look twenty years younger. I don't know how that's possible, but that's who you are."

I've never been looked at so deeply. "Sam was your friend?"

"I admired him."

His dark eyes assessed me. "Wait here."

When he limped from the house, he held a teapot and two cups. He looked so awkward that I reached to help.

We sat in the gazebo. The air felt more cushioned and soothing. My sense of reality was tested. R. J. Wentworth. Could I actually be talking to him?

"How can you look twenty years younger than you are?"

Wentworth ignored the question and poured the tea.

He stared at the steaming fluid. His voice was tight. "I met Sam Carver in 1958 after he found *The Sand Castle* in a stack of unsolicited manuscripts. At the time, I was a teacher in a grade school in Connecticut. My wife taught there also. I didn't know about agents and how publishing worked. All I knew about was children and the sadness of watching them grow up. *The Sand Castle* was rejected by twenty publishers. If Sam hadn't found it, I'd probably have remained a teacher, which in the long run would have been better for me and certainly for my family. Sam understood that. After the accident, he was as regretful as I that *The Sand Castle* gained the attention it did." He raised his cup. "To Sam."

"To Sam." I sipped, tasting a hint of cinnamon and cloves.

"He and his wife visited me each summer. He was a true friend. Perhaps my only one. After his wife died, he didn't come here again, however."

"You sent him *The Architecture of Snow*?"

Wentworth nodded. "Sam wrote me a letter that explained what was happening at March and Sons. You described his stunned look when he was fired. Well, he may have been stunned, but he wasn't surprised. He saw it coming. I sent the manuscript so he could pretend to make one last discovery and buy himself more time at the company."

"But why didn't you use your real name?"

"Because I wanted the manuscript to stand on its own. I didn't want the novel to be published because of the mystique that developed after I disappeared. The deaths of my wife and two sons caused that mystique. I couldn't bear using it to get the book published."

"The manuscript's brilliant."

He hesitated. "Thank you." I've never heard anyone speak more humbly.

"You've been writing all these years?"

"All these years."

He sipped his tea. After a thoughtful silence, he stood and motioned for me to follow. We left the gazebo. Limping, he took me to the small building next to the cottage. He unlocked its door and led me inside. His writing studio. For a moment, my heart beat faster. Then the hush of the room spread through me. The place had the calm of a sanctuary. I noticed a fireplace, a desk, a chair, and a manual typewriter.

"I have five more machines just like it—in case I need parts," Wentworth said.

I imagined the typewriter's bell sounding when Wentworth reached the end of each line. A ream of paper lay next to the typewriter, along with a package of carbon paper. A window directed light from behind the desk.

And in front of the desk? I approached shelves upon which were arranged twenty-one manuscripts. I counted them. *Twenty-one.* They sent a shiver through me. "All these years," I repeated.

"Writing can be a form of meditation."

"And you never felt the urge to have them published?"

"To satisfy an ego I worked hard to eliminate? No."

"But isn't an unread book the equivalent of one hand clapping?"

He shrugged. "It would mean returning to the world."

"But you did send a manuscript to Sam."

"As Peter Thomas. As a favor to my friend. But I had doubts that the ploy would work. In his final letter, Sam said the changes in publishing were too grim to be described."

"True. In the old days, an editor read a manuscript, liked it, and bought it. But now the manuscript goes to the marketing department first. Then the marketing department takes the manuscript to the book chains and asks them, 'If we publish this, how many copies do you think you'll order?' If the number isn't high enough, the book doesn't have a chance."

Wentworth was appalled. "How can a book with an original vision get published? After a while, everything will be the same. The strain on your face. Now I understand. You hate the business."

"The way it's become."

"Then why do you stay?"

"Because, God help me, I remember how excited I felt when I discovered a wonderful new book and found readers for it. I keep hoping corporations will realize books aren't potato chips."

Wentworth's searching eyes were amazingly clear. I felt self-conscious, as if he saw into me, sensing my frustration.

"It's a pleasant day. Why don't we go back to the gazebo?" he asked. "I have some things I need to do. But perhaps you could pass the time by reading one of these manuscripts. I'd like your opinion."

For a moment, I was too surprised to respond. "You're serious?"

"An editor's perspective would be helpful."

"The last thing you need is my help." I couldn't believe my good fortune. "But I'd love to read something else you've written."

The things Wentworth had to do turned out to be raking leaves, putting them in a compost bin, and cleaning his gardens for winter. Surrounded by the calming air, I sat in the gazebo and watched him, reminded of my father. Amid the muted sounds of crows, squirrels, and leaves, I finished my cup of tea, poured another, and started the manuscript, *A Cloud of Witnesses*.

In a slum in Boston, a five-year-old boy named Eddie lived with his mother, who was seldom at home. The implication was that she haunted bars, prostituting herself in exchange for alcohol. Because Eddie was forbidden to leave the crummy apartment (the even worse hallways were filled with drug dealers and perverts), he didn't have any friends. The TV was broken. He resorted to the radio and, by trial and error, found a station that had an afternoon call-in program, *You Get It Straight from Jake*, hosted by a comedian named Jake Barton. Jake had an irreverent way of relating to the day's events, and even though Eddie didn't understand most of the events referred to, he loved the way Jake talked. Jake made Eddie laugh.

As I turned the pages, the sound of crows, squirrels, and leaves became muffled. I heard Wentworth raking but as if from a great distance, farther and fainter. My vision narrowed until I was conscious only of the page in front of me, Eddie looking forward to each day's broadcast of *You Get It Straight from Jake,* Eddie laughing at Jake's tone, Eddie wishing he had a father like Jake, Eddie . . .

A hand nudged my shoulder, the touch so gentle I barely felt it.

"Tom," a voice whispered.

"Uh."

"Tom, wake up."

My eyelids flickered. Wentworth stood before me. It was difficult to see him, everything was so shadowy. I was flat on my back on the bench. I jerked upright.

"My God, I fell asleep," I said.

"You certainly did." Wentworth looked amused.

I glanced around. It was dusk. "All day? I slept all day? I'm so sorry."

"Why?"

"Well, I barge in on you, but you're generous enough to let me read a manuscript, and then I fall asleep reading it, and—"

"You needed the rest. Otherwise, you wouldn't have dozed."

"Dozed? I haven't slept that soundly in years. It had nothing to do with . . . Your book's wonderful. It's moving and painful and yet funny and . . . I just got to the part where Jake announces he's been fired from the radio station and Eddie can't bear losing the only thing in his life he enjoys."

"There's plenty of time. Read more after we eat."

"Eat?"

"I made soup and a salad."

"But I can't impose."

"I insist."

Except for a stove and refrigerator, the kitchen might have looked the same two hundred years earlier. The floor, the cabinets, and the walls were aged wood, with a golden hue that made me think they were maple. The table and chairs were dark, perhaps oak, with dents here and there from a lifetime of use. Flaming logs crackled in a fireplace.

I smelled freshly baked bread and, for the first time in a long while, felt hungry. The soup was vegetable. I ate three servings and two helpings of salad, not to mention a half loaf of bread.

"The potatoes, tomatoes, onions, and carrots—everything in the soup comes from my garden," Wentworth said. "The growing season is brief here. I need to be resourceful. For example, the lettuce comes from a late summer planting that I keep in a glass frame so I can harvest it in the winter."

The fresh taste was powerful, warming my stomach. Somehow, I had room for two slices of apple pie, which was also homemade, the fruit from Wentworth's trees. And tea. Two cups of tea.

Helping clean the dishes, I yawned. Embarrassed, I covered my mouth. "Sorry."

"Don't be. It's natural to feel sleepy after we eat. That's what mammals do. After they eat, they sleep."

"But I slept all day."

"A sign of how much rest you need. Lie down on the sofa in the living room. Read more of my book."

"But I ought to go back to my motel room."

"Nonsense." Limping, Wentworth guided me into the living room. The furnishings reminded me of those I saw long ago in my grandmother's house. The sofa was covered with a blanket.

"I won't be an imposition?"

"I welcome your reaction to my manuscript. I won't let you take it with you to the motel, so if you want to read it, you need to do it here."

I suppressed another yawn, so tired that I wondered if I'd fall asleep on the way to the motel. I wouldn't be alert enough to deal with anyone following me. "Thank you."

"You're more than welcome." Wentworth brought me the rest of the manuscript, and again I felt amazed that I was in his company.

The fireplace warmed me. On the sofa, I sat against a cushion and turned the pages, once more absorbed in the story. Jake was fired from the radio station. He announced that he had only two more broadcasts and then would leave Boston for a talk show in Cincinnati. The upcoming loss devastated Eddie. He hadn't seen his mother in two days. All he had to eat was peanut butter and crackers. He put them in a pillowcase. He added a change of clothes, then went to the door and listened. He heard footsteps. Somebody cursed. Then the sounds became distant, and Eddie did the forbidden—he unlocked and opened the door. The lights were broken in most of the hallway. Garbage was stacked in corners. The smell of urine and cabbage made Eddie sick. Shadows threatened, but the sounds were more distant, just as the crackling in the fireplace came from farther away, mimicking the even farther, fainter tap of a typewriter.

The hand on my shoulder was again so gentle I barely felt it. When I opened my eyes, Wentworth stood over me, but this time he was silhouetted by light.

"Good morning." He smiled.

"Morning?"

"It's eleven o'clock."

"I slept thirteen hours?" I asked in shock.

"You're more tired than I imagined. Would you like some breakfast?"

My stomach rumbled. I couldn't recall waking up with so strong an appetite. "Starved. Just give me a moment to . . ."

"There's an extra toothbrush and razor in the bathroom."

As I washed my face, I was puzzled by my reflection in the mirror. My cheeks were no longer drawn. Wrinkles on my brow and around my eyes were less distinct. My eyes looked bright, my skin healthy.

At the kitchen table, I ate a fruit salad Wentworth prepared—oranges, bananas, pears, and apples (the latter two from his trees, he reminded me). I refilled my bowl three times. As always, there was tea.

"Is it drugged? Is that why I'm sleeping so much?"

Wentworth almost smiled. "We both drank from the same pot. Wouldn't I have been sleepy also?"

I studied him as hard as he had studied me. Despite his age, his cheeks glowed. His eyes were clear. His hair was gray instead of white. "You're seventy-eight, correct?"

"Correct."

"But you look twenty years younger. I don't understand."

"Perhaps you do."

I glanced around the old kitchen. I peered toward the trees and bushes outside. The sun shone on falling leaves. "This place?"

"A similar compound in another area would have produced the same effect. But yes, this place. Over the years, I acquired a natural rhythm. I lived with the land. I blended with the passage of the sun and moon and seasons. After a while, I noticed a change in my appearance, or rather the *lack* of change in my appearance. I wasn't aging at the rate I should have. I came to savor the delight of waking each day and enjoying what my small version of the universe had in store for me."

"That doesn't seem compatible with your gun."

"I brought that with me when I first retreated here. The loss of my family . . . Each morning was a struggle not to shoot myself."

I looked away, self-conscious.

"But one day crept into another. Somehow, I persisted. I read Thoreau again and again, trying to empty myself of my not-so-quiet desperation. Along with these infinite two acres, Thoreau saved my life. I came to feel my family through the flowers and trees and . . . Nothing dies. It's only transformed. I know what you're thinking—that I found a sentimental way to compensate. Perhaps I did. But compare your life to mine. When you came here, when you snuck onto my property, you had so desperate a look that for the first time in many years I was frightened. Your scuffed shoes. The button missing from your jacket. The dirt on your slacks. I knew that homes had been broken into. I got the gun from a drawer. I hoped I wouldn't need to defend myself."

Shame burned my cheeks. "Perhaps I'd better go."

"Then I realized you were truly desperate, not because of drugs or greed but because of a profound unhappiness. I invited you to stay because I hoped this place would save *you*."

As so often with Wentworth, I couldn't speak. Finally, I managed to say "Thank you," and was reminded of how humbly he used those words when I told him how brilliant *The Architecture of Snow* was.

"I have some coveralls that might fit you," he said. "Would you like to help me clean my gardens?"

It was one of the finest afternoons of my life, raking leaves, trimming frost-killed flowers, putting them in the compost bin. We harvested squash and apples. The only day I can compare it to was my final afternoon with my father so long ago, a comparably lovely autumn day when we raked leaves, when my father bent over and died.

A sound jolted me: my cell phone. I looked at the caller ID display. Finally, the ringing stopped.

Wentworth gave me a questioning look.

"My boss," I explained.

"You don't want to talk to him?"

"He's meeting the company's directors on Monday. He's under orders to squeeze out more profits. He wants to announce that *The Architecture of Snow* is on our list."

Wentworth glanced at the falling leaves. "Would the announcement help you?"

"My instructions are not to come back if I don't return with a signed contract."

Wentworth looked as if I'd told a slight joke. "That explains what drove you to climb over my fence."

"I really did worry that you were ill."

"Of course." Wentworth studied more falling leaves. "Monday?"

"Yes."

"You'll lose sleep again."

"Somebody's got to fight them."

"Maybe we need to save ourselves before we save anything else. How would you like to help me split firewood?"

For supper, we ate the rest of the soup, the bread, and the apple pie.

They tasted as fresh as they had on the previous night. Again, I felt sleepy, but this time from unaccustomed physical exertion. My skin glowed from the sun and the breeze.

I finished my tea and yawned. "I'd better get back to the motel."

"No. Lie on the sofa. Finish my manuscript."

The logs crackled. I might have heard the distant clatter of a typewriter as I turned the pages.

Eddie braved the dangers of the rat-infested apartment building. He needed all his cleverness to escape perverts and drug dealers. Outside, on a dark rainy street, he faced greater dangers. Every shadow was a threat. Meanwhile, the reader learned about Jake, who turned out to be nasty when he wasn't on the air. The station's owner was glad for the chance to fire him when Jake insulted one of the sponsors during the program. The novel switched back and forth between Jake's deterioration (a failed marriage and a gambling problem) and Eddie's quest to find him.

This time, Wentworth didn't need to touch me. I sensed his presence and opened my eyes to the glorious morning.

"Did you sleep well?"

"Very. But I'm afraid I didn't finish—"

"Next time," Wentworth said.

"Next time?"

"When you come back, you can finish it."

"You'd like me to come back?"

Instead of answering, Wentworth said, "I've given your problem a great deal of thought. Before I tell you my decision, I want *you* to tell *me* what you think of my manuscript so far."

"I love it."

"And? If I were your author, is that all you'd say to me as an editor? Is there nothing you want changed?"

"The sentences work perfectly. Given your style, it would be difficult to change anything without causing problems in other places."

"Does that imply a few things *would* benefit from changes?"

"Just a few cuts."

"A few? Why so hesitant? Are you overwhelmed by the great man's talent? Do you know how Sam and I worked as editor and author? We fought over every page. He wasn't satisfied until he made me justify every word in every sentence. Some authors wouldn't have put up with it. But I loved the experience. He challenged me. He made me try harder and reach deeper. If *you* were my editor, what would you say to challenge me?"

"You really want an answer?" I took a breath. "I meant what I said. This is a terrific book. It's moving and dramatic and funny when it needs to be and . . . I love it."

"But . . ."

"The boy in *The Architecture of Snow* struggles through a blizzard to save his father. Eddie in *this* novel struggles to get out of a slum and find a father. You're running variations on a theme. An important theme, granted. But the same one as in *The Sand Castle*."

"Continue."

"That may be why the critics turned against your last book. Because *it* was a variation on *The Sand Castle* also."

"Maybe some writers only have one theme."

"Perhaps that's true. But if I were your editor, I'd push you to learn if that were the case."

Wentworth considered me with those clear, probing eyes. "My father molested me when I was eight."

I felt as if I'd been hit.

"My mother found out and divorced him. We moved to another city. I never saw my father again. She never remarried. Fathers and sons. A powerful need when a boy's growing up. That's why I became a grade school teacher: to be a surrogate father for the children who needed one. It's the reason I became a writer: to understand the hollowness in me. I lied to you. I told you that when I heard you coming across the yard, when I saw your desperate features, I pulled my gun from a drawer to protect myself. In fact, the gun was already in my hand. Friday. The day you crawled over the fence. Do you know what date it was?"

"No."

"October fifteenth."

"October fifteenth?" The date sounded vaguely familiar. Then it hit me. "Oh . . . The day your family died in the accident."

For the first time, Wentworth started to look his true age, his cheeks shrinking, his eyes clouding. "I deceive myself by blaming my work. I trick myself into thinking that if I hadn't sold 'The Fortune Teller' to Hollywood, we wouldn't have driven to New York to see the damned movie. But the movie didn't kill my family. The movie wasn't driving the car when it flipped."

"The weather turned bad. It was an accident."

"So I tell myself. But every time I write another novel about a father and a son, I think about my two boys crushed in a heap of steel. Each year, it seems easier to handle. But some anniversaries . . . Even after all these years . . ."

"The gun was in your hand?"

"In my mouth. I want to save *you* because you saved *me*. I'll sign a contract for *The Architecture of Snow*."

Throughout the long drive back to Manhattan, I felt a familiar heaviness creep over me. I reached my apartment around midnight, but as Wentworth predicted, I slept poorly.

"Terrific!" My boss slapped my back when I gave him the news Monday morning. "Outstanding! I won't forget this!"

After the magic of the compound, the office was depressing. "But Wentworth has three conditions," I said.

"Fine, fine. Just give me the contract you took up there to get signed."

"He didn't sign it."

"*What?* But you said—"

"That contract's made out to R. J. Wentworth. He wants *another* contract, one made out to Peter Thomas."

"The pseudonym on the manuscript?"

"That's the first condition. The second is that the book has to be published with the name Peter Thomas on the cover."

The head of marketing gasped.

"The third condition is that Wentworth won't do interviews."

Now the head of marketing turned red, as if choking on something. "We'll lose *Oprah* and the *Today* show and the magazine covers and—"

"No interviews? That makes it worthless," my CEO said. "Who the hell's going to buy a book about a kid in a snowstorm when its author's a nobody?"

"Those are his conditions."

"Couldn't you talk him out of that?"

"He wants the book to speak for itself. He says part of the reason he's famous is that his family died. He won't capitalize on that, and he won't allow himself to be asked about it."

"Worthless," my boss moaned. "How can I tell the Gladstone executives we won't have a million-seller? I'll lose my job. You've already lost *yours*."

"There's a way to get around Wentworth's conditions," a voice said.

Everyone looked in that direction, toward the person next to me: my assistant, who wore his usual black turtleneck and black sports jacket.

"Make out the contract to Peter Thomas," my assistant continued. "Put in clauses guaranteeing that the book will be published under that name and that there won't be any interviews."

"Weren't you listening? An unknown author. No interviews. No serial killer or global conspiracy in the plot. We'll be lucky to sell ten copies."

"A million. You'll get the million," my assistant promised.

"Will you *please* start making sense."

"The Internet will take care of everything. As soon as the book's close to publication, I'll leak rumors to hundreds of chat groups. I'll put up a fan website. I'll spread the word that Wentworth's the actual author. I'll point out parallels between his early work and this one. I'll talk about the mysterious arrival of the manuscript just as his editor died. I'll mention that a March and Sons editor, Robert Neal, had a weekend conference at Wentworth's home in October, something that can be verified by checking with the motel where Mr. Neal stayed. I'll juice it up until everyone buys the rumor. Believe me, the Internet thrives on gossip. It'll get out of control damned fast. Since what passes for news these days is half speculation, reporters and TV commentators will do pieces about the rumors. After a week, it'll be taken for granted that Peter Thomas is R. J. Wentworth. People will want to be the first to buy the book to see what all the fuss is about. Believe me, you'll sell a million copies."

I was too stunned to say anything.

So were the others.

Finally my boss opened his mouth. "I love the way this guy thinks." He gave me a dismissive glance. "Take the new contract back to Wentworth. Tell him he'll get everything he wants."

So, on Tuesday, I drove back to Tipton. Because I was now familiar with the route, I made excellent time and arrived at four in the afternoon. Indeed, I often broke the speed limit, eager to see Wentworth again and warn him how March & Sons intended to betray him.

I saw the smoke before I got to town. As I approached the main street, I found it deserted. With a terrible premonition, I stopped at the park. The smoke shrouded Wentworth's compound. His fence was down. A fire engine rumbled next to it. Running through the leaves, I saw townspeople gathered in shock. I saw the waitress from Meg's Pantry, the waiter from the Tipton Tavern, Jonathan Wade from the bookstore, the barber who was the town constable, and Becky. I raced toward her.

"What happened?"

The constable turned from speaking to three state policemen. "The two outsiders who've been hanging around town—they broke into Bob's place. The state police found fresh cigarette butts at the back fence. Next to a locked gate, there's a tree so close to the fence it's almost a ladder."

My knees weakened when I realized he was talking about the tree I'd climbed to get over the fence. I showed them the way, I thought, sickened. I taught them how to get into the compound.

"Some of the neighbors thought they heard a shot," the constable said, "but since this is hunting season, the shot didn't seem unusual, except that it was close to town. Then the neighbors noticed smoke rising from the compound. Seems that after the outsiders stole what they could, they set fire to the place—to make Bob's death look like an accident."

"Death?" I could barely say the word.

"The county fire department found his body in the embers."

My legs were so unsteady that I feared I'd collapse. I reached for something to support me. Becky's shoulder. She held me up.

"The police caught the two guys who did it," the constable said.

I wanted to get my hands on them and—

"Bob came to see me after you drove back to New York," Becky said. "As you know, he needed an attorney."

"What are you talking about?"

Becky looked puzzled. "You aren't aware he changed his will?"

"His will?"

"He said you were the kind of man he hoped his sons would have grown up to be. He made you his heir, his literary executor, everything. This place is yours now."

Tears rolled down my cheeks. They rolled even harder an hour later when the firemen let Becky and me onto the property and showed us where they'd found Wentworth's body in the charred kitchen. The corpse was gone now, but the outline in the ashes was vivid. I stared at the blackened timbers of the gazebo. I walked toward Wentworth's gutted writing studio. A fireman stopped me from getting too close. But even from twenty feet away, I saw the clump of twisted metal that was once a typewriter. And the piles of ashes that had once been twenty-one manuscripts.

✠

Now you know the background. I spend a lot of time trying to rebuild the compound, although I doubt I'll ever regain its magic. Becky often comes to help me. I couldn't do it without her.

But *The Architecture of Snow* is what I mostly think about. I told March & Sons to go to hell, with a special invitation to my assistant, my boss, and the head of marketing. I arranged for the novel to be privately printed under the name Peter Thomas. A Tipton artist designed a cover that shows the hint of a farmhouse within gusting snow, almost as if the snow is constructing the house. There's no author's biography. Exactly as Wentworth intended.

I keep boxes of the novel in my car. I drive from bookstore to bookstore throughout New England, but only a few will take the chance on an unknown author. I tell them it's an absolutely wonderful book, and they look blank as if "wonderful" isn't what customers want these days. Is there a serial killer or a global conspiracy?

Wade has dozens of copies in his store. His front window's filled with it. He tries to convince visitors to buy it, but his tourist customers want books that have photographs of ski slopes and covered bridges. He hasn't sold even one. The townspeople? The waitress at Meg's Pantry spoke the truth. She isn't much of a reader. Nor is anybody else. I've tried until I don't know what else to do. I'm so desperate I finally betrayed Wentworth's trust and told you who wrote it. Take my word— it's wonderful. Buy it, will you? Please. Buy this book.

And So
with Cries

Clive Barker

And so with cries the world begins,
and angels offer up their skins,
to cover naked Humankind.
As above, below. As in front, behind.
You didn't know this? Yes, we're clothed
in what loving spirits first betrothed
to us. Our skins a glory newly shed,
and to our raw blood sinew wed.
Is it any wonder we're divided
from ourselves? When God decided
we would live with nerves exposed,
and only angels interposed
on our behalf. And dressed us well.
For which, of course, they went to Hell.

One Last Bother

Del Howison

Dark Delicacies III: Haunted is a variation on a theme. There are several meanings to the word *haunted*. What we seem to think of immediately is to annoy or pester a person or place by constantly visiting, the way it happens in a haunted house or possibly the damage I beset upon my favorite saloon. We could be *haunted* by memories of a terrible incident or visions of the past coming back time and again seeking revenge.

It's true that the term *haunt* is most frequently used with a ghost or a spirit as its implied subject. But it also means a lair or a feeding place of animals or other things, possibly because of their returning to the same spot over and over. It means to be present, often.

The one definition that seems to apply to me the most is the adjective *haunting* in reference to something that is often recurring to the mind and not easily forgotten, like a *haunting* tune or the *haunting* stories you have just consumed. There will be more, and Jeff and I will be back to haunt you with yet another selection of ghoulish original tales of terror by the masters of the macabre. But until then we hope you are truly haunted by what you have read and that the ghosts of tales past continue to visit you over and over and over.

Contributor Biographies

Maria Alexander

Alexander's credits include stories in *Chiaroscuro* and *Paradox Magazine*, as well as anthologies such as *Lost on the Darkside* and *Blood Surrender*. An anthology she shares with three other award-winning female horror writers, *Sins of the Sirens*, was released in 2008 to critical acclaim. Look for her work in the queer anthology, *Unspeakable Horrors: From the Shadows of the Closet*. She lives in Los Angeles. For the full literary rap sheet, visit her Web site, www.thehandlesspoet.com.

Kevin J. Anderson

Anderson is the author of nearly a hundred novels. Best known as the author of epic science fiction in his internationally bestselling *Dune* novels with Brian Herbert, his own space opera, *The Saga of Seven Suns*, and numerous *Star Wars* novels, Kevin is also no stranger to the horror field. His first novel, *Resurrection, Inc.*, was nominated for the Bram Stoker Award, and his *X-Files* novels became hugely popular around the world; he has written many horror short stories and edited *Blood Lite*. He has over twenty million books in print in twenty-nine languages. His most recent novels are *Jessica of Dune* (with Brian Herbert), *Enemies and Allies*, and the first book in his epic nautical fantasy saga, *The Edge of the World*.

Clive Barker

Barker was born in Liverpool, England, where he began his creative career writing, directing, and acting for the stage. Since then, he has gone on to pen such best sellers as *The Books of Blood, Weaveworld, Imajica, The Great and Secret Show, The Thief of Always, Everville, Sacrament, Galilee, Coldheart Canyon*, and the highly acclaimed *Abarat* fantasy series. As a screenwriter, director, and film producer, he is credited with the *Hellraiser* and *Candyman* pictures, as well as *Nightbreed, Lord of Illusions, Gods and Monsters*, and *The Midnight Meat Train*. Barker lives in Los Angeles.

Michael Boatman

By day, Michael Boatman dresses up and pretends to be other people on television. He's probably best known as the "gay black guy from *Spin City* or perhaps the "uptight black guy from *Arli$$*." Television addicts of sufficient age may remember him as the "haunted black guy" from *China Beach*. He's been "the black guy" in feature films like *Hamburger Hill, The Glass Sheild, The Peacemaker, Woman Thou Art Loosed*, and the upcoming film *Killing Wendy*. He's darkened up shows like *Law and Order SVU*, *Criminal Minds*, *Gray's Anatomy*, and *The Game* and appeared on Broadway in Athol Fugard's *Master Harold . . . and the Boys*. Much of his fiction attempts to straddle the line between horror and humor. He is the author of the monster-hunter novel *The Revenant Road*. His short fiction has appeared in magazines like *Weird Tales, Horror Garage,* and *Red Scream* and in anthologies like *Sages & Swords, Daikaiju! 2: Revenge of the Giant Monsters, Badass Horror, Voices from the Other Side,* and *Whispers in the Night*. Some of his stories have been herded into his short story collection, *God Laughs When You Die: Mean Little Stories from the Wrong Side of the Tracks*. He lives in New York with his wife and four children, works in LA, writes on airplanes, and heckles angry flight attendants. His website is www.michaelboatman.net.

Gary A. Braunbeck

Braunbeck is the author of eleven novels and eleven short story collections. Among his most popular books are the *Cedar Hill* novels, including *In Silent Graves, Keepers, Mr. Hands, Coffin County, Prodigal Blues,* and the recent *Far Dark Fields*. His third collection of *Cedar Hill* stories, *The Carnival Within*, will see release in 2009, as will the novellas *In Seeing* and *Clipper Girls*. His work has thus far garnered five Bram Stoker Awards, an International Horror Guild Award, three Shocklines "Shocker" Awards, a *Dark Scribe Magazine* "Black Quill" Award, and a World Fantasy Award nomination. He lives in Columbus, Ohio, with his wife, author Lucy Snyder (*Spellbent, Installing Linux on a Dead Badger, Sparks and Shadows*).

Axelle Carolyn

Carolyn has been a horror fan for as long as she can remember. Brought up on a steady diet of scary movies and Stephen King novels, she was for several years a regular contributor to genre publications such as *Fangoria, L'Ecran Fantastique,* and *SFX*, for which she traveled around the world to cover film sets and festivals. Today she still writes a monthly column on horror movies on entertainment website IGN, but she divides most of her time between acting and writing fiction. Her first book, *It Lives Again! Horror Movies in the New Millennium*, a study of horror since 2000, came out in late 2008. She lives in London with her husband, writer-director Neil Marshall.

Simon Clark

Simon lives in Doncaster, England, with his family. When his first novel, *Nailed by the Heart,* made it through the slush pile in 1994, he banked the advance and embarked upon his dream of becoming a full-time writer. Many dreams and nightmares later, he wrote the cult zombie classics *Blood Crazy, Darkness Demands, This Rage of Echoes,* and *The Night of the Triffids*, which continues the story of

Wyndham's classic, *The Day of the Triffids*. His revival of the wickedly ambulatory plants won the British Fantasy Society's award for best novel. Simon's latest novel is *The Midnight Man,* a story of murder, madness, and ghosts, featuring Vincent Van Gogh in the most turbulent year of his life. Forthcoming are *Ghost Monster* and *Whitby Vampyrrhic.* Simon also experiments in short film, and he created *Winter Chills* for BBC TV. Simon's Web site is www.bbr-online.com/nailed.

John Connolly

Connolly was born in Dublin, Ireland, in 1968, and is the author of eleven books, including the collection of supernatural short stories *Nocturnes* and his most recent novel, *The Lovers*.

Mick Garris

Award-winning filmmaker Mick Garris began writing fiction at the age of twelve. He spent seven years as lead vocalist with the acclaimed tongue-in-cheek progressive art-rock band Horsefeathers. His first movie business job was as a receptionist for George Lucas's Star Wars Corporation. Steven Spielberg hired Garris as story editor on the *Amazing Stories* series for NBC, where he wrote or cowrote ten of the forty-four episodes. Since then, he has written or coauthored several feature films (**batteries not included, The Fly II, Hocus Pocus, Critters 2, Riding the Bullet*) and teleplays (*Amazing Stories, Quicksilver Highway, Virtual Obsession,* The Others, *Desperation, Nightmares & Dreamscapes, Masters of Horror*). His directorial credits include many of the above, plus *Psycho IV: The Beginning* and *Sleepwalkers,* and network miniseries *The Stand, The Shining,* and *Steve Martini's The Judge.* As a prose fiction writer, his works include *A Life in the Cinema* and *Development Hell.* Garris lives in southern California with his wife, Cynthia, an actress, musician, composer, and muse.

Jeff Gelb

Dark Delicacies III: Haunted is Gelb's 22nd anthology as editor or co-editor, and his twenty-third published book of fiction. He is still thrilled to work with writers he has admired his entire lifetime.

Heather Graham

New York Times and *USA Today* best-selling author Heather Graham has written over one hundred novels and novellas including category, suspense, historical romance, vampire fiction, time travel, occult, and Christmas family fare. She has been honored with awards from Walden Books, B. Dalton, Georgia Romance Writers, *Affaire de Coeur, Romantic Times,* and more. Heather is the proud recipient of the Silver Bullet from Thriller Writers. Heather has had books selected for the Doubleday Book Club and the Literary Guild, and has been quoted, interviewed, or featured in such publications as *The Nation, Redbook, Mystery Book Club, People*, and *USA Today*. She has appeared on many newscasts including *Today, Entertainment Tonight*, and local television. The complete Flynn Brothers Trilogy has been released: *Deadly Gift, Deadly Harvest*, and *Deadly Night*. This year readers can expect to see *Nightwalker, Dust to Dust, Unhallowed Ground*, and *Home in Time for Christmas*. Her first illustrated book, *There Be Dragons*, will be available for Christmas. Each year she hosts the *Vampire Ball* and *Dinner theater* at the RT convention, raising money for the Pediatric Aids Society, and in 2006 she hosted the first Writers for New Orleans Workshop to benefit the stricken Gulf region.

Simon R. Green

Simon R. Green has written thirty-seven books, all of them different. He has two degrees (one more and he could have been a singing group) and has worked as a shop assistant, bicycle repair mechanic, journalist, actor, and mail-order bride. He lives in the small country town of Bradford-on-Avon in the southwest of England. He has never worked for MI5; don't believe anyone who tells you otherwise.

Joseph V. Hartlaub

Hartlaub is an attorney specializing in entertainment law with special emphasis on musical and literary intellectual property rights. He is also senior writer and reviewer for bookreporter.com and music-reviewer.com. Joe's short story "Crossed Double" will appear in *Thriller Two*, an anthology of original thriller stories that will be published in 2009. Joe made his acting debut in the film *LA-308*, which is scheduled for release in 2009. He lives in Westerville, Ohio, with his wife and four children. A firearm, bladed weapon, and personal protection enthusiast, Joe characterizes himself as "a very boring guy who gets to live a very interesting life."

Del Howison

Del Howison is an award-winning editor and an author. His books have been nominated for or won the Bram Stoker Award, the Black Quill Award, the Shirley Jackson Award and the Rondo Award. He is also co-owner of America's only all-horror book and gift store, Dark Delicacies, in Burbank, California. He can be found at www.darkdel.com.

Del James

Del James is a meat-eating, cigar-smoking, pro-choice, sober atheist. When not out pillaging the free world as the road manager for Guns N' Roses, he can be found lurking in the shadows of Hollywood's seediest dive bars and rock clubs. Depending on his mood, James writes horror fiction, screenplays, and music. Before being reprinted in 2008, his collection of short horror stories, *The Language of Fear*, was among the top ten most sought after, out-of-print horror/sci-fi titles. He lives in Southern California.

John R. Little

John R. Little's first novel, *The Memory Tree*, was published in 2007 and nominated for the Bram Stoker Award. His following four books, *Placeholders, Miranda, The Gray Zone,* and *Dreams in Black and White*, were all recently published novellas. He's been publishing horror and dark fantasy since the early 1980s.

Richard Christian Matheson

Richard Christian Matheson is an acclaimed novelist, short story writer, and screenwriter-producer. He has written and cowritten feature film and television projects for Richard Donner, Ivan Reitman, Steven Spielberg, Bryan Singer, and many others. He has also written pilots for comedy and dramatic series for Showtime, Fox, NBC, ABC, TNT, HBO, FOX, Spike, and CBS. Matheson's critically lauded fiction has been published in major award-winning anthologies, including multiple times in *The Year's Best Horror* and *The Year's Best Fantasy*, as well as *Penthouse* and *Omni* magazines. Matheson's stories have been collected in *Scars and Other Distinguishing Marks* and *Dystopia*. His debut novel, *Created By*, was a Bram Stoker Award nominee for best first novel.

Ardath Mayhar

Mayhar, born in 1930, began her writing career as a poet when she was nineteen. She began writing science fiction in 1979 after returning with her family to Texas from Oregon. She has been nominated for the Nebula Award and the Mark Twain Award and won the Balrog Award for a horror narrative poem in *Masques I*. She has had numerous other nominations for awards in almost every fiction genre and has won many awards for poetry. In 2008 she was chosen by the Science Fiction Writers of America as their Author Emeritus. Mayhar has written over sixty books, ranging from science fiction to horror to young adult to historical to Westerns, with some work under the pseudonyms Frank Cannon, Frances Hurst, and John Killdeer. Joe R. Lansdale says simply, "Ardath Mayhar writes damn fine books!"

David Morrell

David Morrell is the author of *First Blood,* the award-winning novel in which Rambo was created. He holds a PhD in American literature from Pennsylvania State University and taught in the English department at the University of

Iowa until he gave up his tenure to write full time. His numerous best-selling novels include *The Brotherhood of the Rose* (the basis for a top-rated NBC miniseries broadcast after the Super Bowl), *The Fraternity of the Stone,* and *Creepers.* Cofounder of the International Thriller Writers organization, Morrell is a three-time recipient of the Horror Writers Bram Stoker Award. His short stories have appeared in many of the major horror/fantasy anthologies, including the *Whispers, Shadows, Night Visions,* and *Masters of Darkness* series, as well as *The Twilight Zone Magazine, The Dodd, Mead Gallery of Horror, Psycho Paths, Prime Evil, Dark at Heart, Metahorror, Revelations, 999,* and *Redshift.* In *The Successful Novelist,* he describes what he has learned during his almost four decades as a published author. Visit him at www.davidmorrell.net.

Chuck Palahniuk

Palahniuk is the author of nine novels and two books of nonfiction. His latest novel, *Pygmy,* was published in 2009. For more information, go to chuckpalahniuk.net.

Eric Red

Born in Pittsburgh and raised in New York and Philadelphia, Eric Red began his career in the film industry at age nineteen with his nationally distributed urban Western short, *Gunmen's Blues,* quickly followed by a second award-winning short, *Telephone.* After attending the American Film Institute, Red got his start in Hollywood by penning two classic horror thrillers, *The Hitcher* and *Near Dark.* The first feature he wrote and directed was the crime thriller *Cohen and Tate.* Over the past two decades, Red has written and/or directed numerous major films in the horror, thriller, and Western genres. His scripts include *Blue Steel* and *The Last Outlaw.* He wrote and directed *Body Parts, Undertow,* and *Bad Moon.* A second major Universal remake of one of his earlier films, *Near Dark,* is underway. His next original script, the car-chase thriller *Stopping Power,* is currently in pre-production. Red also works in the comic and graphic novel field, where he recently created and wrote the successful sci-fi horror comic series *Containment* for IDW Publishing. Red's latest film as a writer/director is *100 Feet.* He is currently developing the contemporary vampire film *Nightlife* and a film version of Jack Ketchum's *Off Season.* Red and his wife, Meredith, live in Los Angeles.

Victor Salva

Victor Salva had written and directed over twenty shorts and feature-length films before graduating high school in his hometown of Martinez in Northern California. In the late 80s, Salva's homemade horror short *Something in the Basement* won at the Chicago Film festival, picked up an ACE Cable Award, and brought him to the attention of Francis Ford Coppola, who produced Salva's first theatrical feature, *Clownhouse*, a low-budget thriller about killer clowns that kick-started Salva's career as the award-winning writer-director of numerous feature films in various genres: most notably the science fiction drama *Powder*. In 2001, Salva wrote and directed *Jeepers Creepers*, his throwback to the old-style horror films he loved as a boy. Salva followed with *Jeepers Creepers 2*. In 2005, he did the big-screen adaptation of the best-selling book *Way of the Peaceful Warrior*, and in 2007 wrote a teleplay for NBC's short lived horror series *Fear Itself*. In 2008 he penned the modern-day ghost story about Alcatraz Island titled "The Wind at the Door" and, as of this writing, is working on *Jeepers Creepers III: Cathedral*, which will be the final installment in his *Jeepers Creepers* trilogy.

Steven Weber

With a wide range of acclaimed film, television, and theater credits to his name, Steven Weber has established himself as one of the most diverse and respected talents in the industry. In 2007 Weber received critical acclaim for his performance as network honcho Jack Rudolph in NBC's *Studio 60 on the Sunset Strip*. Having starred in several popular series such as *Wings, Once and Again,* and *The D.A.,* he can also be seen in current episodes of *Brothers and Sisters* and *Without a Trace*. He made his New York theater debut opposite Geraldine Page in Odets' *Paradise Lost*. On Broadway he appeared in Tom Stoppard's *The Real Thing*. In 2002 he took over for Matthew Broderick in *The Producers* and later starred in London opposite Kevin Spacey in the Old Vic production of *National Anthems*. Weber made his writing debut with his critically acclaimed film *Club Land*, costarring with Alan Alda as a struggling father-son team of theatrical agents. Alda earned Emmy and SAG award nominations for his performance. Weber's affinity for all things horror and fantasy led to his starring in the ABC miniseries *The Shining* as well as cowriting and directing two episodes of *The Outer Limits*. He recently adapted the famous Bernie Wrightson–illustrated story "Jenifer" for the *Masters of Horror* series. His other forays into the genre include *Reefer Madness* and *Dracula: Dead and Loving It*.